D0442103

JEWELED
FIRE

Ace Books by Sharon Shinn

THE SHAPE OF DESIRE
STILL LIFE WITH SHAPE-SHIFTER
THE TURNING SEASON

TROUBLED WATERS
ROYAL AIRS
JEWELED FIRE

MYSTIC AND RIDER
THE THIRTEENTH HOUSE
DARK MOON DEFENDER
READER AND RAELYNX
FORTUNE AND FATE

ARCHANGEL
JOVAH'S ANGEL
THE ALLELUIA FILES
ANGELICA
ANGEL-SEEKER

WRAPT IN CRYSTAL
THE SHAPE-CHANGER'S WIFE
HEART OF GOLD
SUMMERS AT CASTLE AUBURN
JENNA STARBORN
QUATRAIN

Viking / Firebird Books by Sharon Shinn

THE SAFE-KEEPER'S SECRET
THE TRUTH-TELLER'S TALE
THE DREAM-MAKER'S MAGIC
GENERAL WINSTON'S DAUGHTER
GATEWAY

JEWELED FIRE

Sharon Shinn

ACE BOOKS, NEW YORK

An imprint of Penguin Random House LLC
375 Hudson Street, New York, New York 10014

This book is an original publication of Penguin Random House LLC.

Copyright © 2015 by Sharon Shinn.
Penguin supports copyright. Copyright fuels creativity, encourages diverse voices,
promotes free speech, and creates a vibrant culture. Thank you for buying an authorized
edition of this book and for complying with copyright laws by not reproducing, scanning, or
distributing any part of it in any form without permission. You are supporting writers and
allowing Penguin to continue to publish books for every reader.

ACE and the "A" design are trademarks of Penguin Random House LLC.
For more information, visit penguin.com.

Library of Congress Cataloging-in-Publication Data

Shinn, Sharon.
Jeweled fire / Sharon Shinn.
pages ; cm
ISBN 978-0-425-27705-8 (hardcover)
I. Title.
PS3569.H499J49 2015
813'.54—dc23
2015007962

FIRST EDITION: November 2015

PRINTED IN THE UNITED STATES OF AMERICA

10   9   8   7   6   5   4   3   2   1

Cover illustration by Jonathan Barkat.
Cover photograph: dark stormy sky © Mr Twister / Shutterstock.
Cover design by Judith Lagerman.

This is a work of fiction. Names, characters, places, and incidents either are the product of
the author's imagination or are used fictitiously, and any resemblance to actual persons,
living or dead, business establishments, events, or locales is entirely coincidental.

Penguin
Random
House

To that crazy fan who never expected a dedication.
These are the blessings I pulled for you: intelligence, love, and time.

WHO'S WHO IN THE SOUTHERN NATIONS

IN MALINQUA

FILOMARA, empress
GARAMENO, Filomara's oldest nephew
JIRAMONDI, Filomara's second-oldest nephew
GREGGORIO, Filomara's youngest nephew, son of Morli
ARAVANI AND SUBRIELLA, Filomara's daughters
MORLI AND DONATO, two of Filomara's four brothers
HARLO, the prefect
MARIANA, Harlo's wife
LIRAMELLI, daughter to Harlo and Mariana
BARTOLO AND SATTISI, Filomara's cousin and his wife
SARONA, a high-born young lady
LORIAN, steward of the royal palace
EMILITA, Corene's maid
BILLINI, a tavern owner
RENALTO CORSICARA, head of Malinqua's institute of biological
    research

VISITORS FROM OTHER COUNTRIES

CORENE, a princess from Welce
STEFF (STEFFANOLO KORDAN BORS ADOVA), the son of a
    Welchin farmer and Subriella
FOLEY, a member of the Welchin royal guard
LEAH, a Welchin native acting as a spy for Darien Serlast
ADA SIMMS, a Welchin sea captain

MELISSANDE, a princess from Cozique
CHANDRAN, a merchant from Cozique

ALETTE, a princess from Dhonsho
TEYTA, the daughter of a shopkeeper from Dhonsho
CHEELIN BARLIO, a young man from Dhonsho

IN WELCE

JOSETTA, Corene's sister
DARIEN SERLAST, Corene's father, advisor to the old king,
  currently the regent
ZOE LALINDAR, coru prime and wife of Darien Serlast
ALYS, Corene's mother, formerly the third wife of the old king
DOMINIC WOLLIMER, Alys's second husband
NELSON ARDELAY, sweela prime
KAYLE DOCHENZA, elay prime
TARO FROTHEN, torz prime
RAFE ADOVA, Steff's half brother and the eldest of
  Subriella's sons

Welchin Affiliations and Random Blessings

ELAY (AIR/SOUL)	HUNTI (WOOD/BONE)	SWEELA (FIRE/MIND)
joy	courage	innovation
hope	strength	love
kindness	steadfastness	imagination
beauty	loyalty	clarity
vision	certainty	intelligence
grace	resolve	charm
honor	determination	talent
spirituality	power	creativity

CORU (WATER/BLOOD)	TORZ (EARTH/FLESH)	EXTRAORDINARY BLESSINGS
change	serenity	synthesis
travel	honesty	triumph
flexibility	health	time
swiftness	fertility	
resilience	contentment	
luck	patience	
persistence	endurance	
surprise	wealth	

QUINTILES & CHANGEDAYS

The calendar of the southern nations is divided into five quintiles. A quintile consists of eight "weeks," each nine days long. All the nations observe the quintiles, though each nation calls them by different names. In Welce, the first quintile of the year is called Quinnelay, and it stretches from early to deep winter. It is followed by Quinncoru, which encompasses late winter to mid-spring; Quinnahunti, late spring to mid-summer; Quinnatorz, late summer to fall; and Quinnasweela, fall to early winter. The quintiles are separated by changedays, generally celebrated as holidays. In total, the calendar year is 365 days long.

ONE

Leah crowded onto the dock with half the population of Palminera and watched the ships come in. There were dozens of them, crammed with soldiers, because the empress didn't believe in leaving Malinqua without a formidable force at her back. Even when she was only planning friendly negotiations with the rest of the southern nations, Filomara had always believed that the threat of war was the best way to ensure peace.

A cry went up from the crowd as the most elegant ship in the fleet tacked its way closer to the pier reserved for the royal family. As everyone else surged forward, Leah dropped back, moving from the rough wood planking of the dock to the paved streets of the surrounding harbor. Eventually she came to rest against the warm brick of a dockside tavern and settled in for a long wait. She knew how these disembarkations went; it would be another hour before the boat was secured and the exalted personnel began to exit. First the empress, of course, whose stern face would soften to a smile as she acknowledged the waiting multitudes. Then her attendants, the high-born family members who had accompanied her on her long journey. And finally Princess Corene of Welce. Who had stowed away on the empress's ship without the consent of her family.

It had been common knowledge in Malinqua that Filomara was visiting the nations of the southern seas with the precise goal of bringing princesses back to the royal court. She was looking for eligible foreign young women to marry off to her nephews, and Princess Corene was as eligible as they came. The girl's father had politely declined the invitation on his daughter's behalf—but Corene had accepted it anyway.

Even though it had been five years since Leah lived in Welce, she vividly remembered a twelve-year-old hellion, all fierce will and red hair. She wondered if Filomara had any idea what she'd brought home to Malinqua.

The summer air was starting to heat up, though at this noon hour, it wasn't truly wretched yet. Leah resettled her back against the building, then glanced up as the front door opened. The man who stepped out was wearing a cook's apron and polishing a glass, so she assumed he was the tavernkeeper. He stood there a moment, eyeing the great ship, which was still tacking and rocking its way to the dock. Behind it, the escort flotilla hung back, not a single boat planning to drop anchor until the empress was safely on land.

"Not tied up yet, then?" the bar owner asked. "It'll be sundown before we see a one of them."

"Not quite that long, I think," Leah answered.

He seemed annoyed. "And everyone out in the streets *watching* instead of inside ordering beer."

"I'll come in and order something," Leah offered. "Food, too, if you've got it." There would be no chance of missing the empress's appearance; the crowd would roar out its welcome the minute she showed her face.

The barkeeper looked pleased. "I do. Not yesterday's leftovers, either, but fresh-made this morning."

She followed him inside to find the tavern clean enough, pleasantly cool, and wholly empty. She picked a booth by a window, though it didn't show a view of the harbor, and ordered lunch.

The barkeeper, it turned out, was talkative, but that suited Leah perfectly. Gregarious people were indirectly her source of income. He loitered by her table, holding a broom as if he planned to wield it, but he really just stood there and speculated about the events that might transpire now that the empress was home.

"So she's found three brides," he observed.

Leah affected surprise. "I know about Princess Melissande from Cozique and Princess Alette from Dhonsho," she said, because these two very different creatures had arrived in Malinqua within the past two ninedays and had already taken up residence at the palace. "There's a third one?"

The barkeeper nodded in satisfaction. "A girl from Welce. *A princess*," he corrected himself. "Apparently they have dozens of them over there."

Well, not quite dozens, Leah thought, though it was truly hard to keep track. Before he died, old King Vernon had amassed four wives and four daughters—though it seemed that some of those daughters had been sired by other men to conceal the fact that Vernon was practically impotent. One of the men who had stepped forward to perform this most intimate service was Darien Serlast, the king's closest advisor. It was his daughter who was on the Malinquese ship.

"How'd you hear about that?" Leah asked. "This princess from Welce?"

The barkeeper spared a moment to look self-important. "The empress has been sending news to the palace every nineday since she's been gone—she brought a whole fleet of clippers to carry her messages. I know all sorts of things. I have lots of friends at the palace."

Probably his fish vendor also supplied a merchant who made deliveries to the palace, Leah thought cynically, and his information had traveled a very circuitous route before finally landing here. Still, as she had learned during the past five years, gossip that filtered down from the highest to the lowest levels of society had an uncanny way of being accurate. The lives of the royal heirs and the titled nobility were far less private than they liked to think.

And in this case, the tavernkeeper's information was good, though Leah liked to think hers was better. Since she'd gotten it from Darien Serlast himself.

He'd been the one to suggest Malinqua to her, five years ago when she had wanted to be anywhere but Welce. Vernon had already started to fade, and Darien had clearly been the force behind the throne, the firm hand that kept Vernon steady whenever the old king started to wobble.

"I could use someone in the city of Palminera," he'd told her.

"I'd have thought you already had spies in Malinqua," she'd answered.

"I do. But none of them are—" He'd hesitated, as if looking for a word. Which, of course, was a ploy, because Darien always knew exactly what he was going to say before he opened his mouth. He wanted her to rush right in and supply the words herself.

"Connected to the highest echelons of society," she said bitterly.

He smiled. "Exactly. Able to understand how the machinations at the palace play out in the taverns along the wharf. And how policy in one royal house might have repercussions for royal houses in other nations."

So she'd come to Palminera to spy for Darien Serlast, and he'd sent her a regular supply of gold to pay her expenses and fund her bribes. She'd thought his political clout might fade once Vernon died, but in fact, he grew more influential. First he'd acted as regent while everyone squabbled over who should be the next person to take the throne; very recently, Welce's royal advisors had decided Darien would actually make an excellent king. He hadn't been crowned yet, but Leah thought he was the ideal choice: an intelligent, thoughtful, committed, and righteous man who had an uncanny knack of getting people to do what he wanted. Though apparently that ability didn't extend to his daughter.

She could only imagine how relieved he'd been to know Leah was already in place when he learned Corene had sailed off to Palminera.

It had been only four days since one of his messengers had arrived at her doorstep, bearing the surprising news. Darien had sent his letter via one of the sleek little mail ships that could skim through the ocean much faster than Filomara's heavy warships. Darien was the sort of man who habitually concealed his true thoughts, so she had been astonished to read the bald distress in his first missive.

> *Corene has defied me and set out for Malinqua with Filomara, who claims she is looking to forge alliances through weddings between her nephews and foreign brides. But Malinqua's royal court has an unsavory history of poisoning off its political rivals, and who knows how a Welchin princess will be received? She has her own per-*

*sonal guard with her, so she's not unprotected, but one
man might not be enough. Let me know AT ONCE if
Corene needs to be rescued by force or if a slower extrica-
tion will be safe for all.*

He might as well have claimed he was mad with worry; it could not
have been more obvious.

Leah had wasted no time sending him a reply that should have
assuaged the worst of his fears. Those legendary poisonings seemed to
be a thing of the past, since the last suspected murder among the palace
elite had been more than fifteen years ago. The empress was indeed collecting potential brides for her nephews—two of them were already
present, and so far, they had both been treated like the royalty they
were. Leah emphasized the fact that one of the foreign visitors was
from Cozique, the largest, most sophisticated, and most powerful
nation in the southern waters. It might be considered a coup for a
Welchin princess to stand alongside a Coziquela heiress and look every
bit as desirable.

Two letters had followed in the next two days, each more temperate
and more in Darien's usual guarded style. They included instructions
on how to approach Corene, with helpful details about her preferences
and personality traits. But gaining access to the palace was going to be
trickier than winning Corene's trust, Leah suspected, since—unlike the
boastful barkeeper—she didn't have friends among the staff.

Time to find some, maybe, she thought. She wondered now if the
tavernkeeper might introduce her to his fishmonger friend, and smiled
at the thought.

"Another glass of beer?" the bar owner asked at that very moment.
In the interests of developing the friendship, she accepted.

"If you'll sit and have one with me," she added. "It feels lonely to
drink by myself."

"That it does," he agreed, bringing two glasses over to the table.
"I'm Billini, by the way."

"Leah." She took a sip, wondering how much to tell him, how much
he might already know. He hadn't mentioned the second—and even more
interesting—Welchin traveler on the empress's ship. Was it possible that

Filomara had managed to suppress this news, that she planned to bring the young man ashore without giving her nephews or advisors the slightest hint that he was about to disrupt all their lives? "This beer is very good."

"Brew it myself. A family recipe."

Well, Filomara's secret wouldn't be secret very long. And Billini would be grateful to Leah forever if she gave him a piece of gossip hours before anyone else had it. And gratitude, she knew, was a currency as good as gold.

"I have a friend in Welce—lives near the palace—thinks she knows everything," Leah said. She rolled her eyes and Billini nodded.

"Some folks just like to be ahead of the news. Makes them feel important," he said without any visible traces of irony.

"But she told me the empress is bringing a young man with her. From Welce."

Billini shrugged. "So?"

Leah glanced out the window, as if to make sure no one was outside eavesdropping. "She said this young man is really her grandson. The child of Filomara's dead daughter."

Billini almost collapsed against the back of his chair. *"No."*

"Yes. The daughter who married the prince in Berringey. Everyone thought she was dead, but she just ran away with the baby. And took him to Welce. Now he's grown up and he's coming here."

Billini's face showed rising excitement as he sorted through all the implications. "If he's her grandson—she might name *him* her heir, not any of her brothers' sons. Oh, they won't like that, any of those boys. This could change everything, couldn't it?"

"It could."

Billini took a deep breath. Then he started laughing and waving his hands in a broad gesture that could have meant anything, but Leah knew what he was trying to express. He was indicating the two great towers that stood at opposite ends of the city, invisible from inside the tavern but designed to watch over the city from all vantage points, at all hours. One was topped by a crystal dome that glowed with an eerie white light; one sported a jagged lotus of red and yellow glass and was lit by a fire that never went out. These were the sentinels of Palminera, its guideposts and its metaphors.

"Night and day," Billini said. "Shadow and flame."

"One thing ends," Leah said, "and the next begins."

Almost on the words, they heard an enormous roar of excitement rip through the crowd outside. Filomara must have stepped to the railing of the ship; it was time for the royal party to disembark.

"Ah—that'll be the empress," Billini said, rising. "I suppose you want to see her go riding through town, then."

That was clearly her cue to leave, so Leah came hastily to her feet. "I do! I've been waiting for hours just to catch a glimpse."

"Good timing, too, for I've got to close the place up. I've just remembered an errand I have to run."

I'll bet you have, Leah thought. Off to see his fishmonger friend, no doubt, or someone with even better connections.

"Thanks for the meal. And the conversation," Leah said, digging in her pocket for a few coins.

Billini waved his hands again, this time in magnanimity. "On the house," he said. "But come back sometime and bring your friends."

She grinned. Yes, he could be useful to her indeed. Or—even better—they could be useful to each other. "I will," she said. "Now I want to go get a look at the empress. And everyone she's brought from Welce."

TWO

Y the time the ship docked in Palminera, Corene figured everyone on board hated her. It didn't bother her as much as it should have. She was well aware that, back in Welce, she was generally considered the most unlikable of the princesses, and she had even managed to turn that reputation to her advantage to some extent. If everyone expected you to be sharp-tongued, hard to please, and petulant, you could get away with bad behavior and the people around you would only shrug. *Oh, that's just Corene being difficult again.*

Not that she had *tried* to alienate everyone on the ship. But the journey had taken two ninedays, and Corene had been ready to dive headfirst into the ocean before the second firstday had rolled around. She found it maddening to be cooped up on a small vessel on the limitless sea with nothing to do—except talk to people who hated her.

Actually, it was possible Filomara didn't hate her. In her way, the empress was as hard to read as Corene's father was, though on the surface she seemed so much more open. Filomara spoke bluntly and without any apparent filters of civility; but later when Corene would analyze the conversation, she'd realize that Filomara hadn't given away any of her true thoughts. So maybe she didn't actually dislike Corene. She just hadn't pretended to like her, either.

They had spent a portion of every day together since they set sail from Welce. "You may as well learn the history of Malinqua while you've nothing better to do," had been Filomara's comment that first morning. Corene had obediently joined her in the tiny cubicle that passed for a sitting room and sipped at some beverage that was like nothing she'd ever tasted before—hot and almost flavorless until you loaded it up with honey and milk, and even then something you'd rather clean the floors with than actually *drink*—and listened to her drone on about the history of her country. Corene could tell she was supposed to be impressed by the fact that Malinqua had been trading partners with Cozique for two centuries, the fact that Malinquese explorers had been the first to set foot in Yorramol, but she wasn't, not at all. Who cared about all that old stuff? What mattered was how secure the country was today, how prosperous, how well-run.

"What was Malinqua like before you were crowned?" she asked on their sixteenth day at sea when Filomara paused to take a sip of that abominable brew. "What do you think you've done to make it better?"

The second question made Filomara's eyes gleam with what Corene assumed was hostility. Well, it had been an impertinent thing to ask. But the empress answered promptly enough. "Developed trade agreements with ten more nations—including your own. Doubled the standing army—and deployed it successfully when I had to."

"Commerce and war," Corene said. "The main duties of any government." It was a lesson she'd learned eons ago when she was being drilled in Welchin history in case she was ever named queen.

"Commerce and war and stability," Filomara amended. "But yes."

"'Stability,'" Corene repeated.

"Fair taxes, good roads, a well-regulated legal system, and a royal house that makes a smooth transition between rulers."

And that easily, Filomara had brought them back to the central issue that bound them together: the succession of Malinqua.

"Do you always look outside Malinqua when you want your heirs to marry?" Corene asked, genuinely curious.

"Not always, but every generation or two we have brought in outsiders. It's good diplomatic policy, since it creates strong ties between us and our neighbors, who can be very warlike. And it's good breeding policy."

"*Breeding* policy?"

"Freshens up the blood. Too many small families intermarrying too often results in misfits and lunatics. It's true for cattle, and it's true for men."

Corene wanted to reply huffily that she'd never heard of such a thing, and besides, it was a coarse topic for the breakfast table, but then she stopped and thought about it a moment. Well, the Five Families of Welce had been intermarrying for generations, and there had certainly been a few odd products of all those unions. Consider Kayle Dochenza, who was one eyeblink away from being a madman. And consider Odelia, Vernon's youngest daughter, who seemed to exist in an isolated, empty world inside her own head. Maybe fresh blood was what Welce needed after all.

"Who did *you* marry, then?" Corene asked. "A local man or a foreign prince?"

An expression of distaste flitted across Filomara's face. "A local man. The prefect's son."

"The who?"

"The prefect. By tradition, the monarch's closest advisor. The person who will automatically assume the regency if the heirs are too young to rule when the sitting ruler dies. It is the second most powerful position in the kingdom."

"I'd think that would be a reason for the offspring *not* to marry."

"And generally speaking, you would be right," Filomara acknowledged. "But there had been some unrest in Palminera when I was a young girl—some who were against the idea of a woman taking the throne—and some factions who believed the prefect's family should inherit instead. Uniting the two families appeased everyone, so we were married before I was even twenty."

This was actually starting to be interesting. "So your husband married you thinking that you would stay in the background while he assumed most of the power." Corene surveyed the empress, whose square, strong face showed just the hint of a smile. "I guess he got a surprise."

The smile deepened. "I guess he did."

"Did you like being married to him?"

"No."

"Did you *stay* married to him?"

"We lived together for five years and I bore two daughters," she said. "After that we lived apart until his death some fifteen years ago."

"Did you think about marrying again?"

That faint, sardonic smile was back on the empress's face. "Not for a minute. What few advantages I could wring from a marriage I had already enjoyed. On the whole, I have found my temperament more suited to the solitary state."

"But all you can think about is marrying off everyone around you," Corene pointed out.

"My nephews, certainly. I don't care about the marital plans of anyone else in Malinqua."

"Do *they* want to be married? Your nephews?"

"They all would like to be considered my direct heir, and I have made it clear I will not choose a successor who has not proved he can breed successors of his own—"

"You don't have to be married to do *that*," Corene couldn't help pointing out.

Filomara's expression was not amused. "I have made it equally clear that bastards will never be contenders for the throne."

"*Are* there any? That you know about?"

"No. And I would know."

Corene believed her. You didn't have to spend much time with Filomara to believe she was capable of anything, and that included keeping herself informed about everything that was transpiring within her nation. Corene's father inspired the same faith.

"So you've told them they have to marry or they can't take the throne. Do they have to marry someone you pick out?"

"Not if they choose suitable brides."

"So they could marry for love if they wanted to."

Now Filomara looked pained. "Do silly schoolgirls really believe any king or queen in the history of the world has ever married for love?"

Corene made her voice coldly civil. "I don't know. I don't know any silly schoolgirls."

Filomara loosed a crack of laughter at that. "Your own mother—she married an old king who already had two wives. That could hardly have been the romance she was dreaming about when she imagined herself a young bride."

Oh, if they were to talk about Corene's mother and her notions of the ideal marriage, they wouldn't finish the conversation for at least a nineday. Queen Alys was a schemer of the highest order and completely unburdened by either scruples or sensibilities. She would have married a drunkard, a criminal, a man with a *hundred* other wives, if she'd thought it would place her an inch closer to the throne. It was exactly why Alys had chosen her second husband, why she was even now pregnant with his child: She'd thought he was part of the royal line and her son or daughter might be the next one to wear the crown.

Corene squirmed a little on her chair. How was she any better than Alys? She'd agreed to accompany the empress to Malinqua just on the chance she could make a brilliant marriage for herself. She'd thought she was rebelling against her father, but maybe she was only living up to her mother's legacy. She'd probably made Alys proud with her rash and ill-considered act.

It was enough to make her want to order the ship to turn around and take her home.

She straightened her spine and lifted her chin defiantly. It didn't matter what her mother thought. Or what her father thought. She had decided to travel to Malinqua because she was tired of Welce—of the people who pitied her because she was never going to inherit the throne, of the people who courted her because she was still connected to the most powerful families in the country. Of the people who disliked her because of her blunt manners. She didn't know her place in Welce anymore, so she'd gone looking for a better one somewhere else. Would she find it in Malinqua? She'd been less and less sure of that as the voyage progressed—but she wasn't going to call the journey a mistake before they'd even arrived at their destination.

The empress was watching her somewhat quizzically, and Corene realized she'd been quiet too long. "My mother," she said with an easy laugh, "never expected that she would marry for love, or that I would, either. I'm not sure it's a concept that anyone has ever explained to her."

"Good," Filomara said. "Then you might be just the sort of bride my nephews are looking for."

So the empress might not hate her, but Filomara's attendants most certainly did. Filomara's cousin Bartolo and his wife, Sattisi, had been reticent and quiet during the visit to Welce, but once they were onboard the ship, headed back to their own country, they had proved to be autocratic and opinionated. Filomara had tasked them with teaching Corene the Malinquese language, and the lessons were not going smoothly. Corene had never enjoyed sitting in a classroom, and her efforts to master other languages had rarely gone well. She could scarcely remember a word of the Soechin she had studied five years ago, when they expected her to marry the viceroy of Soeche-Tas. She had done better at learning Coziquela, which was the common tongue of the southern nations, mostly because it was a lovely language and she thought she looked pretty speaking it. She didn't read it well, though, and she knew her accent was atrocious.

Malinquese was much worse. Or else her tutors were.

"No! We went over this five times yesterday!" Sattisi fumed that same afternoon when Corene's understanding seemed particularly dull. "You cannot call a man a *buffoon* when you mean to call him a *genius*."

"Can I call *you* a buffoon?" Corene asked in the polite voice she used when she was trying to be particularly irritating. "Because I certainly don't mean to call you a genius."

"Perhaps no one in your own provincial nation cares about manners, but they're very important in Malinqua," Sattisi shot back.

"Really?" Corene said, still in that polite way. "I wouldn't have thought so judging by the way you treat me."

As she'd hoped, Sattisi was so angry that she dismissed Corene for the day; that was how their sessions usually ended. She did manage to say, "Come back this afternoon to continue your studies with Bartolo—perhaps he will have better luck knocking some knowledge into your brain." They both knew this wasn't true. If anything, Bartolo had even less patience with Corene than Sattisi did. But Corene nodded and made her escape. She headed straight to the main deck so she could lean against the railing and watch the water glitter in the sunlight and feel its immensity restore some of the balance to her soul. She liked the ocean; no matter how placid it seemed on the surface, you could never forget its capacity for uncontrolled turbulence. She was a sweela girl, aligned with fire far more than water, but she appreciated anything with the potential for chaos.

She wondered if Steff would join them for the afternoon tutoring session. The lessons usually went better when Steff was on hand, though he had been studying Malinquese even before they set sail, so he was more advanced than Corene. And in the past day or two, when Corene had started tallying up the people who hated her, she'd wondered if the list should include Steff.

Well. Steffanolo Kordan Bors Adova. The empress's grandson.

Filomara had discovered his existence in the most tortuous way possible. Some thirty years ago, she'd married off her daughter Subriella to a prince of Berringey. When Subriella began to fear for her life and that of her newborn son, Rafe, she'd faked her own death and escaped to Welce. There she met a lonely farmer, married him, and produced Steff. She'd died a few years after that, though Corene was hazy on the exact date. The brothers might have lived in obscurity for the rest of their lives except that, a couple of quintiles ago, someone from Berringey had recognized Rafe's distinctive birthmark. People started trying to kill him to keep him from taking the Berringese throne, and naturally that had caught Darien's attention, and Darien—of course—had figured out who was related to whom.

Filomara had wanted to bring both of her grandsons back to Malinqua, but Rafe had had plenty of reasons to stay behind in Welce. But Steff had been eager to leave the farm life behind him, eager to explore the heritage he never could have guessed was his. Corene strongly suspected that he had no idea how grueling, tedious, dangerous, and demanding life as a royal heir could be. When people weren't trying to get close to you so they could use you to their advantage, they were trying to kill you—or undermine you—or marry you off. And when none of *those* exciting events were under way, you were attending hideously boring state dinners or trying to learn the history of the world or having yet another discussion about the royal succession.

Really, could a farmer's son learn how to balance the desperate days with the dull ones?

She had posed that question to Steff, almost that bluntly, and he'd laughed. "I guess you've never lived on a farm," he said.

She'd eyed him with disfavor. "Do I *look* like I have?"

"Days and days and *days* of nothing but plowing fields, watering crops, and tending livestock. Seeing only the people who live right there on your land, because you don't have time to visit a neighbor or a friend. Then the brook floods or the barn catches fire or there's an early freeze, and you have to work like crazy to save the animals or cover the crops or build a dam between your house and the water. That's exactly what it is—dull as dirt until it's desperate as death. If that's what it's like to be heir to a throne, I already understand it."

But it's a much more sophisticated kind of boredom, she'd wanted to say. *A more elegant form of urgency. You have to speak Coziquela while you're enduring an endless dinner or fending off assassins.*

But she didn't. She wanted Steff to like her.

He had, at first. When they'd met, before he'd discovered his astonishing origins, he'd been awestruck and bashful—almost worshipful—having never so much as glimpsed a princess in the flesh before. It had been pleasant to have someone pay such close attention to her, listen to her with such reverence, almost stumble over his own feet in his willingness to serve her.

And it wasn't his sudden elevation to high status that had changed him, because he was still kind of a goofy, bashful, wide-eyed, unspoiled teenaged boy. No, he'd just started to find Corene troublesome and difficult.

"Why do you have to make Sattisi so mad all the time?" he'd demanded after one particularly contentious language lesson.

"She's rude to me! She treats me like some kind of uneducated slum girl."

"Only because you won't listen to her."

"I'd listen to her if she didn't yell at me for being stupid."

"She might not think you were stupid if you ever did the lessons before you came to class."

"I *hate* learning Malinquese!"

"Then why are you going to Malinqua?"

He had asked the question in a reasonable tone, but she could see the exasperation in his face. The real answer was too complicated to boil down to under an hour, so she'd made a flippant reply.

"Because nobody thought I would. That's why I do everything."

"Well, nobody thinks you'll learn Malinquese," he'd said. "Does that mean you will?"

He'd made her so mad that, for the next three days, she really *had* tried to master her lessons, just to prove all of them wrong. But Sattisi kept scolding and Bartolo kept frowning and pretty soon there weren't enough incentives to make her keep trying.

She had learned how to conjugate all the irregular verbs during those three days, though. So maybe the little burst of temper had had some benefit after all.

Though it hadn't made Steff like her any better.

Actually, he'd told her recently that she reminded him of his little sister, a half sibling born to his father's second wife. It shouldn't have bothered her because, even before they left Welce, she'd fallen into the habit of treating him like an annoying younger brother; but she'd wanted *him* to have a higher opinion of *her*. But she had a dreary suspicion that from now on he would view her as a twelve-year-old farm brat with ratty hair and bare feet, throwing a tantrum because she had to go milk a cow.

So maybe Steff didn't actually *hate* her (since he seemed to be fond of all his siblings), but he certainly didn't worship her anymore.

Well, who cared? She didn't need people fawning over her—she'd had plenty of that in her life. She needed someone to size her up and decide she would be the perfect royal bride and forge an alliance with her that would see them both on the throne.

The longer she was on the ship, the easier it became to silence the small, wistful voice at the back of her mind. *But you don't want to be the empress of Malinqua,* the voice whispered, in direct opposition to everything Corene had ever said or thought or dreamed. *You might not know what you want, but it's not that.*

It was. And she wouldn't let anyone, even herself, try to convince her otherwise.

She stood at the railing so long that she could feel her face turning scarlet from the sun and the abrasive ocean air. The wind was so strong that the ship's flag streamed out from the mast at an almost true horizontal; it was easy to make out the crossed swords, the symmetrical white flowers, sewn onto the bright field of red. Corene thought it was gaudy; she greatly preferred Welce's simple rosette of five interlocked colors.

The wind was also playing havoc with Corene's hair, and she didn't even want to think about how bad it looked. Even when she was inland on Welce, far from the ocean or the river, her dark red hair had a natural curl. Here on the water, it was a mass of frizz and knots, impossible to tame, and she'd started wearing it pulled into a tight knot at the back of her head. It was not a good style for her; it left her looking stark and startled, her brown eyes too big, her fair skin too white, her sharp chin too pointed.

So today she'd left her hair loose, and now it floated around her head like a bed of algae, though redder and even more tangled. She'd never get a comb through it. Maybe she'd just cut it all off. Filomara wore her gray hair straight and short; she'd probably approve of the practicality.

Corene had just decided it might be time to go below and seek her cabin when she heard footsteps behind her on the deck. Turning, she found she'd been joined by the one person on the ship who *didn't* hate her—didn't even seem to find her irksome. Foley. A member of the royal guard of Welce, and formerly assigned exclusively to her sister Josetta. Corene was pretty sure that if he hadn't agreed to accompany her to Malinqua, she wouldn't have had the nerve to come. He was the one person who always made her feel safe, no matter how strange and precarious her circumstances were.

If she'd been a shopkeeper's daughter instead of a princess, she would have been mad for him, attracted to his size, his steadiness, his preternatural calm. But of course, she *was* a princess, sailing the world in search of a throne. She certainly allowed herself to think of her guard as a friend, but she'd never entertain other thoughts about him.

Well, not very often.

"Has somebody been looking for me?" she asked him.

"The empress's cousin said you were expected for a lesson."

She grimaced. "I'm sure he's just as delighted at the prospect as I am."

Foley merely grinned. Although he was an alert listener, he tended not to talk a great deal. Sometimes Corene made a game out of drawing him into a conversation, trying to see what she could get him to say. Usually it wasn't much.

She sighed and turned back to the ocean, resting her arms along the railing. "I suppose I need to learn *something* this afternoon. It would be good if I understood *some* of the conversations going on around me while we're in Malinqua."

He didn't answer, and she glanced up at him. "Have you picked up any of the language since we've been on the ship?"

He answered in Malinquese, which surprised her so much she almost pitched overboard. "I can ask for food and water and beer," he said. "Count to a hundred and name the quintiles and ninedays."

"That's excellent!" she exclaimed. "But what do you mean—'name the quintiles'?"

He switched back to Welchin. "The Malinquese have quintiles and ninedays, like we do, but they have different words for them," he explained.

"I never thought of that," she said. "I guess I should have. The Malinquese don't care about elemental affiliations. I don't understand it."

In Welce, everyone was presumed to fall under the influence of one of the five elements—fire, water, air, earth, or wood—and exhibit the corresponding character traits. Corene was a sweela creature, a child of fire, and her quick temper certainly attested to that. Foley was all torz, all earth, as steady and dependable as the land itself. Steff was coru through and through, as fluid and adaptable as water.

The influence of the elements also spilled over into the seasons. They were just now coming to the end of Quinnahunti as summer reached its high point. In Welce, they would soon be observing the Quinnatorz changeday as they moved into the next quintile. In fact—

"It's Quinnatorz changeday, isn't it?" she demanded. "And nobody noticed! Not even a special dish at breakfast this morning! Do they even *have* changedays in Malinqua?"

"They acknowledge changedays, but they don't celebrate them as holidays," Foley answered.

She nodded glumly. "They don't seem like particularly lighthearted people." Almost without her volition, her hand came up to touch the necklace she wore under her tunic. A slim silver chain holding three simple charms. "And I suppose they don't have blessings, either?" she asked. She could tell that her voice sounded small and childlike, which annoyed her, but somehow she couldn't make herself sound scornful and derisive, as she would prefer.

Foley's only answer was to shake his head.

No blessings. Really, it was hard to imagine how the Malinquese made it through their days. In Welce, all infants received three blessings a few hours after they were born, and these blessings would sustain and guide them for the rest of their lives. People also could drop by a temple at any time and draw fresh blessings for daily guidance if they were dealing with some vexing problem. There were eight blessings associated with each of the five elements, and three extraordinary blessings on top of those.

Most of Corene's life she'd carried the sweela blessings of imagination and intelligence, and one hunti blessing of courage, no doubt a reflection of her father's unbreakable heritage of wood. But her life had been so turbulent this year, and she'd been so unhappy—she'd wanted to be someone new, someone different, someone who could leave old burdens behind. So she'd insisted that Josetta draw new blessings for her as a sign of her planned metamorphosis. The first one to come up had been clarity—a sweela gift—and something Corene would be deeply grateful to possess. The coru trait of change followed right on its heels, and Corene had been glad of that; she'd been more than ready for change to shape her life. She'd been surprised at how happy she was that her third blessing was courage, for she'd hated to give that one up. And she thought she'd need it if she really did develop the clarity to make wholesale changes to her life.

She'd thought all her blessings had coalesced when she'd decided to leave Welce. It had seemed so clear to her, two ninedays ago, that traveling to Malinqua would be just the thing to set her life on a new path. She was seventeen now, almost eighteen—it was time to take up an adult's responsibilities. It was time to stop trying to impress her father and please her mother. It was time to plunge into the future.

But now she wasn't so sure.

"It'll be so different there, won't it? In Malinqua," she said softly. "Nothing at all will be familiar."

Foley glanced down at her, sober as always, and for a moment she thought he might not reply. Then he said, "But isn't that why you wanted to go?"

THREE

The harbor at Palminera, when they reached it two days later, looked much like the harbor in Welce, except three times its size. The piers stretched on and on; Corene thought they might accommodate a thousand boats, whereas she'd never seen more than a couple hundred at one time in Welce.

And the city that was laid out behind it was magnificent, much bigger than Chialto back home. The harbor, at sea level, was slightly lower than the surrounding countryside, so the city seemed to rise slowly from the edges of the water and spill out in a lush and varied display. And it was densely packed with buildings—tall, short, wood, stone— crammed together like children at a carnival display. From shipboard, Corene couldn't tell which were the wealthy districts, which were the slums, but it was clear there were demarcation lines created by walls, canals, and roadways, each laid in with its own distinctive colors.

She was back on the deck, staring her eyes out, as the ship made its final, excruciatingly slow approach to land. Steff had joined her as soon as they'd gotten close enough to see anything, and he was staring just as hard as she was. Inexplicably, Sattisi and Bartolo had also chosen to stand at the railing with them—although maybe, Corene thought, they were just keeping Steff company. The empress had remained below.

"Magnificent, isn't it?" Bartolo said in his self-satisfied way.

Corene couldn't take issue with him. "It really is," she admitted. "I've never seen such a big city."

"This is small by the standards of Cozique—but few other countries in the southern seas boast a town much bigger," Bartolo said.

Steff pointed. "What are those two big towers? There and there?"

"They represent day and night," Sattisi piped up. "Fire and ice. South and north. Flame and shadow. Flesh and spirit. Life and death. The duality of existence."

This *duality* idea had wound through some of the most recent lessons, but Corene hadn't thought it would manifest in such a physical way. The towers were impressive, though. If she'd correctly identified her compass directions, the one to the north stood for ice and death and spirit and shadow. It appeared to be constructed of white marble, from this distance utterly smooth; it was crowned with a half-moon of some clear material that seemed to emit an opal light.

No surprise that she preferred the southern structure, which looked as if it had been built of warm, rough, reddish granite. On its roof, open to the sky, were huge flower petals of stained glass—red and yellow and orange—and at the center of the great blossom writhed an enormous fire. It was an eye-catching sight even in the middle of the day, against a summer sky practically drained of color by the afternoon sun. She'd bet it was really impressive by night.

Steff's attention had already moved on. "Look at all the crowds," he exclaimed. That was when Corene realized that the streets were packed with people, all gathered to witness the ship's arrival; more gawkers stood on the roofs or hung out of upper-story windows, watching and waving. "Are they here to see the empress?"

Bartolo seemed smug. "Yes. Anytime she departs, there are throngs to welcome her when she returns. She is much beloved."

Steff and Corene exchanged quick smiles. It was the one point they'd agreed on during the journey—Filomara was easy to admire, but difficult to like, at least for those who knew her intimately. But her subjects might not care that she was cold and calculating in her personal relationships. If she kept her people safe, treated them fairly, and never lost faith with them, they would love her anyway.

Corene couldn't resist poking at the others. "Maybe they're not here to see Filomara," she suggested. "Maybe they want to catch a glimpse of Steff."

Steff looked briefly horrified and Sattisi displeased. Bartolo just shook his head. "They know nothing about him," Bartolo said.

"Really? She didn't send the news ahead?" Corene asked.

Bartolo pursed his lips, thinking over his answer. "The empress wished to introduce her grandson to everyone at court at the same time, to personally explain the circumstances surrounding his birth."

"She didn't want to give anyone time to start scheming against him," Corene translated. "So she wanted him to be a surprise."

Sattisi's frown grew darker, but Bartolo, unexpectedly, nodded. "It's possible that not everyone at court will be entirely pleased by my cousin's great good fortune," he said carefully.

"Anyway, she wants proof, doesn't she, before she starts introducing me around?" Steff interjected. "She said that the doctors here would be able to trace my blood. Or something."

Bartolo nodded again. "Yes. She wants to be absolutely sure you are who you claim to be before making great fanfare about your existence."

It sounded vaguely insulting, as so many of Bartolo's comments did, but Steff just nodded. Malinqua might have advanced scientific and medical abilities, but Welce had the primes—the heads of the Five Families, the people most in tune with the elemental affiliations. Darien's wife, Zoe, was the coru prime, a woman with strong ties to both water and blood; she could lay her hand on anyone and instantly identify his or her family bloodline. That was how she'd figured out Rafe's heritage, and then Steff's. If Zoe said Steff was Filomara's grandson, it was true. But Corene supposed she couldn't blame Filomara for wanting her own kind of proof.

"Honestly, I'd just as soon arrive quietly," Steff said. "Not have people staring at me the minute I step off the boat." He glanced down at Corene and grinned as he said, "Nobody knows about you, either, since you came along at the last minute. The servants at the palace won't be expecting a Welchin princess. They won't have your rooms ready for *hours*. Maybe you'll have to sit in the courtyard with all your baggage."

Sattisi took the bait. "They might not be expecting Princess Corene, but palace servants are always ready for unexpected guests of high quality," she answered swiftly.

"Oh, they know about me," Corene said. "Didn't you see the small boats come and go while we traveled? Filomara might have wanted to keep Steff a secret, but she told people I was on the way."

"Maybe some of the crowds are out there to see *you*, then," Steff suggested.

"No," Sattisi snapped. "They are all for the empress."

Corene couldn't help grinning at the spite, but she did wonder.

Filomara had had plenty of time to send news ahead—and so had Corene's father. A small, swift cutter could have completed the journey from Welce to Malinqua days ago; the spies that Darien no doubt kept in Palminera surely knew his daughter was on her way. Corene had even wondered if he might send a contingent of royal guards to await her arrival. The minute she disembarked, they would close ranks around her, not listening to her protests, and escort her to their own vessel. She would be whisked back to Chialto before she'd even had time to visit the royal palace.

She had spent hours on the journey trying to decide if she would be furious at that turn of events, or glad. If Darien sent the guards, did that mean he loved her too much to let her go? If he didn't, did that mean he admired her spirit and wanted her to succeed in an adventure she had picked out on her own? That he trusted her to navigate a tricky foreign court, secure alliances there, and strengthen Welce's position in the world?

Or did it mean that he didn't care where she was, what she did? He had a new baby daughter now—already named the next heir to the throne of Welce—he might not have any time to spare for the troublesome, unpopular princess who had no defined place at court. He might have been glad to see her go.

They were at the pier now, and cadres of men both onboard and onshore were dashing around, securing ropes, and shouting. A line of Malinquese soldiers held the common crowds at bay, so the royal party could disembark onto a relatively clear dock. Corene scanned the crowds closest to the soldiers and farther back along the city streets, clustered against walls and between buildings, waving, calling, chanting Filomara's name.

She didn't see anyone wearing the Welchin rosette. No one standing still and focused, staring only at *her*. No one waiting for her, no one looking for her at all.

Good. She would be all on her own in Malinqua, and she would be just fine.

They rode in open carriages from the harbor to the palace, and hordes lined the streets every mile of the way. For the first few blocks, Corene had waved and smiled at the crowds, since that was what a princess was supposed to do, but pretty soon she realized that no one was paying attention to anyone except Filomara, who sat in the lead carriage with Bartolo and Sattisi. She and Steff and Foley might as well be invisible for all the attention they were receiving. So instead, she leaned back against the cushions and looked around with great curiosity.

The buildings nearest the harbor hadn't been all that impressive, mostly one- and two-story structures that appeared to be warehouses and shipping offices. Past the commercial districts were blocks and blocks of run-down residential neighborhoods filled with multistory buildings that appeared to be crammed with people. Corene guessed these were the cheap areas where the working families took small apartments and dreamed of better days. The buildings became progressively more distinctive, more impressive, and better maintained the farther they traveled from the harbor.

The architecture didn't get *really* interesting until they passed through a pair of iron gates that had to be twenty feet high. They were set into walls that curved in from the north and south and obviously enclosed the heart of the city.

The wall extending from the northern border was made of heavy white stones, more powdery and pitted than marble, and irregular enough that they were probably boulders that had rolled down from some mountain. The southern wall consisted of enormous blocks of reddish granite, uniform in size and perfectly mortared together.

Corene nudged Steff, because he was the sort of boy who generally noticed *things*, even though he wasn't paying attention to people. He nodded and said, "Just like the towers."

"I think the whole city is like that."

Indeed, it was quickly obvious that the route they followed made a straight dividing line down the interior of the walled enclave. The roads to their right, the north side, were paved with some kind of silver-white amalgam; those on the left, with material that incorporated crushed red rock. Most of the northern buildings were white or off-white in color, whether constructed of stone or painted wood; those in the southernmost streets featured warmer colors: terra-cotta and cinnamon and stained oak.

"I find this a little peculiar, don't you?" Corene asked.

"It makes me wonder why they set up the city this way," Steff agreed.

"I wonder if one side is considered good and one side bad. If you spend your whole life wanting to move from a red house to a white one, for instance."

Foley spoke up. "Everything looks pretty well-kept, though. Like the two sides are equal, just different."

"I think they carry this *duality* idea a little too far," Corene said.

Steff laughed. "Well, in Welce everything is about your blessings or your affiliations. It's sort of the same thing."

Corene couldn't help a small sniff of disapproval. She had the feeling Steff didn't give all that much weight to the blessings, either; the country folk usually didn't. She glanced at Foley, who had taken the less desirable backward-facing seat when they climbed into the carriage. He was watching the city roll past, studying with acute interest the buildings, the people, the very layout of the streets. He'd probably paid enough attention to their route that he could find his way back to the harbor without a misstep. She didn't think Foley worried overmuch about blessings, either.

"Well, I just think it's *odd*," she said, and flounced back against the seat.

"Just different," Foley said. "Not the same thing."

The palace, when they finally arrived, was enormous, easily twice the size of the one in Chialto where Corene had lived for the first eleven years of her life. Like the towers and the city itself, the palace was split in two: the north wing built of smooth white stone glittering with embedded crystals, the southern one of a polished red marble veined with gold and black. The two halves were perfect mirror images of each other, with doors and windows placed in corresponding locations on each story. Even the shrubs that flowered in front of the two wings were distinctly different, the northern hedge covered in white star-shaped flowers, the southern hedge with delicate red blossoms.

"I mean, it's excessive," Corene muttered as the carriages came to a halt in a courtyard that was easily big enough to host a changeday festival.

"I like it," Steff said.

There was no more time to talk, because the minute they stopped, they were completely engulfed in people—footmen to help them down from the coaches, servants with trays of food and drink. The ride from the harbor had been miserably hot, and Corene was grateful to the young woman who offered her a glass of something sweet and fruity and divinely cold. There was more than enough for everybody; Steff and Foley took one glass each, and Corene had two.

While she sipped at the second glass, she watched Filomara, who was already out of her carriage and deep in conversation with someone. He was a tall, slender man with sharp features and a decisive manner— probably the empress's chief of staff. The one who made the palace function, the one Filomara would trust to accomplish any task she might send his way.

He was the one who would not be nonplussed to learn he must conjure up quarters suitable to house an unknown man who could very well be heir to the throne.

Corene had just handed her empty glass to a serving girl when Filomara brought the tall man over to meet them. Close up, he looked to be in his early sixties, with a little silver in his thinning black hair. His gray eyes were bright with intelligence, and his face was utterly impassive.

"My steward, Lorian," Filomara introduced him. She did not bother supplying names for Corene and Steff; clearly she had already shared this information during their whispered colloquy. Her eyes gleamed with faint humor. "Of the far too many men in my life, he's the only one I've ever found to be completely reliable. Go to him with any requests you have or any issue you can't resolve."

"Excellent," Corene said, giving him a friendly nod and a half-smile. Steff watched her and followed her lead—not too familiar, not too patronizing. He was still figuring out how royalty was supposed to behave to nobility; he had no idea how he was supposed to treat the servants.

"Lorian will show you to your rooms, which are near each other, since you know no one else in Palminera," Filomara went on. The humor grew more pronounced. "And he will find staff to serve each of you, since, regrettably, neither of you has attendants of your own."

Well, *Corene* did—back in Chialto. But she hadn't wanted to bring anyone but Foley on this adventure, so she'd left her maid behind. Steff had never had his own valet, as far as she knew. He'd shared one with Rafe when they were in Chialto, meeting Filomara for the first time. But he'd been uncomfortable with the notion that someone was always going to be waiting there, "ready to pounce on me every time I step into the room."

Lorian gave them each respectful bows. "I have just the right candidates in mind. You will let me know if they are unsuitable for any reason."

"Well, say, I don't know if—" Steff began, but Corene elbowed him and he shut up.

"Thank you. That's most kind," she said. "I admit I'll welcome a bath and a chance to change clothes."

"Yes, I always want to wash the sea air from my face," Filomara agreed. She surveyed Corene and Steff a moment, as if wondering whether they might look different now that they were standing on Malinquese soil. "We are not very fancy here," she said. "We do not have all the pomp and grandness you have come to expect at your own royal court."

Corene let her eyes roam over the palace, its white walls, its red ones. "I find that a little hard to credit," she said. "Your palace seems grand enough to house extraordinary amounts of pomp."

Filomara smiled. "It is the heart of Palminera—almost a city in its own right," she said. "Maybe five hundred people live here—my cousin, my nephews, my closest advisors, all in the royal wing." She gestured first at the glittering white walls, then waved at the red walls of the southern wing. "On the other side, the top city officials and their family members reside on the upper floors, and they have offices and conduct business on the bottom stories. Of course, there are public spaces and kitchens and storage rooms. If we were under siege, which I devoutly hope we never are, we could keep this small city fed and clothed for— How long is it, Lorian?"

"Three ninedays," he answered smoothly.

Steff's practical nature was intrigued, Corene could tell. "You must have a water supply, then—something not easily poisoned or cut off?"

Filomara nodded as if pleased he'd thought of that. "An underground spring deep beneath the foundations," she said.

"That's handy," Foley said.

Corene saw Lorian's attention shift to Foley as the steward tried to decide exactly how to categorize this particular new arrival. So she helped him out. "Lorian, this is Foley, a member of my father's royal guard, and here as my protector. Please provide him quarters very near to mine."

"Of course, Princess," Lorian said.

"Now that that's all settled, let us see you to your rooms," Filomara said. "As I started to say, we are not an ostentatious court. Dinner will be a small affair, with only family and a few guests in attendance. I do not have parties or entertainments planned. I hope you are not disappointed."

"So far nothing in Malinqua has disappointed me," Corene said. "I'm sure dinner won't, either."

"Good," the empress said. "Then I will see you again in a few hours."

It would have taken a few hours to navigate the whole of the palace, Corene thought, but fortunately Lorian took them by a straightforward route to their suites on the fourth floor of the northern, royal wing of the palace. Along the way, he pointed out rooms and hallways that might be of some interest to them—the ballroom, the library, a smaller dining parlor—but Corene figured she'd try to absorb all of that at a later date. For now, she allowed herself to be impressed by the pleasing proportions of the interior hallways—all high ceilings and thick carpets, giving an unexpected feeling of softness and warmth to a place so forbiddingly large.

Similarly, her quarters, halfway down a long hallway, could not have been more charming. The suite included a sitting room, a bedroom, a bathing room, and a maid's chamber; each one was filled with furniture of simple design but the highest-quality materials. Her windows overlooked the expansive courtyard.

"Excellent," Corene said. "And Foley's quarters?"

Lorian opened a door right across the hall from Corene's to show them an interior two-room suite with no window, but there was nothing shabby about it, either. Probably bigger than the spaces Foley had called his own when he accompanied Josetta to her various residences.

"Excellent," she said again.

Then the steward led them to Steff's rooms, adjacent to Corene's, and she looked around curiously. If the servants had had to scramble to put his suite in order, there was no sign of hasty cleaning. It was just as bright and well-kept as Corene's, though decorated in more masculine colors. Lorian glanced at Steff as if awaiting approval. Steff could only think to copy Corene. "Excellent! Really!" he managed. Corene had to smother a laugh.

"Your luggage is being carried upstairs and will arrive momentarily," Lorian informed them. "Emilita will wait on the princess and Andolo will serve—" He hesitated a moment, and then just nodded in Steff's direction. "You."

They thanked him solemnly and he finally departed. The three of them stood motionless in the hallway until he disappeared.

Then Steff collapsed against the wall. "Corene! Did you see the *size* of this place? It's monstrous! It was all I could do not to stare like a half-wit!"

She grinned at him. "And to think, you might be lucky enough to inherit the whole thing."

"Forget inheriting! I only hope I don't get so lost I end up starving in a dark hallway, terrifying some poor servant girl when she finds me dead."

"The size is dramatic but the layout seems simple," Foley said. "I think there are only two turns off of any main corridor—at any intersection, go twice in the same direction, and you will either end up near the grand stairwell or a dead end. And then just reverse."

"Well, that helps," Steff said. "But I'm still terrified."

Corene surveyed him with a half-smile. "What did you expect? You've seen the palace in Chialto. This is bigger, but it's the same idea. A lot of space, a lot of people, and someone watching your every move, even when you think you're alone."

Steff glanced nervously over his shoulder, which made Corene and Foley laugh. "I didn't think about it much," he admitted. "I just knew I wanted to see Malinqua. Learn more about my mother." He shrugged. "Get away from the farm and do something interesting with my life."

"Well, this is about as far from the farm as you'll ever get," she answered. They could hear footsteps coming down the hallway, and quiet voices speaking Malinquese. The servants assigned to them, Corene guessed.

She lowered her voice. "Don't forget what I said. Someone is always watching. Someone is always listening. This valet coming to wait on you? A spy for the empress."

"That seems harsh."

"She pays him. He'll tell her anything he learns about you."

Steff heaved a sigh just as the servants stepped into view. Two men, pushing carts full of luggage, and one slim young girl. They were all dressed in dark clothing unrelieved by the slightest decoration. "Lucky I don't have anything to conceal," Steff said.

Corene laughed at him silently. "There is always something to conceal." That was a lesson she'd learned from her mother, practically while she was still in the cradle. Always something to conceal, always something to learn, always something to turn to your advantage if you could just figure out how.

Foley gave them both a short bow. "I'll let you settle into your rooms now. Call or knock if you need anything."

Corene nodded, but paused in the act of turning away. "Let me know if *you* need anything," she said. "If the servants are rude to you or don't do what you ask."

Foley showed a faint amusement. "I think I can fend for myself."

She couldn't help smiling in return. "But if you can't, I am always ready to save you."

Emilita proved to be quiet, competent, monosyllabic, and too deferential to respond to Corene's attempts to draw her out. She also couldn't speak any language but Malinquese, which severely limited Corene's conversational gambits. She wouldn't be able to grill the girl about the rest of the occupants of the palace. A pity.

Until a few years ago, Corene had never given servants a second thought. They were just there, all the time, like air or sunshine, and they did whatever you told them to with admirable efficiency. Her mother treated staff with the same careless cruelty she treated anyone who didn't offer her an immediate and obvious advantage—which had been fine while they lived at the royal residence, where there were servants galore. Once Alys remarried and moved in with her new husband, maids and butlers frequently quit on her without warning. It hadn't been the greatest source of stress in that household, but it had been a constant one.

It wasn't until Corene started spending time with her father and Zoe that she realized even the lowest kitchen maid, even the rawest footman, was an individual person with thoughts and feelings and dreams just as distinct and real as Corene's own. It had been quite a shock. But nobody was invisible to Zoe; no one was worthless. If possible, Corene's sister Josetta felt even more strongly on the subject, since Josetta spent half her days in the slums of Chialto, ministering to the poor.

Corene knew she wasn't as bighearted as either one of them, but this was a lesson she'd embraced with zeal. She'd started acknowledging housekeepers, merchants, restaurant owners, beggars on the street— meeting everyone's eyes like an equal. She hadn't changed her behavior expecting any kind of payoff, but the rewards had been huge. Cooks saved the best portions for her, footmen warned her when there were unexpected guests in the parlor. Every single person in her mother's employment was devoted to Corene, and hadn't *that* proved handy when Alys's husband—well. When he took an inappropriate interest in Corene and her bedroom habits. The maids had taken turns sleeping in Corene's room with her to make sure Dominic couldn't surprise her in the night. And they'd been only too happy to pack up her things when Darien learned the truth of the situation and permanently removed her from her mother's house.

Now Corene had permanently removed herself from Darien's house as well. Time to charm a whole new set of servants—or not, if Emilita's diffidence was anything to go by. Maybe Corene would have better luck once she'd managed to learn the language.

She had washed up in the deliciously hot water of the bathing room, and now she was wrapped in a robe of Emilita's providing, surveying the contents of her luggage. The maid had hung everything in the huge closet that took up one whole wall of the bedroom. Corene hadn't been traveling with a very big wardrobe when she made the spontaneous decision to leave with Filomara, so her clothes filled only a fraction of the available space. But at least she had some of her finest tunics and trousers with her, since she'd been planning to attend several formal events as the elite of Welce said goodbye to the visiting empress.

"What should I wear to dinner tonight?" she asked Emilita in halting Malinquese. "My best? Or something more—" She didn't know how to say *simple* in this stupid language. "Something else."

"Princess?" Emilia replied, her delicate face looking worried. It was the word she had used most often during their restricted conversation. It seemed to be the most respectful way she could think of to convey, *I have no idea what you're trying to say.*

"Never mind," Corene said with a sigh. "With any luck someone will take me shopping someday soon."

"Princess?"

Corene had never been so grateful to hear a knock on the door. Steff, probably, with sartorial challenges of his own, but at least he'd understand her rantings when she vented her frustration.

But Steff wasn't the one standing on the other side when Emilita opened the door. It was a young woman, maybe a year or two older than Corene, peering in around Emilita's small form.

"You are the princess from the quaint little country of Welce, are you not?" she said in beautifully enunciated Coziquela. "This is where Lorian said he would put you, and I have been waiting days and days and *days* for you to arrive. Can I come in? Are you too weary? I am going simply mad with boredom, you know."

On those words, and over Emilita's faint protests, the woman stepped inside. She was quite literally the most beautiful person Corene had ever seen. She was small and delicately formed, with a heart-shaped face exquisite as a doll's and blue eyes so dark they shaded into purple. Her clothing was deceptively simple—a sleeveless indigo sheath gathered into hundreds of pleats that fell without any kind of tailoring from her shoulders to the floor. Her hair was a silky black, full of wispy curls, and her red mouth was curved in a hopeful smile.

"You must be the princess from Cozique," Corene said.

The woman laughed and sashayed deeper into the room. "I am! Is it my accent that gives me away, or my clothing, or the fact that I am so very badly behaved?"

"All of those things, all together. I'm Corene." She came forward and offered a slight bow—one member of royalty to another—and the Coziquela princess responded in kind.

"And I am Melissande. You have no idea how glad I am to see you. Please tell me you are not as dull as the very quiet, very dour Princess Alette of Dhonsho."

Corene laughed out loud. "And if I am? And easily offended on top of it?"

Melissande heaved an exaggerated sigh. "Then I shall have to hope Filomara sails to many other countries and brings back more candidates for her nephews to consider. But I was watching from my window when you arrived, and I made note of your red hair. I have never in my life met a redhead who was boring. I have very high hopes of you."

That made Corene laugh even harder, though Emilita looked uncertain and anxious. "Princess?" she said. "Shall we now dress you for dinner?"

Melissande turned her graceful little body and gave Emilita a warm smile. "Oh, she does not need to dress for another hour at least, I am very sure," she said in Malinquese. "I must talk to her and discover everything about darling little Welce! Would you be so kind as to give us privacy—just for a while?"

Emilita looked inquiringly at Corene, who nodded. "Yes, please. I will see you again in an hour."

Emilita bowed and slipped out the door, shutting it quietly behind her. Corene opened her mouth to speak, but Melissande held up a hand for silence, and appeared to be concentrating intently. "Some of them listen at the door," she breathed.

Corene was amused. "Of course they do."

"And some of them speak Coziquela, even though they pretend they do not."

"Of course," Corene said again. "Too bad you don't speak Welchin."

"But I do!" Melissande exclaimed, instantly switching to that language. "Not very well, I am afraid, but you are right—it is undoubtedly much safer."

She spoke it perfectly. Corene grinned. "Safer?" she echoed. "What will we be saying that no one should overhear?"

Melissande crossed the room to fling herself into one of the plain, well-made chairs, and smiled up at Corene. "We shall be gossiping about the empress and the nephews she is trying to marry off, of course! Do not tell me you are not about to expire with curiosity."

Corene pulled the sash of her robe tighter and dropped onto a settee across from Melissande. "Oh, but I am," she assured her guest. "*What* have I gotten myself into?"

Melissande trilled with laughter. "I suppose you know how the situation stands? Filomara's daughters both died, leaving no children of their own behind, so Filomara must choose her heir from among her nephews. There are three of them."

"Why doesn't Filomara name one of her brothers her heir? I had the impression she was the oldest of several siblings."

"Indeed yes, which is why the crown came to her all these years ago." Melissande's blue eyes glittered with amusement. "She had four younger brothers, though two of them are dead and the other two never come to court. No one will say exactly why that is, and I am so very curious! At any rate, many years ago, apparently, Filomara declared that she would not saddle Malinqua with some doddering old fool for a leader, so she cut the brothers from the succession. Everyone thinks one of her nephews will take the throne next."

"But she hasn't said which one?"

"No! She wants them to prove that they are worthy to rule, but so far there is no clear favorite."

"What are the three nephews like?"

Melissande resettled herself in her chair, stretching her legs before her so her feet peeped out from the pleated fabric. She was wearing cloth shoes dyed the same color as her dress, and intricately embroidered with a design of leaves and flowers. For an adult, she had the smallest feet Corene had ever seen.

"What are they like as potential heirs or potential husbands?" Melissande asked.

Corene grinned. "Either, I suppose."

"Each one has a—trait—that might be considered a drawback in a monarch, but that I personally would find an advantage in a mate. Though not all women would think as I do, I am very sure."

"Oh, this ought to be interesting."

When Melissande smiled, *wicked* was the word that came to Corene's mind. "The oldest is Garameno. He is thirty-two or thirty-three, I think, the smartest of all of them, very ambitious. He sits on the council and stays informed about everything that happens in Malinqua. Filomara seems to value his advice."

"So what's his disadvantage?"

"He was injured ten or twelve years ago and his legs never fully recovered, so he must use a wheeled chair to get around. He can walk for a few steps at a time, they say, though I have never seen him attempt it."

"So his subjects might perceive him as weak because he could not lead them to battle, for instance," Corene said.

"That is what seems to worry Filomara," Melissande said. "I cannot tell how he is regarded by the prefect and other council members. I have only been here in Palminera for a nineday and a half."

Corene studied the other woman for a moment. Melissande was being surprisingly candid and helpfully informative, but there was no way to know if she was being truthful. She might have an ulterior motive for sharing her insights in such an open way; she might be lying; she might be trying to enmesh Corene in her own machinations. She was such a charming package that Corene imagined most people were delighted to be singled out for her confidences. The trick was figuring out what she might want in return.

"I can see why some women might think a wheelchair would be a liability in a husband," Corene said. "Why do you consider it an advantage?"

Melissande laughed. "Because the idea of being stronger than my husband very much appeals to me!" She lifted her bare arms above her head. "Look at me! I am so very delicate! I would be wholly at the mercy of a brutish man. But I believe I could outrun Garameno in his chair."

Corene spared a moment to think Melissande would probably find ways to outmaneuver a brutish husband as well, but she didn't say so. "Well, that's a good point," she said. "So, what about the other two?"

"Jiramondi—"

"Why do they have such *names*?" Corene burst out. "Filomara and Bartolo and Jiramondi—these soft, beautiful names when *none* of them, as far as I can tell, are soft or beautiful. When their clothing is plain and their houses are plain and they make a point of telling you they are not ostentatious people—"

"No, it is quite ironic," Melissande agreed. "And they seem to be quite unaware of the irony, which makes it even more annoying. And yet, those are their names. After a while you get used to it."

"So. Jiramondi—"

"The middle nephew. The most sophisticated of the three. Not as smart as Garameno, but not stupid, either. He is most often the one who deals with foreign ambassadors as he has more tact than almost anyone else in court."

"And his liability?"

Melissande seemed to debate. "I do not know how this is viewed in Welce, but in Malinqua it is considered quite a disgrace when a man or a woman is—I do not know your word for it. In Coziquela we call them *sublime*."

Corene was wholly at a loss. "I don't know what you're trying to say."

"I suppose I must be cruder. When a man wants sex only with another man, or a woman with another woman. What do you call such people in Welchin?"

Corene shrugged. "We don't have a word."

"*Really?* No one comments and no one cares?"

Corene shrugged again. "There are comments, I suppose—like there are comments anytime someone picks someone out. 'Why'd she choose *him*?' 'She looks like she'd be cold in bed.' 'Wouldn't want to live in *that* household.' But I never heard—it's just—why would anybody care?"

Melissande was smiling. "To think everyone in Malinqua considers

Welce such a backward little country! But that is very progressive, don't you think?"

Corene decided to let the insult pass. "So, Jiramondi is—what did you call him? 'Sublime'? And this offends Filomara and the people of her country?"

"Yes, and here we have more irony!" Melissande exclaimed. "Because Filomara never had much use for her husband, so I would not have been surprised to learn she was sublime as well—and sadly could never take the opportunity to show her true self."

"Maybe," Corene said. "But I'm not sure she would have loved a wife any better than a husband. I'm not sure she would have loved anybody." Filomara might have adored her daughters, but maybe not; she'd sent Steff's mother off to Berringey knowing full well that the girl's life could be forfeit. Even Corene's own mother wouldn't have been that callous.

Probably.

"You are doubtless correct," Melissande agreed. "And yet, Jiramondi labors under a stigma that might prevent him from taking the throne."

"And if he *is* sublime—well, I can see where most women would consider that a drawback in a husband," Corene said. "But you don't?"

That wicked smile again. "I am the most cosmopolitan of women! I am not shocked when people tell tales of taking lovers or experimenting in the bedroom. I have always thought it would be utterly tedious to be married to one man for eternity. But a sublime man who does not wish to sleep with me himself? And who is grateful that I make no demands on him? How is that not ideal?"

Corene burst out laughing. "Ideal if he doesn't mind that you take other lovers," Corene said. "And if he isn't worried about siring his own heirs."

Melissande was smiling. "If the rumors about Welce are true," she said, "your old king did not worry about that so very much, either."

Corene gave a small sigh and leaned back against her settee. "Oh, they're true. Vernon certainly had help producing his own daughters." She gave Melissande an inquiring look. "But I understand that in Malinqua they have techniques they use to test the blood—to make sure that an heir is legitimate?"

"They do? Well, then, I am certain a cautious woman could make sure not to conceive outside of the marriage bed. And a determined one could convince her sublime husband to get her with child at least once. Those seem like very minor obstacles to me."

"I can hardly wait to hear about the third nephew."

"Greggorio. The youngest, though his father was the oldest. He is very well-liked and very good-looking. He also is *very* interested in women, though he is quite young still, only eighteen, I believe. From what I have observed, he is a favorite with the prefect and other members of court."

"But?"

Melissande spoke slowly, consideringly. "But he is not very intelligent, which sometimes makes him stubborn and sometimes means he cannot grasp—subtlety."

Corene raised her eyebrows. "I can hardly wait to see how you turn this liability into an advantage."

Melissande laughed. "A stupid man who likes women is easily controlled by a beautiful, clever wife. I think we would suit very well."

Corene took a deep breath. "So! These three are the only contenders for Filomara's crown?"

She asked the question to see if Melissande had an inkling of Steff's existence, but she was surprised at Melissande's answer.

"No, there is a faction that will only be happy if Liramelli is named Filomara's heir."

"Who?"

"The daughter of the prefect. Apparently, there are some who feel the prefect's line has a better claim to the throne."

"That's who Filomara married," Corene said. "Someone from the prefect's family."

"Yes! You have been studying your Malinquese history, I see. If I understand correctly, Liramelli is the great-niece of Filomara's husband."

"And what are *her* defects and advantages?"

"Well, her chief disadvantage is that she would not want to marry either of *us*, given the way the Malinquese treat their sublime!" Melissande replied, bubbling with laughter.

"Aside from that."

"She has no disqualifiers. She is sincere and intelligent and kind—really, her list of virtues goes on and on. She is not particularly beautiful—though I think if they would give her to me for just an afternoon I could do *something* to make her fashionable. She would make a most excellent empress, I think—but Malinqua is not the sort of country that would be happy to see a woman follow another woman to the throne."

"Then that's the biggest disadvantage of all."

"Yes—but if she marries one of the nephews they would form a very powerful alliance. So she is the one I would consider our main rival."

"Who are the other bridal candidates?" Corene asked. "You mentioned a girl from Dhonsho. What's she like?"

"Alette? Who can tell? She will not speak. Seriously, I do not believe she has uttered a syllable in my hearing. I think all three of Filomara's nephews have given up any notion of trying to charm her."

"She would not seem to be a serious contender, then."

"Ah, but Malinqua and Dhonsho have skirmished for years over some disputed border." Melissande waved a hand toward the window, as if Corene could spot that boundary from there. "A marriage might end all hostilities, who knows? So Alette might be Filomara's favorite."

"Well," said Corene. "We cannot *all* be crowned. So, then, will we be enemies? You and I and the others?"

Melissande shrugged. "To be entirely honest, I am not so sure I would like to live in Malinqua the rest of my life. I am playing this very amusing game, trying to guess who will catch Filomara's attention and seeing if I can make him choose me as his bride—but it is no more than a game to me. I would rather go home to Cozique when all this is over."

"Why did you agree to come here in the first place?"

Melissande appeared to debate her answer. "My mother thought it would be a good idea for me to be somewhere other than Cozique for a quintile or two."

Corene couldn't help smiling. "A scandal, then."

"A very small one. Though my mother did not see it that way."

"If you don't marry here, will she take you back?"

There was the briefest pause before Melissande laughed and said airily, "Oh, I am sure she would! I could go home at any time."

Corene had the sense that Melissande was lying, but she merely nodded and said, "So the stakes aren't as high for you as they could be."

"No. How high are they for you?"

It was the first direct question Melissande had posed, and she asked it so lightly that it would be easy to think she didn't care about the answer. But Corene was pretty sure the other girl was burning with curiosity.

She didn't have anything to hide, so she answered honestly. "As high as I want them to be, I think," she said. "I was raised knowing I might very well take the throne, so it's been something of a shock to be pushed out of the running. I like the idea of being empress in Malinqua—though not if I don't like Malinqua."

"And you? Could you go home?"

"I could," she said. "I don't know that I want to." *No one would prevent me from returning, but maybe they're just as glad that I'm gone.*

"And how did your parents present to you this grand opportunity of sailing away to a foreign court to try to win favor with its heirs?"

Corene laughed soundlessly. "Filomara told my father she wanted a blood alliance, and he flatly refused to let me go. So I stowed away on her ship without his permission."

Melissande sat up in her chair, practically bouncing with excitement. "A runaway princess! Oh, that is so much better than an obedient daughter! Your mother? Was she also reluctant to see you go?"

For the life of her, Corene couldn't prevent her bitter expression. "My mother—is only interested in what advantage I can bring to her. I assume she was delighted to hear what I'd done." She lifted her eyes to meet Melissande's. "My parents are not married, you understand. My father was an advisor to the old king, and my mother was one of the queens who needed help to conceive. Now that Vernon is dead, my father has been chosen to be the next king, and he is already siring his own line of heirs. He has a new wife and a new daughter, and everyone loves them all."

"Ah," Melissande said. She nodded, clearly familiar enough with court dynamics to fill in all the details to that story. "Yes. I, too, would have run away at the first opportunity! What woman of spirit would not?"

That made Corene grin, banishing the bitterness. "Exactly! So there are the two of us—"

"The rebellious ones," Melissande supplied.

"There is also the silent but valuable Alette, and the well-behaved, well-liked Liramelli. Very clear choices for the nephews, I would imagine. Is there anyone else who might be competing with us?"

"Any of the high-born women of Malinqua would be suitable brides, so in theory the possibilities are infinite," Melissande replied. "Until recently, Sarona was considered a top contender to marry Greggorio, but lucky for us, she is gone now."

"Gone where?"

Melissande spread her hands. "I cannot be certain! Some people say she ran away with a lover because she did not really care about Greggorio and she could not bear to pretend any longer. Some people believe Filomara paid her parents to send her away because she wasn't good enough to be a royal bride. It is most mysterious."

Melissande spoke lightly, but Corene felt an uneasy chill gather between her shoulder blades. "Mysterious indeed," Corene said slowly. "Girls from well-connected families don't usually just vanish overnight."

For a moment, Melissande's expression was deadly serious; in that instant, Corene read on her face stark knowledge about all the ways and all the reasons a young woman might disappear from court. "They do not," she agreed.

"Should we worry that someone might find *us* unsuitable candidates for the Malinquese throne?" Corene asked bluntly.

Melissande opened her blue eyes in an expression of exaggerated shock. "If I were to disappear under suspicious circumstances, my mother's navy would burn Palminera to the ground!" she exclaimed. "Welce might not have the same military might, but surely your disappearance would also invite reprisals. Filomara is looking to form alliances, not gain enemies. I am certain we are quite safe. No matter what happened to Sarona."

Corene shrugged her shoulders, managing to dislodge the chill. "You're probably right."

Melissande offered her bright smile again. "And all that matters is that Sarona has left the field clear for *us*," she said. "It will be interesting to see if either of us snares a royal husband."

FOUR

The first dinner at the palace in Malinqua was every bit as uncomfortable as the worst state dinner Corene had ever sat through in Chialto, despite Filomara's boast about how simply she maintained her court.

Corene followed Melissande's advice and wore one of her plainer outfits, though it was still very fine—an off-white tunic and matching pants in a loose, flowing fabric, every hem and border heavily ornamented with ivory beads and raised stitching. But most of the Malinquese contingent seemed to be competing with each other to see who could put together the most severe ensemble. Almost everyone wore either unrelieved black or white; the short, close-fitting jackets hid physical flaws as well as assets, while the plain trousers didn't flatter anyone.

"Looks like I could have worn my work clothes and fit right in," Steff muttered to Corene as they stepped from a small anteroom into the larger dining room. You certainly couldn't call his blue tunic or black trousers very fancy, but in this group, any splash of color was as dramatic as a scream. Melissande, who was there before them, looked just as vivid in her own indigo dress.

No servants bothered to announce them, so they stood in the

doorway for a moment and looked around. It was a pretty enough space, not too big, with more of that plain but well-made wood furniture softened by a thick rug and fluttering drapes. All in all, it looked like the casual dining room at some nobleman's hunting lodge in the far provinces, Corene thought—comfortable but hardly elegant. Not what she would have expected from anyone with taste or money.

There were probably twenty people in the room, grouped together in casual conversation. After Melissande's detailed descriptions, Corene found it easy to pick out the three nephews who were vying for a place on the throne. The remaining individuals were probably council members, the prefect and his wife, and one or two other high-ranking officials. She was delighted to note that Sattisi and Bartolo were nowhere in sight. Not important enough to join this elite group—or perhaps so sick of Corene that they begged off this particular meal. Both possibilities made her smile.

Corene caught a few surreptitious glances thrown their way, but no one actually addressed them until Filomara came over to greet them. "Here you are," she said. "I hope you're all settled in?"

"Yes, thank you," Corene said, and Steff merely nodded.

"Let me introduce you around," the empress said.

Everyone else gave up pretending to talk to each other and faced the door, motionless and curious. Filomara went around the room, simply pointing at people and giving their names. The acknowledgments were shallow bows or polite nods, depending on how high the individuals ranked, and Corene copied their responses. Steff copied her.

Garameno was the last to be introduced, and he pushed his wheelchair closer to them as soon as his name was sounded. "Welcome to Malinqua," he said. Corene thought he looked too much like the empress to be handsome—square-jawed and somewhat craggy—but he had a slightly friendlier aspect. His dark brown eyes were alert and intelligent, and he looked inquiringly from Steff's face to Corene's.

"This is Princess Corene, daughter of the third wife of King Vernon, late of the country of Welce," Filomara said. "She'll be staying with us awhile." She glanced at Steff. "And this is Steffanolo Adova, an interesting young man I met in my travels through that country."

She doesn't want to identify him until his blood's been tested, Corene realized. It left Steff in a somewhat awkward position—but not as awkward as it would be if he'd been introduced as her grandson then proved to be a fraud.

"What makes him so interesting?" Garameno asked.

"Perhaps just the fact that I like him," Filomara said, which elicited a ripple of laughter.

"That makes him rare and special indeed," Garameno said, and again the others laughed lightly. Garameno lifted a hand from his armrest and gestured at Steff. "Come sit by me at dinner and tell me how you entertained my aunt on the long journey from Welce."

Steff cast a swift despairing look at Corene, then followed Garameno. There were twenty place settings at the table but only nineteen chairs; Garameno rolled up to that open spot, and Steff took the seat beside him.

"I'm not that entertaining," Steff said. "So I hope you're not expecting much."

"I'm sure you're more fascinating than you realize," Garameno replied.

If possible, Steff looked even more alarmed at that, but Corene's gaze narrowed as she studied Garameno. *He knows about Steff,* she thought. Despite the empress's extraordinary efforts to keep Steff's existence a secret, somebody had learned the truth.

Jiramondi stepped up to Corene. "Perhaps the princess from Welce would be willing to sit by me?" he said. "*I* won't expect you to be entertaining. I know you've had a long journey."

"Of course," Corene said, and followed him to the table.

Within moments, the others had seated themselves as well, picking chairs and dinner partners apparently at random. Corene couldn't tell if there was some secret protocol they were all following; at the palace in Chialto, the matter of who would sit where at a state dinner might take days to determine. The informality here would be refreshing except for the high level of tension.

Once they were all in place, servants appeared and began serving. Most of the food items looked familiar enough that Corene could identify the meats and vegetables, but the sauces and spices were decidedly foreign. She cautiously tasted a strip of baked fish and felt the seasoning burn so hot against her tongue that she hastily reached for her water glass.

"Oh—someone should have warned you about the zeezin," Jiramondi said sympathetically. "If you're not used to it, it can flay the roof of your mouth."

"Anything else that I ought to know about?" she asked, willing herself not to cough.

"Take a bite of the strained fruit—it's always paired with a zeezin dish to negate the burn," he recommended.

She did as he instructed and her mouth instantly cooled. "Thank you. That helped."

He nodded toward someone sitting across the table and several places down—a dark-skinned girl wearing brightly colored clothing that in no way matched the funereal expression on her face. She concentrated on her plate and did not look up, even when she was addressed by the young man sitting beside her.

"Alette won't touch zeezin," Jiramondi said. "The cooks make up special dishes for her so it doesn't contaminate anything she eats."

"Does it make her sick?"

Jiramondi shook his head. "I think it's just a—cultural bias, you might say? She comes from Dhonsho, where zeezin is used in rituals for the dead. So to taste it is practically a desecration of the living body."

"Well, I don't have a cultural bias against it, but I do think it desecrated my body," Corene said.

Jiramondi laughed. "And maybe don't have any of the brown gravy—it's an acquired taste even for locals. But everything else should be safe."

"Thanks," she said again, giving him a grin. He smiled back. As Melissande had said, he was a handsome man. The family resemblance was there in the strong features and dark eyes, but the proportions of his nose and chin and cheekbones were more pleasing. And his amiable expression instantly made him more attractive than his aunt.

"Let me know how you would like to proceed," he said. "I can prattle on about the beauties of Malinqua, if you're in the mood to listen. Or I can inquire about the wonders of Welce, if you'd rather talk."

"First, I'd like to thank you for speaking Coziquela," she said. Filomara had introduced them in Malinquese, and Corene had figured dinner conversation would be painstaking at best. From what she could overhear of the discussions around them, everyone else was employing the native tongue. "Someone must have told you how badly I speak Malinquese."

His smile widened. "Sattisi, in fact. She still seems offended that it is not the language you have used since birth."

"I did try to learn it," Corene said. "But Sattisi—well, I guess I wasn't a very good pupil."

"I can't imagine Sattisi was a very good teacher," he said. "She is not—mmm—an easy person to be around. I have known her my whole life, of course, since Bartolo is my father's cousin, and I can't say I've ever had a conversation with her that I would have labeled as pleasant."

That made Corene laugh. "Well, now I feel much better about the whole journey," she said.

"And you'll be happy to know they're rarely at court, so you might never lay eyes on either of them again," he added.

She affected dismay. "Then how will I continue my language lessons?"

"I'm sure we can find you a more congenial tutor," Jiramondi answered. "In fact, I'll take up the role, if you're willing to learn from me."

Corene took another sip of water and smiled. "What an excellent idea," she said. "I'm supposed to be getting to know all of Filomara's nephews, and this seems like a good way to start."

"Indeed it does. And once we're tired of language lessons, I can give you tours of the city. Though you probably saw some of its grandest sights on the way in from the harbor."

"We certainly noticed the towers, if that's what you mean."

"I'm biased, I admit, but I think they're spectacular."

"They are," she agreed. "And the palace, with its red half and its white half. And the houses. And the streets. Is there anything in the city that isn't split in two that way?"

"Once you get outside of the inner walls, the distinction is not so pronounced," Jiramondi said. "But inside it's precisely organized for that perfect balance of flame and smoke."

He sipped from his wineglass before continuing. "In fact, you probably couldn't tell it from the carriage, but the streets inside the walls are laid out like two halves of a labyrinth, though each half leads to the center, which is not how most labyrinths are constructed. When the palace was first built—centuries ago, of course—everything inside the walls was part of the royal grounds, and two winding pathways led from the gate to the courtyard. The north one was constructed all of white rock, the south one of crushed granite. These immensely high hedges lined every loop, so you couldn't just cut across the roads and get straight to the palace. According to convention, carriages arrived from the southern side and departed on the northern route. They say that, when traffic was heavy, it could take half a day to make it from the gate to the doorway."

Corene tilted her head as she listened. "I like the theory," she said. "But it seems impractical for daily living."

"You're right, of course, and Filomara's great-grandmother eventually razed all the hedges and invited the wealthier families to begin building homes closer to the palace. At that point, new roads were constructed over some of the old ones to make it easier to cross from one side of the city to the other. But there are still districts where you have to follow the old loops and bends for a couple of miles before you intersect with one of the straight roads."

"And the city is still very much split in two, with its red houses and white houses," Corene pointed out. "Is one color perceived as better than the other?"

"Certainly, but not by the same people," Jiramondi said. "There are families who have lived in the southern city for generations who would never move to the north—they won't even let their sons and daughters marry across the dividing line."

"So then do people align themselves with the towers as well? Do they identify themselves that way—as smoke or fire? Dark or light?"

"Broadly speaking, yes," he answered. "Folk of flame think of themselves as people of action, and those of shadow consider themselves more thoughtful. If you claim fire as your symbol, you are likely to talk a great deal and be open about what you're feeling. If you prefer smoke, you are more likely to listen and to keep your own counsel."

"It seems very limiting," Corene commented. "And somewhat extreme."

"Ah, but part of our philosophy is the understanding that people are neither all one thing or all the other—no matter what their general tendencies, they are almost always leavened by the other. An outspoken man might have a very good reason to keep a secret, whereas a quiet woman might someday wail with grief or sing with joy. No matter what you are, you are also the opposite. No one is ever wholly one thing or the other."

"So what are you?" Corene asked casually. "Flame or smoke?"

He spread his hands as if to indicate his whole body as well as the soul inside. "Flame, of course! In fifteen minutes of conversation, you couldn't tell?"

"I would think anyone who lived in a royal palace and was competing for a throne would have to be part shadow as well."

He raised his eyebrows and leaned back against his chair, regarding her for a moment. "That was a dagger thrust from a hand in a silken glove," he said, but he didn't sound offended. "You are not the innocent you appear to be."

She was smiling. "I have spent my life at court, learning how to pick the truth from the lie," she said. "Or—no. Learning that it's sometimes impossible to tell the truth from the lie, but that someone is always lying."

"If you were willing to be truthful about it," he said, smiling in return, "would you consider yourself flame or shadow?"

Her hand went to the necklace at her throat, strung with three delicate rings stamped with the glyphs for courage, clarity, and travel. "In Welce, we're not so restricted," she said. "We affiliate ourselves with one of five elements—fire, water, air, earth, and wood. My element is fire."

"I would have guessed that, I think."

"But there's more to it than that. Each element corresponds to a physical component. Fire and mind. Water and blood. Air and spirit. And so on. So the sweela folk—the people of fire—are thinkers as well as lovers. They're creative and passionate and full of imagination. But we're never *just* one element or another. In fact, we go to temple to meditate ourselves back into a sense of balance. We realize that we need all of our elements, all of our physical selves, to function in harmony."

Jiramondi smiled again. "I think our philosophies are not so different, if you look at them closely," he said. "It is merely a matter of discovering where you stand on a spectrum of choices and deciding how honest you want to be about those choices. In the end, it is not the color of your house or the element you select that defines who you are. That color, that element, reflects what you have chosen to be."

Corene listened closely. "I hadn't thought of it that way," she said. "But I agree with you."

"But I like your elemental affiliations very much," he added. "What would I be, if I were in Welce?"

She surveyed him a moment. A slim, handsome, charming man whose quest for power had forced him to hide a side of his personality that was strongly condemned in his corner of the world. "At first glance, someone would think you sweela," she said slowly. "But I would bet there is a lot of coru thrown in."

"Coru?"

"The sign for water. Adaptable, open to change, and full of surprises."

His smile was back. "Interesting. I think I shall take that as a compliment." He nodded to where Filomara sat halfway around the table. "What about my aunt? How does she fit in your world?"

Corene almost laughed. "Oh, there's no doubt that she's hunti! Wood and bone. Strong, powerful, and determined. Hunti people are utterly reliable—but so stubborn that trying to change one is like trying to kick a brick wall down with your bare feet."

He couldn't restrain his laughter. "If I didn't know better, I'd think you'd just spent a couple of ninedays with my aunt in close quarters. That describes her perfectly."

"My father as well," she said. "My guess is that hunti folk are commonly found among the monarchy. It takes great strength of will to rule a country."

Jiramondi glanced thoughtfully around the table, his gaze resting briefly on Garameno and Greggorio. Greggorio, who seemed to have run out of things to say to Liramelli, stared right back. "I suppose you're right," he said. "But I don't think either of my cousins are any more— What did you call it?—hunti than I am. I wonder what that says about our chances for success as rulers."

"You said it yourself," she answered. "You make your own choices about who you want to be. And, I would think, how you want to rule." She toyed with the stem of her water glass. "Or you could choose a hunti bride."

"Someone whose assets make up for my deficits," he said. "Yes. A wise course of action, I'm sure."

Greggorio leaned across the table, offering an attractive smile. He was so good-looking he was almost pretty, and his face held none of the sharpness that characterized both of his cousins. "Princess Corene!" he exclaimed in Malinquese. "I haven't said a word to you all night. Tell me how you like Palminera so far."

The conversation became more general at that point, and more stilted. The tête-à-tête with Jiramondi had been unexpectedly enjoyable, even more so by contrast with the rest of the meal. Corene labored through the unfamiliar language, well aware that she missed a good third of what was being said, and tried to keep her expression civil as she accidentally took another bite of that wretched zeezin. There was no dessert served at the end of the meal, as she was accustomed to, though the servants came through pouring some sweet, heavy wine that seemed to signal the final course. Everyone else at the table sipped it with obvious pleasure, but Corene found it syrupy and cloying.

So far, there wasn't much about Malinqua that she actually *liked*. She thought she liked Melissande, but the other girl might not be trustworthy—and, anyway, Melissande wasn't even from Malinqua.

Not the best way to start a quest for a foreign crown.

She found herself fighting off a yawn and hoping the meal was almost over so she could seek her room and collapse. She was delighted when Filomara came to her feet and everyone—except Garameno—followed suit.

"It was a pleasure to see you all," she said, showing no pleasure. "Good night."

"Oh, but wait," Garameno spoke up. "I had a question."

She looked impatient. "Yes?"

He was smiling as if he knew he was about to delight her. "Why didn't you tell us your good news? Even for you, this can't be a trivial thing."

Everyone else was staring at him, but Corene watched Filomara. The empress mostly kept her expression under control, but Corene saw her lips tighten and her eyes grow colder. "Maybe it's news that's not ready to be shared."

"But it *is*!" Garameno exclaimed. He made a sweeping gesture with both hands. "Everyone—you should know. Filomara has returned from Welce with a living grandson in tow. Sadly, as we all know, Subriella is dead, but what we *didn't* know is that she had two sons—and one of them has come to visit us today."

Naturally, that caused pandemonium as everyone burst into conversation at once. *What? Subriella has living offspring? A grandson? Another heir? What was that? What did Garameno say?*

Corene saw bewilderment on Greggorio's face, calculation on Jiramondi's, and angry satisfaction on Garameno's. She interpreted that to be a message to his aunt: *You cannot outmaneuver me. Include me in your plans or see those plans upended.* Clever, Corene thought.

Corene glanced at the others to try to assess their reactions. Steff, of course, was trying to hide flat dismay under a stoic demeanor. The prefect and the other city officials were offering Filomara congratulations, but she saw worry under their smiles; what they wanted was a stable succession, and too many heirs threatened that stability. Alette showed no expression at all, but Liramelli looked intrigued. Maybe she thought Steff might be a more attractive marriage prospect than the three young men she'd known her whole life. Melissande, predictably, appeared delighted, at both the new candidate and the chaos. When she caught Corene's eyes on her, she laughed and pursed her mouth into a kiss.

Filomara raised her hands for silence, and everyone subsided. Her face was set in grimmer than ordinary lines. "Yes. My daughter did indeed escape her marriage in Berringey and keep two sons alive. One remains in Welce, and one has accompanied me here." Now she gestured at Steff, whose face became even more masklike.

"But this is so exciting!" Jiramondi exclaimed. "Weren't you going to tell us?"

"Of course I was," she snapped. "But I wanted to conduct tests. I wanted to be absolutely certain." Her dark eyes rested on Steff a moment and Corene thought she saw a flicker of pain. "The story put forth by Steffanolo and his family was convincing, yet I am sure you all would agree that science trumps anecdotes. If he is not in fact mine, I do not want to embrace him."

The prefect spoke up. "You said Subriella bore *two* sons. Will we have the opportunity to meet this young man's brother?"

"If you sail to Welce, you will," Filomara replied with a trace of humor. "There are circumstances that prevent him from traveling beyond those borders."

"Then you don't expect him to join the long and ever-growing list of contenders for your throne?" Garameno said a little too sharply.

Conversation died to nothing. Filomara and her oldest nephew locked gazes. "Lerafi will never leave Welce," she said deliberately. "If he ever wears a crown, it will be in that country, for he is attached to one of the old king's daughters."

"But I don't understand," Greggorio said. "Are you thinking of passing the crown to this stranger? Instead of one of us?"

"Yes, Greggorio, that's exactly what she's considering," Garameno said, his voice edged. "He is directly in line for the throne."

"I have made no decisions yet," Filomara snapped. "I have not even verified his lineage. I would thank you to not presume to know my own mind before I know it myself."

"And yet, everyone will want to learn about him," Jiramondi said smoothly. "Everyone will want to lionize him. I mean, he'll be so popular. Just look at him."

Of course, when everyone turned to stare at Steff, he looked like nothing so much as a small boy caught stealing the baker's pies—chagrined and nervous and braced for terrible consequences. *I warned you this would not be easy,* Corene thought.

Melissande's laugh trilled out, and she strolled around the table to lay her hand on Steff's sleeve. Surely it was random coincidence that her indigo dress paired so nicely with his blue tunic. She could have had no idea who he was or what he might be wearing to this dinner, could she?

"I for one will be happy to look at him," she said gaily. "A handsome prince! Every girl's dream come true. Hello, Steffanolo, I am Melissande. I am sure we will be the best of friends."

Despite the fact that Filomara was clearly ready for the evening to end, everyone else obviously wanted to stay and talk, so the whole party eventually adjourned to another room. It was a bit bigger and more informal, full of simple but comfortable furniture, and featured two huge windows that gave a spectacular nighttime view of the northern half of the city. The most impressive sight, of course, was the bright beacon of the white tower, with the eerie light of its crystal dome glowing like a low half-moon.

"Isn't it pretty?" said a voice from behind Corene. She turned to find Greggorio had joined her at the window. Everyone else had fallen into one of two clusters: some around Filomara, some around Steff. It was hardly a surprise that, generally speaking, the women encircled Steff and the men gathered around the empress.

"Truly impressive," she said, answering in Coziquela. "I'm sorry, I don't speak your language very well."

"I don't speak yours at all," he said, obligingly following suit. He gave her a rueful smile. "I haven't had much chance to talk to you. Kind of a strange evening."

She decided to be forthright. "You didn't seem very happy to hear the news about Steff."

"Who?"

"Steffanolo."

The rueful expression grew more pronounced. "It just makes things more complicated, and they were already complicated enough."

"That tends to be the way of it when there's no clear succession," she agreed.

He leaned against the window, his back to that incredible view. "Garameno says it *used* to be clear," he said. "When my cousin Aravani was alive."

It was a moment before Corene recalled that Aravani was the name of Filomara's eldest daughter—the one who *hadn't* been sent off to marry a murderous Berringese prince.

"I don't know anything about her," Corene said. "I think the empress said she died of a fever."

"I don't know much about her, either," Greggorio said. "I was born the year she died."

Corene was having a hard time doing the math in her head. "How old was she? Shouldn't she already have been married and had an heir or two of her own by then?"

"I think she was thirty? Thirty-two? Something like that. And she *was* married. And had two daughters. They all died, and so did her husband."

"So you were a baby and the other two—"

"Jiramondi was ten and Garameno was fifteen."

"I would have thought Garameno would have been the likeliest heir, since he was the eldest nephew."

"Yes, Harlo said that once."

"Harlo?"

"The prefect. Liramelli's father. He said Garameno would have been an even better ruler than Aravani—at least until he got injured."

"What happened?"

"He was riding and his horse fell on him. It took him forever to heal and he's still in a lot of pain."

"And the good people of Malinqua don't like the idea of a ruler who has a broken body."

Greggorio looked uncomfortable. He himself was the picture of perfect health, with fine shoulders and muscular arms not entirely disguised by the tailored jacket. "It's such a hard job," he said earnestly. "I think people just want to be sure he can do it."

"So when Garameno's horse fell on him, people started looking at you and Jiramondi."

"Harlo says I am the next natural heir. My father was Filomara's oldest brother, and if something had happened to her, the crown would have gone to him. My father's dead now, but Harlo says I should still be next in line."

Harlo sounded like he enjoyed meddling in the succession, Corene thought. Out loud, she asked, "Do you *want* to be king? Or—no—you don't call yourselves 'king' and 'queen,' do you? Would you be 'emperor'?"

Greggorio nodded. He was smiling. "Garameno always says it's a grand title for a small nation. We used to be kings and queens until a hundred years ago, and then the king decided he was going to consolidate the nations of the southern seas. So he called himself emperor and started wars with all his neighbors, but he couldn't conquer a single one. The new title stuck, though. Garameno says it's silly."

"I like the story," Corene said, "but he was probably a horrid man."

Greggorio laughed. "I think a lot of rulers *are* horrible people."

"And so? Do you want to be one?" she repeated.

He looked briefly confused. "I suppose so. I mean, who wouldn't? There are people to help you through the hard parts. And you have all that money and all that power, and people love you."

"Well—people probably don't love you if you're a tyrant."

"I wouldn't be," he said earnestly. "I would be kind to everybody. And fair. And I would only raise taxes if I had to."

This boy doesn't have a clue what it takes to be a king, Corene thought. His general likability kept her from feeling true contempt, but she couldn't help thinking he would be a bad choice for Filomara. Unless two minutes in his company didn't accurately convey the kind of man he really was . . .

"Is there any reason we need to raise taxes?" asked a voice behind them, and Corene and Greggorio turned to see who had joined them.

It was Liramelli, the prefect's daughter. Corene surveyed her critically, not making any attempt to hide her curiosity. Liramelli appeared to be about twenty, though her serious expression might make her look older than her years. She was dressed all in white, the color accentuated by her ice-blond hair, and didn't seem to be wearing a single personal adornment. Corene thought Liramelli might be the plainest person she had ever seen. She remembered that Melissande had expressed a desire to make her over, and she longed to see what the Coziquela girl might do if she had the chance.

Greggorio greeted Liramelli without enthusiasm and then added, "No, I don't think we need more taxes—that was my point."

Corene tried a smile to see if Liramelli would respond. "We were talking about all the responsibilities that fall to a ruler. Just in general."

Liramelli nodded and didn't lose her solemn expression. "Of course, it's not just the empress who decides to raise taxes. The mayor and the prefect and the council offer advice. As they do in all matters of state."

"Of course," Corene answered.

Someone called Greggorio's name from across the room. Corene thought it might have been Jiramondi. "Well, I better see what he wants," he said in relief. "Maybe we can talk tomorrow."

That left Corene alone with the deathly serious potential heir. For the longest moment of her life, she couldn't think of a single thing to say.

Liramelli tried to fix a look of interest on her face. "So did you have a pleasant journey from Welce?"

Not by any measure, Corene thought. She tried another smile. "I've never made a long trip by sea before," she said. "I had no idea what to expect! The rooms were small, but the food was very good. And I never got sick enough to throw up. So I think that counts as pleasant, don't you?"

Liramelli's lips quirked up slightly, but the smile did almost nothing to lighten her expression. "Most of my ocean travels have been less than a nineday, but I agree, the quarters are very cramped. I would not want to be a sailor and spend all my days at sea."

"Where did you go?"

"I've been to Dhonsho twice and Cozique once. Someday I'd like to see Welce. I know hardly anything about it."

"No, it seems like no one here does," Corene answered.

"I'd like to learn, though."

"Then you should spend an afternoon with Steff and me," Corene said. "I grew up in the city and he grew up in the country, so we can tell you everything."

Liramelli had turned so she could watch the knot of women clustered around Steff. "I would like that," she said. "I wonder how long it will take the empress to have his blood tested."

Because you wouldn't want to waste your time getting to know him if it turns out he's not in the running after all, Corene thought. "I don't know," Corene said. "But I can tell you this—he's Subriella's son. My father's wife has an ability—I can hardly explain it—all she has to do is a touch a man to know who his ancestors are. I can understand that Filomara wants her own proof, but Steff is her grandson. Don't hold back from him just because you're not sure."

Liramelli shifted her gaze to look directly in Corene's eyes, clearly hearing the barb in that last comment. "You're a stranger here, so you can't possibly know," she said quietly. "But I would die for Malinqua. My family has served the crown for more generations than I can count. All I care about is that the next person to sit on the throne is the *best* person. Whether or not I am attached to him is immaterial."

It was the first time Corene found herself liking the prefect's daughter. But then, Corene always liked people who showed a little spirit. She had the thought that this girl was probably elay, possessing such traits as honor and vision.

"I imagine that, one way or the other, you'll end up near the throne," Corene said. "Won't you serve the crown after your father?"

Liramelli nodded. "Yes. And my children after me and their children after them."

"That's what people like—stability in the realm."

"Is that what you have in Welce?"

Corene was tired of going into all the details about the Welchin succession, so she abbreviated. "Mostly. The old king died, and the regent has been chosen to be the next king. And since he was the chief advisor to the old king, everybody knows him and everybody trusts him." She laughed soundlessly. "Not everybody *likes* him, but I don't suppose that matters."

"Exactly," Liramelli said. "There are so many more important things than being liked."

Oddly enough, Corene agreed with Liramelli on that point, too. *Though I bet people would dislike us for different reasons,* she thought. She couldn't help but laugh and Liramelli, cautiously, smiled in return. It transformed her face so much Corene almost didn't recognize her.

A lthough Corene had begun to think the evening would simply never end, a few moments later Filomara strode from the room, obviously using that tactic to avoid answering any more questions. Corene slipped out immediately afterward, giving no one else a chance to approach her, and hurried up to her suite. At her own door she hesitated. Both Melissande and Steff were likely to come knocking, and she didn't feel like answering questions for her or offering reassurances to him. So she crossed the hall and tapped on Foley's door.

He answered as quickly as if he had been standing on the other side, awaiting her. She wondered if he had spent the evening prowling the corridors just outside the dining hall, ensuring her safety, returning to his room just steps before she arrived. She liked the idea, in the general way, but she supposed he needed time to eat and attend to his own basic needs. He couldn't shadow her every second of every day.

"How did it go?" he asked.

"Fine. Can I come in? You're the only person I can stand the idea of talking to."

He stepped aside to let her pass—and none too soon, as she could hear voices down the hall before he shut the door. He dialed up the gaslight to brighten the room, and she dropped into the closest chair. He settled nearby.

"You're not acting like it was fine," he observed.

"It was just tiresome. All these new people, and half the time talking in a language I don't understand, and wondering who's lying and who's telling the truth."

"Except for the language, it doesn't sound that different from Chialto."

She laughed. "No! Maybe that's why it was so tiresome. I thought it would be more fun."

"Did you learn anything interesting?"

"Hard to say," she said, launching into a summary of the conversations she'd had over the course of the evening. Foley listened closely, only now and then asking her to clarify who had made some remark.

"A little odd," he said when she was done.

"What in particular?"

"All those bodies."

"Bodies? What?"

He counted on his fingers. "The empress's husband, dead. Her daughters, both dead. The one girl's children, all dead. Two brothers, dead. That's a lot of heirs to be eliminated."

Once again, Corene felt a chill of uneasiness between her shoulder blades. "When you put it like that, it is a little unnerving," she said slowly. "But—I think some of those are just coincidence. I mean, Subriella was sent off to another country to marry. No one could have expected her husband to want to kill her."

"Why not?" Foley said mildly. "Berringey is just across the mountains from Malinqua. Surely it would be easy for someone here to discover the way the succession is handled there. Isn't it common for potential heirs to be killed off once the new king is named?"

"Well—yes—"

Foley shrugged. "So maybe someone knew that, and that person advised Filomara to make the marriage anyway."

"And Aravani died from a fever—"

Foley looked skeptical, and Corene's discomfort deepened. She said, "I suppose that could have been faked. She could have been poisoned instead. And all her family."

Foley nodded. "Four heirs dead. And then two of Filomara's brothers. How did they die?"

"No one has told me."

"Two more heirs gone."

"But everyone says she was never going to name her brothers her successors."

"Maybe not. But if something suddenly happened to her, surely one of them would take the crown."

Corene felt herself actually shiver. "So you're saying that someone arranged to have Subriella sent off somewhere she was likely to get killed—poisoned Aravani and her entire household—and murdered Filomara's brothers? All to clear his own way to the throne? That would take someone with a lot of patience and cold-blooded ambition."

Foley shrugged. "People like that abound in royal courts."

"As we both know," she said. She reviewed the list of likely candidates. "I suppose one of her brothers could have been scheming all this time—or maybe the prefect. But whoever it is seems to have given up, because I don't think anyone's died for almost twenty years."

"You said Garameno was injured ten years ago."

"Yes, but that was an accident . . ." Her voice trailed off. "Or maybe a botched murder attempt."

"And for all you know, there have been other deaths among the nobility—names you haven't even heard yet."

She shivered again, and this time Foley gave her a questioning look. "Melissande told me," she said in a quiet voice, "that some high-born woman disappeared a couple of ninedays ago. No one knows where she went."

"And why would someone want to get her out of the way?"

"She was close to Greggorio. Maybe someone didn't want her to end up next to him on the throne."

"They wanted him to marry a princess instead."

Corene stared at him, remembering what Melissande had said. "Then that means I'm safe, doesn't it?"

"Unless whoever is going around murdering people decides he doesn't like you, either."

She held the stare a moment longer, trying to tamp down a complex surge of emotions: fear, anger, bewilderment, and a touch of self-loathing. *If someone's killing unlikable people, I will surely be on that list.* She attempted a smile. "I see I acted with my usual good judgment when I decided to run away to Malinqua," she said.

His unexpected smile was amazingly sweet. "It's true that things tend to be a little more dramatic when you're at the heart of them."

That made her laugh, which instantly changed her mood. "Poor Foley! I always think of you as so calm and so still. And here I've plunged you into chaos."

He shrugged slightly. "You don't become a royal guard if you expect life to be ordinary and dull," he replied. "Part of you likes the chaos. Or at least likes the challenge of taming it."

"Maybe that's why I always feel so safe when you're around," Corene said. "Because I'm always at the center of a whirlwind, and you seem like you can settle down any storm." She spoke lightly, but in truth she was much struck. That explained it exactly, the way she'd always reacted to Foley's presence. She felt steadier. More sure of herself. Certain that he could keep her from careening off the edge, no matter how events unfolded around her.

It hadn't occurred to her that he would be drawn to tumult, but it made a certain kind of sense. So maybe he didn't mind so much that she'd dragged him off on this adventure—even if it turned out to be more dangerous than either of them had expected.

Foley gestured toward the door, indicating the whole palace that lay outside these walls. "We don't know yet if there will be any storms here in Malinqua," he said. "But it's best to be prepared."

"Prepared for storms *or* murderers," she agreed. "Well, you kept Josetta safe for five years, and people really *were* trying to kill her. So I think I'll be just fine as long as you're around."

"I hope so," he said seriously.

She came to her feet and headed for the door, Foley right behind her. She found herself suddenly exhausted after what had been a very long day. "In any case, I'm glad I brought you with me."

He didn't reply until she had crossed the hallway, opened her door, and stepped into her own room. Then he said, "I'm glad you invited me to come."

FIVE

Everyone else cursed the rain, but Leah welcomed it, because it gave her more time.

It had seemed likely that within a few days of her arrival, Corene would visit some of the more popular sites of the city—specifically, the towers and the Great Market. Leah had concluded that her best chance of making contact with the princess would be to pose as a vendor at the market, but it wasn't so easy to slip into the role.

The Great Market was a massive structure a couple of miles south of the wall that enclosed the heart of the city—though there were those who considered the market itself to be Palminera's heart. Everything could be bought and sold there, from livestock to opals. The four levels were constructed of contrasting layers of red and white stone and featured great arched openings that admitted sunlight and rain with equal impartiality. A wide metal stairwell spiraled up the center, taking prospective buyers to progressively more well-ordered and expensive levels.

A butcher might do all his shopping on the bottom story, where cattle and chickens created a wild cacophony and a distinctive smell. One level up were booths carrying household goods from baking pans to common spices. Above them, shoppers could find glassware and small furnishings and shoes and clothes. And on the top level the items sold were things that only the very wealthy could afford: jewels, imported fruits and trinkets, fine musical instruments, drugs for every imaginable use.

Leah needed to make a friend on the fourth level, where the royal visitors would inevitably shop.

The problem was that most booths were owned by vendors whose families had occupied the exact same spaces for decades, if not centuries. They were suspicious of strangers and unlikely to let a foreigner borrow counter space for an afternoon.

The very day that Corene arrived in Malinqua, Leah headed toward the market, climbed to the top level, and browsed through the merchandise on display. She had dressed in her absolute finest clothes, by Malinquese standards—made of simple but expensive black silk—and visited as many booths as she could. She could usually get a sense of when people might be willing to deal, but none of the merchants on Great Four struck her as being open to trades or bribery.

So she returned to the harbor to ask her new friend Billini for help.

She had sized him up as a man who dealt in information, which meant he would respond to a truth better than a fabrication. So she was honest with him, up to a point.

"I just want to meet the new princess—the one from Welce," she said to Billini over a beer. It was late by this time and the bar was nearly empty again, though Billini had had a packed house once the royal party finally cleared out of the harbor. "I want to be able to tell my friend back in Chialto that I didn't just *see* the princess, I spoke to her. She'll be so jealous."

Billini was wiping down the counter while keeping an eye on the few remaining patrons. He grinned. "That she will."

"And I thought, surely she'll go to Great Four, right? And if I was working at one of the stalls when she walked up—" She heaved a sigh of self-pity. "But I was there today and I didn't see a booth where an owner looked friendly enough to ask."

"They're a pretty closed-off lot," Billini agreed.

"I'd pay," she said glumly. "I'd pay a lot to have a chance to say five words to the princess."

A man at the end of the bar called out for another beer, so Billini stepped away for a few minutes. That was fine; Leah hoped it gave him time to think. When he came back, she changed the subject.

"I have the stupidest landlord," she said. "He wants to start charging me extra if I keep food in my rooms. Says it brings in the mice. I said, No, *you* not clearing garbage out of the alley is what brings in the mice."

"Landlords are assholes," Billini said, nodding. "That's why I'm so lucky I own this place."

They swapped a few stories about the general unlikability of the rich and powerful, then Billini tapped his finger on the counter a few times.

"I might be able to help out," he said.

Leah affected surprise. "With what?"

"At Great Four. I know somebody who wouldn't mind doing me a favor."

She let herself show excitement. "Someone who has a booth? Where I might meet the princess?"

He nodded. "If you mention my name, Chandran will listen. But he won't give anything away for free."

"Of course! I wouldn't expect him to. But I don't want to seem cheap. What should I offer him? What should I say to him?"

In between Billini's next few customers, they discussed the protocol and price ranges of bribery, which wasn't nearly as expensive as Leah would have thought. When she finally departed for the night, she left an exorbitant tip as thanks, but both of them knew very well she had already paid Billini in advance with her information about Steff's arrival.

Just as she'd hoped. This was going to be a profitable relationship.

Billini's friend in Great Four was a commandingly tall, heavily bearded man who spoke with a trace of a Coziquela accent. Leah was intrigued by the idea that Billini only collected friends from foreign lands, but it made sense. They would tend to have less loyalty to the crown and much more loyalty to hard cash. She wondered how Chandran had managed to acquire a booth in the Market. Married for it or murdered for it, she supposed.

She didn't ask.

He traded in foreign fripperies—embroidered scarves, painted vases, tiny glass music boxes that threw off prisms of light while their interior mechanisms spun with melody. He listened without expression as Leah laid her offer before him.

"One day only?" he asked when she was done.

"Unless I don't manage to speak to the princess on the first day she comes here."

A very small smile showed through the thick beard. "The royal party *always* stops at my booth."

"Then one day only."

"Would you pay in Welchin coin?"

She almost said, *No, of course not—I have Malinquese money*, but she stopped herself in time. "Would that be an advantage to you?"

"I have a supplier who would be happy if I were to buy his goods in that currency."

"Then that's what I'll bring."

"You will need to work while you are awaiting the princess's arrival," he warned her. "You will need to be courteous and knowledgeable about the items for sale."

She glanced at the variety on display. "You might need to spend a few hours training me, but I'm generally quick to learn."

"I have time today," he offered. He jerked his head in the direction of the open wall, where unrelenting rain was making the whole city miserable. "Not many will venture to the market in this weather."

"I'm free as well."

So she slipped inside the booth, which was the size of a small bedroom. Chandran and his neighbors had created divisions by lining up tall cabinets, back to back with each other, to delineate their own spaces. Some of Chandran's cabinets had drawers, some had doors, and all were heavily locked. Instead of a back wall, there was a curtain, and through it Leah could glimpse a storage area filled with locked trunks and a very small seating area. On the other side of the curtained area, she surmised, was a vendor whose space backed up to this one. Chandran had one of the coveted middle aisles, close to the stairwell that delivered wealthy buyers and a comfortable distance from the open archways where bad weather came blowing in.

The front of the booth was a polished wood table laid out with samples of Chandran's exotic goods. They were designed to catch the eyes of passersby, but Leah suspected that they were the least interesting of the items he had for sale. The very best pieces would be kept under lock and key and only brought out for the discriminating buyer who knew what to ask for.

The rain never let up and traffic remained slow, so Chandran had plenty of time in between customers to explain what he was selling and how it was priced. Leah was interested to learn that he accepted payment in any kind of currency and could convert monetary amounts rapidly in his head.

"Most of my customers pay in Malinquese coins, but some of my wealthiest patrons are from Dhonsho and Cozique," Chandran explained. "They are willing to pay more for the convenience of using their own money."

Leah had a chance to practice her math skills late in the day when an older woman accompanied her petulant granddaughter to Chandran's booth and began picking through the music boxes. They wore the long, flowing clothing that Leah had learned to associate with Cozique; that, more than the fact that they spoke Coziquela, gave away their national origin. Nothing pleased the little girl until Chandran brought over a music box made of deep red glass and featuring a small gold rabbit that spun slowly on the lid while the melody played.

"I want that. Can I have that?" she demanded.

"Of course, anything to make you happy," the older woman said. She seemed amused rather than irritated; Leah herself would have been tempted to push the little girl down the stairwell if they'd been anywhere near the center of the building. "I can purchase it with Coziquela coins, can I not?"

Chandran nodded and looked pointedly at Leah, who made a guess at the right multiplier and named a sum. She wasn't sure if it was correct or not, but the woman handed over her payment without argument.

As soon as the customers were out of sight, Chandran gave her a nod of approval. "Nicely done."

"I thought the number might have been too high."

Chandran offered his buried smile. "She did not think so."

The rest of the day brought a handful of additional customers, but they all possessed Malinquese funds, so the transactions weren't too difficult. Still, by the time the floor cleared and merchants started closing up their booths, Leah admitted to herself that she was feeling fatigued. She wasn't used to standing in one place all day, trying to look welcoming. Her cheeks hurt from the unaccustomed smiling.

That says something about you that you don't want to think about too much, she thought ruefully.

"I usually reward myself with a cup of keerza at the end of the day," Chandran said. "Would you like some?"

Leah didn't care much for keerza, which she considered either bitter or flavorless, depending on how it was brewed, but she never missed a chance to cultivate a friendship. "I would," she said. "Thank you."

Chandran stepped back into the little curtained area and set a kettle over a tiny portable firepit. Leah dragged out a pair of stools and arranged them in the middle of the booth, so she and Chandran would have room to sit comfortably. About half the other merchants were engaged in similar rituals, she noticed, taking this hour to wind down or tally up accounts or visit with neighboring vendors. The rest of the shops were completely deserted.

"How do you know your merchandise will be safe overnight?" Leah asked as Chandran handed her a steaming cup and settled in the chair across from her. "A determined thief could break into any cabinet he wanted."

Chandran blew on his cup to cool it. "There is a ring of guards outside the market every night. Thefts are few."

Leah sipped her keerza, which was on the strong and bitter side. *Why would anybody drink this stuff?* "Guards? Paid for by the merchants?"

"Originally," Chandran said. "But given the importance of the Great Market to the economy of Palminera, it has become an expense borne by the crown. Of course, the rents we pay to lease our spaces are a source of income for the crown, so in some sense we *are* funding the guards."

Leah took another swallow. It might not be so bad if she had a sweet to go with it. When she came back tomorrow, she would bring something sugary—enough to share with Chandran. "How long have you had a booth here?" she inquired. That seemed safe enough to ask; if he felt chatty, she might learn how he'd managed to acquire the space.

But he didn't. "For ten years. A very lucrative ten years."

She grinned. "I imagine so." There was only about half the cup left and she chugged the rest of it down, just to get it over with. She felt her stomach turn over in protest. Welce and Malinqua had healthy trading arrangements, but Leah couldn't imagine this particular item catching on in her home country. "So what time should I be back tomorrow? When would the royal party arrive?"

"They might come at any time—or they might not come until the next day, or the day after. It is hard to gauge."

"Then I guess I'll just keep returning until they do."

He nodded. "As I expected. Be here when the market opens. I will give you a pass that will see you through the guards in the morning." He gave her a stern look. "It will *not* get you past the perimeter at night, should you be thinking of returning and appropriating a few items from my fellow merchants."

That made her laugh. She appreciated suspicious people; they reminded her of herself. "What, you don't know me well enough to trust my good intentions?"

"I don't know you at all," he said. "As you do not know me. Either of us might be much different than we seem."

She acknowledged that with a rueful look.

"Would you like more keerza?" he asked.

"Thank you, no. I need to get home." And the sooner the better; the keerza was not agreeing with her stomach at all. She gathered her feet under her, preparing to push herself off the stool, but he held out a hand.

"One moment," he said, his voice darkly serious.

She tried not to show the tension that suddenly tightened all the muscles in her back. "What is it?"

His black eyes studied her as if he wanted to read her soul. "Why are you so interested in meeting the Welchin princess?"

"I told you—"

"The truth," he said. He gestured at the empty cup still in her hand. "I put poison in the keerza. If I do not like your answer, I will call the guards. I am not interested in playing any role in an attempted assassination."

Poison! Oh, she'd been a fool for not even suspecting. Even by keerza standards, this cup had tasted foul. Malinqua's early history was rife with tales of deadly drinks served to unsuspecting rivals, and even today a fatal brew was the preferred weapon for murder. She was an idiot.

Leah's mind raced as her gut cramped. She had a whole range of medicines in her lodgings—including more than one antitoxin—but judging by the way her abdomen was clenching, she wouldn't be able to make it that far without puking her guts out. Or worse.

"I am not interested in assassination, either," she said, trying to keep her voice calm. He hadn't specified if the drug he'd administered would kill her or just incapacitate her, and his solemn bearded face didn't give away any clues. "The truth. I am in Malinqua as an agent of the Welchin crown. I send back any useful information to the regent, Darien Serlast—who will shortly become king."

"You're a spy."

"I am."

He considered that a moment. "Relations between Welce and Malinqua have been generally friendly."

"That's right. And there's been nothing damaging in my reports. Just—information." As he thought that over, she added, "The empress has spies in Chialto as well. You know that. Just as she has spies in Cozique and they have spies here." *You might be one of them,* she thought, but decided it was more prudent not to say so. Her stomach was really knotting up now, and her hands felt sweaty. One way or the other, this was not going to be pleasant. She tried to push down the panic that kept rising at the back of her throat. It would only make the situation worse.

"Why do you want to make contact with the Welchin princess?"

Leah rubbed her hands on her trousers. "She's Darien Serlast's daughter, and she came here without his permission. He's afraid for her safety. He wants me to discover if she is well, and to offer to be a friend to her if she isn't."

His gaze sharpened. "Why did she run away from her father's court?"

Now Leah could feel perspiration building up in her armpits; her breathing was coming faster. If she survived this, she was never again leaving her lodgings without a general-purpose antidote stashed in her pocket. "I don't know. I haven't lived in Welce for five years. I don't know the politics of Chialto anymore."

"Why did *you* leave Welce?" he wanted to know.

She stared at him. No one had asked her that question the whole time she'd lived here. Even Darien hadn't asked—although he knew, and everyone she'd left behind in Welce would suspect. She didn't want to talk about it, not with this clearly ruthless stranger, but she also didn't want to die. "I'll tell you," she said, "but first get me a bucket or something, because I'm going to vomit."

He did better than a bucket—he handed her a small pink capsule. "Swallow this," he directed. "You'll feel better very quickly."

She eyed it doubtfully, and Chandran actually smiled. "No need to be suspicious," he said. "I wouldn't poison you twice."

She took the drug from his palm and he poured her another cup of keerza. It didn't taste much better even without the noxious additives, but she gulped it down along with the medicine. It was surprising how fast it worked; her stomach calmed almost immediately.

"I think I'll tell Billini that he shouldn't send any more friends your way if he wants them to remain his friends," she said.

Chandran actually laughed at that. She hadn't thought laughter was in his repertoire. "Billini might not know me as well as he thinks," he replied.

"I'm guessing very few people do," she retorted.

That amused him, too, but his nod was solemn. "Now. Your reasons for leaving Welce."

She shrugged. "I fell in love with a man and I thought he loved me back. There was a baby. It turned out the man didn't want me, and I didn't want the baby. So I gave the child to people I trusted, and I ran away someplace I wouldn't have to think about any of them again."

Of course, she did think about them, all the time. That small face, so red and angry, so impossibly beautiful. One glimpse, that's all she'd allowed herself, and it was the image she saw every night before she fell asleep, every morning when she first woke up. Her lover's face she'd had a little more success erasing, but sometimes it visited her in her dreams.

"And who besides the regent knows you're in Malinqua?" Chandran asked.

Leah shrugged. It was becoming easier to breathe, easier to sit up straight; the antidote was faster than the poison. "I don't know. Darien can usually be relied on to keep a secret, and I asked him to tell no one, but he might have felt compelled to let my family know where I am. Or maybe not. No one has come looking for me."

"Did you want them to?"

Leah narrowed her eyes and surveyed him. A big man with an unreadable face and no doubt a whole catalog of secrets of his own. She understood why he would want to know her motives, but she was surprised he would ask after the state of her heart.

"I didn't," she said.

"Do you think you might go back someday?"

"And leave Malinqua?" she replied flippantly. "Where everyone has been so kind to me?"

He smiled again at that. "You are feeling better, I see."

She came to her feet—still shaky, but not so bad she thought she'd fall over. "I am," she said. "But I'm tired—I'm sure you understand. I just want to get home."

He rose, too, subtly reminding her how imposing he could be. "I'll see you tomorrow, then?" he asked without inflection. The question behind the question was obvious enough: *Even though I tried to kill you, are you still planning to return?*

She made him a mock bow. "I'll see you tomorrow. I'll bring my own food and drink with me, though."

The smile showed briefly through the beard, then disappeared. "Somehow, I thought you might."

Leah walked slowly through the stubborn rain and let it sluice away the last side effects of Chandran's mystery drug. She still felt a little wobbly, but her stomach had relaxed enough that she could imagine being hungry before long, so she made a slight detour through the Little Islands part of town. It was a polyglot neighborhood filled with immigrants from a whole host of southern nations. Here you could find shops carrying the bright fabrics of Dhonsho, boutiques selling books in Coziquela, and cafés serving the traditional dishes of Welce. She would swing by one of those cafés and pick up something for dinner.

But first she made her way to a side street to visit a small, squat building with no windows and a single door. Painted on the plain white stone exterior was a simple mural featuring a sturdy tree planted beside a flowing river; a small bonfire burned next to a plot of freshly turned earth, while a flock of unidentifiable birds circled overhead.

The five symbols of the elemental affiliations signified that this was a Welchin temple. Leah didn't often bother to slip inside and pull blessings—these days she rarely felt like she deserved blessings—but today she felt the need for a little guidance.

She stepped quietly inside, dropping a few coins into the tithing box. Three visitors were already there, all congregated on the green torz bench. They weren't speaking to each other, at least at the moment, but they seemed to be enjoying the silent communion all the same. Well, that was the torz gift—the connection of one person to another person, to all people, part of the great human chain of being.

Leah had been born torz, was still torz as far she knew, but she felt like she had severed all connections five years ago and still hadn't figured out how to reknit them. Wasn't sure she wanted to. She hadn't had anything approximating a real relationship in five years, and she'd done just fine.

Everyone looked up when she walked in, and two of the other visitors offered tentative smiles. She knew what they were thinking, and it annoyed her. She nodded brusquely and moved as far away from the others as she could, taking a seat on the red sweela bench. But it was a small place and there was almost no way to avoid staring across the room at the others.

They wanted her to pull blessings for them from the weathered wooden barrel in the middle of the room. You could choose your own blessings, of course—just dip your hand in the big pile of coins and draw out whichever ones felt right against your fingers—but superstitious folks always wanted to have three blessings pulled by three differ-ent people. Three *strangers* was best of all.

On the rare occasions Leah dropped by a temple, she preferred to be there alone, so she could move from element to element without hav-ing to share the experience. *A torz woman who welcomes solitude,* she thought with a twist of her mouth. *That must make me a rare creature indeed.*

But if she had learned anything during her five years in Malinqua, it was to do favors anytime she had the chance. So she nodded again to the other visitors—*Once I am in a state of balance, I will gladly work with you*—and then closed her eyes.

She always started on the sweela bench; it was the element of fire and mind, and she always thought more clearly when she sat there. Chandran's little trick had seriously unnerved her. How had she become so careless? She scarcely knew Billini, and here she was trusting him *and* his circle of friends. She needed to be smarter than that, less vul-nerable. If Chandran decided to turn her over to the empress's guards, her useful time in Malinqua was over.

And then she would have to make the staggeringly difficult decision about what to do next with her life.

She could fail to return to the market tomorrow. If guards were there to apprehend her, they would wait in vain. Chandran might track her down through Billini, but Billini knew nothing about Leah, includ-ing her address. Neither of them would be able to find her if she never showed up on their premises again.

But she'd miss her best opportunity to make contact with the Welchin princess. There might be chances to approach Corene on the street as she visited the famous sites of the city, but Leah doubted that the royal guards would allow a random stranger to get close enough to whisper introductions.

The market was her best option.

She would return tomorrow, but she would be prepared for betrayal. She'd bring more than her usual complement of weapons under her clothing, and she'd wear her sturdiest shoes. If she had to fight and run, she'd fight and run. It wouldn't be the first time.

That settled, she felt better about the day. She nodded decisively and moved to the white bench. Elay. Air and spirit. Never an element that spoke to her clearly, and today was no different; she just wasn't the kind of person who thought on an ethereal plane. But she stayed there a few moments anyway, taking in long, slow, calming breaths, just to say she'd tried.

The black bench next—hunti. Bone and wood. Strength and unflinching determination. Leah hadn't had much hunti in her before she'd come to Malinqua, but she'd toughened up considerably since then. She stiffened her spine, hardened her resolve. She wouldn't let Chandran's antics scare her off. She'd be prepared for anything when she returned to the market tomorrow—but she would return.

She slid easily over to the coru bench, silky blue to reflect the element of water. The coru virtues had always appealed to her, even more so these days; she liked to think she'd learned to adapt no matter what came her way. The trick with embracing coru was to avoid becoming so flexible that you lost sight of your goals and your personal morality. You might bend and rearrange, but you had to hold to that hunti certainty or you'd be lost.

No delaying it any longer—time to join the people on the torz bench. They squashed up against each other to give her space, but of course her leg brushed against someone else's knee anyway. *Sorry,* he mouthed, trying to draw even farther away, but she just shook her head and smiled. It was almost a relief, actually, to be forced to remember that there were other people in the world—people with their own hopes and fears and disreputable secrets. Why had *these* particular individuals abandoned Welce? What terrible memories had *they* left behind? And what comfort did they draw from this brief interaction that would gird them for their private battles during the rest of the nineday?

She wouldn't ask, of course. But she felt a strong surge of affection for all of them, just because they were there—seeking, like she was; trying, just like she was. Fighting to stay human and do something with their lives that mattered.

She sat a moment with her head bowed and her hands folded, slightly apart from the others, then she looked up and summoned a broad smile.

"So? Shall we draw each other's blessings?" she invited, and they beamed back at her in gladness and relief.

She didn't even pay attention to who pulled what coin for whom, even when the young girl clapped her hands and the older woman exclaimed, "Oh, my!" She just handed over the bits of stamped metal when it was her turn to choose and cupped her palm when it was time for her to receive. She civilly declined an offer to head out into the rain and find a place that might still be serving food, and she waited till the three of them had left before she examined the blessings that had crossed her palm.

Hope. Serenity. Change.

She flipped through them a second time, a third. What an unexpected set of blessings. She couldn't remember the last time she had felt either hopeful or serene, but change had dogged her for the past five years. For the past six years, really, since her final few quintiles in Welce had been turbulent in the extreme. But she would dearly love to have both of those unexpected blessings visited upon her, unlikely though it seemed. She would take these as reflections of her hidden desires and a reminder that, if she lived long enough, she might one day win her way back to peace.

She dropped the coins one by one in the barrel and headed back out into the rain.

SIX

The bad weather kept them inside for three days.

Corene didn't mind too much, since she was still exploring the enormous palace. She thought she might stay within its walls for a quintile and never visit all its music rooms, libraries, studies, and dining areas—there was even a greenhouse so humid and warm that she thought it would be her favorite spot on cold Quinnelay afternoons. Now, of course, the weather was hot and naturally humid, but she liked the conservatory anyway.

But everybody else seemed edgy and morose at being cooped up indoors. By *everybody* Corene meant the small group of people who quickly came to constitute her particular circle: Steff, Melissande, Jiramondi, and Liramelli. Corene was not the kind of person to make friends easily, but she liked this group; she found it enjoyable to pass the time in their company.

"I do not care if it is raining. I do not care if my shoes are ruined and my clothes are simply *plastered* to my body," Melissande declared on the third day as they sat in one of the smaller parlors and played a listless game of penta. It was a Welchin card game Corene and Steff had taught the others, and they were all bad at it. No one could win enough hands in a row to amass a fortune of any significance. "I must get outside—I must see the world! I must breathe air that has not been breathed a thousand times by someone else."

"It's supposed to be nicer tomorrow," Liramelli offered in her serious way. "We can get out then."

"Can we go someplace where I can buy clothes?" Corene demanded. "The empress has kindly provided me with a few Malinquese jackets and trousers, but I am so tired of the few outfits I brought from Welce."

"I hope you plan to buy more Welchin clothing," Melissande said. "I like all those decorations on your tunics. I like your distinctive look. We foreign beauties must constantly remind our hosts that we are different and unique."

Jiramondi bowed in her direction. "Trust me, no one forgets that you are unique."

"Are there Welchin shops here?" Corene asked.

"At the Great Market," Liramelli said. "They're expensive, though."

There was a moment's silence. Corene couldn't remember the last time she'd had to think about money. Her mother had married a wealthy man and her father controlled the Welchin coffers, so her every need generally was cared for. She hadn't had much money on hand when she decided to slip away to Malinqua, and it hadn't occurred to her that this would be problematic. But while she could reasonably expect the empress to feed and house her—and perhaps even clothe her—she couldn't expect Filomara to indulge her whims and fancies. Especially when Filomara was not, herself, either whimsical or fanciful.

"Well, maybe I won't buy much," Corene said at last. "But I'll *look*."

"So we shall shop tomorrow. Rain or no rain," Melissande said. "Most excellent."

Steff shuffled the cards again. "Until then—more penta?"

Melissande stretched her arms on the table and laid her head on top of them. "I cannot bear it," she said mournfully. "Not another round of cards. Not another book. Not another conversation about the rain. It is all so dreadfully boring."

Liramelli actually looked concerned at this; she patted Melissande's arm. "Come with me to the smaller music room and I'll play for you," she suggested.

Melissande tilted her head up just enough to look at the other girl. "But happy songs only, yes? Nothing dreary? No ballads of brave heroes falling to their deaths?"

Liramelli laughed, but she had, indeed, played just such a song the day before. "I must know one or two happy songs," she said uncertainly.

Melissande groaned and turned facedown again, but Steff came to his feet and tugged on her shoulder. "Come on. I'll go with you. We'll lock her in the music room if she doesn't play something lively."

The prospect of violence cheered Melissande right up, and she flowed to her feet, Liramelli beside her. "Come with us?" Melissande said to the others.

"Corene should stay and do her lessons in Malinquese," Jiramondi said, mock stern, and Corene nodded glumly and remained in her chair.

The other three tripped off together, talking easily. Corene watched them go and sighed.

"You'll hurt my feelings," Jiramondi said.

"It's just that I hate doing what I'm not good at, and I'm not good at languages."

"But if you only do what you're good at, you never learn new things."

"Who needs new things?"

Jiramondi eyed her, his handsome face creased in a smile. "Oh, I think you're more adventurous than that," he said. "Or you wouldn't be here to begin with. You strike me as the kind of girl who throws herself into fresh experiences."

Corene leaned her chin on her hand and thought about that. "Well, when you grow up in a royal palace, you aren't allowed to have that many fresh experiences," she said. "Someone's always watching to make sure you behave. And someone else is always watching to make sure you're safe. Life can be very dull."

"And yet you do not seem dull."

"Odd things have happened to me now and then," she admitted. "When I was eleven, one of the king's wives planned to make me marry the viceroy of Soeche-Tas, who was an old man and *quite* disgusting. But my father's wife rescued me and sent me off with some merchant traders so no one could find me. That was the most fun I ever had. We traveled around Welce and visited small towns and camped out at night when we couldn't find an inn. There were days I wanted to give up being a princess and just spend my life as an itinerant peddler."

Jiramondi was supposed to be teaching her grammar, but this story caught his attention. He leaned back and regarded her with interest. "An eleven-year-old princess—and some merchants—alone on the back roads of Welce?" he said incredulously. "And this wasn't a scandal that rocked the entire country?"

She grinned. "There were a few other scandals going on at the same time. Anyway, my sister Josetta was with me. And Foley, of course."

"Foley? Ah, the taciturn guard who follows you around the palace. He has been with you all this time? I'm impressed."

"Actually, he'd been assigned to Josetta. For something like five years, anytime you saw her, you'd see him, too. So of *course* he went on the trip with us."

"And where was the guard assigned to you?"

Corene made a face and hunched her shoulder. There must have been *someone* that day whose sole task had been to keep her safe. Her mother was careless, of course, and might not have requested a guard, and Darien hadn't been sure just then that Corene was his daughter, so he wouldn't have thought to demand one—but even so, she was a princess of the realm and *every* princess deserved royal protection. Right? So surely someone had been watching over her; he just hadn't been able to react when the situation deteriorated. He hadn't been able to keep Corene in his sights as the water rose and Zoe grabbed her, grabbed Josetta, and plunged them all into the raging river. They were swept away and he simply couldn't follow.

But *Foley* had followed them. When the water disgorged the three of them, coughing and shaking with cold, Foley had been only moments behind them. So why hadn't anyone come after Corene?

She tried to push the thought away. Foley had watched over both of them during those next ninedays of travel, guarding Corene as closely as he had guarded Josetta. It was the first time in her life Corene remembered ever feeling entirely safe. There *should* have been a guard for her, no question, but Foley had been enough. He was always enough.

"We outwitted the rest of the soldiers," she said lightly. "We were better off without them."

"So did this untrammeled trek across the Welchin wilds inspire in you a desire to go off on other adventures?"

Corene laughed. "I wouldn't say that. Until I ran away to come to Malinqua, I was always very well-behaved." She reconsidered that. "Well, no, not exactly. But I didn't do *drastic* things."

"Maybe you'll find that drastic appeals to you, and you'll want to try something else."

"Maybe," she said pessimistically. "Let's see how well this visit turns out first."

"No doubt it will turn out better if you learn to speak the language," Jiramondi said, deftly turning the subject.

Corene sighed and agreed. She had been improving under Jiramondi's daily instructions, but she still had a long way to go.

They hadn't been conjugating verbs for more than an hour before Lorian approached in his usual stealthy fashion. Corene had probably encountered him a dozen times in the past three days, and each time it was as if he materialized from nowhere. It was beginning to give her a serious dislike of him.

"Princess," he said. "A shipment has arrived for you."

She was more than happy to push aside her books. "What do you mean?"

"Trunks from Welce. A courier just brought them to the palace."

She felt her face light up. Her father hadn't sent Welchin troops to bring her back, but he hadn't forgotten her entirely. He had let a few days pass while his temper cooled, then sat down to write her a letter while someone else in the house organized clothing and other necessities. She jumped to her feet. She could hardly wait to see what had arrived.

"The items have already been delivered to your rooms," Lorian said. "They have not been opened, of course. The courier delivered this expressly to my hands." He handed her a keyring.

Well—they probably *had* been opened, but Corene assumed the contents had been searched very, very carefully. Whoever had assembled them on the Welchin end had surely anticipated that, and had packed accordingly.

"Thank you," she said, taking the keys, then smiling down at Jira-mondi. "Class is over for the day."

"I find I am not surprised."

She hurried to her suite to find Emilita there before her, staring hopefully down at three heavy chests. Two were enormous, and one was small enough that Corene could probably carry it herself.

"Princess?" Emilita asked in very slow Malinquese, to make sure Corene understood. "Do you think there might be clothes inside?"

"I hope so," Corene said, and they both knelt down.

She unlocked the big ones first and threw back the lids, and she and Emilita both crooned over the contents. Oh, clothes indeed—tunics and trousers in a dozen colors and multiple weights, some heavily beaded and embroidered, others severe and plain. There were also shoes, scarves, hair clips, and a box of her favorite cosmetics. Corene held a dark burgundy scarf against her face and smiled.

"Princess? Shall I begin to hang these up?"

"Yes, thank you."

While Emilita began happily arranging the new acquisitions, Corene carried the smallest trunk over to the bed. It was heavier than she'd expected, and when she opened it, she saw why. It was filled almost to the brim with bags of coins—most of them golds and quint-golds, with a few quint-silvers thrown in. She sucked in her breath. Zoe—and possibly Josetta—had obviously picked out the clothing, but the money had probably come straight from Darien's hand. She didn't read the largesse as approbation of her actions, however. She was visiting at a foreign court and he didn't want her to embarrass him; thus, he would fund her accordingly.

It certainly made the prospect of tomorrow's shopping expedition much more enjoyable.

It was a moment before she noticed the thick cream envelopes tucked against the back of the chest. One bore her name written in Zoe's handwriting, one in Josetta's.

Nothing from her father, then. Nothing from her mother, either, but that had been even less likely.

She opened Zoe's first. It was brief and scrawled in Zoe's intemperate, almost illegible handwriting.

You ran away like a coru girl! I'd be angry with you, but I've run away myself. Please please please take care of yourself, since I'm not there to drown anyone who mistreats you. Send us news whenever you can.

> *Love you always—*
> *Zoe*

The letter sounded so exactly like Zoe that Corene felt a wave of homesickness strong enough to drown in. She scowled against the threatening tears and opened Josette's note as a distraction.

I can't believe you left without giving me a chance to say goodbye! I miss you so much! I can't wait till you come back and tell me about all your adventures.

I'm sure Malinqua will be wonderful, but different from Welce, and I don't want you to miss us too much. So I'm sending you a bag of blessings—yes, a full set! If you don't see them at first, it's because I'm sure Darien stuck them at the bottom of the trunk. Put them in a bowl in your room, so you can draw one every day.

Then I thought it might be a good idea for me to pull blessings that would govern your whole trip to Malinqua— just to give you some context, you know. Actually, Rafe and Zoe and I each pulled blessings for you. They're in the little bag inside the bigger bag. And then we picked some for Foley, but I didn't bother sending them along. You already know what they are: loyalty, loyalty, and loyalty. I don't know why I even bother. I'm glad he went with you on the trip.

> *Love you. Stay safe.*
> *Josetta*

Corene was smiling by the time she reached the end of the letter.

She was still a little homesick, but she felt buoyed by affection, too. Josetta could always be counted on to rebuild your confidence. Corene pawed impatiently through the pouches of gold till she found the small velvet sack at the bottom of the chest. Red, of course, and closed with a gold drawstring. A gift for a sweela girl.

She opened the bag and poured the coins onto the bed in a bright metallic splash. They were miniatures, the size of her little fingernail, and brassy bright—they looked like a set someone might buy for the nursery. Corene loved them instantly, and laughed as she picked them up by the handful and let them drip through her fingers, cool and full of promise.

Stuck in the bottom of the velvet sack was a smaller bag, this one made of white linen and tied shut with a yellow ribbon. A gift from an elay sister. Inside were three slim rings, like the ones Corene used to wear—one gold, one silver, one bronze—and perfectly sized for her fingers. Trust Josetta to get the smallest detail right.

Trust Josetta also to remember that Corene wasn't as conversant with all the symbols as she should have been; she had thoughtfully included a folded piece of paper that depicted each of the glyphs and explained what each one represented. Corene scanned it quickly, expecting to find her new blessings to be in the sweela category, as most of her blessings were. But not these three.

Vision. Courage. Luck.

What a very odd combination. Corene slipped the three bands on her fingers and studied the symbols again, wondering what they might signify. She couldn't help thinking about her conversation with Foley a few nights ago, when they debated what murderous schemes might be under way at the Palminera court. Perhaps she would need vision to see who was plotting what, courage to confront an adversary—and luck to survive the encounter.

Well, that was exciting. Disconcerting, but exciting.

She gathered up the tiny blessings and dribbled them back into the red bag before bouncing off the bed and giving Emilita a big smile.

"See anything you like among my new outfits?" she said, not sure she had used the right word for *outfits*. "What do you think I should wear to dinner?"

. . .

Sunshine, glorious sunshine, danced over the city on the following day, and Corene and her companions set out almost as soon as they'd finished breakfast. Of course, it wasn't just the five of them—*all* the candidates for the throne had expressed a desire to visit the market, and such a congregation of ranking royalty required an extensive guard. Corene thought there might be two soldiers for every titled man or woman in their party, as well as Foley, Melissande's maid, and Gara-meno's personal attendant. Then there were drivers for the two large, open carriages and horses for all the soldiers, and pretty soon they were the size of a changeday parade.

Somehow Corene ended up in a carriage with the people she didn't know as well: Garameno, his attendant, Greggorio, and Princess Alette. The three men had gallantly crowded into the backward-facing seat so the women could travel in more comfort for a ride that Corene had been told would take about forty-five minutes.

At first, she tried to make conversation with Alette. The Dhonshon princess was very tall, with rich dark skin, huge blue eyes that could be unnervingly direct, and very short, very curly black hair. Her Malin-quese was worse than Corene's, but her Coziquela was flawless.

"Have you been to the Great Market before?" Corene asked.

"Yes."

"Did you like it? What did you buy?"

"Nothing."

"I'd think someone there would carry Dhonshon items, if that's what you were looking for."

"I brought with me everything I need."

Well, this wasn't a very illuminating conversation. Corene tightened her lips in exasperation, and was annoyed to see Garameno had caught the expression. He was facing her, almost knee-to-knee; he would prac-tically have to shut his eyes to avoid looking at her.

"Indeed, there are vendors at the market with delicacies from all the southern nations," Garameno said smoothly. "I'm sure you can find Welchin goods if you already miss the tastes and scents of your home country."

"I'd much rather buy things from Cozique and Berringey," Corene replied. "Things I couldn't get at the Plazas back home."

"The Plazas?"

"The markets where we shop."

He seemed interested, so she described some of Chialto's landmarks and customs, interrupted by Garameno now and then when there was some Palminera attraction he wanted her to notice. After clearing the massive gate set into the city walls, they turned south. Their pace was slow, as the wide streets were cluttered with vehicles—mostly one- or two-horse wagons, a few fancier carriages like their own, and a number of small four-wheeled conveyances that seemed to be powered by human riders diligently pedaling. Onlookers waved and cheered as the royal procession passed by, but they were nowhere near as enthusiastic as they'd been when Filomara was riding through town.

No matter what the skyline, Corene could always see the tower of fire dominating the southern landscape, its restless flame visible even against the clear morning sky. She tried not to turn her head too often to gaze at it, but the incessant flickering kept catching the corner of her eye.

They'd been outside the walls about fifteen minutes when Garameno slewed around to stare ahead of them. "Usually by the time you've gone this far, you can catch a glimpse of it—yes, in front of us and a little to your left. See the building with all the levels? That's the Great Market."

Corene shaded her eyes and took in the sight of the multilayered, multicolored structure. She supposed the word *Great* should have prepared her, but she hadn't anticipated anything quite so big. "It's enormous," she said.

"They say if you pack people in as tightly as they will go—chest to back and shoulder to shoulder—you can fit five thousand people on each level. I tend to doubt that," he added, "and no one's ever tried it, as far as I know. But it is big."

Their pace became excruciatingly slow as they drew close to the market, since apparently everyone else in the city had spent the last few rain-soaked days wishing they could get out and go shopping. Their coach had been sitting in the same snarl of traffic for ten minutes when Corene came impulsively to her feet.

"I'll go on foot the rest of the way," she said.

Greggorio looked up in alarm as she set her hand upon the door. "Princess Corene—royalty can't just walk unescorted through the market. It's not safe—"

She didn't even have to look to know that Foley would already be off his borrowed horse and at the carriage door, ready to help her down. But, of course, she looked and, of course, he was there. "I'll be fine," she said, taking Foley's hand and swinging both legs over the side of the carriage.

Garameno watched her with hooded eyes. It would probably be difficult for him to maneuver his wheeled chair through the traffic, so he had to remain with the coach, but he let his reproachful expression be his only rebuke. "We'll see you there," he said.

She gave him a saucy smile, tightened her grip on Foley's fingers, and jumped down.

There was a sudden scramble from the second vehicle. "Wait for us!" Melissande cried. A moment later she and Steff had exited more conventionally through the carriage door. A handful of soldiers detached themselves from the larger contingent and fell in behind them as they picked their way though the welter of carts and wagons and made for the market.

Close up, it was even more impressive, with the huge archway of the main entrance big enough to drive six carriages through, three stacked on top of three. Through the immense opening, Corene could see people everywhere—not quite stomach to spine and shoulder to shoulder, but not much more spread out, either. Corene was glad to feel Foley at her back, a solid shape of safety and reassurance. Still, she wasn't surprised when Melissande reached out to take hold of Corene with one hand and Steff with the other.

"I am terrified that we will get separated among all these millions!" Melissande exclaimed. "I have never seen so many people here!"

"Well, let's see what they've got that everyone's so eager to buy," Steff said practically, and they stepped through the giant archway and into the tumult of the bottom floor.

It was a little cooler inside, but the odor was overpowering. Corene thought it consisted of equal parts sweat, manure, and frying meat.

"What—they've got livestock here?" Steff asked, amused. He sniffed. "And horses somewhere."

"I do not see horses," Melissande said faintly. "Only cows."

"I'd know that smell anywhere."

"It is not quite so unbearable when you climb up to the next levels," Melissande told them. She pointed. "See? There's the stairway."

Corene glanced back over her shoulder, but she couldn't see if anyone else from their party had abandoned the carriages and followed them in. They probably should have made a plan for reconvening at some designated place or time—although surely the others wouldn't dare to leave them behind?

"And all the best stuff is on the upper stories, too, right?" Corene said. "Let's go."

"I want to look at the horses," Steff said.

Corene glanced at Melissande, who rolled her eyes and said, "Boys."

"But I don't think the three of us should get separated," Corene added. "So let's go with him."

They fought their way through the throngs to find one whole row of the market given over to horses. Melissande, it turned out, was a rider, so she could admire the fine-boned geldings and soft-nosed fillies who poked their heads over the stall doors. She was less enthralled with the burlier animals who could be harnessed to plows and threshers, though Steff was impressed by a matched pair of large brown working horses and spent ten minutes discussing their weight and strength with the owner.

"My father would *love* a pair like that," he told Corene and Melissande when they finally managed to drag him away. "Probably have to feed them a ton, but it would be worth it in time saved. You might plow a field in half the time."

"A little piece of advice for you," Melissande said, linking her arm through his and guiding him toward the central stairwell. "When you are courting various princesses and noble ladies, try not to talk *too* much about farm animals and plowing dilemmas and other so very mundane topics."

Steff grinned. "Liramelli and I talk about farming all the time."

"I can't imagine why," Corene said candidly. "You couldn't wait to get off your father's farm."

Steff rubbed his jaw with his free hand, considering. "Maybe, but

I'm seeing it differently now. I don't want to go *back*, but I don't mind so much that I was there. That I had that life. It seems a lot more real than some of this." He swept his hand out to indicate the market—or perhaps all of Malinqua. Or, Corene thought, all the trappings of this new royal life.

"Well, I do not think you should waste your time talking to Lira-melli when Corene and I are so much more interesting."

He grinned. "*You* think you're more interesting."

Corene laughed. "He has a little sister," she said. "And it shows."

The spiraling metal staircase was wide enough for the three of them to climb side by side while others passed them going down. Corene glanced over her shoulder but, yes, Foley was just a pace behind.

"I do not think we should bother with the second and third floors," Melissande said. "The really fine items are on the top."

Steff looked like he might want to see what was on display here even so—not because he was interested in shopping, Corene thought, but because he was generally curious. He liked to understand how things worked, and she had the feeling he viewed the whole of Malinqua as one big puzzle. He was trying to put the pieces together, and the market was one of the most colorful pieces on the board.

But he allowed Melissande to tug him away from the second-floor landing. "If you worked here, you'd be running up and down these stairs all day," he commented.

"It would be very tiresome," Melissande agreed.

He laughed. "I was thinking it would keep your muscles in good shape."

Melissande glanced over at Corene and sighed loudly.

All of them—except Foley—were panting by the time they made it to the fourth floor, but Corene could immediately see that the exertion had been worth it. Everything about this level of the market had an elegance that had been lacking on the lower stories. The colors were more muted, the proportions were more pleasing, and the scents of incense and potpourri masked the animal odors drifting up from below. Best of all, it was much less crowded up here, with only a handful of well-dressed customers browsing through the booths, some of which were as big as the shops back in Chialto.

"Oh, *yes*, this is where we want to spend our time," Corene said.

"And our money," added Melissande.

They passed a delightful twenty minutes strolling down the first row of booths, fingering bolts of silken fabric and sniffing at exotic perfumes. At first Corene thought Steff might be bored, but he almost immediately struck up a conversation with a Berringese clockmaker and started discussing the mechanisms used in his intricate creations. Melissande and Corene exchanged smiling glances, then moved on to the next row.

"The last time I was here, there was a man selling the most lovely little music boxes—made of glass, so dainty!—and I want to show them to you," Melissande said. "Even Steff would like them, I think, because you can see inside them and watch the gears turning."

"Those do sound nice," Corene agreed. "I'm thinking I should buy presents to send back to Josetta and Zoe."

"There will certainly be something here to suit them. And here is the booth I mentioned! And see? Are these not exquisite?"

The glass music boxes were, indeed, delicate and charming, though the man who seemed to own the booth was neither. He was large and bearded and rather alarming-looking, and Corene was glad when Melissande's incessant questions took up all his attention.

A young woman—his assistant or maybe his wife—moved over to wait on Corene. "Are you looking for anything in particular?" she asked.

She spoke Malinquese, but Corene detected a familiar accent. "Are you Welchin?" she asked in her native tongue.

The assistant smiled. She looked to be in her early thirties, a little slimmer than she should be for her sturdy frame. Her rich brown hair was drawn back in an unflattering knot; her hazel eyes were brimful of curiosity. "I am. I don't get many chances to speak the language, though."

"Well, I'm getting better at Malinquese, but I'm still not good at it," Corene said. "I'm so grateful when someone will speak Coziquela instead. But Welchin is even better!"

"I saw you looking at the music boxes. Did one catch your eye?"

"I need gifts for a couple of women—one elay, one coru."

"Oh, the music boxes are very elay. Wait, I have the perfect one."

She stepped away to search through a tall wooden cabinet and returned with a tiny item cradled in her hands. "This is my favorite one," she said, holding out a crystal box scarcely bigger than her thumb. It was graced with touches of gold—four small filigree feet, a tiny crank, and the inner workings, clearly visible through the glass. Etched on top of the lid were three birds in flight. "The song it plays is so pretty, too. Try it."

Corene obligingly turned the little handle, and a lilting melody drifted out, sweet and ethereal. Without question, an elay creation.

"I have to have this for Josetta," she said. "But I need something else for Zoe. She's much more—robust."

"If she's coru—I know! We just got a shipment of hammered metal pitchers from Cozique. There's a whole shelf of them behind the curtain in back. Would you like to come into the booth and see them all?"

Corene glanced around. Melissande was still absorbed in negotiations with the large bearded man and Steff was nowhere in sight, but Foley stood just a foot away, both patient and watchful. It didn't seem like she could come to any harm by stepping into the stall.

The woman sensed her hesitation. "Or I can bring a few of them out to show you! It's no trouble."

"No, I'd like to see them all. How do I get inside?"

The assistant drew her to the side of the booth and swung open a hidden gate. "How long have you been in Malinqua?" she asked as Corene came through.

"Half a nineday. I arrived right before the rain."

Two steps took them to the rear of the booth. The woman held back the curtain and motioned for Corene to precede her into a cramped, overcrowded storage space full of shelves and boxes. "Is this your first trip to the Great Market?"

"It is! It's been so much fun."

The woman let the curtain fall, and Corene had the sudden illusion that—in this very crowded, very public place—they were suddenly alone and private. The woman said, "And has anyone tried to sell you any red gemstones?"

Corene froze.

It was a code phrase, one she and Josetta had concocted years ago. It could mean almost anything—*Are you in danger? Have you been hurt? Is the person so casually standing beside you actually holding a knife against your ribs?*—and they had employed it a half dozen times in the past five years. If this woman knew to ask it, she could only have learned the question from Josetta.

Or from Darien, who had asked Josetta what sentence would make Corene trust a total stranger.

Unless—it was just barely possible—it was a random question a merchant might ask any wealthy customer on her first visit to a famous shopping district.

"No," Corene answered, trying to keep her tension out of her voice. "But I haven't been shopping very long."

The woman had already dropped the obsequious manner of a shopkeeper; her expression now was deadly serious. More natural to her, Corene thought. "I have messages from your father."

"Who *are* you?"

"My name is Leah. I have been in Malinqua for five years, working for the regent."

"He sent you to look for me?"

Leah gestured at a pair of stools stacked on top of each other in the corner. "Would you like to sit? We can talk a few minutes before your friends start to worry about you."

Foley is probably already worried, Corene thought. But she nodded, and sank to the stool when Leah set it before her.

"I've received several letters from your father, informing me you were on your way and asking me to make contact with you," Leah said briskly. "He was most worried that you might have been brought to Malinqua against your will and he wanted me to ascertain your state of mind and the level of your safety. If you are in any danger at all, we will find a way to remove you from Malinqua and get you home."

Corene felt a tightness in her ribs, as if her lungs had stopped functioning or her heart had swelled to an uncomfortably large size. Darien hadn't sent her gifts and letters—oh, no—he had mobilized agents across the southern nations to look out for her. He was efficient, not emotional, but she had the sudden unshakeable conviction that he would rearrange the continents of the world if that was what it took to ensure her well-being.

"No—not in any danger—at least I don't think so," she added, thinking about the murdered heirs and missing girl. "And I certainly came of my own free will. I thought I made that clear in the note I left behind."

"You could have been coerced into writing something. He's been very worried."

"Darien doesn't seem like the type to worry."

"Maybe you don't know him as well as you think."

"Maybe he's never worried about me before."

Leah narrowed her eyes and studied Corene for a moment. Corene straightened on her stool, wondering what the other woman saw. "His secret sweela daughter by a ruthless manipulative woman," Leah finally said. "I would think he's been worried about you since you were born."

And didn't that cast much of her life in a wholly different light? Corene would need to think about that at some more leisurely moment. "You can tell him I'm doing well. Everyone has been very kind." *No one's tried to harm me. So far.*

"He'll be glad to hear it. Can you come and go from the palace at will? "

Corene blinked. "I don't know. I haven't tried. This is the first day I've been out. Naturally, guards accompanied our entire party."

"Naturally," Leah echoed, but her voice sounded doubtful.

Corene, who had allowed herself to enjoy the outing without reservation, now found a little tension creeping into her shoulders. It hadn't occurred to her there might be anything sinister in the fact that so many soldiers had been assigned to their carriages, but maybe the number was excessive. Certainly, she'd been allowed to roam Chialto with only a guard or two at her back, and she hadn't expected to be guarded by anyone other than Foley while she was in Palminera. So why had so many soldiers come along on this excursion to the Great Market? To keep them all safe—or to keep them all contained?

"You raise an interesting question," Corene said finally. "Someday soon I'll try leaving the palace without a royal escort and see what happens."

"And if you find that your movements are restricted, let me know."

"That might be hard to do if I can't get out," Corene pointed out.

"You have your own guard with you, don't you? Send him to me with a message."

"Send him here?"

Leah seemed to debate. "Probably not. Let me give you a different address." She scribbled information on a scrap of paper and handed it over. "If I send messages to you at the palace, do you think they'll get delivered?"

Corene pocketed the paper and thought that over. "I think any messages would be *read*," she said at last. "So you might have to be careful about what you say."

Leah smiled briefly. "Of course they'd be read. We need a code."

"Red gemstones always mean danger."

Leah nodded. "Then if I think you need to get out of there quickly, I'll send you a message about rubies or garnets. Come to that address as soon as you can."

"I will. Thank you."

"And it's probably wise to stay in touch regularly."

"I could send you a note at least once every nineday."

"And if I don't receive one I'll know there's trouble."

"All right," Corene replied. She shook back her hair and defiantly shook off her slight uneasiness. "Though I don't actually believe I'm in danger. Which you can tell my father. You can also tell him I'm learning a lot about Malinqua and doing my best to charm the heirs to the throne."

"I'm sure they *do* find you charming," Leah said in a quiet voice. "But if it turns out you don't like them as much as you hoped, you can always go home."

"Is that one of the things my father said in his letters to you?"

Leah appeared to choose her answer carefully. "He seemed to think you might not consider that an option."

"I'm not sure it *is* an option," Corene said. "I didn't care much for the life I was living in Chialto."

"Sometimes it seems like any other life would be better," Leah agreed. "But sometimes the old one follows you."

"Did yours?"

Leah's face instantly shuttered, leading Corene to feel a sudden surge of curiosity. "Not so far."

Corene had the feeling the other woman wouldn't share much more personal information, so she settled for the one question everyone from Welce would answer. "So what are your blessings?"

"Endurance, honor, and time."

One torz, one elay, and one extraordinary blessing. And none of them exactly comfortable. Someone with blessings like those seemed well-suited to espionage, patiently watching events unfold so she could report them back to her employer. A spy or an executioner, waiting for decades, maybe, before enacting justice.

"I can't tell your affiliation."

"Torz."

"Well, I'm glad to have met you, Leah. And glad to know my father has someone in Malinqua he trusts—that I can trust, too."

"He's an interesting man, the regent. Soon to be king now, I understand."

"Yes—and no doubt one of the best kings Welce has ever had."

Leah nodded, but she looked puzzled. "What happened to the little girl? King Vernon's youngest daughter? Odelia, that's her name. I thought she was the heir."

"She was," Corene said. "But it turns out Odelia has a condition—it's hard to describe. She's lost in her own mind, and she can't easily get out."

Leah looked shocked. "How sad for her."

"Yes, and quite an upset to the court, since none of us knew there was anything wrong."

"But surely—she must have been at the palace attending functions and meeting people. I mean, I know she's only a child, but—"

"She and her mother had been living in the provinces and came to court only rarely," Corene explained. "Whenever they *did* come to Chialto, her mother brought Mally instead."

"Mally?"

"A little girl who looked so much like Odelia you couldn't tell them apart. A decoy princess. It was Darien's idea, of course."

"It's odd to hear you call your father Darien."

"I was eleven before I knew he was my father. I'd always called him Darien before. It doesn't seem odd to me."

Leah watched her a moment. "You're not close."

Corene hunched a shoulder. "It's complicated. Are you close to *your* father?"

Leah's smile looked painful. "He's dead now. But it was complicated."

"Maybe it always is."

Before Leah could reply, the curtain was swept back, and the large forbidding man looked in. He cast Leah one unreadable look but spoke to Corene. "Your friends are asking after you, Princess."

She peered around him to see not just Melissande and Steff waiting anxiously on the other side of the counter, but all the other occupants of the royal carriages, who had apparently managed to catch up with them while she and Leah got acquainted. "So sorry," she said brightly. "I was just enjoying the chance to speak to someone else from Welce! I'm almost ready to leave."

She offered a quick wave to Melissande, who made an imperious gesture that meant *Come out here right now!* "We didn't even look at pitchers," Corene said. "Just pick one and I'll buy it for Zoe. And the music box, too."

A few moments later she had made her purchases from the merchant, made her apologies to her companions, and taken a few steps down the broad aisle toward the next set of booths. When she could do it without seeming too obvious, she dropped back to where Foley was trailing behind the others.

"You'll never guess who the shopkeeper's assistant was," she murmured.

"An old friend from Welce? I noticed her accent."

"From Welce, yes, but not someone I knew. She's one of my father's spies."

He raised his eyebrows, then nodded emphatically. "Good. I knew there must be some in the city, but I didn't know how to contact them."

She slipped him Leah's piece of paper. "This is where you can find her. She wants to hear from me at least once every nineday." She didn't bother explaining why. Foley was already on the lookout for constant danger; he would hardly be surprised to learn Leah was equally watchful.

"Good," he said again.

She nodded at the untidy group preceding them down the aisle. Garameno's servant was pushing the wheeled chair at an even pace;

Melissande walked beside him, chatting with great animation. "How'd he get up the stairwell? Can he walk that well?"

"His man carried him and a soldier brought the chair."

"He must hate that. He seems so proud."

Foley glanced down at her. "He seems like he would hate even more being confined to the palace, left out of events. I think he seems willing to make whatever concessions are necessary."

"A good trait, I suppose."

"Or a dangerous one."

"You see danger everywhere."

"I imagine it as a possibility, certainly."

She jerked her head toward Leah's booth. "So. Back there. I stepped behind the curtain. What did you think when I was gone so long?"

His smile was faint. "As I say, I noticed that you spoke to her in Welchin, so I thought it was most likely that you were exchanging news. But I also considered the possibility that she had somehow rendered you unconscious and carried you through the curtain to the booth that I presume is on the other side."

Corene was laughing. "I'm not sure she would be strong enough to drag my body very far."

"No, but she could have had accomplices nearby."

"I don't see how you could have saved me if that had actually happened!"

"I would have gotten Steff's attention, which would have gotten the guards' attention, and several of us would have raced after you. It would be hard for kidnappers to conceal the fact that they were carrying the lifeless body of a young woman through the Great Market. I don't think we would have had much difficulty finding you."

"It sounds exciting," she said buoyantly. "I'm almost sorry it didn't happen."

He glanced down again, no longer smiling. "I'm not."

She touched his arm. "I'm joking. I wouldn't want to put you to that kind of trouble."

He was still watching her. "I wouldn't mind the *trouble* of rescuing you," he said. "I wouldn't want *you* be hurt or afraid."

"Well, fortunately, nothing of the kind occurred," she said.

Just then, Melissande turned around to look for her. "Corene! Up here is a booth you *must* visit. Candies with a taste I cannot describe."

She hurried to catch up with the others and fell in next to Melissande. "I'm starting to think you've spent every day here at the market, buying things."

"Well, perhaps not every day, but many of them."

"We rely on Melissande's openhanded purchases to maintain the balance of trade between Cozique and Malinqua," Garameno said with a grin.

"How unfair! You come here as often as I do!"

"My purpose is different. I am collecting information from the vendors and assessing the level of satisfaction of the buyers."

"So how is the Great Market regulated?" Corene asked curiously. "How do you choose the merchants? How long are their contracts? Do they pay rents or percentages?"

"*Corene!*" Melissande exclaimed in horror. "That is too absolutely boring!"

"It's not," she insisted. "I used to listen in all the time when my father and the council would talk about the best ways to tax the shop districts in Chialto. It's not as simple as it seems."

"Well, it is just as dull as it seems," Melissande said. "I am going to find Jiramondi and have a much more enjoyable conversation."

She flounced off, but Corene stayed behind, accommodating her steps to the slower pace of the wheeled chair. "The Great Market has two models," Garameno told her. "There are the booths that have been run for generations by the same families and that bring in such a steady stream of revenue it seems reasonable to assess an annual tax. But there are a few booths on every level that are more temporary, changing hands every few years, and these are taxed on a percentage basis."

"Of course, anytime you just take a percentage, you have to be sure the vendor isn't lying to you about his receipts," Corene pointed out.

Garameno laughed. "Hence the reason I often visit the market, trying to ascertain who is running a flourishing business and who is not." He lifted his hands from the armrests and gestured briefly. "It is one of the duties I perform for my aunt. In several capacities, I act as her business advisor."

She lifted her eyebrows. "Formally or informally?"

"A little of both. I sit in on the council meetings with my aunt, the mayor, the prefect, and certain elected officials from various districts, so I have a formal voice there. But we also meet for keerza every morning and talk over pressing issues."

"Do your cousins meet with her, too?"

Garameno smiled. "They do not have—I want to put this kindly— minds that are as analytical as mine. Many other good qualities, of course, but they don't think as strategically as I do."

It was a blatant attempt to show himself indispensable to the empress, though in all honesty Corene had to admit that he was probably right. She hadn't spent much time with Greggorio, but *analytical* was a word that had never once crossed her mind when she was with him. Jiramondi was smarter than he was given credit for, she thought— but she didn't think she'd put him in charge of accounting for the revenue of the whole country.

"So how does it work? Do different council members represent the interests of different guilds, or different regions of Malinqua? Is someone responsible for regulating foreign trade?"

Garameno laughed loudly enough to cause Melissande and Steff and Jiramondi to look over their shoulders in curiosity. "Princess Corene, you surprise me. I would have thought you were only interested in fashion and frivolity, not the wealth and commerce of nations."

"That's what everybody thinks about me," she agreed. "I *hated* history classes and every single lesson about economic incentives and imbalances. But when I went to live at my father's house, it was all different somehow. He was the regent, you know, and everyone with a complaint or a scheme dropped by to talk things over with him. He didn't mind when I would sit in his study and listen. Once I realized that all this stuff was about real *people*, I thought it was fascinating."

"Yes, real people with real lives," Garameno said. "You can raise the tax rate by one percent and put a small merchant out of business. And he closes shop and his family suffers and his children starve. But if you don't charge adequate taxes, you can't fix your roads and you can't preserve the water supply and you can't pay your navy, so when Dhonsho or Berringey shows up in your harbor with a fleet of warships, you can't protect your land. It's a very delicate balance."

"What would you change," she asked, "if you were emperor?"

He lifted his head to look up at her. A slight smile lingered around the corners of his mouth, but she couldn't determine what he meant by it. Maybe he was just amused that a seventeen-year-old girl was intrigued by issues of governance. "I try not to look that far ahead," he said, "in case I am never emperor. Since—now that we have joyfully welcomed Steffanolo into our midst—my chances are only one in four."

"It's hard not to, though," she answered frankly. "I mean, I was one of four heirs, too, and I always knew my chances of taking the crown weren't good, but I *thought* about it a lot."

"And yet here you are, not even in Welce anymore," he said lightly. "See what all that thinking got you?"

Before she could come up with a reply to that, Melissande turned around again and impatiently motioned her forward. "Corene! You must see these hairpins! They look like something that would suit a sweela girl."

They spent another two hours at the Great Market before everyone confessed to weariness and a desire to return to the palace. Melissande made sure Corene rode in her carriage for the return visit, practically shoving Liramelli toward the other one, so they could sit together and examine the items they'd picked up during the course of the day. Corene had ended up with not only the pitcher and the music box, but also the hairpins and a couple of scarves.

And a small pouch of red glass beads that had been cut and polished to look like rubies.

She'd found them on the second level—where Steff had insisted they stop so he could look at some seedlings on display in the agricultural section. The beads were so cheap that Corene could buy a handful for less than a quint-silver.

"If you wanted jewels, they have beautiful ones upstairs," Melissande had said.

"I don't want to wear them. I want to decorate with them."

Which was a lie, though she might, in fact, put them in a dish on her dressing table and add a candle or two. Red beads and fire—anybody would call that a sweela combination.

But she really wanted them in case she needed to send a message. To Leah, to Josetta, even to Darien—all of whom now knew the code. *Here are some pretty little beads I picked up at the market. Put them in a jar and think of me.* How would an innocuous note like that raise anyone's suspicions? But any of those recipients would instantly know that Corene was in danger—and act accordingly.

Though she didn't really think she was in danger. Despite the soldiers. Despite the missing girl. Anyway, she was safe as long as Foley was nearby. She glanced over her shoulder, to locate him among the accompanying guards, and found him at the very front of the line, within easy reach of her voice.

No danger at all.

Melissande was yawning as the carriages pulled up before the palace, where the wing of red stone and the wing of white stood in stark contrast under the sultry afternoon sun. "I think I shall be very lazy and sleep until dinner," she announced.

"Since you are always very lazy, I think none of us are surprised," Jiramondi replied.

A half dozen footmen stepped forward to help them from the carriages and escort them to the enormous doors. Lorian was waiting for them just over the threshold, and he offered a slight bow as soon as he spotted Steff.

"The empress requests your presence in her study. Immediately," he said, his voice heavy with portent. "Please come with me right now."

SEVEN

Corene watched Steff as he grew perfectly still, assessing what Lorian's words might mean. He turned his head to look at her, and she nodded. The day after they'd arrived, the empress had had Steff's heritage tested by two very odd men who had arrived in the driving rain. Steff said they had taken samples of his blood, his hair, and his fingernails—and that it had been the creepiest experience of his life. They had explained the kinds of testing they would attempt, though none of it made sense to him. All he knew was that the empress trusted these local diviners to tell her the truth; Zoe's coru conviction was not good enough for Filomara.

Corene suspected it wasn't good enough for Steff, either. He hadn't grown up watching the primes work their subtle magic; he might wonder if Zoe had misread his blood. He might wonder if he was not, after all, the lost grandson who had miraculously returned—if he had any place in this court at all.

Corene put a comforting hand on Steff's arm. "It will be all right," she promised.

"Come with me," he begged.

Lorian spoke in a polite but chilly tone. "She wishes to see you alone."

Steff glanced at Corene, then back at Lorian. "I'd really like to have her with me," he said. "No matter what the news."

Corene didn't feel like pleading with the supercilious Lorian. If Filomara didn't want her in the room, let the empress say so to her face. "I'll come," she said. "Let's go."

"This is very exciting!" Melissande exclaimed. "Perhaps I won't nap after all, but merely sit and wait in *agony* until you return with the news."

Corene handed her various bundles to Foley, then followed Steff and Lorian through the palace doors. She could feel the three nephews staring at their backs with an intensity that made her spine itch. This was a conference that meant as much to them as it did to Steff.

Lorian led them to the second story of the white wing and down a long hallway that Corene hadn't explored yet, though it was clear that this was the region of the palace where the empress spent the bulk of her days. The rooms she glimpsed behind half-closed doors were large, full of light, and sparsely but comfortably furnished. Both grand and severe—exactly how Corene viewed Filomara.

The empress waited for them in a room that seemed to be nothing but high ceilings, white walls, and sunlight. The only color was supplied by the garden greenery visible through windows that took up an entire wall. At first Corene didn't even see any chairs or places to sit.

The empress was standing in the middle of the room, dressed in such a plain ivory jacket and trousers that she almost blended in with her surroundings. Close enough, and dark enough, to be her shadow stood a slight, stooped man with the wrinkled face and hunched posture of the very old. But his eyes were searching and curious; Corene would bet there wasn't much he missed.

Lorian felt compelled to announce them formally, perhaps for the benefit of the visitor. "Steffanolo Adova and Princess Corene of Welce."

Filomara glared in Corene's direction. "I didn't ask for your presence, Princess."

Corene bowed politely, a conciliatory gesture. "I thought Steffanolo might like to have a familiar face nearby."

Filomara frowned a moment longer, then shrugged. "I suppose you may as well stay." Not until then did Lorian withdraw, closing the door quietly behind him. Corene tried to smile at the thought he had lingered long enough to throw her out if Filomara had asked him to, but she was too tense to be amused.

Filomara gestured at her companion. "This is Renalto Corsicara, who oversees the institute of biological research."

"The what?" Steff said, moments before the words came out of Corene's mouth.

The old man grinned. It made his face surprisingly likable. "In your country, so I hear, most of the research centers around mechanical things. In Malinqua, the top scientific minds bend themselves to understanding living creatures. Humans, animals, and plants. We have not built flying machines, as I understand the Welchins have, but we know more about the body than any of your experts do."

I bet the primes know things about the body your researchers wouldn't even think to ask about, Corene thought. "So were you one of the people who tested Steff's blood?" she said.

"Not the first day," Filomara answered. "I brought in two respected biologists who do commercial research—they're very involved in animal breeding programs."

"The best in their fields," Renalto murmured. "The most up-to-date testing facilities."

"They said Steffanolo's blood doesn't carry the same markers as mine," Filomara said baldly.

For a moment, Corene thought she'd heard wrong. "They said—what? That Steff isn't related to you?"

The empress nodded. Her square face was carefully blank of emotion, and Corene wondered if she was trying to hold back rage or pain. *I thought he was my grandson and I started to love him, but he's just an imposter . . .*

"But that can't be," Corene said urgently. "He *is* your daughter's son—"

She could feel Steff's hand on her shoulder, tugging her back; it seemed she had taken a couple of hasty steps forward. "Maybe Zoe was wrong," he said in a small voice.

"She's *never* wrong."

"No, and she's not wrong in this case, whoever Zoe is," Renalto said. He looked like he very much wanted to follow that line of inquiry once they were done with this particular conversational thread. "I ran my own tests and drew much different conclusions."

Now Corene was confused, and she could feel Steff shift his balance beside her. "What?" she said faintly.

Filomara's face relaxed to a grim smile. "Have you never wondered why my two living brothers are never seen at court? They are under a lifetime ban because of all their scheming to take the crown away from me. They don't live here, but they have many allies who do, and I knew they would have learned of Steff's existence—and my attempts to prove his bloodline. I thought it highly probable they would find some way to contaminate the evidence, or pay someone else to do so." She snorted. "You see I was right."

"So then—how did you find out the truth?" Corene demanded.

"I had Renalto come here in secret to take additional samples from Steffanolo."

Corene glared at Steff. "You didn't tell me that!"

"I don't tell you everything."

"Well, you should."

Renalto seemed amused at this byplay. "I conducted my own tests, and the results were very clear." He spread his arms as if to draw the others together in one familial hug. "Steffanolo is closely related to the empress, most likely a direct descendant. As his story is the only one that makes sense, I consider it true."

"As do I," Filomara said gruffly. "You are my grandson. Subriella's boy."

Again, Corene felt Steff shift his balance next to her, as if he might want to dash for the exit, as if he might want to sink to the floor. As if he might want to run across the room and throw his arms around his mother's mother. Trying to be subtle about it, she nudged him forward. He took one short, stumbling step, then another—and then Filomara held her arms out to him. Two more steps brought him close enough to clasp her hands and gaze down at her, seeming unsure about what he should do next. Filomara was not a woman to welcome fervent embraces.

Slowly, staring at Steff the whole time, the empress clutched his hands and cradled them against her heart. "Subriella's boy," she said again. "It is like having her back again to have you stand before me."

Corene thought—she could hardly believe it—she could see tears collecting in the empress's stern eyes. One slipped down her cheek, leaving behind an almost invisible track. Filomara lifted Steff's clasped hands and rested her wet face against his folded fingers. No one else in the room moved or spoke, and they stayed like that a very long time.

Since she was sure this was news the empress wanted to announce herself, Corene lied to Melissande when she found the Coziquela girl in her room, already dressed for dinner.

"Filomara wouldn't let me stay," she said. "So I don't know what the blood tests showed."

Melissande sat up very straight on the settee where she had settled in to wait. She'd brought a book and letter-writing materials with her in case that wait took hours. This was a woman who liked to stay informed. "But you yourself are convinced of the veracity of his claim?"

"Completely."

"Explain to me again why that is?"

It was so hard to put into words things that Corene had always considered to be foundational truths. "In Welce, we are all affiliated with one of the five elements. And for every element, there is a prime—someone who can practically bend that element to his or her will. My father's wife is the coru prime. She has power over water and an affinity with blood. She can lay her hand on a man's arm and tell him who his relatives are, who he belongs to. She knows that Steff is Filomara's grandson."

"But even if you are right, that does not mean Filomara's experts will interpret his blood correctly," Melissande pointed out. "They might not be as good as she thinks—or they might have an incentive to lie." She clapped her hands together. "Someone might pay them to say Steff is not at all who he says he is!"

Not for the first time, Corene thought that behind her flighty exterior, Melissande possessed a quick brilliance. She was most certainly sweela. "That occurred to me," Corene said, as if worried about the possibility. "One of her nephews—"

"Or the prefect, or the mayor or someone else who has a stake in the game," Melissande agreed. "But if you and I thought of that, surely Filomara did as well."

"And fifty more things that never crossed our minds," Corene said.

"Then I think dinner tonight will be very interesting."

To nerve herself for the occasion, Corene chose one of the more formal tunics Zoe had sent and kept her hair in place with one of the jeweled pins she'd bought at the Great Market. *Was that just this afternoon?* Corene thought. *This has been the longest day of my life.*

The usual contingent of palace residents had gathered outside the small dining room, awaiting Filomara's appearance—the empress's nephews, the mayor and the prefect and their own family members, the aloof Alette. Corene lied to all of them when they sidled up to ask what Filomara had learned. *I don't know anything. It's very unsettling.*

"If he's an imposter," Greggorio asked, "what will happen to him? Will she have him executed?"

"*What?*" Corene exclaimed.

"Well, it's treason," he argued. "Isn't it? Lying to the empress?"

"I think she'd merely send him packing," Jiramondi said, but he sounded uncertain.

"It would be an act of war, would it not, to execute a foreign national?" Melissande asked, her voice sweetly puzzled. But of course she knew—they all knew—that such an action would be tantamount to a declaration of hostilities.

"He would be banished, nothing more," said the mayor. She looked pointedly at Corene. "And diplomatic relations with Welce would most certainly deteriorate."

Corene offered the woman her brightest smile. "Oh, but you do not know my father. He would never be so clumsy as to send an imposter to Malinqua if there was any chance the ruse would be uncovered."

That brought everyone to a brief halt as they tried to parse her words. Would Darien Serlast ship a pretender off to Palminera if he thought he could get away with it? The mayor's face gathered in a scowl.

"I have complete faith in our researchers," the mayor said. "Whatever the truth is, they will discover it."

Remember you said that, Corene thought as she heard footsteps approaching. Moments later, Filomara and Steff stepped into the ante-room where everyone waited. Steff pulled up short, uneasy at being the center of so much concentrated attention, but Filomara just nodded, not at all discomposed.

"I suppose you've all guessed that I've received the results of the tests conducted to verify Steffanolo's heritage," she said without preamble. "And he is Subriella's son. My grandson. And potentially my heir."

A single cry of *"Wonderful!"* came from Melissande, who also clapped her hands together. Everyone else seemed stunned. Corene glanced quickly from face to face, thinking that anyone who showed anger or disbelief would have been involved in trying to compromise the results. But in fact, everyone seemed equally surprised. Had they all thought Steff to be a fraud? Or had the whole roomful colluded to try to skew the results?

"Naturally, I will want to celebrate this momentous news in some suitable fashion," Filomara went on. Corene thought she detected a faint quaver in the empress's voice. "We must plan a gala event to welcome my grandson."

She paused, as if waiting for congratulations that did not come, and then held her arm out to Steff. "You may escort me in to dinner."

Steff's face was so serious and self-conscious that Corene wanted to laugh, but no one else seemed remotely amused as they followed the empress and Steff into the dining room. Corene found herself sitting beside Jiramondi, who seemed to have chosen a chair as far from his aunt as the table would allow.

"Everyone seems so astonished," she observed in a low voice once the others began stilted general conversation. "Did *none* of you believe he was telling the truth?"

"You must admit the story is farfetched," Jiramondi said. "A daughter who did not die when we all thought she did and a lost grandson who is miraculously alive. I don't know who my aunt entrusted to deliver her news, but I'm afraid she has been lied to by someone who thought to profit by giving her the results she most desired."

Now, that was a version of the story that hadn't occurred to Corene—that *Renalto* would falsify the tests, while the eminent scientists told the truth. "I would find that supposition more alarming if I didn't have complete faith in the woman who first discovered Steff's identity," Corene said. "As it is, I never had a moment's doubt that he is who he says he is."

Jiramondi gave her a shrewd look. "Yet a cynical man might say you have some incentive to lie as well," he said. "I don't mean to give offense."

She laughed. "And you don't. I understand how these court games work."

"Yes," Jiramondi said on a sigh. "And so the game continues, though with an entirely different set of rules."

"So what will your strategy be, now that there are four heirs instead of three?" she asked, teasing a little. "Will you spend more time flattering the empress or will you try instead to make Steff your friend?"

"I shall flirt with the foreign princesses in hopes of making a quick match and winning my aunt's favor that way." He saluted her with his wineglass before sipping from it. "I shall start by saying how beautiful you look. I admire that jeweled clip in your hair."

She patted the hairpin and batted her eyes. "I shall be happy to flirt with you, if it will do you any good," she said. "But would it really influence Filomara if you made an alliance with one of us?"

He smiled, but she thought she saw a shadow flit behind his eyes. "Of course it would!" he said. "Isn't that why she brought you here, after all?"

"Well, so far I like you best of Filomara's nephews, but that could change any day," she said. "You'll have to be *very* nice to me if you want to keep my favor."

They continued to banter throughout the meal, a pastime Corene found highly enjoyable—more so because it earned them speculative and disapproving looks from half the other people at the table. But while she laughed and flirted, she couldn't help wondering about the shadow that had crossed Jiramondi's face. Was it possible his aunt had imported a raftload of foreign women for some other reason than to marry them off to her nephews? Was there a whole different kind of danger here in Malinqua that Corene hadn't even considered yet? She didn't show her sudden uneasiness. She merely took another sip of her wine and smiled.

. . .

The next day, of course, all the talk was about Steff and his certification as heir. He wasn't around to hear the endless speculation, since Lorian had fetched him from the breakfast table and he seemed set to spend every hour with Filomara.

"I don't envy him," Garameno said lightly when he unexpectedly joined Jiramondi and Corene for her language lessons. "I can generally only take a few hours of uninterrupted time with my aunt before I want to roll myself straight out of the palace, down to the harbor, and into the ocean to drown."

Corene was only too glad to give up grammar in favor of gossip. "He has a lot to absorb," she said. "When I was growing up, my sisters and I had lessons every day on everything from past history to current politics."

"It can take a lifetime to master it all," Jiramondi agreed.

Garameno brooded a moment in silence, and then shook his head as if shaking off a mood. "Well, it is not like Steffanolo needs to learn everything in a single quintile," he said. "Since Filomara clearly intends to retain the crown at least another decade. She has *years* to teach him all her secrets."

"Will she trust him, do you think?" Corene asked curiously. "Merely because he is her grandson? People betray their parents and grandparents all the time."

"And their siblings," Jiramondi added. When Garameno gave him a sharp look, Jiramondi merely shrugged. "Well, it's true."

Finally, an opening to ask about Filomara's missing family members. "Are you talking about the empress's brothers? I know two are dead and two are banished, but I don't know any details."

The cousins exchanged glances again; this time Garameno shrugged and looked away. Jiramondi answered. "They were always arguing over the throne. They were constantly making alliances with each other, and then breaking them off. Garameno's father was the youngest, but the first to produce a son, so he felt that *he* should be Filomara's heir. Then my father had me and claimed he had just as much right to the throne. But Morli and Donato—the two oldest brothers—said they shouldn't be left out of the calculations just because they were childless. In fact, Morli married three times until he found a woman who could bear him a son. Then he went on and on about how he was the oldest, so he should be heir and Greggorio after him."

"An argument with which many at court were in full agreement," Garameno put in.

"So what happened?"

"There was a dinner party that all four brothers attended," Jiramondi said. "Probably to talk, as always, about who deserved to be emperor. Morli and Donato ended up dead."

"Poisoned, in the grand tradition of Malinquese courts," Garameno said. "Have you gotten that far in your history lessons yet? At least twenty-five suspicious deaths over the past two hundred years have been attributed to that single cause."

So Foley had been right in some of his speculations. Corene tried not to show her dismay. "Who killed them?"

"Who knows?" Jiramondi said. "My father or Garameno's father were the obvious suspects. Which is why they've been banned from court for life."

"But it could have been a servant in someone else's employ," Garameno put in. "One popular theory was that they poisoned each other. No one can be certain—which is why our esteemed parents were merely banished and not executed for murder."

The way he said "our esteemed parents" made her wonder what kinds of relationships the two men had with their fathers, but there were so many other questions to ask and she didn't want to get distracted.

"But none of this makes any sense to me," she said. "Did they do all this maneuvering for the throne even when Filomara's daughters were alive?"

"Oh, yes," Jiramondi said. "But Morli really stepped up his efforts when Greggorio was born. And by then, of course, we thought Subriella was already dead."

"But Aravani was alive *and* she had children of her own," Corene pointed out. "So why didn't everyone expect *them* to be the natural successors?"

Jiramondi assumed an exaggerated expression of shock. "Another woman on the throne? Are you mad?"

"You can't be serious," Corene answered.

Garameno nodded. "Filomara was not a popular choice. Not with the council, at any rate—though the people love her. Even she knew it would be risky to name Aravani her heir. And once Aravani died, everyone assumed she would have no choice but to pass the crown to a man."

"A strong, virile man," Jiramondi said.

"A whole one," Garameno added.

They didn't have to list their defects to make it obvious why they, too, might seem like risky choices as Filomara's successors. "So Greggorio has become the favorite," she said. "But you two still consider yourselves in the running. How do you win Filomara's favor? Or the favor of the council?"

"As I said last night—by marrying well," Jiramondi said promptly. "And producing heirs of our own."

The mood had lightened just a little; Corene felt it was safe to smile. "So why haven't you all rushed into matrimony?"

Jiramondi laughed. "Because we can't tell who the best bride would be! If we were to pick from among our foreign visitors, Melissande would be the obvious choice, because Cozique is the most powerful nation in the southern seas."

"And yet we have excellent relations with Cozique," Garameno interrupted. "Whereas many times we have been on the brink of war with Dhonsho. In which case, would it be better to marry Alette?"

"Though you could hardly find a less congenial woman to take as your bride," Jiramondi said frankly. "And I am not convinced her father didn't send her here to marry one of us and then stab him in the heart some night when he was sleeping."

"A very expensive way to harm your enemy," Corene said.

Garameno shrugged. "He has something like fifteen children. I'm sure he could spare one or two if it meant making Malinqua suffer."

"But perhaps it would be better to take a domestic bride," Jiramondi said. "The prefect is very popular. Perhaps Filomara and the council would be happiest if one of us married Liramelli."

"Maybe there is no way to know what would please them," Corene said. "Maybe it would be better to marry to please yourselves."

"All that would please me is being named my aunt's successor," Garameno said flatly. Jiramondi merely nodded.

Corene could hardly fault them for that sentiment. She'd crossed an ocean in search of a crown, after all, since she didn't seem likely to inherit one at home. But she couldn't help thinking that such single-minded focus on the pursuit of power wasn't particularly attractive in either man. It made her squirm to think how unattractive it must be in *her*.

Steff remained closeted with Filomara for the next series of days, and without him the afternoon penta tournaments seemed oddly flat. So they were all delighted when he finally joined them in the sun-filled room where they had gathered to play cards.

"Did you escape, or did my aunt throw you out?" Jiramondi inquired when Steff pulled a chair up to the table and practically collapsed in it.

"I think I escaped, but it's hard to tell," Steff said with a groan. "Some fellow showed up to discuss—something—and at first she invited me to listen. But then she changed her mind and said I might be excused."

They laughed, and he went on. "It's been like that for days. Every time a visitor arrives, she'll spend five minutes telling me who he is and why he's important, and then she'll have me sit in the room and listen in. Then he leaves, and she questions me about what I heard and what I learned and whether or not I thought he was lying. It's more exhausting than plowing the entire farm by hand."

Liramelli gave him a serious look. "But it must have been instructive."

Steff ran a hand through his hair, which—until that moment—was neater than Corene had ever seen it. In fact, now that she looked him over closely, she could see that his whole appearance had been subtly altered. He was wearing highly tailored, completely unadorned Malinquese clothing; the dark colors suited his face and made him look older and more sophisticated. Or maybe that was the effect of his intense concentration on everything the empress was trying to teach him.

"I suppose so," he answered Liramelli. "I can't tell how much I'm actually *learning* and how much I'm just listening in bewilderment."

Jiramondi shuffled the cards and raised his eyebrows in a silent question. When everyone nodded, he began dealing another hand of penta. "If Greggorio can learn the intricacies of Malinquese politics, you can, too, because Greggorio is as stupid as an ox," Jiramondi said. When the three women protested, he shrugged. "He *is* stupid. I'm fond of him, and he doesn't have an ounce of cruelty in him, but he'd make a terrible emperor." He flicked a card at Liramelli and challenged her, "Tell me I'm wrong."

Corene watched Liramelli's earnest face crease with worry. Corene supposed the other girl was capable of lying, since *everyone* was capable of lying, but she didn't seem to be able to do it when Malinqua was the topic at hand. "He would probably be a very popular ruler," she offered at last.

"He certainly *looks* the part," Jiramondi agreed. "But I don't think he could negotiate a trade agreement to save his life."

"He simply needs to marry well," Melissande decreed. "Handsome, stupid men always benefit from marrying intelligent, resourceful women."

Steff sorted his cards and gave her an impudent grin. "Are you volunteering to take him in hand?"

She swatted him lightly on the arm. "I *am* very clever," she answered, then nodded across the table. "But so is Corene, and so is Liramelli—and Liramelli, besides, has the advantage of understanding the whole of Malinquese politics. In fact, the match is so obvious, I cannot believe it has not been promoted before now."

Liramelli's face suddenly assumed a closed expression, and even the easygoing Jiramondi looked to be momentarily at a loss.

"Ah," Melissande said. "So there is some unhappy history here."

Steff looked up from his cards. "What, were the two of you betrothed or something? What went wrong?"

Corene punched his shoulder. "Stop talking. Just play your cards."

"I wish people would stop hitting me all the time," Steff complained, ostentatiously rubbing his arm.

"Then shut up when people tell you to."

Liramelli had regained her usual composure. "Everyone knows the story anyway. Yes, you're right. Filomara and my father had decided

that Greggorio and I would be an excellent match. It had not been formally announced but—"

"Everybody knew," Jiramondi supplied.

"But Greggorio didn't—he wasn't—he didn't seem to have realized
how beneficial such a match could have been to the kingdom," Liramelli said carefully.

He thinks you're plain and boring, and it broke your heart, Corene
thought. *Were you in love with him? You seem too smart to care only
about a pretty face.* Though she supposed even the smartest woman
could be dumb about love. To help Liramelli through the painful part
of the narrative, she said flippantly, "He rebelled at the idea of being
tied to one woman for the rest of his life, and he started flirting madly
with anyone who crossed his path. And since he's gorgeous and might
be emperor one day, everyone flirted back."

"Yes," Liramelli said. "My father was angry, the empress was furious, and Greggorio—" She shrugged.

"Greggorio didn't notice," Jiramondi said. "Since, as we've already
established, he's stupid."

Melissande leaned back in her chair, somehow managing to look
artlessly fetching as she did so. This sort of intrigue was absolutely delicious to her, Corene thought. "I think perhaps you do not give young
Greggorio enough credit," she said. "I think he saw the road that had
been laid out before him, did not want to travel it, and took whatever
steps he deemed necessary to change his course."

"Think that if you like," Jiramondi said dryly, "but never in the
eighteen years I've known him has he ever thought that clearly or that
far ahead."

"So what happened?" Steff asked, as blunt as ever. He caught Corene's
hand as she lifted it to swat him again. "I mean it. What happened?"

Liramelli glanced at Jiramondi. "There was a girl named Sarona.
The daughter of one of the richest merchants in the city. He began
spending so much time with her that no one could overlook it. Filomara
was angry, but it didn't deter him. I even heard him tell Filomara that he
could marry Sarona if he wanted—she was certainly high-born enough.
Which happened to be true."

Corene and Melissande traded looks. As if she didn't know, Melissande said, "But this Sarona, where is she? I do not remember meeting her at court."

Liramelli glanced at Jiramondi again, clearly trying to decide how much information to share. "The stories differ. Everyone *believes* Filomara told her parents that she had to be removed from Palminera or Filomara would ship the girl off herself. The empress claims she never gave such an ultimatum."

"At any rate, she's gone now," Jiramondi said.

"How long ago did she leave?" Corene asked.

"A nineday or two before you arrived," Jiramondi answered.

Corene raised her eyebrows. "Not very long. Is Greggorio heartbroken?"

Liramelli looked sad. "I do think he's lost some of his—his *brightness* since Sarona left," she said.

"So maybe he did love her," Corene said.

"And who would want to marry a man in love with someone else?" Liramelli asked.

"It would not bother me particularly," Melissande said briskly. "People fall in and out of love all the time. It is to be expected! And a king—well—he might have *many* loves over his lifetime. I don't think you should marry a royal ruler and think to find romance."

"One has to admire the practical Coziquela spirit," Jiramondi said, saluting her with his penta cards.

She gathered up her own cards and began sorting them into suits. "Yes, I think one does," she said serenely. "Now, shall we play this round? Oh, we must, because I have a *very* good hand."

When people weren't speculating about Steff's audiences with Filomara or Greggorio's affection for Sarona, they were talking about the upcoming gala. Apparently it was rare for Filomara to plan a celebration of any size, and this one would be massive. The main event would be at the palace, of course, but there would be additional venues throughout the city where she would arrange for food, music, and entertainment, all paid for by the crown. The scale of the event required so much planning that it might not occur until a nineday or two before Quinnasweela.

Corene expected that she and Melissande would spend hours determining what to wear to the grand fete, but she was surprised when Liramelli seemed to be fretting about the same topic. Well, she hadn't figured Liramelli out yet, she knew, so the Malinquese girl was always surprising her.

Once was when Liramelli asked her to dinner. She'd managed to loiter behind with Corene after one particularly raucous penta round, maneuvering so that the two of them were alone together, putting away the cards.

"My mother and father would like to invite you to their apartment for dinner sometime in the next nineday," she said, her serious voice making the request seem even more formal.

Corene had only had a few brief conversations with Liramelli's parents, and they'd all been so desultory that she couldn't imagine sitting through a whole meal, but, of course, there was only one answer. "I'd be delighted! Simply pick a day."

That was quickly settled; it took longer for Corene to decide what to wear to the meal. Liramelli exemplified the Malinquese fashion of severe unadorned simplicity, so Corene wanted to show respect by wearing her plainest, darkest tunic and trousers. And yet, the prefect and his wife might be *expecting* their foreign guest to look exotic. So Corene compromised by adding a brightly colored shawl covered with winking sequins. A gift from Zoe, who loved anything gaudy.

Liramelli had offered to meet her at her door and escort her to the prefect's suite in the southern wing of the palace. Corene was positive she wouldn't find her way otherwise, so she gratefully accepted. But when she answered the knock on her door that evening, she found Foley there instead of Liramelli.

"Just wanted you to know I'm ready," he said.

"You're coming with me?"

He nodded. "I'll wait in the hallway."

She tilted her head to one side. "I'm trying to decide if they'll find that rude or impressive."

"I don't much care," he responded.

His tone was polite but his posture was unyielding; clearly, nothing would dissuade him from accompanying her. But she liked the thought of him prowling along behind her as they traversed the palace's endless halls. She liked knowing he would be within call of her voice for the duration of the meal. "Then I'll hope they think it's impressive."

Liramelli arrived just then and cast only a cursory glance at Foley; it seemed she was used to him by now. "I love that shawl," she said instantly. "I've never seen anything like it."

"My stepmother gave it to me. I love it, too."

Liramelli set off toward the end of the hall, not the direction Corene usually went. "I'm already lost," she said with a light laugh.

Liramelli produced her usual serious smile. "There are two stories that connect between the red wing and the white one," she said. "One is the ground level, of course, but the sixth one also connects."

"I didn't know that."

"You didn't grow up here, chasing other children down the halls and learning where all the stairwells and passages run."

Corene laughed. "That sounds like fun."

"Greggorio and I knew every inch of this palace. We've been on the roof, we've been down in the foundations. I don't think there's a single room we haven't been inside."

"Even the empress's suite?"

For a moment, even Liramelli's strict face looked merry. "*Especially* the empress's suite."

She took them through an unmarked doorway that Corene would have thought opened onto another bedroom, but that led instead to a stone stairwell, chilly with disuse. Thin tubes of gaslight provided adequate but uninviting illumination and contributed to a somewhat haunted feel.

"Up," Liramelli said, and they climbed two more stories before arriving at the sixth-floor landing.

"This door is always tricky," Liramelli commented, wrestling with a heavy metal handle.

"Maybe it's locked," Corene suggested. "The empress probably doesn't like people roaming where she can't see them."

"You're supposed to *think* that," Liramelli said. "But it's always like this."

"Let me try," Foley said, and stepped between them. Two good pulls and he wrenched the handle in place with the satisfying *click* of the catch disengaging. The door swung open.

The sixth-floor hallway was almost as spooky as the stairwell. At least half of the sconces appeared to have been turned off, leaving great stretches of the corridor in darkness. In what light remained, Corene could see dozens of thick doors, all of them shut tight, guarding who knew what secrets or horrors? She was even more grateful Foley had come along. Maybe Sarona wasn't the only young woman who had suddenly vanished from this palace.

"I suppose you and Greggorio went into all of *these* rooms, too?" she asked.

Liramelli didn't seem at all affected by the dramatic lighting and lurking shadows. "Every one!" she answered, leading them forward. "Most are moldy old bedrooms that haven't been used in decades. Some are just storage rooms, though I can't imagine that anyone remembers what's inside them."

"Isn't this the top floor?" Corene asked. "I would have thought it would hold the servants' quarters."

"It is," Liramelli said. "And it *used* to. But now they're all on the fifth floor."

"Which doesn't connect between the two halves. That seems inconvenient."

Liramelli gave her a swift, unhappy glance. "Jiramondi says he told you about the poisonings. Filomara moved all the servants down a level after her brothers died. She thought if she restricted access between the two wings, maybe everyone would be safer."

That actually makes sense, Corene thought. Before she could say so, there was a sound from behind one of the closed doors—a noise that was half moan, half rattle. Corene spun around to stare, actually pressing her hand to her heart in momentary fright. "What was that?"

"Wind in the casement. Greggorio and I would shriek and go running every time we heard it." Sensing that Corene wasn't entirely convinced, she asked, "Do you want to look inside and make sure everything's all right?"

"No," Corene answered instantly, then added, "I don't want to be late for dinner." She glanced down at her tunic. "And I don't want to get dust all over my clothes."

Liramelli nodded, then loosed a sigh. "Everyone keeps talking about what they'll wear to the celebration," she said. "It's making me feel panicked."

"Why? It should be fun."

"Because I always look like a dull and quiet mouse, and that night won't be any different, but I *wish* it would be," Liramelli said in a rush. Before Corene could recover from the surprise of that, the other girl added, "I don't suppose you'd be willing to help me dress for the gala, would you?"

"Of course I would! I'd love to. But, you know, Melissande is much more fashionable than I am. She's really the one you should ask."

Liramelli was quiet as they passed a few more of those ominous doors. "I don't think Melissande likes me," she said at last.

"What? Of course she does. Melissande likes everybody." *Or nobody,* Corene thought. At any rate, the Coziquela girl treated everyone with equal warmth, whether or not it was genuine. Even Alette.

"I just feel awkward and unsophisticated around her," Liramelli said. "I would much rather spend that time with you."

Corene was having a hard time remembering the last time someone had preferred her company over anybody else's. She was usually the one whose sharp tongue and abrupt manners made people hastily seek out more congenial company. "Well, I'll be happy to help you dress the night of the celebration—and go shopping with you beforehand, too! But you have to promise you won't mind if I'm very honest about what looks good and what doesn't. It's one of the things people tend not to like about me."

Liramelli gave her a shy smile. "It's one of the things I *do* like about you," she said. "You and Steff. You don't play the same kinds of games everyone else does."

"Steff doesn't, but sometimes I do," Corene admitted. "Don't forget, I've been at court most of my life."

Liramelli cast her one keen sideways look. "Don't forget, I have, too."

Was that a warning, Corene wondered, or just a reminder that Liramelli wasn't quite the fumbling innocent she appeared to be? "So when would you like to go shopping?" she asked.

"Let's get through dinner first."

In another few paces they passed the broad archway that led to the majestic stairwell that served the white wing of the palace. Six stories below them they could hear voices and footsteps, the clatter of everyday court life. It sounded very far away.

A few yards beyond the stairwell an ironwork door blocked the entrance to the red wing of the palace. In the corridor where Corene's rooms were, the corresponding space was a solid wall guarded by a slim bronze statue of a boyish soldier wielding a thin silver blade. It hadn't occurred to Corene before that the soldier was literally forbidding her passage.

The door opened with a groan of disuse, and they passed into a corridor that was even gloomier and more unwelcoming than its twin. Corene was happy beyond measure when they made it to the grand stairwell that served the southern wing, and followed it down to the third floor. Here, the hallway was brightly lit and buzzing with conversation that seeped out past the closed doors.

"Well! It's already been an adventure," she observed. "I hardly think the dinner itself can compare."

But the meal was more enjoyable than she'd expected. For one thing, the prefect and his family were housed in an expansive suite that was probably almost the size of the empress's own quarters, and they didn't share Filomara's minimalist tastes. The colors were warm, the furniture was plush, and the whole atmosphere was much homier than any other rooms Corene had been in at the palace.

For another, her hosts had made an effort to please her by preparing Welchin foods with Welchin spices. They had even placed glasses of fruited water on the table, a touch of elegance Corene had missed at all of the formal dinners. And finally, they exerted themselves to be gracious.

"We're delighted you could join us for dinner, Princess Corene," the prefect's wife greeted her. Like her daughter, she was fair-haired, plain-featured, and not very tall; it would be easy to pass her on the street without noticing her. But her smile was wide and her eyes seemed kind. She looked, Corene thought, like someone who had seen a great deal of life and watched it with compassion.

"Oh, please! Just call me Corene."

"And you must call me Mariana. I suppose you must use titles when you're in the empress's presence, but here"—she gestured at her husband—"he is simply Harlo."

The prefect came close enough to take her hand, but he didn't. Malinqua might be less formal than Welce, but even here, no one casually reached out to touch royalty. Harlo was a big man, probably in his late forties or fifties, and powerful-looking. Corene often thought he should be out striding through fields or breaking horses instead of trying to hold a delicate china cup in the empress's dining room.

"Indeed, we are glad you could join us," he said. He had an attractive voice, low and resonant. It was one of the things Corene had found to like about him in their rare interactions so far. "It's hard to get to know anyone when Filomara and her whole family are watching."

"Yes, I've started to dread dinner every night," Corene replied. "I'm used to either very grand meals where you don't expect to enjoy yourself, or very small ones where just a few family members are sitting around the table. And that's not always fun, either, particularly if the baby is crying, but it feels more *real*."

"Baby?" Liramelli repeated.

"My father and his wife have a little girl named Celia. When I left, she wasn't talking yet, but she was pretty good at crying."

"That's the way of babies," Mariana said, shepherding them past a large formal dining room and into a much more intimate space. They took their places at a small, square table where they could sit so close their knees almost touched. It reminded Corene of dinners with Darien and Zoe, and for a moment she was so homesick she almost couldn't catch her breath.

"So your father remarried and you have a half sister," Liramelli said. "Do you like them? Your stepmother and the little girl?"

"Darling," Mariana said in a reproving voice.

But Corene appreciated the question. She would have asked it herself. "I love Zoe—my father's wife," she said honestly. "She's so much nicer than my own mother. Celia—I don't know. I'm not very good with babies. And sometimes it's hard to watch Darien playing with her, because I know she has so much more of his attention than I ever had."

Servants had stepped into the room and began serving the food. Fish and fruit and bread, and not a flake of zeezin in the whole meal.

"You didn't grow up with your father?" Harlo asked.

Corene sampled the fish. Perfect. "It's complicated," she said. "This tastes wonderful."

"I always thought you were the king's daughter," said Liramelli.

Corene grinned. "It's *really* complicated."

"And you certainly don't have to discuss your family with us," said Mariana.

"Oh, I don't mind talking about it. I just don't want to bore you."

Mariana leaned across the table. "I love hearing about other people's odd families. It makes me feel so much better about my own."

"Well. My mother was one of four wives that King Vernon had."

"Four!" Harlo boomed. "Isn't one challenging enough for any man?" Mariana frowned at him, and he laughed.

"It turned out he couldn't sire children, which alarmed his advisors, so they found ways to—I don't know how to put this delicately—"

"They bred his wives to other men," said the prefect.

"*Harlo,*" Mariana exclaimed.

"I'm an old farmer. I know how these things are done."

"And he's right. That's what they did," Corene said. She could tell that her easygoing response to Harlo's earthiness made Mariana relax a little. "So between them, his wives had four daughters—though the youngest baby, it turns out, was really his. But after Vernon got sick, everyone found out the truth, and I learned that Darien was my father."

"And was that a good day or a bad day?" Mariana asked.

No one had put the question to her in such a way before. Corene toyed with the stem of her water glass and thought it over. Well, so much else had been happening then. She'd almost been sold off to Soeche-Tas, and Zoe had saved her. And Josetta—after years of being the fretful older sister Corene had been taught to despise—Josetta had turned out to be her staunchest ally and truest friend. The things she'd thought she could always depend on had been yanked out from under her, and supports she had never known existed had loomed up out of nowhere to serve as bulwarks against chaos. But it had taken her a while to come to terms with the idea that Darien was her father—and planned to take that role seriously.

"I'd known him my whole life, of course. He was Vernon's most trusted advisor, so he'd always been at court. But he'd never been *part* of my life before. It was strange at first. Darien is very strong-willed. Very used to getting his own way. And he didn't approve of everything my mother did to raise me. So—there were some tense moments." She sipped at her fruited water. "But, on balance, I liked my life a lot better once Darien and Zoe were part of it."

Mariana signaled one of the servants, who noiselessly approached to refill Corene's glass. "So if I'm understanding you correctly, your mother and father were never married and perhaps they don't get along very well now."

Corene laughed. "They *hate* each other. But to be fair, most people hate my mother."

Liramelli looked shocked. "Even you?"

Yes, except on the days I'm afraid I'm just like her. Except on the days I wish she would love me—or maybe I hate her even more on those days. She didn't answer the question directly. "I suppose you must have people here in Palminera who never stop scheming. Who are always three steps ahead of everyone, trying to guess what the next power play will be." She saw Harlo and Mariana exchange rueful glances, apparently recognizing an acquaintance in that description. "That's my mother. So she's hard to love."

"Well, now I think I understand a little better," Liramelli said, taking another helping of the fruit compote. "I thought it would be difficult for you to be so far away from home, but maybe it's the kind of home you *want* to get away from."

And that, Corene realized, was the best reason she'd heard yet to explain why she had run away from Welce in Filomara's company. "So tell me more about *your* family," she invited.

Mariana lifted her water glass. "Where to even start!" she exclaimed. But she launched into a colorful recital that involved multiple marriages, mysterious disappearances, an uncle who turned out to be an aunt, and the occasional illegitimate child conveniently adopted by a wealthy cousin.

"I honestly couldn't believe Harlo had the nerve to propose to me, given my family's eccentric past," Mariana said. "Whereas there has not been a single scandal attached to Harlo's ancestors going back for a hundred generations."

He nodded. "It's true. An unbroken line of the dullest, most insipid men and women you could ever want to hear about. I married Mariana hoping she'd stir up a little controversy, but so far she's been a complete disappointment on that front."

He said it with such palpable fondness that it was clear he was joking—was maybe even relieved, Corene thought. She said, "Maybe Liramelli will cause some turmoil for you."

All three of them laughed, and Mariana reached over to pat Liramelli's wrist. "She has been the best daughter anyone could have. I think she'll have to marry badly before we have any hope for scandal on her part."

"Of course, if she marries one of Filomara's nephews, she's ruined that plan," Corene pointed out.

Liramelli groaned. "Can we just have *one* meal where we're not talking about the succession and who might marry whom?"

Corene laughed. "And we'd done so well up to this point! Forget I even mentioned Filomara's heirs."

Harlo was shaking his head. "I've said it many times. I'd be happy to see my girl paired with Greggorio, but the other two? I'd rather she married a country farmer and lived the rest of her life outside of Palminera than wed one of them."

"Harlo," Mariana said.

"Garameno's broken and Jiramondi's unnatural, and there's no point in pretending otherwise," Harlo said. "In fact, Jiramondi's the worst of the lot by far. There are days I have trouble looking at that boy, knowing what he's like."

Liramelli cast Corene an agonized look, but Corene knew better than to challenge a man in his own house. She merely took another bite and waited for someone else to turn the subject.

Mariana obliged. "I do like the new heir—Steffanolo," she said. "He's so polite and thoughtful. As you might imagine, he and Harlo could talk land management and crop rotation for hours."

Corene's face must have showed her surprise, because Liramelli quickly explained. "We've had Steff to dinner a couple of times because my father wanted to get to know him better. And to let the rest of the family meet him, too."

Which was when Corene finally put it together. "Of course! Filomara's husband was Harlo's—uncle?"

"That's right," Harlo said.

"So Steff is your second cousin, or something like that."

"I know some people make fun of him for being a farmer's son, but that's why my father's relatives liked him so much," Liramelli said.

"He's unpretentious," said Mariana. "That's the word I was looking for."

"He is that," Corene agreed. "It's one of the reason he's so likable—but might be one of the reasons Filomara decides not to name him her heir."

"We're not talking about that tonight, remember?" Liramelli demanded.

"Do you think he'll stay?" Harlo asked. "If Filomara doesn't choose him?"

"I don't know," Corene said. "It might be hard to go back to being an ordinary man in Welce after being a prince in Malinqua."

"I don't think he'd actually be ordinary," Harlo said. "My uncle—Filomara's husband—had assets that have been kept in trust since his death but will now devolve on Steffanolo, since he has been declared legitimately to be Subriella's son. He will be a man of some wealth, and I imagine he could be an ambassador of sorts between our nations, if nothing else." Harlo sipped from his glass. "Relations have generally been good between our countries, but things could always be better," he went on. "In the area of commerce, for instance. I imagine there are a lot of possibilities there."

Corene sat up straighter in her chair. This, then, was the real reason she'd been invited to the meal. "Well, as my father says, there are three types of goods that countries exchange," she said. "Living things, mechanical things, and knowledge. You and Steff have already talked about livestock and crops, but mechanical things might be where the money is. Surely Filomara has told you about our smoker cars and flying machines?"

"*Flying* machines?" Mariana repeated. "Oh, just the words sound dangerous!"

"They're pretty scary," Corene admitted. "Steff's brother is a pilot. We watched him fly once, and I was sure he was going to crash and die."

"I understand they're still experimental," Harlo said. "But those smoker cars sounded intriguing."

"I have no idea what 'smoker cars' are," Liramelli said.

"Vehicles that run on compressed gasses," Corene explained. "So you don't need horses. They were invented by the elay prime, so they're also known as elaymotives."

"I think the Malinquese people would definitely embrace elaymotives," Harlo said. "What do you think the Welchin folk would like in return?"

"I met someone the other day—Renalto?" When Harlo nodded, Corene went on. "He talked about biological science and some of the advances you've made in medicine. I'm sure there are researchers in Chialto who would love a chance to learn from him."

"If some of your scientific leaders wanted to come here to study, I'm confident that could be arranged."

They talked for another twenty minutes about the items their own countries might be willing to export, might be looking to import, and which individuals at which end might make those exchanges happen. Corene would have said she was the last person in Welce who could talk knowledgably about trade, so she was somewhat surprised that she was able to answer most of Harlo's questions, at least in general terms. Maybe she had absorbed more than she realized during those afternoons spent in Darien's study. Maybe she was smarter about finance and economics than she, or anyone else, had ever realized. She fingered the blessing rings hanging from her silver necklace, separating them out by feel until she located the one she wanted. *Clarity.* Maybe it meant something different than she had thought all along.

EIGHT

In a conspiratorial moment, Corene and Liramelli had decided they would slip off to the Great Market without any of their usual companions by claiming they were going to tour the two great towers of the city. Melissande had already made the obligatory visit to the landmarks, and Filomara's nephews had seen them so often they couldn't be expected to work up any interest in the jaunt. Once they were free of the palace, the two of them could head to the market alone and shop. Corene had even mentioned this clever plan in a note she'd sent to Leah the day after her dinner with the prefect's family.

So at breakfast a few days later, they proposed an outing to the towers and had to hide their glee when Melissande actually yawned. But Steff expressed interest in going, which made Melissande suddenly want to join them. Jiramondi excused himself, but Garameno and Greggorio both surprisingly attached themselves to the expedition. Most astonishing of all, Alette looked up from her almost-empty plate and said, "May I come, too?"

"How lovely it would be to have you with us!" Melissande exclaimed. "Please do."

So, once again, they required two carriages and *platoons* of soldiers to make the slow journey through crowded streets to a destination

Corene wasn't even sure she wanted to visit. Once again, she'd ended up in Garameno's carriage, and this time he filled her in on the history of the towers: when they had been built, and when the gas lines had been added so neither one had to be tended by human workers but would burn eternally on inexhaustible fuel.

"So the white light is also flame?" Corene asked. "It doesn't look like any fire I've ever seen."

"It is not flame so much as heat," he replied. "The top of the dome is made of a dense crystal that is unimpressive until the temperature reaches a certain point. Then it begins to glow in the way that you've seen. A few very wealthy individuals have much smaller lighting systems in their houses built along similar principles."

"It seems like a spooky sort of illumination," Corene commented. "I'm not sure I'd want to live by it."

"I tend to agree."

They headed first to the southern tower with its magnificent crown of fire. Up close, it was even more impressive, built of solid chunks of cinnamon granite, each one bigger than a coffin. A large arched doorway showed a glimpse of a stone floor and a spare stairwell curving upward into darkness. The base was at least the size of Corene's suite of rooms, though the spire seemed to taper as it climbed toward the sky. Or perhaps that was just the extreme perspective; Corene was squinting upward and couldn't be sure.

Melissande leaned as far back as she could, craning her neck to see. "Yes, flame, just as there is always flame, night and day," she decreed. "Now we have seen it, let us move on."

But Steff had hopped nimbly from the second carriage, then thoughtfully turned to help both Alette and Liramelli alight. "We can climb to the top, can't we?" he said. "I want to do that."

Melissande looked at him in horror. "No, you do not! Who would want to do that?"

He grinned. "Corene, I bet."

She was already out of her seat and accepting Foley's hand to swing down to the cobblestones. He looked amused; he knew this wasn't how she'd really planned to spend the day. "You're right," Corene said. "I'm here, I'm going up."

Liramelli looked indecisive. "I've been so many times. I think, today—"

"Today you will wait with me and Garameno and be very entertaining," Melissande said firmly. "Come. Sit with us."

"I'm climbing," Greggorio said. He glanced at Steff. "I'll race you up."

Steff grinned. "You're on."

Alette spoke up in her soft, heavily accented voice. "I would like to go to the very top of the tower, please. But I will not run."

"No, I'm not running, either," Corene said. "Those two are idiots."

"Well, come on, then," Steff said, and the four of them stepped through the archway.

They paused a moment to let their eyes adjust. The stairway, which hugged the wall as it spiraled upward, appeared to be built predominantly of wood reinforced in various spots by cast metal. It was wide enough for four people to walk abreast if none of them was afraid of being pushed off the interior edge, where there was no banister. In counterpoint to the stairway, on the opposite wall, a single thin tube of gaslight wound up the spire, providing enough light to see by but not enough to chase away all the shadows. Way, way up, at the very apex of the tower, a coruscating red announced the presence of fire.

"Hold up at the bottom of the stairs. Have one of the women give the signal to go," Greggorio commanded, and he and Steff lined themselves up, each with one foot on the lowest step.

Corene glanced at Alette, who didn't seem to have heard the directive. So she said, "Go!" and then laughed to see the two men leaping up the stairs as fast as their legs would carry them.

"I hope they don't fall and break their necks," she commented. "Still want to make the climb?"

"Yes," Alette replied, and side by side they stepped onto the first riser and began the ascent. They could hear the laughter and ringing footfalls of the men as they charged upward; Corene even fancied she could feel the stairway shake from the vigor of their passage.

She had taken the outside edge just to prove she wasn't afraid to fall, but she started to regret it before they were halfway up. The wood and metal framework felt less and less substantial, and through its slats Corene could see the floor so far away beneath her feet. It was akin to being suspended unsupported in midair, and vertigo swirled through her head.

"You go on ahead, I'll fall a step behind," Corene said, suiting action to words. The world stabilized a bit once she could put her hand against the wall. The key was to not look down, she decided. She focused on the colorful print of Alette's robe and the feel of the granite against her fingertips. "Aren't you dizzy?" she couldn't help asking.

"No."

"I'm not usually afraid of heights, but I feel like I could lose my footing at any minute," she went on. She could tell she was babbling, and probably annoying Alette, but she couldn't stop. "Though I guess I'm a *little* afraid of heights. I mean, I wouldn't go up in the flying machines we have in Welce. Well, that only makes sense. They're not safe—people crash and die all the time. But I've never worried about *stairs* before."

Alette didn't bother answering, just kept moving surely and smoothly up the tower. Corene wondered what kind of shoes the other girl was wearing. The soles of her own pretty slippers felt decidedly slick; maybe Alette was so steady on her feet because her shoes provided a better grip. Or maybe Alette had grown up on a mountaintop and spent her days running up and down narrow pathways like a wild creature. Corene knew nothing about Dhonsho. She should study it. *I will, as soon as we get safely back,* she told herself. *If I haven't gone completely mad from fear before we make it to the top.*

They were almost there—she could tell by the thick, smoky heat and the heavy, fluttering sound of a massive flame. The color of the air around them had darkened to a translucent ochre that they passed through like fish swimming through tinted water. For the final few steps, the heat was so oppressive that Corene found it hard to breathe, and the metal patches of the stairwell felt hot beneath her feet. Then they burst through a rectangular trapdoor to the roof and found the world on fire.

Truly, that was how Corene felt when she first laid eyes on the raging blaze that crowned the granite tower. Behind the jagged glass screens of crimson and saffron and orange, the flames leapt up, taller than a man, whipping wildly in an invisible wind. Over the loud whuffling of the fire Corene could hear the faint hiss of the gas jets paying out their fuel. It was the most spectacularly beautiful sight she had ever seen.

"About time you got here!" Steff called out. Corene dragged her eyes from the mesmerizing rise and fall of conflagration to inspect her destination. The roof of the tower didn't feel a whole lot safer than the stairwell. There was a wooden lip, wide enough for three people to stand shoulder to shoulder, that encircled the leaping flames. Above it was a metal fence, barely waist-high, consisting of only two flat rails and occasional vertical supports. Past this flimsy barrier the city spread out in all directions below them, looking like nothing so much as a painting of a city in a child's picture book. The heat was so intense that Corene moved as close to the railing as she could without scalding herself on its broiling edges.

"Who won?" she called back.

Greggorio pushed past Steff, looking pleased with himself. "I did. By two steps."

"You went up on the inside edge," Steff argued. "You had an advantage."

"We'll race up the white tower, too," Greggorio retorted. "I'll take the outside, and then we'll see who's fastest."

Corene moved carefully past them so she could locate the one landmark she was sure to recognize: the palace. As the largest building in Palminera, it wasn't hard to find. And from this vantage point, she could also get a better appreciation of the walled city that enclosed it, could clearly see the loops and whorls of the labyrinthine streets that wound their way to the palace grounds and away again.

She liked this distant view better than the day-to-day close-up one, she thought. Maybe because it made more sense to see it than to live it.

Not quite resting her hand on the hot railing, she slowly walked the perimeter of the tower, studying the landscape below her as the view shifted. She liked the haphazard arrangement of city streets and neighborhoods, and the colorful border of the harbor. From here, she could barely see the ocean, just a smudge of blue against the long horizon. If she squinted, she thought she could make out white sails against the indigo of the water.

She would never be able to see far enough to catch a glimpse of Welce.

That thought had just crossed her mind when Steff yelped with alarm, and she whirled around to see what was wrong. And then, even in this hellishly hot place, she felt herself freeze with fear.

Alette had scrambled up from the wooden floor of the tower to the frail metal of the railing and stood poised upon it with her arms outstretched. She stared down at the city below, her dark face suddenly alive with emotion, twisted with anguish. Her balance was so delicate, her pose so impossible to hold, that even the whipping flames seemed like they could create enough wind to knock her over.

"Alette," Corene whispered, afraid to speak any louder, afraid to startle her. "Don't."

Alette just closed her eyes and swayed forward.

Corene shrieked, but Greggorio lunged. He grabbed Alette's arm and wrenched her backward as she screamed and twisted to get free. Steff leapt to help, and together they dragged her to safety, though her arms and legs bumped heavily against the metal railings and Corene was sure she would be covered with burns and bruises. Alette fought them, moaning something in a language Corene couldn't understand, but it was clear enough that she was begging them to let her go.

To let her die.

Corene was shocked motionless, but Greggorio, of all people, seemed calm and in control. Once Alette was safely off the railing, he took her in his arms, then sank to the wooden floor, holding her so closely that her flailing hands were immobilized against his chest. He leaned his head over hers and murmured something in her ear—reassurances, surely, promises that everything would be fine, that whatever troubled her could be fixed—and did not look up until she grew quiet and passive in his embrace.

Corene just stood there, still staring, but Steff crouched beside them, and the two men conferred. "How can we get her down?" Steff asked.

"I'll carry her."

"If she starts struggling, you could both fall."

"You go ahead to catch us."

"I can carry her part of the way," Steff offered.

"I'll do it."

Steff straightened up and threw Corene a single look of distress. She just nodded—*It's as good a plan as any*—and said, "Should I go first? To let the others know what happened?"

"No," said Steff. "We don't all want to come crashing down on top of *you*."

"We won't fall," Greggorio said quietly. "But you might have to help me to the stairwell, and guide my feet down the first few steps."

Corene watched helplessly as Steff dropped through the trapdoor and found his footing. Still sitting on the wooden floor and holding Alette in his arms, Greggorio inched over and let his feet dangle into the stairwell until he, too, caught his balance. He rose cautiously to his feet and slowly disappeared.

Corene came after them, far enough back to keep out of Greggorio's way. They made a slow, strange procession down the steps that the men had run up so merrily just a few minutes earlier. Corene could see that Steff was descending backward, one hand against the wall, one hand on Greggorio's arm to keep him steady. She could tell that Greggorio was feeling his way down blindly, keeping one shoulder against the rough granite of the stone. She could glimpse the top of Alette's dark head pressed into Greggorio's shoulder, could see the bright fabric of her robe fluttering around her thin legs, but the girl didn't speak and scarcely moved and might not even be breathing.

Corene's thoughts chased themselves wildly through her mind as she followed them down. Had Alette come to the tower this morning specifically so she could throw herself off? What had made her so miserable that she wanted to die? Had she received terrible news from home? Been treated badly by Filomara? Was she simply an unhappy girl, unstable and wretched, unable to manage the normal blows and disappointments of daily life?

Unbidden, fragments of a recent conversation with Jiramondi floated to the top of her mind. He had said, *I am not convinced her father didn't send her here to marry one of us and then stab him in the heart some night when he was sleeping.* Alette could do almost as much damage to international relations by killing *herself.* That would most surely provoke enough outrage to invite hostilities from Dhonsho.

You have spent too much time at court suspecting everyone's motives, Corene scolded herself. *She's probably just a troubled girl who could not endure some tragedy the rest of us know nothing about.*

It seemed to take a year to navigate the stairwell, but finally they safely reached the ground. As soon as Greggorio strode out into the sunlight with his burden in his arms, cries of consternation rose from the waiting carriages.

"What happened?" Melissande called. "Did she faint?"

"Was she dizzy? The heat is so intense up there," Liramelli spoke up.

Steff and Corene glanced at each other, wondering if it would be better to conceal the truth. But Greggorio didn't hesitate.

"She tried to jump," he said. "We were barely able to stop her."

"Jump!" Garameno exclaimed. "Why? What's wrong?"

Alette loosed a low moan and began to sob uncontrollably into the front of Greggorio's jacket. For the first time during this whole terrible interlude, Corene saw him look uncertain. He could cope with a wild woman, she thought, but not a weeping one.

"Oh, the poor girl," Melissande said. In a moment, she was on her feet and out of the carriage she had shared with Garameno and Liramelli. Climbing into the empty coach, she gestured imperiously at Greggorio. "Bring her to me. I'll take care of her."

"Maybe we should—" Corene began, but Melissande shook her head.

"She and I will ride together. I am sorry, but the rest of you will have to crowd together in the other carriage. Come now. Do as I say."

When Melissande spoke in that confident voice, it was impossible to gainsay her. Soon enough, Melissande and Alette were in the lead carriage, heading back to the palace, and the other five had folded themselves into the second coach. Corene couldn't settle in place until she'd scanned the ranks of accompanying soldiers and spotted Foley among the lead riders. Then she sank back against the seat cushions with a sigh.

"She tried to *jump*?" Liramelli demanded as soon as the first carriage was out of earshot.

"I heard Steff cry out, and then I turned around and saw her standing on the railing," Corene said. "I have no idea why she didn't topple over."

"How did you stop her?"

"Greggorio and Steff hauled her down."

"Greggorio, mostly," Steff said.

"Then my cousin is a hero," Garameno said softly. "You must be praised for your quick actions."

Greggorio didn't answer. Like Steff, he was sitting in the backward-facing seat, but he had twisted around so he could watch the other carriage.

"Did she say why?" Liramelli wanted to know.

"No, she just started crying," Steff answered.

"I can think of a number of possibilities, but they're all pure speculation," Garameno said.

"Well? Don't keep them to yourself," Corene said.

He seemed amused at her sharp tone. "Perhaps she's had a letter from Dhonsho containing bad news. Or perhaps she recently wrote asking to come home, and the reply she received merely said, 'No.'"

"And *has* she received such a letter?" Corene asked. "Surely someone in the palace is monitoring all the mail."

Garameno put a hand to his heart and looked pained. "Princess! I am shocked that you have such a low opinion of the empress!"

Corene just waited.

Garameno managed a lopsided grin. "To my knowledge, no such letters have arrived."

"She might just be homesick," Liramelli said. "It's obvious she's not happy here."

"Maybe she's ashamed of something that's happened," Garameno said. "Maybe she's done something that she knows would render her an outcast at home."

"Well, I can't imagine what," Steff said.

Garameno shrugged. "Maybe she's pregnant."

They all cried out at that, and even Greggorio swung around to enter the conversation. "You've got a nasty mind," he said angrily.

Garameno spread his hands. "How so? Pregnancy is an unfortunate side effect of certain very human activities, and Alette would not be the first woman to find herself in such a predicament."

"Well, since she's hardly *spoken* to anyone, I can't imagine she's taken a lover," Liramelli said.

Garameno's gaze was fixed on his cousin. "She sees three eligible men on a daily basis. It's certainly possible that she would develop a fondness for one of them."

"I suppose that's true," Liramelli said, but she didn't sound convinced.

Corene didn't speak; she was fascinated by the interplay between Filomara's nephews. Greggorio looked flushed and angry, and maybe the slightest bit guilty. Garameno appeared calm and relaxed, but Corene sensed that he, too, was hot with anger. It was yet another reminder of how intensely Filomara's heirs were competing for her crown, how clearly they saw their cousins as rivals.

"Who would be the likeliest seducer?" Garameno went on. He gestured at his lap, where even on this hot day, a light blanket covered his twisted legs. "The man who needs a great deal of cooperation before he can take a woman to bed?" He flung a hand out to indicate the palace where, presumably, Jiramondi was engaged in some useful pursuit. "The man who does not even *like* women? Or the handsome, whole, attractive specimen who kisses any girl who stands still long enough for him to embrace her?"

"I ought to punch you," Greggorio said fiercely. "And if you *were* a whole man, I'd do it."

Corene felt Liramelli flinch beside her, but neither of them interrupted. Steff was similarly silent, though his troubled gaze passed back and forth between the cousins.

"And yet I don't hear you saying that, as far as *you* know, there's no reason Alette could possibly be with child," Garameno said.

As if he couldn't help himself, Greggorio swiftly glanced at Liramelli, then away. "It's insulting to her that you would even say that. But, no, I would have no reason to think she might be pregnant."

"Yet you do have a relationship with her," Garameno pursued. "I have seen you talking in the conservatory, and in the gardens, and you escorted her to the market not three days ago."

That got all of them staring at Greggorio. Although it had never been explicitly stated as a rule, shopping expeditions tended to be group outings—and *no one* else had been able to engage Alette in a private conversation. Again, he flicked a look at Liramelli.

"So what if I talk to her? If I'm nice to her? Nobody else in this whole city is. If she's lonely and sad, it's because she's been treated so badly. I was just trying to befriend her."

"Which is admirable, of course," Garameno said. "Since you've *befriended* so many other women."

"And she hasn't been treated badly—you shouldn't say that," Liramelli said. "I can't tell you the number of times I've tried to talk to her. And my mother has tried, and Jiramondi, too! She's always aloof."

"We'll all try harder, after today," Corene said.

Garameno glanced at her. "And have even less success, I'd wager," he said. "She strikes me as the type who grows more silent as she grows more desperate."

Corene met his eyes squarely and smiled. "Maybe so," she said. "But I think you're off on some of your calculations. Alette doesn't spend her days with three eligible heirs—there are four, or don't you remember? Surely you haven't forgotten Steff?"

"Hey, I never did anything to Alette," Steff said in alarm.

Garameno inclined his head in Corene's direction. "My mistake. Of course I haven't forgotten Steffanolo. I just thought it unlikely he had been here long enough to establish himself in Alette's good graces."

"Well, I haven't been. I mean, I'm going to try to be her friend, but that's *all*."

"Don't worry," Garameno said softly, seeming to speak to Corene alone. "I don't forget how many people are playing this game."

She broke the stare, sighed, and leaned back against the seat cushions. "No," she said. "I don't suppose any of us do."

Naturally, there was no going on to the white tower this day, and Corene suspected that her expedition to the Great Market with Liramelli would be postponed indefinitely. The minute they returned to the palace, Melissande disappeared with Alette, Greggorio headed to his quarters, and Garameno rolled off to find his aunt. Steff and Liramelli and Corene were left feeling odd and unsettled, and even the prospect of playing penta didn't lift their spirits.

"Let's go out to the gardens," Liramelli suggested. That sounded as good as anything, so they did.

While the front of the palace was little more than stone and courtyard, the back was mostly vegetation. It was as if the architects who drew up plans for the grounds couldn't decide what sort of garden would be best, so they'd laid in every kind they could think of. There were the neat rows of vegetables and spices occupying a fenced area near the kitchen. There were multiple flower gardens all clustered together, each spilling over with its own particular color and variety of blossom. And on the far back edge of the lawn there was a hedge maze with high evergreen walls and twisting pathways that led to a secret heart.

Between the rain and the heat that had constituted Malinqua's weather since she arrived, Corene hadn't bothered spending much time outdoors. But as the ninedays marched through Quinnatorz, the temperature had become much more tolerable, and today's weather was downright pleasant. Perfect for a garden stroll.

Liramelli led them straight to the hedge maze and said, "This has always been my favorite place on the palace grounds."

Foley had followed them this far, but he glanced at Corene and said, "I'll wait out here."

She laughed. "Afraid you'll get lost inside?"

He smiled back. "Afraid to have my movements restricted. Not much space for maneuvering."

All she could think to say in reply to that was, "Oh." *Fighting for my life* was never the first activity she considered whenever she was about to enter a new environment. Apparently it was always Foley's.

Steff stepped into the maze right after Liramelli, but Corene, who was last, saw him glance back several times as if to find markers that would delineate his passage. "I don't mind admitting that *I'm* a little afraid I'll make it to the middle but never be able to find my way back," he said.

"You could always break your way out through the bushes," Corene said. "If you were that desperate."

"Then everyone would *know* how stupid I am," he retorted.

"They already know," she said, laughing when he stuck his tongue out at her.

"Don't worry, there's a pattern," said Liramelli. "The first turn is a left, but then you take right turns the whole way until you get to the center."

"Even *you* ought to be able to remember that," Corene said to Steff.

"I was thinking I ought to write it down for *you*," he answered.

Liramelli glanced back at them, appearing slightly amused and slightly appalled. "You two argue like brother and sister," she said.

"That's about right," Corene replied. "His brother is in love with my sister."

"But maybe that means you should be flirting instead of fighting."

"He liked me when he first met me," Corene remarked. "He was falling all over himself to be nice—it was all *Princess Corene* this and *Princess Corene* that. He'd never been off the farm, you know, and I was the first royalty he'd ever met. But *now*—"

Steff was grinning. "But now that I'm surrounded by princesses and high-born women, I'm not so impressed," he said. "Anyway, she treats me like a servant. Like I'm only useful when I'm not annoying."

"Actually, that's not true," Corene said. "I'm nicer to the servants than I am to you."

"I think I was right the first time," Liramelli said. "You act like brother and sister."

"I'm sure that would make Garameno happy," Corene said dryly. "He doesn't seem to want any more romantic competition from Filomara's other heirs."

Almost on the words they stepped into the center of the maze. It was a pretty little clearing, featuring a gazebo built around a small, playful fountain. Though the rest of the hedge had been a determined and unrelieved green, red and purple flowers flourished around the outside of the white gazebo and twined up the wooden slats of its walls.

"Well, isn't this lovely," Corene exclaimed. "Worth the risk of getting lost trying to find it."

"Greggorio and I used to come here all the time. I still do, when I want to be alone," Liramelli said. "Almost no one else ever goes to the trouble of walking the maze, so I usually have the place to myself."

They stepped inside the welcome shade of the gazebo and took seats on the bench that made a semicircle around the fountain. The maze itself was torz, Corene decided, but the gazebo was all coru. An unexpected favorite spot for a girl like Liramelli. Corene inspected her with interest, as if seeing the broad, honest face and the clear, direct eyes for the first time. "What do you think, Steff?" she asked. "Wouldn't Liramelli be elay?"

"That's what I've thought from the beginning," he agreed.

"I don't know what that means."

"I told you that in Welce we all claim some affiliation with the elements. Elay people are creatures of air and spirit, and they have all these admirable traits like honor and kindness. They just reek with goodness. Like my sister Josetta."

Steff was grinning. "Yeah, but don't forget that some of them are locked-in-the-madhouse crazy, too, like Kayle Dochenza."

"I don't think Liramelli is that kind of elay."

"Too bad there isn't a temple here—we could draw blessings for her," Steff said.

"I think there is, though," Liramelli said. "There's an international district not far from the wharf where you can buy food from at least ten different countries. It's called the Little Islands. It also has all these sanctuaries and shrines, and I'm pretty sure there's a Welchin temple."

"We don't need a temple, because my sister sent me a whole set of blessings," Corene said. "I've been drawing one every morning just to feel close to her."

Steff jabbed her with his elbow. "Oh, thanks for telling me that! Maybe *I* would have liked to pull a coin now and then, but I didn't know you had your own private blessing barrel in your room."

"Well, come on in before dinner, then, and pull as many as you like."

"What do the blessings tell you?" Liramelli asked.

"They just—if you feel like you need guidance for the day. If you need some kind of inspiration or—or—well, it's hard to explain, really," Corene said. "They just make you feel better."

Steff scooped up a dead branch that lay under the stone bench and began stripping it of its withered berries, then tossing them one by one into the fountain. "So what did you draw for this morning's blessing?" he asked. "Since this would have been a good day to have some guidance."

She laughed. "It was surprise," she said. "So I guess I should have known."

"I'm worried about Alette," Liramelli said seriously. "Is it even safe to leave her alone? Someone who would jump off a tower could find a lot of other ways to kill herself."

"What did you think of Garameno's idea?" Steff asked. "Alette and Greggorio?"

Corene elbowed him sharply, but it didn't have the desired effect. "What?" he demanded. "What did I say?"

Liramelli smiled sadly. "She thinks it will break my heart to hear of Greggorio pursuing other women."

"Well, you'll just have to get over that," said Steff, insensitive as ever. Corene wanted to hit him. "From everything I hear, he's never going to be the kind of man who settles down with one woman, so you either accept that about him or you stop caring about him. It never does any good to hope people will change."

Corene changed her mind about hitting him; that was actually pretty good advice. "I vote that you stop caring about him," she said. "Just wash your hands of all the royal men! Let's concentrate on finding you a nice rich boy who also happens to be handsome. And thoughtful. And interesting to talk to. Maybe you'll meet one at the gala, whenever Filomara decides to hold it."

"Hey, wait. I'm one of the royal men," Steff said. "She doesn't have to wash her hands of *me*."

"She's got too much sense to be interested in you," Corene informed him.

"Just because you don't have *enough* sense to be interested—"

Liramelli was laughing. "I will be happy to keep Steffanolo on my list of potential husbands if he keeps me on his list of potential brides," she said.

"Well, if I had to choose from the ones gathered here at the palace, I'd pick you first," he said frankly. "I mean—Alette? The crazy woman? I don't think so." He jerked a thumb at Corene. "And you can see how well *we* get along."

"I would expect Melissande to be the one everyone falls in love with," Liramelli said with a little sigh. "She's so beautiful and—and delightful. I always feel like a giant lump when she's in the room."

"Everybody feels like they're a giant lump when she's in the room," he assured her. "She's much too sophisticated. It's very intimidating."

"So you can see how pleased you should be when he calls you his top choice," Corene said. "It's not that he actually *likes* you, it's that everyone else has a flaw he can't abide."

"I noticed that," Liramelli said. Her voice was grave but her eyes were dancing. "I'll try not to be too flattered."

Steff sighed heavily. "This is why it's impossible to talk to women," he said. "They twist everything you say."

"Well, if you didn't say stupid things—"

The conversation went on like that for the next half hour, until the angle of the sun reminded them that they were perilously close to the dinner hour. As they came to their feet and followed Liramelli out through the hedge, Corene reflected that this had been the most relaxed and happy space of time she had spent since she arrived in Malinqua. It surprised her. She hadn't realized how much she'd missed her easy camaraderie with Steff during all the days he was closeted with Filomara—and she hadn't expected the reserved and solemn Liramelli to be someone she would enjoy getting to know.

Actually, she'd never had much experience with making friends, so she hadn't realized how pleasant it could be to have some. It had just been one more thing she didn't think she needed.

One more thing she'd been wrong about.

Emilita fussed and scolded, but worked efficiently even so, with the result that Corene was dressed and ready for the evening meal in record time. She excused the maid, then knocked on Foley's door to let him know she was going down to dinner. And to snatch a moment to discuss the events of the day.

"I'm so distressed about Alette," she said. "Why do you think she might have done such a thing?"

"People can have a lot of reasons for not wanting to live anymore."

"Garameno thought she might be pregnant."

Foley nodded again. "I heard that theory down at the stables."

"He all but accused Greggorio of seducing her."

"Maybe," Foley said. "Or maybe she left a lover behind in Dhonsho. Or maybe—" He paused, looking troubled.

"What?"

"Someone here could have assaulted her, and she was too ashamed to speak up."

Entirely without warning, Corene was flooded with fury. "You're right," she exclaimed. "She's alone in a place that she clearly hates—she has no one to protect her and no one to turn to if something goes wrong. And there are always men who will prey on young women and think no one will punish them for what they do."

Foley looked down at her and she saw remorse and compassion on his face. "Like your stepfather," he said, "who came after you."

Corene repressed a shudder. She hadn't realized Foley knew that story—then again, she'd taken steps to make sure *everyone* knew it, so she supposed she shouldn't be surprised. "I had protectors, though," she said. "I had people I could tell and places I could run to."

"You wouldn't have had to run," Foley said. "If I'd been assigned to you back then."

"Really? In my mother's own house?" she said. "You'd have stood guard at my bedroom door?"

"If you'd needed me."

"You wouldn't have known. No one knew, except some of the maids."

"I would have known."

She narrowed her eyes and looked up at him, assessing. But his face was perfectly serious, his gaze level. "What exactly would you have done," she asked slowly, "to keep him away from me?"

"Whatever I had to do," he said.

"You'd have—punched him in the face?" she guessed. "Stabbed him in the ribs?"

"Thrown him out a window. Any of those things," Foley said.

"But he could have had you arrested for assaulting him."

Foley shrugged.

"Although," she went on, "the instant my father knew *why* you'd assaulted him, you'd have been out of prison."

"Even if I rotted in a cell, I still would have done it to keep you safe from him."

The words sent a warm rush all the way down her spine, but she laughed it away. "Now I wish you'd been stationed at my mother's house! I would have liked to see you beat up Dominic Wollimer."

He smiled faintly. "If we ever go back to Welce," he said, "I'll do it anyway, if you like."

She was still laughing when Steff stepped out of his room. "Oh, good, I thought I was late," he said. "Let's go down to dinner."

To no one's surprise, Alette was not at the meal, which was even more silent and uncomfortable than most dinners at the royal palace. This evening, there were no outsiders present, only Filomara, her nephews, Melissande, Steff, and Corene.

Filomara set the tone at the beginning by saying flatly, "You will oblige me by not speculating on the unfortunate actions of Princess Alette while we are trying to enjoy our food." Since no one could think of a single other topic, the table was almost wholly silent. Even Melissande and Jiramondi, the two easiest conversationalists, gave up after a few attempts and just concentrated on their meals.

"Steffanolo, I'd like to speak with you," Filomara said as the strained dinner finally came to an end and everyone pushed away from the table. Corene noticed the sudden intense interest of the empress's three nephews, but no one said anything as Steff merely nodded and followed her out the door.

Corene was the next one to leave, and was unsurprised to find Melissande at her heels. They walked in silence to Corene's room and then collapsed on the pretty furniture.

"This day! So terrible from start to finish!" Melissande exclaimed.

"So what happened to Alette?" Corene demanded. "What did she say to you?"

"Very little," Melissande answered with a sigh. "While we were traveling home she was sobbing too much to speak, and once we returned to her room, other people joined us right away. Her maid was there and some woman with a cup of keerza—which I suspect contained drugs that would make her sleep."

"Do you think she's pregnant? That's Garameno's theory."

"It would be. But I did not get the sense that that was her concern."

"Will she try to kill herself again?"

"That is my greatest fear," Melissande admitted. "But I do not think she will be given the freedom to try it. Her maid will most certainly be sleeping in her room now, and I imagine discreet Malinquese spies will trail her wherever she goes."

"Maids fall sleep," Corene said. "Spies can be outwitted. If she's eager enough for death, she'll find a way."

Melissande spread her hands in an eloquent gesture of uncertainty. "It is not a way I think I would ever choose," she said, unwontedly serious. "Would you?"

"I'm more likely to lash out at someone else than hurt myself," Corene agreed. "But if I felt totally powerless? And greatly afraid? I might. It would depend on how deep the pain was."

"I think you have just described how Alette feels."

"Then we should do what we can to let her know she's *not* powerless and shouldn't be afraid."

Melissande's light laugh was incredulous. "If you think that, Corene, you have not been paying attention. We *are* powerless—the three of us. We are closely watched and oddly isolated. We have complete freedom within the palace, but none outside it, so much so that the palace might almost be considered a prison. Surely you must have noticed."

"I've noticed how many soldiers accompany us anytime we step out the door," Corene admitted, feeling her uneasiness build. She'd been a little on edge ever since arriving in Malinqua, but she'd managed to ignore the feeling most of the time. After today's events, that might be more difficult. "And I've found it strange."

"Have you also found it strange that no one from Welce has come to visit you?"

"I hadn't paid attention to that. But I've only been here a couple of ninedays."

"Well, I have been here somewhat longer than that, and no one from Cozique has arrived to visit *me*. Why is that, I wonder? Ships from Cozique come and go every day in Palminera harbor. Why have none of their passengers come to the palace? We are receiving mail—at least I am—but it is very dull stuff. Are the incendiary letters being withheld? One does have to wonder."

"I have assumed the empress reads our correspondence—"

"Of course she does."

"But so far I haven't written anything that I wouldn't want her to see. If I wanted to send a private message to my father, I would slip from the palace and go to the wharf and entrust a message with a Welchin sea captain."

Melissande rose to her feet, shaking out the folds of her silken dress. "Try that," she advised. "And see how far you get."

Corene stood up also, feeling more and more troubled. "I've never heard you talk like this. How long have you felt this way?"

Melissande had headed toward the door, but now she paused and looked thoughtful. "About a nineday," she said at last. "When my father answered my latest letter but did not address a specific question I had asked. Which is very unlike my father. And I began to wonder if my mail had not only been read but—edited. I find myself wondering—"

"Wondering what?"

"If we are not free to come and go, we are not simply guests of the empress. We are not here simply to flirt with her nephews and possibly cement an alliance. We are playing some other role."

"But what? Why would she want us if not as brides?"

Melissande's pretty face showed no trace of laughter now. "As hostages."

For a moment, Corene didn't breathe. "For what reason?"

"I haven't been able to guess."

NINE

"I want to try an experiment," Corene said to Foley the next morning. She had woken up practically with the dawn, despite the fact that she had lain awake for hours, wondering about Alette and thinking over Melissande's words. But she wasn't tired. Curiosity and disquiet stalked through her mind, leaving her energized and on edge. She hadn't waited for Emilita to arrive, but had dressed herself in one of her unadorned Malinquese outfits. She'd pulled her curly red hair back in an unflattering style and tried to look as inconspicuous as possible, and then she'd gone knocking on Foley's door.

"All right," he said.

"When I first met Leah, she asked if I could come and go freely from the palace. And last night Melissande as good as said that I wouldn't be able to leave the grounds without an escort. I want to find out."

He surveyed her a moment, noting her ensemble and assessing what it meant, and nodded. "We should go out a less public way than the front entrance, then," he said.

She laughed. "Of *course* you have found such a route already."

He grinned. "Of course I have."

He led her toward the end of the corridor, to the door that Liramelli had used the other night, but he followed the stairwell down instead of up. They emerged into a warren of hallways that she guessed the servants took as shortcuts to the various sections of the white wing. Indeed, she could hear voices and footsteps, the occasional clatter of china, drifting to them from invisible sources, but they didn't encounter anyone on their stealthy journey.

They finally exited through a door that opened from the northern wall of the palace and onto a graveled walk bordered with vigorous vegetation. Corene wouldn't have classed it with the other gardens behind the palace—it was more like greenery that had been pressed into service to make a workaday pathway appear to be a pleasant promenade. Here they *did* run into maids, footmen, and gardeners, already hard at work at this early hour. They all looked startled to see Corene, and none of them seemed fooled by her unassuming attire.

"Someone will inform the empress's staff that you're leaving the premises," Foley murmured when they passed a footman wrestling a heavy box toward one of the side doors. The young man stared at them wide-eyed before remembering to drop his gaze in respect.

"I suppose that's good," she answered. "If they don't see me go, how can I know if they'll try to stop me?"

Foley knew a back path that skirted the courtyard, though it quickly looped back to intersect with the main road leading from the palace. By this time they were a few hundred yards from the front doors—not easy to spot, if someone was looking.

"Do you want to stay within the walls of the inner city, or try to get past the soldiers at the main gate?" Foley asked.

"For today let's stay inside," she decided.

His only answer was a nod, but another fifty yards down the road, he veered to the right. Corene followed, looking around with interest. They were in the red granite part of town, and all the sturdily built houses seemed to glow with a friendly warmth. It was still early, but windows were being opened and doors thrown back; she could catch the cheerful sounds of women talking to each other over their chores and men coaxing their horses to behave. The scents of baking bread and frying meat drifted from the kitchens, and she suddenly remembered she hadn't had breakfast.

"Do you think there are bakeries or cafés around here?" she asked.

He glanced down at her. "Did you bring any money with you?"

She was crestfallen. "No."

"I did," he said, amused. "I'm not sure there are shops, but I think vendors drive in every day. Delivering milk and eggs and meat and flowers."

"Let's look for vendors."

She was quickly distracted from that task just by noticing the path they were taking. The road wasn't particularly wide—barely big enough for two small carriages to pass—and made of red cobblestones worn smooth with centuries of use. And since it was part of the giant labyrinth that enclosed the palace like two cupped hands, it followed a constant gentle curve instead of a straight line.

Until they came to a corner that wasn't a corner, but the road doubling back on itself, parallel to the way they'd just come, but one street farther from the palace. Such a tortuous route would make it difficult to achieve any real distance from their starting point, she thought. Of course, Jiramondi had told her that several straight new roads had been constructed to overlay the old ones, allowing residents to travel through the walled city with more efficiency. She and Foley hadn't come across one of those useful spokes yet, though she *had* spotted dozens of straight-line footpaths cutting between houses, connecting one whorl of the road with another. Some of the footpaths were paved, some were dirt and gravel, and all of them looked well used.

"This would be an easy city to get lost in," she commented.

Foley shook his head and pointed at the pillar crowned in fire, much closer here than when she viewed it from the palace. "You might not know exactly where you are, but you can always orient yourself by the towers," he said.

"Oh, yes. That's good to remember."

He glanced down, his face serious. "If we ever get separated—if you leave the palace for some reason when I'm not with you—go to the tower of fire and I'll find you there."

"I can't imagine I'd ever leave the palace without you."

"I hope not."

Corene spotted another of those shortcut footpaths—this one

mostly mud, though at least it had dried during the past two days of sunshine—and tugged Foley down it. The houses they passed between were close enough to touch on either side. If the windowsills had been low enough, Corene wouldn't have been able to resist the temptation to peek inside.

They emerged onto a street that was a little more run-down and a lot more lively than the ones they'd traversed so far. Corene guessed it was more of a workingman's neighborhood, and residents were rushing off to their jobs as shop owners, sales clerks, ladies' maids, groomsmen, artisans, brewers, and milliners. About half the people were on foot; many of the others rode clever four-wheeled contraptions that they pedaled furiously to keep in motion. Horses were rare, and usually pulling a wagon instead of serving as somebody's mount.

One of the wheeled conveyances skimmed past them, ridden by a middle-aged man and hung with five big wicker baskets. Corene inhaled the appetizing aroma of fresh-baked bread, and on impulse she ran after him.

"Are you delivering bread? Can I buy some?" she panted in halting Malinquese when he noticed her and came to a stop.

He named a sum that she couldn't convert quickly in her head, but she thought it was probably shockingly high. She didn't care. She motioned Foley over, said, "Don't even haggle," and practically snatched the loaf out of the baker's hands. She'd ripped it in half and swallowed her first very large bite before the man pedaled off. Foley pocketed his change and joined her where she sat on a bench at the side of the road.

"I saved some for you, though I really think I could eat the whole thing," she said, handing over his portion.

"I should probably let you have it all, but I'm starving, too," he said, and tore into it.

That made her laugh. "No, no, you should never let me be rude and selfish! I'm too inclined to be both. I don't need the encouragement."

He chewed for a moment, gazing down at her thoughtfully. "I don't think you're rude and selfish," he said at last.

That made her eyes widen. "You *don't*? Everyone else does."

He just shrugged and took another big bite.

After a moment's silence, she said, "So how *would* you describe me?"

He thought that over, too, but not as if he was trying to decide how to word a polite answer. "Outspoken," he said at last. "Unafraid. Intelligent. Angry. Sad."

She had lifted the bread to her mouth to take another bite, but at that she dropped her hand and just stared at him. She would have said *outspoken* was just a more courteous way to say *rude*, and even the people who didn't like her would generally concede she was intelligent. But she wasn't used to the other adjectives.

Most people didn't care if she was angry or sad. She had figured that out a long time ago. Her mother certainly didn't; her father would have expected her to fix, or ask him to fix, whatever situation was troubling her. Zoe and Josetta cared—maybe too much. They would have wrapped her in soft cotton and patted her hair and soothed her to sleep if they had seen her raging or weeping. And both of them (if she was being perfectly honest) *had* seen her throw a tantrum or two; but they had put her ill-humor down to a seventeen-year-old's moodiness, or an overreaction to some specific irritation.

But Foley was right. Corene couldn't remember the last time she *hadn't* felt both emotions, coiled inside her rib cage like malevolent snakes, hissing through her blood. Oh, she had plenty of days where she could be delighted or amused or astonished; she did not walk the world in some perpetually morose and snarling state. But they were always there, those unattractive serpents, undulating through her thoughts and dreams.

She was not who she wanted to be. And not only did she not know how to make herself over into someone else, she wasn't even sure who she wanted to become.

She didn't say any of that. She didn't even pose the question that had intrigued her since they embarked on this adventure: *Why did you agree to come with me to Malinqua?* Instead she asked the one thing she'd always wanted to know. "Why were you never in love with Josetta?"

That took him by surprise. He actually coughed on his last bite of bread, and gave her a reproachful look. "I don't think that's suitable conversation," he said.

"I don't care. I want to know." When he still didn't answer, she elucidated, "Josetta is *perfect*. She's kind and good-natured—much stronger than people give her credit for—and absolutely loyal. If you're not steady on your feet and you need to lean against someone, you can lean against Josetta until the world falls down."

"That makes her sound hunti," he said. "But she's not."

"No, she's elay. She looks inside people's souls. And she loves them for the right reasons—because of who they are, not for what they have. And she's beautiful, and she's gracious, and she's a *princess*, and it doesn't make sense that you could be around her all that time and not fall in love with her. But you never did."

"As you said. She's a princess. Not meant for someone like me."

"Oh, phooey," she said inelegantly. "People fall in love all the time with people who are too good for them. And the history of Welce is full of stories about royal heirs who took commoners as lovers. It just doesn't make sense that you weren't in love with Josetta."

"Sometimes people don't make sense," he said.

"Is it that you prefer men? In Cozique, Melissande says, such people are called sublime. Isn't that nice?"

"No. I mean, yes, it's nice, but no, I don't prefer men."

"Is it that you can't love *anybody*? Because some people can't."

A small smile played around his mouth. "I've changed my mind. You are rude."

"Well, I want to know. And you know I'll keep asking until you answer."

He was silent a moment, regarding her, as if trying to decide if she would make good that threat. She met his gaze squarely, her own expression unyielding. *Yes. I really will.*

Finally he spread his hands. "When I was first assigned to watch her, she was just my job. But I quickly began to feel protective of her—because back then, until Zoe took a hand in her life, she was as lost and at risk as anyone could be. It was a pleasure to watch her come into her own, to figure out who she was and what her place in the world should be, and to do it so gracefully."

Corene was listening closely. "You sound more like her—her uncle than her lover."

"That isn't a bad way to describe how I feel about her."

"But you're only a few years older than she is! Are you even twenty-five yet?"

"That's exactly how old I am."

"Hardly an *uncle* to someone who's twenty-two."

"Well, I can't explain it any better than that. I admire her, I care about her, and I would have died to keep her safe. But she has found the man who can love her in a way I never did, and I'm glad for her. Glad for both of them."

"I still don't understand it."

"Nobody said you had to."

She wrinkled her nose at him. "And there's something else I don't understand."

Foley eyed her warily. "What's that?"

"You should have girls all over Chialto madly in love with you."

"I should?" He kept his face perfectly straight, but his voice was amused. "You think that's respectable behavior? I wouldn't have expected that from you."

She brushed this aside. "I didn't mean you *ought* to. I meant you could if you *wanted* to. I mean, look at you!"

He glanced down at his neat, severe uniform and brushed away a stray crumb. Then he looked back at her, appearing sincerely puzzled. "What about me?"

"You're tall, you're well built, and you look great in royal livery," she said bluntly. She wanted to see if she could embarrass him, or at least rattle him a little, by making the observations that had long been in her mind. "Plus, there's this steadiness about you—when you're nearby, you make it seem like everything will be fine, no matter what else is going on. Don't you know how attractive that combination is? And you don't lose your temper and you listen when other people talk and you don't try to make people do things just because *you* think they're right. If I was some ordinary girl, some merchant's daughter living in the shop district in Chialto, I'd snatch you right up. I'd follow you around, night and day, trying to make you fall in love with me."

His face had shuttered at her first words; if she was having an impact, he wasn't showing it. When she finished, he nodded seriously. "But then, you're not an ordinary girl," he said. "What's more, you've never wanted to *be* ordinary."

She felt a little defensive. "So?"

"So there wouldn't be any point in trying to make me fall in love with you, would there?"

For a moment there was absolute silence between them. She narrowed her eyes and studied him. He surprised her by not looking away. "Well, it might be enjoyable, even so," she said slowly. "Just to see if I could do it."

"Maybe not so enjoyable for me," he suggested. "Just to be part of a game you were playing."

She shrugged. "Maybe I wouldn't care."

"That's not true," he said softly. "You always care what people think about you. You know when you'll make someone angry and you know when you'll hurt someone's feelings. And sometimes you go ahead and act anyway. But you're never unaware of consequences."

"Maybe I don't think the consequences would be so bad."

"Think harder," he said.

"I always thought—"

He interrupted her by flinging a hand up, and she fell silent. His attention was fixed on something down the road, and as soon as she looked that way, she saw it too: a group of four Malinquese soldiers, all mounted, trotting slowly along the curved street and staring intently at everyone they passed. It was a moment before she spotted the fifth one, on foot, jogging up to each straight-line alley and peering down it to check if anyone was hiding in its shadows.

Much as Corene wanted to continue their previous conversation, it was clear they had more pressing matters to deal with. "Are they looking for us?" she breathed.

"Looking for someone. Maybe you."

She glanced around. "Not many places to hide."

"They're working their way down from the palace. If we want to stay ahead of them, we need to keep going instead of heading back."

She met his eyes. "Or we could let them find us."

"Up to you."

She debated. "I'm sure they'll just say they're concerned for my safety."

"Which they might be."

She came to her feet and he followed suit. "Let's see if we can elude them."

"Behind us and to the left. There's another alley. We can cut through there."

She hadn't even noticed that walkway, but of course he was right. Moving as casually as possible, trying not to attract attention, they sauntered toward the alley and ducked in, then raced between the houses to come out on the next block. This one was just as busy as the last, crowded with wagons and pedestrians, and downright noisy. Corene and Foley fell into a brisk walk as they hurried along the outer spine of the curved road, continually glancing between buildings in search of the next shortcut. But this particular road didn't seem to be linked to the adjacent street by any such means. They picked up the pace. If they had to head all the way to the next place where the road doubled back on itself, the mounted soldiers would have rounded the bend onto *this* stretch. Good thing there were so many people bustling about; two fugitives would not be easy to spot.

Corene had just had the thought when the soldier on foot popped out of an alley in front of them and stood with his hands on his hips, looking around.

Corene swallowed an *eek* and quickly spun around to hide her face. They either had to go forward and pass this fellow, or head back, and run straight into the oncoming soldiers. She wished she'd brought a scarf to cover her distinctive hair. She could almost feel it waving for attention here in the bright morning air.

Foley touched her sleeve and then pointed to the road behind them. A large horse-drawn wagon was headed their way, the driver cursing and shouting as he slowly navigated the crowded street. The vehicle was piled high with what looked like every stick of furniture from someone's house, broad armoires lashed together in the back, chairs and tables tied in a wild tumble, their spindly legs pointing up at the clear sky.

"Fall in beside the wagon," Foley whispered. "Keep it between us and the guard."

She nodded and obeyed, ducking her head low to hide it behind the imperfect cover of an open bookcase. It was a trick to keep pace with the wagon, which sometimes came to a complete standstill and sometimes moved fast enough that she had to trot to catch up. She didn't even dare look around to see where the soldier might be now. Within five minutes they were past the spot where he had emerged, but who knew how quickly he might have canvassed the street?

They rounded the next curve and started back in the other direction, still loitering in the shelter of the wagon. Until it came to a dead halt and didn't move for five minutes. Foley reconnoitered and came back with the bad news that a couple of passing carts appeared to have collided, and a horse was down, and only pedestrians were getting through for the moment.

"Though I suspect men on horses could also ease by," he added. "We better keep moving."

They abandoned the shadow of the wagon and strode down the street, looking for another cut-through. This loop was longer than the ones they'd followed so far and looked like it might circle the entire palace before it doubled back—but that suddenly that didn't matter anymore since they finally encountered one of the paved spokes that sliced directly across the meandering route. It was wider than the labyrinthine streets and even more heavily traveled; most of the traffic consisted of carriages and other horse-drawn vehicles, though the high number of pedaled contraptions ensured that none of the conveyances traveled too fast. Anyone on foot stayed on the sides of the road, out of the way of hooves and wheels.

"At last," Foley grunted, steering Corene into the moving stream of pedestrians. "I think this will take us to the outer edge of the circle and then south to the gate."

"Maybe we *should* try to get outside the walls," she said. "Just to see if we can."

His only answer was a nod, but she could tell he was looking around alertly, trying to assess danger. There were dozens of other pedestrians keeping pace with them, most carrying bundles or tools; it would be easy to think the whole city was on the move. Corene had just started to relax when she felt Foley stiffen beside her.

"What is it?" she whispered.

"Soldiers. Different ones. Coming in our direction."

"Looking for us?"

"Hard to say. Might just be doing a routine patrol."

She lifted her gaze to look for them and spotted the three soldiers some distance ahead. They were riding down the middle of the road, forcing traffic on both sides to squeeze away from them, and they were intently gazing at the faces of all the passersby. While Corene watched, one of the soldiers hastily dismounted and stopped a plainly dressed woman carrying a basket of fabric. After what looked like a brief but heated exchange, he let her go, swung back onto his horse, and caught up with his companions.

"She had red hair," Corene said.

"I noticed."

"So they *are* looking for me."

He nodded. "Now that you've learned what you wanted to know, we could just go back to the palace."

She grinned. "Now I'm curious. I want to see how far we can make it."

Two blocks later, the straight road intersected the outermost ring of the labyrinthine route, and they were suddenly in a throng of people moving in a double migration—half of them in one direction, half in the other. Corene and Foley fell in with the traffic following the gentle curve of the red wall straight to the iron gates. It was moving so slowly that pedestrians and single horses intermingled with carts and carriages in one untidy, ill-tempered mass.

"I can't believe it's so crowded," Corene said, raising her voice so Foley could hear her over the muttering of the throng. "It wasn't even this bad the day the empress came back."

A man passing in the other direction overheard her and paused to chat. He was carrying a massive wrapped bundle over his shoulder—impossible to guess what was inside, though he was bowed slightly under its weight, so it must have been heavy. "The guards are checking every outbound coach and wagon," he said. "Looking for someone, I guess. It's going to snarl traffic all day."

Corene feigned alarm. "Someone dangerous? A *criminal*?"

The man shrugged and shifted his burden to his other shoulder. "They didn't say."

"This is our first nineday in the city. How often do you have a road-block like this?" Foley asked.

"Oh, it doesn't happen but once or twice a quintile. Never fun, though." He resettled his bundle, nodded, then stepped away, whistling cheerfully. Corene and Foley continued forward a few steps, pausing again when the crowd in front of them came to a halt.

"They might *not* be looking for me," she said at last.

"Only one way to find out."

"But how humiliating! To be stopped at the gate by common soldiers! What do you suppose they'd even *say* to me?"

"Again, one way to find out."

She glanced up at him. She couldn't tell from his expression what he thought about any of this. Did he think she was foolish to try to leave the palace in the first place—and even more foolish to play this game out to its conclusion? Did he think the empress was wise to make sure soldiers kept track of her foreign visitors? Or did he find it worrisome that Filomara wanted to keep Corene under close surveillance?

"What do you think we should do?" she asked.

"Go out some other day and find another way past the walls."

That surprised her into a laugh. "Another way out? You think there is one?"

"I guarantee there is. Every perimeter has its porous spots. Otherwise you wouldn't need guards to keep anybody safe."

"Huh. I never thought about it that way."

"Your friend Leah might know alternate ways in and out."

"Of course, we'd have to get outside the palace to *ask* her about those ways."

He grinned. "I'm sure you can leave anytime you like if you're properly escorted."

The crowd was on the move again, and Corene numbly followed it forward. "I suppose there's no need to go to the gate this morning, though."

"Probably not," he agreed. "But we don't need to take the very long way back. This street should intersect with the main road that leads directly to the palace. That seems the better way to get home."

She nodded and allowed him to shepherd her through the crowd, which grew denser and more unruly the closer they drew to the gates. It was particularly chaotic where the outer curved road met the inner straight one, mingling two streams of traffic into one irate whole. Much easier to be on foot at this particular juncture, Corene thought, as Foley threaded his way past carriages and wagons and restless horses, pulling her along behind him. The impatience of the drivers and riders was palpable and spilling over into shouts and shoving matches as the bottleneck showed no signs of easing soon.

"And to think, this is all my fault," Corene murmured. "If any of these people realized *I* was the reason they were stuck here at the gates—"

He grinned down at her. "You'd be wishing you had the protection of the soldiers after all."

She laughed. "I don't think so. I think you're all the protection I need."

He was still smiling, but she thought his voice sounded serious. "I hope so."

TEN

Somewhat to Leah's surprise, Chandran had invited her to continue working for him at the Great Market.

"There are difficulties in staffing a booth as a solitary shop owner," he had explained. "I cannot easily have long conferences with individual patrons, or leave to meet with merchants delivering new shipments. It would be useful to have a trusted employee to cover for me."

"You don't trust me," Leah pointed out.

"And you don't trust me," he replied. "It makes for a mutually cautious—and beneficial—arrangement."

At first, she wasn't so sure. She didn't need the money, so the idea of holding down a daily job didn't appeal to her; it would restrict her movements too much. On the other hand, what better place to observe the wealthy and powerful of Palminera than from a stall on the fourth floor of the Great Market?

"Part-time only," she said. "Certain days and hours."

"As long as you inform me in advance when you won't be present."

"Mmmm, I don't know that I can always promise that. But if *you* tell *me* the days you most want me here, I can do my utmost to honor that."

He agreed to the compromise, and their partnership continued.

Leah found herself unexpectedly enjoying her working days and spent a little time figuring out why. At first she thought it was because she relished the chance to walk the wide aisles during slow times and visit with the other merchants, learning names, learning trades, picking up scraps of information that might one day be useful for Darien.

Then she thought it was the camaraderie. Although she had many carefully cultivated acquaintances throughout the city, none of them were friends; she rarely saw any of them twice in the same nineday. But at the market, she could follow the unfolding lives of her fellow workers. She learned when their wives were sick or their sons were getting married. She could commiserate with them when the weather was bad and offer congratulations when they made big sales. She still wouldn't say she had friends, but she had a circle, and that was almost as good.

Later she thought it was the sense of accomplishment. She'd never had a job when she lived in Welce, so the only way she'd ever made a living was by spying for Darien Serlast. It was an altogether different experience to earn money through actual labor. She hauled boxes, counted money, cleaned tables, and waited on customers, sometimes for ten hours at a stretch. She wouldn't have thought the work was that demanding, but after a long day spent in Chandran's booth, she would go home and topple, exhausted, onto her bed.

She liked those days. She liked being so tired that she fell asleep almost instantly; she liked sleeping through the night without dreaming.

But more than that, she liked the feel of coins in her pocket, coins she practically felt she had minted herself because she could equate each one to an hour of work. The first time Chandran had handed over her nineday's pay, she had spent nearly all of it on a Berringese necklace that she had admired for three days. It was made of thin, curling strands of gold wire wrapped protectively over dozens of small emeralds, and it was the least practical thing she could have selected from a market full of impractical things. Yet she loved it, and every single time her eye fell upon it, she would smile.

It was the end of the second nineday before she realized what she really liked about the job at Chandran's booth. It was having structure to her days. For five years, her life had been utterly shapeless; unless Darien sent her a specific request, she had nothing to dictate how she spent her hours. She had fallen into a routine of sorts, visiting certain parts of the city during certain days, checking in with all her contacts two or three times a quintile, but there had been nothing and nobody to ensure that she kept to a schedule.

Nobody to notice if, one day, she failed to show up at all.

Although she and Chandran were still wary of each other, they quickly fell into an easy rhythm. When the market was slow, Leah would work the counter, waiting on customers, while Chandran tallied accounts in the back or logged in new inventory. He handled all the transactions with his regular suppliers, sometimes entertaining them in the curtained-off "office" and sometimes departing for a few hours to meet them at other rendezvous points. Occasionally a new supplier would come peddling down the aisles, offering treasures from Cozique or Dhonsho and swearing that he wouldn't sell them to any other merchant in the market if only Chandran would promise him favorable terms.

Leah was surprised the first time Chandran asked her opinion about potential new wares. These happened to be small, finely crafted wooden boxes with hidden drawers barely big enough to hold a gold coin.

"What do you think?" he asked her. "Is this something a rich woman would buy?"

"I'm not a rich woman," she answered, but she inspected the merchandise anyway. She instantly loved the little boxes, so varied in woodgrain and color, so smoothly finished, so delicate in her hand.

"If you decide to carry them," she told Chandran, "you should invest in a few rings or charms or loose jewels, too. Men looking for gifts for their wives and daughters will be happy to have all the work done for them in advance." She glanced at the supplier, whose pale face looked hopeful at the thought of a sale. "And then even if he *does* sell boxes to someone else on Great Four, yours will still be distinctive."

"Clever thinking," Chandran approved. "Let's buy twenty. You pick them out."

So she spent a pleasant half hour carefully checking out each individual box, pulling out the drawer to be sure it didn't stick, examining the joints, and making her selections. The next hour passed even more enjoyably as Chandran sent her out to buy trinkets to fill the secret compartments.

"Now I'm a little nervous, though," she told Chandran as she filled about half the boxes with her new acquisitions. "If nobody wants them, I'll be the one to blame."

"Which is why I expect you to work hard to sell each one," he said imperturbably. "You now have a stake in the game."

"*You* won't make an effort, too?"

"Oh, I will. But I have noticed that the more I myself like an item, the more eagerly I display it to customers—and the more frequently it sells. I do not know if my enthusiasm for a product makes me a better salesperson, or if my unwillingness to be wrong just makes me try harder."

She laughed. "Maybe both of those things."

"That is what I suspect."

In any case, Chandran was right. Leah was so enamored of the wooden boxes that she had no trouble finding buyers for them, and all of them were gone within a nineday.

"You have an eye," Chandran told her. "If you see other items you think we should sell, bring them to my attention."

It shouldn't have pleased her so much—Why did she care if a Coziquela merchant working in a Malinquese market had a profitable quintile?—and yet it did. She might be good at something after all. Something besides spying. Something besides watching other people live their lives and wondering what they knew that she had never learned.

As Corene had promised, she sent updates to Leah once or twice every nineday, but since she was trying to be circumspect, sometimes her messages were obscure. For instance, the first one:

> I bought some lovely beads when I was at the market. I might send you some one day if I think you'll like them.

Leah assumed the beads were red, and if she received a packet of red stones, she should understand that Corene was in danger. But she hoped any real request for rescue would be worded a little more clearly.

A few letters later, Leah received a note that was even more difficult to decode.

*By now, the whole city knows that Steff has been certified
as Filomara's grandson, and she's planning a celebration.
I wanted to buy something special to wear at the gala, but
there was such a crowd I found it impossible to get past
the iron gates. Maybe someday I will ask the palace
guards to escort me out and I'll have more luck.*

What did the princess mean by that? Had she tried to leave the
palace on her own and been stopped at the exit? That was the way Leah
read it, anyway. It raised the very real question: If Corene ever *did* need
to be rescued, how would Leah manage it?

Time to put some strategies in place.

Leah spent the next few afternoons down at the wharf, paying attention to how often Welchin ships were at the harbor. There were usually
one or two tied up at the dock, most of them small private vessels,
doubtless ferrying cargo between Welce and some of the other southern
nations.

She picked the ones that looked most prosperous and asked to come
aboard to meet the captains. If, after a little general conversation, she
judged them reasonable and relatively honest, she started asking her
real questions: *How often are you in port? How quickly can you make
it back to Welce? What kind of payment would you require to carry a
delicate cargo back to Chialto on very short notice?*

"What kind of cargo?" was the inevitable question at this point.

"Human."

"Criminal?"

"No."

"Worth something to the empress?"

"Worth something to Darien Serlast."

That always got their attention. If the captains immediately jacked
up their prices, she mentally crossed them off her list—though, if the
time came, she might not be able to be too choosy. If they showed great
willingness to do a favor for the regent-who-would-one-day-be-king,
she paid a few coins on deposit as a good-faith gesture.

One of the captains was a blunt red-faced woman who looked strong
enough to wrestle a sea monster and who had introduced herself as Ada

Simms. Captain Simms had obviously pieced the whole puzzle together with no trouble. "It's his daughter, then, that he's worried about?"

Leah played dumb. "Excuse me?"

Captain Simms nodded in the direction of the palace. "His oldest girl. Princess Corene. She's not liking Malinqua after all? Thinking about leaving suddenly?"

"The princess is happy at the present moment," Leah replied. "But as you know, the situation at a royal court can change unexpectedly. I'm just helping to prepare her against any contingency."

"Well, that's wise," the captain said. She rubbed her great raw hand over her weather-beaten jaw. "But you'll have a harder time getting her out if Berringey sets up another blockade."

Leah cursed under her breath. Every few quintiles, or so it seemed, Malinqua and Berringey started threatening each other with war, which mostly resulted in skirmishes at sea and a choke hold on trade. Until now, Leah had never found the hostilities to be more than inconvenient. But if she was trying to spirit Corene out of the country—

"Does that seem likely?"

Simms shrugged her burly shoulders. "There's some talk about a Malinquese ship that disappeared last quintile, then a Berringese ship that disappeared a couple ninedays later. There were some shots fired at us as we came sailing in. They seemed to be just for show, but it wouldn't take too much of the Berringese navy to set up an effective blockade."

"And then no ships get in or out?"

The big woman grinned. "We-elll, I wouldn't say that. It's just harder to move merchandise."

"There's a smuggler's port?" Leah asked.

The captain regarded her steadily for a moment and clearly came to the conclusion that this whole conversation might have been the bait for an elaborate trap. "There might be," she answered finally, "but *I* wouldn't know where it is."

More she wouldn't say, and Leah knew better than to badger anyone for details; such tactics only made the informant grow more stubbornly silent or start handing out lies just to get rid of her. She was sure she could find out about the smuggler's port from other sources, but she liked Simms. She wanted to win her over.

"I wonder," Leah said. "Do you think we have any acquaintances in common in Chialto? Someone who might vouch for me?"

The captain looked interested. "Might be."

"What kind of cargo do you carry?"

"Mostly mechanical parts," the woman answered. "Valves and small motors and such. Although—" Suddenly her rough face softened with a grin. "My next trip out I might be carrying an elaymotive. One of those smoker cars that run on gas? I hear the empress is dying to have one of her own, but she's been negotiating with Kayle Dochenza about his price."

Leah's head snapped back. "Kayle Dochenza? The elay prime?"

The captain couldn't help looking pleased with herself. "One and the same. We've been doing business for five years now. He's as odd as they say, but smarter than most people realize. And any contract he writes is good as a quint-gold. He never reneges."

Leah leaned back in her chair, feeling like she'd finally stumbled on a little coru luck. "I know Kayle Dochenza," she said. "I'll give you a letter for him, and he'll vouch for me. Then you'll know you can trust me."

The woman looked impressed—but not entirely won over. Anyone could *claim* to be a friend of Kayle Dochenza's, after all. "Good enough," she said. "I'm heading for Chialto in the morning. I'll be seeing the prime in a couple of ninedays."

"Good," Leah said. "I think this will be a very profitable arrangement."

Chandran, of course, knew all about the smuggler's port, though he insisted he preferred not to do business with the captains who used it. "When the taxes are equitable and the system is fairly managed, it benefits everyone to abide by the rules," he said. "My business will only thrive if there are roads to bring customers my way and guards to keep them safe. The nation will only thrive if there is a strong commercial class and successful international trade. We help each other. I have no desire to operate outside the system."

"So you've never bought or sold illegal goods?"

"When there was no other option."

"For instance, during the last blockade."

"Yes," he said reluctantly.

"Then introduce me to somebody who can help me when I have no other options."

She didn't much like the man Chandran produced a few days later, thin and nervous, with a hoarse, raspy voice that sounded like a permanent side effect from being nearly hanged. In fact, she suspected that Chandran had chosen the least prepossessing individual from his short list of smuggling contacts in the hopes of discouraging Leah from cultivating such an acquaintance. She found the thought amusing—and oddly touching.

The rogue was a font of information, though, telling her where she might find him on certain days, what prices he charged for various services, and what kinds of goods were most likely to pass through the illicit venue.

"Can you tell me the next time a ship from Welce comes to the smuggler's port?" she asked. "I'd like to meet with the captain."

"I *could*," he said doubtfully. "But it's not like any of them linger. The ship would be gone before I'd made it halfway to the city."

She throttled her irritation. "If I gave you a little money to share with the captain," she said, "would he or she stay long enough to meet me?"

"That might change things," he agreed. "Most of those bastards will do anything for money."

As was so often the case, she had to hide her amusement at his complete unawareness of irony.

"Then here are a few coins. See that they're liberally distributed— keeping whatever amount seems fair to you, of course. I'll be in touch again in a nineday or so."

He pocketed the money, looking quite cheerful. "Pleasure to work with you," he said. "I'll see you soon."

All these preparations meant little, Leah knew, if she couldn't get Corene out of the walled city. Assuming the princess could escape the palace itself, she wouldn't find it easy to elude the guards at the main gate. But the stone wall that enclosed the inner city wasn't completely secure; Leah knew of several places where it was possible to slip across the border, and she spent some time visiting each of them.

Most were along the red wall, where the mortar holding the stones in place had loosened over time. There were always sections where the wear of centuries had been aided by the zeal of miscreants, and just enough blocks could be moved to allow someone to wriggle through. Of course, the empress's men were constantly on the lookout for such breakdowns, and the bolt-holes were always being patched over with stronger materials, but new ones would spring up just a couple of yards farther along. A few discreet inquiries, a few coins judiciously handed out, and Leah was able to find three spots in the wall where someone who was desperate or enterprising could find a way in or out.

After she'd inspected the third escape route, Leah leaned against the sun-warmed stone and watched the afternoon traffic amble by in the summer heat. In the improbable event that Corene had to escape from the palace, Leah would tell the princess to meet her at one of the weak points in the wall. They would slip through the breach and run for whichever port was open, and there Corene would board a friendly Welchin ship that would immediately set sail for Chialto.

Leah frowned. There was a lot of ground to cover between the palace and the harbor—easily ten miles, and the smuggler's port was even farther out. Leah would need to provide a conveyance of some sort—a wagon, a horse, one of those four-wheeled contraptions. Something that she didn't need to care for or think about on a daily basis, but that she could commandeer at a moment's notice if she needed.

As soon as the thought occurred to her, she muttered a Coziquela curse and slumped against the stone. This might take a little cogitation. She knew plenty of people with carts and wagons—and horses, when it came to that—but most of those were in daily use and none of them were conveniently near the palace. She would have to send out some delicate inquiries and come up with a pretty good lie if she was going to provide transportation on demand for a fleeing princess.

She was still thinking the problem over a few days later when a palace footman brought her an envelope from Corene. Inside was the usual opaque message—and a single red bead.

The princess had written:

*I've decided I MUST go back to the market tomorrow
and buy more of these red gemstones. Wouldn't it be fun
if I ran into you there?*

Leah rolled the smooth bit of glass between her thumb and finger
and felt a prickle of anxiety scratch through her veins. Despite all her
preparations, she hadn't really expected this. She hadn't truly believed
Corene could be in danger.

Would the princess really be at the market in the morning? Would
she be able to make it out of the palace after all?

ELEVEN

After some thought, Corene decided not to mention her little adventure to anyone. She could hardly put the details in a letter to her father, of course, since she suspected that Filomara or Garameno read her mail. In her next note to Leah, she made a light reference to the unsuccessful outing, but since her wording was so vague, she couldn't be sure Leah would take her meaning.

She found herself equally reluctant to relate the story to anyone living at the palace. She didn't want to accuse the empress of keeping her a prisoner, didn't want Steff to leap to Filomara's defense, didn't want Melissande to start speculating as to why they were being watched so closely. So she just didn't talk about the escapade.

There were plenty of other things to talk about, anyway. Hardly a day passed without someone sharing some new tidbit about the upcoming gala, which was currently rumored to be a masked festival. But an even more interesting topic was Alette.

Corene and Melissande and Liramelli had decided it was up to them to comfort Alette—whether or not they knew why she needed comforting—and they'd started to drop by her room every afternoon for determinedly cheerful visits. The first few days didn't go particularly well. Servants stayed nearby the whole time, limiting conversation to trivialities, and Alette was both listless and monosyllabic.

But the fourth day went noticeably better, due to Melissande's brilliant idea. "We will have a cultural afternoon in which we celebrate something special about all our countries," she proposed. "There is a shop by the Little Islands where they sell foods from Dhonsho, and Jiramondi and I went down there yesterday. I bought these odd little cakes that the woman assured me are very popular, and a pretty little tablecloth to put them on. My mother just sent me some boxes of dried lassenberries from Cozique—they are *so* good. Liramelli, perhaps you can bring some keerza for us to drink, and Corene—"

"I'll bring blessings," she said. "We can't *eat* them, but they will make for an interesting activity."

"Excellent," Melissande said. "Maybe we can nudge Alette out of her melancholy."

Certainly the bustle of setting up their afternoon extravaganza was impossible for Alette to overlook, because Liramelli and Melissande had engaged servants to help them set up tables and arrange plates and bring in the hot keerza pot. Somehow, as Liramelli laid items on the brightly printed tablecloth and Corene pulled four chairs from various corners of the room, Melissande managed to thank the maids and kitchen workers and push them all out the door.

So for the first time since Alette's aborted jump from the tower, they were alone with the Dhonshon princess.

"Come, come! Let us sit!" Melissande invited, and they took their places around the table. Alette moved with a sort of cautious uncertainty, perching on the edge of her chair and staring at the items spread before her as if she couldn't believe they had materialized.

"All this—for me?" she asked in amazement. She took a fold of the tablecloth between her fingers and rubbed it as if it was silk and soothing to the touch. It was really some kind of cheap cotton, Corene thought, but maybe what Alette was trying to absorb through her fingertips was the color, which was a happy riot of reds and purples and blues.

"We wanted to cheer you up," Melissande said. "So we each brought in something from our own countries that we could celebrate together."

"That was very kind."

Melissande turned to Liramelli. "Shall you begin by pouring keerza?"

Liramelli nodded at Alette. "I thought Alette might start? At meals, before you eat anything, you always say something silently. A prayer, perhaps? And I thought, if you wanted to, you could say it out loud today."

Alette went absolutely motionless, her big eyes fixed on Liramelli's face, and for a moment Corene worried that it had been the wrong thing to say. Perhaps Alette hadn't realized her private moment had been observed; perhaps what she was praying for was to see everyone at the table die painfully from an ingestion of poison. Then she dropped her gaze and bowed her head.

"I would like that," she said in a subdued voice. The next sentence she spoke was in Dhonshon, and Corene didn't understand a word. But she saw the multilingual Melissande nod, and Melissande echoed Alette's final word as if it were a benediction.

"*Now* the keerza," Melissande said, and Liramelli poured steaming cups for all of them.

"This doesn't taste nearly as bad as most of it does," Corene remarked after her first sip.

Liramelli grinned. "It's a special blend that most purists despise, but people who aren't used to keerza tend to prefer it," she answered.

"Indeed, it is almost tolerable," Melissande agreed. "I can envision asking for a second cup."

"My father will disown me if he realizes I've served it to anyone, so don't tell him."

"It will taste even better with dried lassenberries on your tongue," Melissande said, prying the lid off a white wooden box she had set in the center of the table. Inside were nestled brownish-yellow globes of fruit that were about the size of Corene's fist. They were sprinkled with some kind of raw sugar and smelled like citrus and honey. "I promise, you will love these."

The lassenberries were sticky and messy and such an odd color, but they tasted like the distillation of delight, and Corene took a second one out of the box before she'd even finished the first one. "Your father has to send you some every nineday," she spoke around a full mouth. "I'm not joking."

"Alas, they are only in season for about half a quintile and there are never any left because people eat them all up. As you can imagine," Melissande replied.

"I can't believe you were generous enough to share them with us," Corene said.

"I know. I am already regretting it."

Alette spoke up without being prompted. "I think you will like the seed-wax cakes as well," she said. "Unless the cook was not very good."

Like the lassenberries, the seed-wax cakes weren't much to look at—hard, flaky biscuits flecked with bits of black and drizzled with a dried red sauce. But they made a satisfying crunch when you bit into them, Corene found, and loosed a complex medley of sweet flavors on the tongue. A sip of bitter keerza between bites enhanced the taste of both.

"This is the best meal I've had since coming to Malinqua!" Corene exclaimed.

"I am not sure lassenberries and seed-wax cakes really constitute a meal, but I think I agree with you," Melissande said.

Alette's face relaxed into something resembling a smile. "It is certainly the most enjoyable one I've had," she said. She actually addressed a question to Corene. "But did you not bring some delicacy from Welce for us to share?"

"Not food," Corene said. "A ritual."

She had carried the blessing coins in the red velvet bag Josetta had provided, and now she poured them all into an empty bowl in the center of the table. The small brass coins made a happy clinking sound against the china.

"In Welce, as some of you know, everyone is affiliated with one of the five elements of earth, wood, fire, air, or water, and each of the elements is associated with eight blessings," Corene said. "When children are born, their parents find a temple and have three strangers pull blessings for them, and these blessings are considered theirs for a lifetime. We also go to temples anytime we need guidance, and pull a blessing or two for that particular day. You can pick your own blessings, but it is always considered best if others do it for you—and because three is one of our propitious numbers, it is even *better* if three people pull them." She gestured around the table. "There are four of us. I thought we should all choose for each other."

Alette looked grave. "What if we pick the wrong ones? Bad ones?"

Corene shook her head. "It's impossible. They're all blessings. They're all good." She didn't bother to mention the ghost coins that lurked in the blessing barrels at some temples—very old coins that had been worn so smooth by much handling that it was impossible to tell what the original glyphs had been. The ones Josetta had sent were all freshly minted; no troubling ghosts lurked in this bowl.

"I will go first," Melissande said. "All of you pick blessings for me."

Liramelli and Alette watched closely as Corene swirled her fingers through the pile and pulled out a coin. "Charm," she said, and laughed. Of course this was a blessing that would be bestowed on Melissande.

Liramelli went next, and showed Corene the coin she'd drawn. "Beauty," Corene deciphered.

"Accurate so far," Liramelli said.

Alette focused seriously on the task of mixing the coins and pulling a single one from the bowl. "Flexibility," Corene said. "Accurate on *all* counts, I would say."

"Indeed, I like these very much!" Melissande said. She had pulled out a piece of paper and was jotting down the attributes. "I am quite sure I would like someone who had all these traits."

"Me next," Liramelli volunteered.

Corene was hardly surprised when Liramelli turned out to be endowed with gifts of honesty, loyalty, and kindness. "We hardly even had to pull blessings to learn *that*," she said.

"Of course, you could just be making these up as they occur to you," Melissande pointed out.

Corene laughed and dug in a pocket of her tunic. "I knew you would think that! So—here—I brought Josetta's list of the blessing glyphs and what they mean."

Melissande flattened the paper on the table between her and Liramelli, and they studied it intently. "Indeed, she appears to be telling us the truth," Melissande judged. "How much fun this is! I would enjoy drawing a blessing every day, I think."

"That's what I do. Well, unless I forget. Now the three of you pick blessings for me."

This was quickly done, and in a moment Corene was looking at the symbols for vision, courage, and luck. A little thrill went down her back. These were the same coins Josetta, Zoe, and Rafe had drawn for her before sending the bag of blessings to Malinqua. The same ones stamped on the gold, silver, and bronze rings she wore on her right hand. She didn't mention this fact, merely thanked the others and tossed the little disks back in the bowl.

Then she turned casually to Alette. "Would you like us to pull some for you?"

Alette hesitated a moment before nodding. "Yes, please."

Corene didn't know about the other two, but she felt nervous as she swished her fingers through the bits of brass and hoped she picked out something useful. The one that came to her hand wasn't exactly reassuring—and awfully familiar. "Courage," she said.

Melissande pulled a coin and searched for it on Josetta's list. "Hope," she pronounced.

Liramelli did the same. "Love," she said softly.

There was a long silence while Alette thought over their words and the rest of them tried not to breathe. Finally Alette said, "I would be grateful to be given such blessings."

"You can have them made into charms or rings or paintings or anything, really," Corene said. She tugged on her necklace to show them the blessings stamped into the metal; she didn't draw their attention to the rings on her fingers, though, because she was still a little spooked by that coincidence. "See? My lifetime blessings are clarity, change, and courage, and I wear them all the time. You could do something similar."

"I will think about that," Melissande said. "Some sort of memento to remind me of my time in Malinqua."

That caught Liramelli's attention. "Remind you? Does that mean you plan to leave us sometime? Go back to Cozique?"

Melissande shrugged with her usual elegance. "Perhaps. I like Malinqua—very much!—but will I want to stay if I am not chosen as bride to the next heir? I am not so sure."

Liramelli looked oddly sad at this news, despite the fact that scarcely a nineday earlier she had mentioned that she didn't think Melissande liked her. *We have become friends in these last days,* Corene thought. She would bet Liramelli was as surprised as she was.

Liramelli glanced at Corene. "What about you? Do you plan to stay or go?"

Corene shrugged, too. "Depends on whether or not there is a role for me here. I like the idea of being the next empress, but if I'm not picked for that job—" She lifted her hands in a gesture of uncertainty.

"Would you go back to Welce?" Liramelli asked.

Ah, that was the question Corene wrestled with every time her thoughts reached this juncture. "I don't know what I'd do."

Melissande nodded at Alette. "What about you? Would you stay or go home?"

And that was the point of this whole exercise, Corene thought, admiring how artlessly it had been done. *Trying to pry information out of Alette.*

Alette's face went very still and for a moment Corene thought she wouldn't answer. When she did speak, her voice was so low that they had to lean forward to catch her words.

"I cannot go home," she said. "My father would not have me."

They all exclaimed out loud at that, speaking over one another as they expressed shock and demanded to know how such a thing could be.

"It would be a failure to return, and my father does not tolerate failure. Just ten days ago he had my mother and my sister put to death."

They should have cried out again, but the words were so stark that they could only stare at her.

Alette briefly lifted her eyes, saw their expressions, and dropped her gaze again. "You are wondering what their crimes were," she said, her voice even softer. "But there were no crimes. My sister failed to win the interest of a Berringese suitor, and my mother failed to prepare her well enough that she would succeed in that task. Thus the order for their executions."

"But—but—that is so awful, I have no words," Liramelli stammered.

Melissande's voice was hard. "Your father has many wives, does he not? And many children? Does he consider them all expendable?"

Alette nodded. "Ten wives when I left—nine now. Twenty-one children. Sixteen living."

Another strained silence.

"He's had five of his children put to death?" Corene asked.

Alette merely nodded.

"Then it is good you are here in Malinqua," Liramelli said firmly. "We won't send you back no matter who gets married and who is sitting on the throne. You can just stay here as our guest."

Alette's face looked even more sad. "You cannot protect me if he wants me dead. If I am not married to the man who is chosen as heir, he will send assassins to dispose of me. You do not understand what a blot it is on his honor to have his children fail."

"Oh, I think there are many more *blots* on his *honor*!" Melissande exclaimed.

"Maybe you should run away from Malinqua," Corene said urgently. "To Welce or Cozique or even Berringey—though I don't know that they treat people any better in Berringey, to tell you the truth."

"I think he would find me anywhere in the southern seas," Alette said. "To be truly safe, I would need to flee to Yorramol."

It was a country so far away none of them had ever met anyone who had actually lived there, though now and then exotic shopkeepers claimed to sell wood or jewels obtained in that unlikely place. The journey could take half a quintile, and who knew what kinds of savages might await travelers on those mysterious shores?

"You could never go so far," Liramelli said. "Not by yourself."

Alette was silent for a moment. "There is someone," she said at last. "Who would travel with me. Who would keep me safe. But first I would have to leave Malinqua undetected, and there appears to be no way to do that."

Melissande flicked a look at Corene, and said in the airiest voice, "Yes, I have noticed that! The empress's guards are *most* attentive to the comings and goings of Filomara's guests. It would be quite difficult to leave the palace and head for the wharf and book passage on a ship without royal soldiers trying to prevent you from leaving."

Liramelli frowned. "That's not true."

"I assure you, it is."

"I agree with Melissande," Corene said reluctantly. "The empress does seem to keep a very close eye on us."

"Only to guarantee that you're safe. Think what trouble there would be if you were harmed while under her care!"

"I think it is more than that," Melissande said. "I think she does not want us to leave the city—or the country."

"But that's ridiculous," Liramelli said. "If you want to go home, tell her that. But you can't blame her for having guards watch you closely while you're her guests and she's answerable to your families."

She seemed so upset that Melissande made a graceful gesture. "Perhaps you are right. I am not used to so much—supervision—in Cozique. Perhaps any monarch would be so assiduous when hosting foreign guests."

Corene laughed. "I promise you, if you were visiting Chialto, my father would know where you were at all times. He wouldn't care *where* you went, and he certainly wouldn't stop you from leaving, but he'd pay attention. My father pays attention to everything."

"You see?" Liramelli said. But Corene thought she sounded troubled. "It's not so sinister after all."

"It does not matter what Filomara's guards do or do not do," Alette said. "I am watched by my father's men at all times, and they will do whatever he asks."

Melissande looked straight at Alette. "Yes, let us return at once to the pressing topic of your safety," she said. "You say there is someone who would spirit you away if you could get out of the palace undetected? We pulled the blessing of love for you. Is it a man—or perhaps a woman—who would act so heroically on your behalf?"

Alette's dark face flushed and she looked down again at the scraps of food on her plate. "A man," she said softly. "And I do love him."

"Then you should never have been sent to Malinqua to try to make a match with one of Filomara's heirs," Liramelli said.

Alette glanced at her. "He is not royal. He is not *cocho*—unworthy—but my father would never have let me marry him. My mother told me that if my father knew—"

But just speaking the words "my mother" made her voice choke up and her words trail off. She covered her eyes with her hands and turned her face away. Liramelli jumped up and flew around the table to hug her, though it wasn't clear Alette welcomed the embrace. Corene just sat there in horror, staring; for a few moments she had almost forgotten the bitter news that had made Alette so grief-stricken she wanted to die. She and Melissande exchanged brief glances full of wretchedness and pity.

Liramelli was patting Alette's back and making useless promises into her dark hair. "We'll work something out, you'll see. We won't let you go home to be killed. You'll be all right now."

Alette pulled away and tried to put herself in order, scrubbing her face with the heels of her hands and tugging her clothing back in place. "I do not wish to be rude after you have all been so kind to me," she said at last. "But I find I am anxious to be alone."

Corene and Melissande quickly stood up and the three of them made disjointed, awkward goodbyes. "I'll leave the lassenberries, if you'd like them," Melissande offered.

Alette attempted a smile. "That is generous indeed."

"Oh, I have two more boxes in my room that I will not share with anyone."

"Then I accept."

The three of them headed toward the door, but Liramelli turned back to brush her hand along Alette's shoulder. "Come talk to me anytime. I mean it. I will help you anyway I can."

"Yes—me, too," Corene said.

"And I. All of us. We shall be your champions from now on," Melissande added.

"Thank you," Alette said. She sounded sincerely grateful and utterly exhausted. "It is very good to know."

A few more offers of friendship, a few more expressions of gratitude, and the three of them were finally out in the hallway and heading back toward their rooms. The minute they considered themselves out of earshot they began voicing their outrage over Alette's impossible situation. "We must do something," each of them said at some point, though it was hard to think of exactly what that might be.

"I'm glad she told us, at any rate," Liramelli said as they came to a halt outside Melissande's door. Melissande and Alette both had rooms on the third floor of the white wing, but they were so far apart from each other they were hardly neighbors. "All this time I just thought she was unfriendly. And it turns out she's horribly sad and in fear for her life. It makes me feel terrible for not trying harder."

"I am not sure she would have told you much, no matter how nice you were to her, until she became desperate," Melissande said. "But she no longer cares if she lives or dies, so she has little left to lose now by speaking the truth."

"We have to do something," Liramelli repeated.

"We'll come up with an idea," Melissande replied, opening her door. "Corene, do you want to come in and get that hairpin you asked to borrow?"

Corene had asked for no such thing. "Oh, sure. Thanks."

Liramelli waved and headed toward the stairwell. "I need to change before dinner. I'll see you both later."

Corene stepped inside the room, Melissande shut the door, and they stared at each other a moment in silence. "There is still a piece of this puzzle missing," Melissande said quietly.

Corene nodded. "Garameno told us Alette hadn't received any news so dreadful she would want to leap from the tower," she said. "And we know he's been reading her letters, or *someone* has. So either he didn't think she would be upset by learning that her mother and sister had been executed—"

"Or she's getting mail from another source."

"So she has at least one ally within the palace or without."

"Not enough, though," Melissande said. "Not someone with the power to set her free."

"I'm not sure we have that power, either," Corene said.

"Perhaps not," Melissande said. "But we are very clever. We will think of something."

Naturally, Corene recounted the whole conversation to Foley before dinner. She had gotten in the habit of telling him everything that transpired during her day; he often had insights that hadn't occurred to her, and she liked to see things from his perspective. And oddly, sometimes it seemed that things hadn't actually *happened* until she'd told Foley about them. Even to herself, she didn't try to explain why that might be.

He listened closely, and when she finished, he said, "It seems Princess Alette would have an even better reason to try to escape from the palace than you would."

"Yes! But we still haven't figured out how *I* could do it."

"I keep wondering about something," he said. "The day we arrived, Lorian mentioned that the palace is safe from a siege because it has an underground water source. Maybe it's time to look for that and see if it offers any possibilities."

"Excellent idea," she said. "I'll get Jiramondi or Liramelli to take us to it."

"Will they wonder why you're curious?"

She laughed. "I'll think of a way to work it into conversation."

He grinned. "I admit, I'd like to see how you do that."

"Oh, this is the sort of thing I'm very good at. You'll be surprised how easy it will be."

TWELVE

A few days later, on a lazy afternoon when rain had kept them all indoors, Corene threw down her penta cards.

"A dreadful hand. I don't want to play anymore. Let's *do* something," she said, letting petulance edge her voice.

Jiramondi gathered up the cards while Steff, Melissande, and Liramelli regarded her with varying degrees of exasperation. "Naturally, I would be happy to *do* something as well, but we seem confined to the palace," Melissande observed.

"It's a big building," Steff said. "There must be things we haven't seen."

"The storerooms on the sixth level," Liramelli suggested. "They're full of odd stuff."

"They're *creepy*!" Corene exclaimed.

"Oh, then I want to see them," Steff said.

"Not creepy in a fun way," Jiramondi told him. "In a dull, depressing way."

Liramelli was smiling. "Anyway, we should go late some night when it's dark and we have to carry candles and every little noise is terrifying."

"I, perhaps, might ask to be excused from such an excursion," Melissande said.

"There's the conservatory," Jiramondi suggested. "Plenty of new flowers in bloom. You could pick bouquets to take back to your rooms."

"Yes, and have the gardeners chase us out with their hoes!" Liramelli answered. "If they had their way, anyone who plucked a blossom would be executed on the spot and their bodies used as fertilizer."

Corene bounced in her chair. "I know, I know—let's go *down*," she said. "Do you have dungeons here? I'm sure no one is locked up in them *now*, but we could tour the cells where they used to keep prisoners."

"Now, *that* I'd like to see," Steff said.

Liramelli and Jiramondi exchanged a brief glance. "No dungeons," he said lightly. "Just more storerooms. Ones that are actually filled with useful items."

"What kinds of items?" Melissande asked.

"Grain, seeds, dried fruit, paper, fabric," Jiramondi answered. He hesitated a second, then added, "Ammunition."

Melissande's delicate brows rose. "Siege preparations," she said.

"Exactly."

"There's water down there, too, isn't there?" Steff asked. "I'm sure Lorian mentioned that once."

"A spring," Jiramondi said. "Though I, for one, don't relish the idea of carrying buckets of water up from the bowels of the earth should the need ever arise."

"Should the need arise," Melissande said with asperity, "I imagine you will be exceedingly grateful that there is something to fill those buckets with."

"Well, now I'm curious. I'd like to see this spring," Steff decided.

Corene shrugged. "It sounds more interesting than just sitting here, at any rate."

"It's an awfully long way down," Liramelli warned. "And then climbing back up."

"It can't be worse than the red tower," Steff asked. "And I managed that."

Corene jumped up. "I want to do it," she said. "Who else wants to come?"

Steff was immediately on his feet. Melissande and Liramelli stood more reluctantly, and Jiramondi kept his seat. "I do *not* think it sounds like fun," Melissande said. "But I hate to be left out of anything, so I will join you."

Jiramondi faked an elaborate yawn. "I don't have any interest in clambering around underground," he said. "You go, and then tell me how much you enjoyed yourselves."

"I suppose I'll have to lead the way, then," Liramelli said.

Jiramondi eyed her. "Surely you can find it. You and Greggorio must have spent half a quintile down there when you were younger."

Liramelli nodded. "I do wonder if Filomara would think this is a good idea, though."

"Well, that makes it somewhat more interesting," Melissande drawled. "If our little outing is *forbidden*."

Jiramondi yawned again. "I hope the four of you have fun."

Of course, five of them actually set out on the adventure because Foley was lurking in the hallway and he fell in with them as soon as they emerged. As usual, he stayed somewhat to the rear of the group but within easy calling distance.

"If we don't want to draw attention to ourselves, we should take the back stairs," Liramelli said, leading the way toward the far end of the corridor.

"Back stairs? Who knew there were back stairs?" Steff asked.

"*I* did," Corene said smugly.

"Someone had to tell you about them. You never found them on your own."

"So? I still found them."

"If the two of you are just going to argue the whole time, I will not come with you," Melissande said.

"We're not arguing," Steff replied with a grin. "This is how we talk."

"Keep your voices down," Liramelli said softly. "We'll be going past the servants' hallways, and there could be guards anywhere. Just follow me and stay quiet."

The women all wore soft-soled slippers that made almost no noise, but Corene could tell Steff and Foley had to take extra care to keep their boots silent on the stairs. Liramelli guided them down the back passageway that Corene and Foley had used on their own adventure, but when they got to the second level, she began weaving through a warren of corridors that branched off in all different directions. Corene was lost by the third turn, and her sense of direction plummeted when they climbed down yet another unfamiliar stairwell to what she presumed was the ground level. They found themselves in a narrow, poorly lit hallway whose rough walls seemed to have been hastily constructed of blocks of flaky gray stone. No doors or cross-corridors interrupted the endless march of dull rock; this was a passage designed to lead to one destination only. It happened to be a tall wooden door with a single brass plate where the handle should be. It was hardly a flight of fancy to think it looked judgmental and disapproving, Corene thought, as if it strongly discouraged anyone from trying to push past its threshold.

"I find myself thinking—maybe even hoping!—that this is the kind of door that is always left locked," Melissande observed.

Even in the inadequate light, the amusement on Liramelli's face was easy to see. "It is! But Greggorio and I know where the key is always kept."

She stretched up to run her fingers along the narrow lintel above the door, but sank back to her heels empty-handed. "That's odd. It's not here."

"Did it fall to the floor, perhaps?" Melissande asked. They all gazed down at their feet and scuffed at the dust with their toes.

Steff eased Liramelli aside and stooped down to squint at the lock. "It doesn't look very complicated. I could probably pick it if I had a knife or a long pin."

"So you are a thief as well as a farmer!" Melissande observed.

He grinned at her over his shoulder. "I'm good with mechanical things. I used to be able to fix almost anything that broke down on my father's farm. This is a pretty simple mechanism."

Foley glided forward and offered Steff a choice of weapons—a dagger, Corene thought, and something long and thin and wicked that looked suited for putting out a man's eye. Steff's grin grew wider.

"That'll do nicely, thanks," he said, choosing the slimmer tool and setting to work.

Liramelli and Melissande—who usually had so little in common— wore matching expressions of doubt as they glanced at Foley, then Steff, then Foley again. Corene thought they were having trouble deciding which one made them most uneasy at this particular moment.

Faster than Corene would have predicted, Steff said, "Got it," and the lock snapped back. He returned the tool to Foley and pried the door open with his fingertips. It required some effort before the door swung wide enough for them to see to the other side.

Melissande peered through. "Better and better," she pronounced. Corene stood on tiptoe to look over her shoulder.

A thin runner of gaslight continued past the doorway and into the gloom on the other side. It threw just enough ghostly illumination for Corene to make out what appeared to be a tunnel hewn straight from the rock of the palace foundation. No blocks, no mortar, no seams—just a low, arched opening in smoky gray rock that stretched forward into a corridor.

That curled down onto a ramp.

Steff had stepped confidently through the door, but Corene saw him quickly falter. "How far down does this go?" he asked.

Liramelli brushed past him, ready to play the leader again. Corene guessed at the thoughts in her mind. *You want to see what lies under the palace? I'll show you, then, but don't blame* me *if it gives you nightmares.* "The equivalent of three stories, I think. Maybe four."

"And the water is at the bottom?" Corene asked.

"All the way down."

Corene pushed past Steff, too. "Then let's go."

Liramelli moved forward slowly, the fingertips of one hand trailing along the curve of the wall as she traversed the short corridor and began her descent. Corene quickly followed suit; the passageway was so uneven that the extra contact made it easier to stay upright. About half the time, the floor was a downward grade, and then there would be a random section where steps had been carved out of the bedrock, fanning out from the center axis in rough triangular shapes. The thin tube of gaslight spiraled down with them, its faint glow adding to the overall eeriness.

Corene lost count of the downward twists they'd taken by the time the tunnel widened out into a reasonably sized cavern. Here, indeed, were the siege supplies Jiramondi had described—barrels of wine, stacks of cloth, huge wooden crates that might hold anything. The illumination was better here, since the single artery of gaslight split into multiple veins that wrapped around the high walls. At any rate, it was bright enough for Corene to see the small dark shapes that scurried away from the disturbance of their presence. Mice or rats, she figured. She didn't even want to think about what other kinds of creatures might be roaming these shadowed hallways.

"Well, I know where I'm coming next time I'm hungry in the middle of the night," Steff joked.

"I think I would rather risk the displeasure of the cook and sneak food from the kitchen," Melissande said faintly.

Corene sniffed. "It smells funny in here. Like there's fruit rotting."

"I wouldn't think there's any fresh fruit down here," Liramelli said. "I know some of the stores get used up and new ones laid in every quintile or so, but I suppose a few items go bad now and then."

"So where's the water?" Steff asked.

Liramelli gestured. "Another level down. If you still want to go."

"Of course."

They fell into single file again and resumed their circular descent. Corene was sure they weren't *really* so far underground that she was running out of air. They weren't *really* about to be crushed by the tons of stone crouching overhead. Nonetheless, she was finding it hard to breathe; the narrowness of the passageway, the dimness of the light, just added to the oppressive sense of danger.

The odor was getting worse, too, the deeper they went underground. Sickly sweet and sulfurously foul at the same time. She wanted to hold her breath but she was already panting slightly and needed all the air she could get.

Liramelli's voice floated up to her. "It doesn't usually stink so much down here. Mostly it smells sort of moldy and dank."

"Probably a dead animal," Steff said in what Corene suspected he intended to be a comforting voice. "There were a bunch of rats a level up. Maybe a whole nest of them died."

"Dead rats!" Melissande exclaimed. "I am even happier that I decided to accompany all of you."

Steff laughed. "You could go back to the surface and wait for us. Or even just back up to the supply room."

"And be alone with the *living* rats? I do not think so."

Another twist of the stairwell and Corene could see that they had reached the end of their journey. The tunnel emptied out into a second, smaller cavern with a low ceiling. Echoing back from the rough walls she could hear the trickling sound of running water. She glanced around to try to find the source, moving aside as Melissande bumped into her from behind.

"Utterly charming! Entirely worth the effort!" Melissande pronounced. "Now, let us go."

"Wait—I want to see where the water comes in," Corene said. "I can *hear* it—but the light is so bad—"

Liramelli gestured over at what looked like a blank face of rock. "See? There's an opening in the wall and the water just bubbles out."

Corene stepped closer, bent down, and put her hand against the chilled and bumpy wall. Liramelli was right. There was a small natural spout at about knee height where a thin stream gurgled out. She would have expected the water to be frigid, but, in fact, it was lukewarm, almost pleasant against her skin. She cupped her hand to take a sip, and thought she could taste copper and dirt mixed into the wetness.

Foley stepped up beside her, and he also filled his hand with water. But he opened his fingers and let it fall, watching as it splashed into a narrow trough at their feet. "Where does it drain to?" he asked, turning his head to the right to follow the course of the underground stream. It appeared to wind around a bulbous outcrop then disappear under a low overhang, but since the gaslight didn't extend that far, it was hard to be sure.

"Too bad we didn't bring matches and candles," Corene murmured.

"I did," Foley answered.

In a moment, he'd lit a slim taper and paced around the outcrop, Corene at his heels. It was instantly clear that the channel the water followed would not accommodate a fleeing princess. The flickering candlelight revealed what looked like a small cave with naturally rounded sides and ceiling, and only the tiniest opening in the far wall where the stream could run through.

"No exit," Corene said.

Foley held the candle higher, his attention caught by a shadow pooling on the floor against the wall, only visible now that they'd moved past the outcrop. "Something tried to get through, though," he said.

She pressed even closer to Foley, straining to see through the half-dark. "Is that what smells so bad?"

It definitely was. The ripe, rank, sweet stench was intense at the distance of a few feet, and there was no doubt that the poor creature was dead. Whatever it was. It was the size of a large dog, though it was hard to figure out how an animal of any mass had gotten through the locked door and made its way down to this level. Corene didn't think it was a dog—too long and thin, though somewhat curled into itself—and whatever it was, it had dragged some kind of white fabric down with it, maybe a blanket to sleep on—

Suddenly Foley moved forward to block her view and edged her back toward the others. "Step away," he said, his voice grim.

But she had seen enough. "Foley," she whispered. "That's a person, isn't it?"

"Yes. Take the others and go back up to the surface. I'll stay here. Send one of Filomara's guards down."

But Corene had never been particularly good about following orders. She came closer and stood on tiptoe, trying to peer over his shoulders. "Can you tell what kind of person? A man, a woman, a child?"

"I'd have to look closer. And—" He hesitated a moment. "The body has decayed pretty far."

"But then—how long do you think—I wonder who it is?"

Their low-voiced conversation had caught the attention of the others. "What have you found? A rotting corpse?" Steff asked jovially.

But his smile faded fast when Corene turned to stare at him. "There's a body," she said. "We think it's human."

"*What?*" Liramelli exclaimed, pushing past Melissande, who looked ready to vomit. "It can't be!"

"Of course it can," Corene said. "Someone could have come down here to explore, and then tripped and fell. Hit his head and died."

"His heart could have given out suddenly," Steff said. "That happens sometimes."

"Any number of things could have happened, but I don't think you want to be the ones to examine the remains," Foley said.

"But I do," Liramelli said, brushing past Foley and Corene. "Whoever he is, I probably know him—"

"*Her*, I believe," Foley said gently. "Judging by the length and style of the hair."

Liramelli gasped and took two running steps before falling to her knees at the side of the body. "Bring the candle closer," she said, and Foley obliged.

Corene and Steff crowded as near as they could, but in this light, from this angle, it was hard to see much. The face was so dark and bloated that the features were hard to make out, but the hair certainly seemed to belong to a woman. It was a fine wheat-blond color caught in a long braid and tied with a ribbon. The rest of her body was concealed by a white blanket that the woman appeared to have drawn up to her chin in an effort to stay warm. When Liramelli peeled the coverlet back, Corene could catch glints of gold at the woman's throat and around the wrist, so this had obviously been a person of wealth. She appeared to be wearing traditional Malinquese clothing—a jacket and trousers—mostly black with random splashes of white.

"That's blood," Steff said suddenly. Corene barely had to turn her head to look at him, he was standing that close to her. "On her clothes. I thought it was a pattern in the cloth, but it's blood."

Foley nodded. "I think so, too."

"She bled to death down here?" Corene asked sharply. "Was she—was she murdered?"

"That," Foley said, "or she took her own life."

"Either way, it's awful," Corene said. "I wonder who she is."

Liramelli came shakily to her feet, murmuring a thank-you when Foley reached out to steady her. "It's Sarona," she said in a small voice. "She often wore her hair like that, and I recognize the necklace."

"Sarona?" Corene repeated. "The woman everyone assumed ran off a few ninedays ago?"

Liramelli nodded. She looked as if she was trying very hard not to dissolve into hysteria. Corene was frankly astonished that she hadn't done so already. "Yes. She didn't run. She died."

Just speaking the words was enough to push Liramelli over the edge. She dropped her face into her hands and started crying, thick choking sobs that shook her sturdy shoulders. Before Corene could even react, Steff had squeezed around Foley and taken Liramelli in his arms.

"It's horrible, I know," he said, smoothing a hand over her hair and cradling her against his chest. In the murky light, Corene couldn't be sure, but she thought he kissed the top of her head. "I wish you hadn't seen it."

Liramelli's voice was rough with tears. "I was glad she was gone, don't you understand? I tried so hard not to hate her, but then when she disappeared, I was so happy! And all this time—she was down here alone and *dead* and I wasn't even sorry—"

Steff had shifted his hold on Liramelli and now he was guiding her away from the body, back toward Melissande and the stairwell. "Just because you didn't like her doesn't mean it's your fault she's dead," he said.

Melissande had come forward with her arms outstretched, as if she would take Liramelli from Steff and comfort her. But Steff, Corene noted, was not willing to relinquish the weeping girl.

"It is Sarona?" Melissande asked Steff in a low voice, and he nodded. "How very dreadful. We must tell Filomara."

"And her parents," Liramelli said on a sob. "And—and—Greggorio. And everyone."

"Very well," Melissande said. "Upstairs we go. Now. We will leave Foley to guard the door at the top until one of Filomara's soldiers can be dispatched to bring the—to bring Sarona to the surface."

At that, Liramelli looked up and tried to wrench away from Steff's hold. "No—she's been alone too long. Someone should stay with her."

Melissande stepped closer, took Liramelli's face between her hands, and spoke with utter solemnity. "That is merely Sarona's body. She no longer inhabits it. It is terrible that she died in such a way, and we will help Filomara however we can to figure out exactly what happened. But you cannot help her by sitting down here in the dark and crying. You must go up and let the living do their part for the dead."

For a moment, their gazes stayed locked, then Liramelli started crying again, but more quietly. She nodded and seemed to droop against Steff's shoulder. "Let's go up, then," he said.

They were a mostly silent procession as they wound their way to the surface, alternately climbing the rough stairs or sliding their feet along the smoother ramps. The only noises were their shoes against the stone, Liramelli's occasional sniffle, Steff's intermittent murmurs of encouragement, and the distant sound of rats chittering in the walls.

Corene had never in her life been so glad to reach a doorway and step through it. Even though this windowless hallway was almost as low and shadowy as the underground stairwell, it felt airy as an elay bower; she felt a thousand times lighter, bathed in sun, and finally, finally able to breathe.

Liramelli sagged against the wall as Steff and Foley shoved the thick door back in the frame until the lock snapped in place. The girl looked pale as death herself, Corene thought. She could hardly imagine how Liramelli was still staying upright.

Melissande had drawn the same conclusion. "Steff, you must go to the empress," she said. "Corene and I will take Liramelli to her parents before she collapses in the hall."

"I'm all right," Liramelli said faintly.

"You're not," Corene said. "But I want to wait here with Foley. If someone knows what we've discovered—well, two people are more difficult to overcome than one."

Steff snorted. "I hardly think *you* would be able to fend off an attacker who overcame Foley."

"Maybe not, but I could scream loud enough to rouse the whole palace."

"All right," he answered. "Melissande—are you sure you can get her that far?"

Liramelli pushed herself away from the wall to prove she could stand on her own. "I'm fine," she said, her voice a little stronger.

Melissande put an arm around her shoulder. "We will manage," she said. "You go to Filomara."

In a few moments, the other three had disappeared down the low hallway. Corene stood tensely as she listened to their footsteps fade away, then she looked over at Foley. He was standing with his back against the door, his feet planted solidly on the floor, his hands casually at his sides. She remembered the weapons he had offered Steff, and wondered if there were more blades concealed on his body. She'd never actually seen him fight, but she'd always believed he could defeat as many assailants as he had to. She'd been so jealous of Josetta—to have someone so committed to her well-being. To have that someone be *Foley.* She had constantly imagined what that must be like.

She shook away the wisp of longing. "What do you think?" she asked. "Suicide or murder?"

"It seems like an odd place and an odd way to choose to die," he said. "I'm inclined to think murder, but I can't be sure."

She nodded. She had formed the same opinion. "I wish *you'd* been guarding her," she said quietly. "No one could have killed her if *you'd* been there."

"I hope that's true," Foley answered.

"Of course it is. You would have followed her everywhere she went."

He regarded her silently a moment. "She could have gone to the bed of a lover. I wouldn't have followed her into that room. He could have killed her and spirited her body out a window or a secret door. She could have joined a party for dinner in private rooms and swallowed poison. I wouldn't have been in that room, either. There is no way to keep anyone completely safe unless you are standing next to her, beside her, no more than an inch apart, every minute of every day. And even then, there is no guarantee. If you stand in front of her, the arrow might arrive from the back. Or the first arrow might pierce your throat, and when you fall, the second one buries itself in her heart. No one is ever safe, no matter how closely the guard is watching."

Corene nodded and slumped against the wall. All of her muscles felt sore and tired, as if she had spent hours holding up these stone ceilings so that the others could walk beneath them. "You're warning me," she said. "You're telling me to be careful."

"Yes," he said.

"If somebody killed that girl," she said, "can you guess who?"

"Someone who knew where the key was kept, for starters."

She nodded again. "That might be a lot of people. Lorian, of course. Probably the head chef, too, and the housekeeper and anyone who might have reason to visit the underground storeroom."

"I would assume Lorian and the housekeeper have their own keys to every door in the palace," Foley said.

"You're probably right," she said. "So maybe this was someone who didn't have a key, but knew the door would be locked. And knew where the key was usually kept." She shrugged. "Greggorio, for one. Liramelli said something to that effect."

"I would guess all three of the empress's nephews knew."

"Though Garameno couldn't have reached the key if it was hidden above the door. Or carried a body down the stairs," she pointed out.

"No. But he could have paid someone else to do it."

"To commit a *murder*? Or cover it up?"

Foley shrugged. "Someone faithful to him. That man of his who goes with him everywhere—he might have done the deed out of love or loyalty."

She tried for a smile, which wasn't very successful. "You wouldn't kill anyone for those reasons, would you?" she asked. "Even if I asked you to?"

He watched her steadily and didn't answer. But it wasn't reprimand she read in that gaze.

"You *would*?" she breathed. "I think I'm horrified."

"If it was someone who had harmed you badly enough and there was no other way to keep you safe," he said.

"Did you ever kill anyone for Josetta?"

"At the end. When soldiers from Berringey came after Rafe and she was in danger, too."

"Did she know that?"

"I imagine so."

"You never talked about it?"

"There were a lot of other things going on just then."

"I hope you don't have to kill anyone for me."

"I hope so, too," he said. "Mostly because I don't want you ever to be so much at risk."

"I'm beginning to think Malinqua is a more dangerous place than I was anticipating."

"So am I. Maybe it's time to leave."

This time she almost managed the smile. "We can't, remember? The empress's soldiers would stop us."

"I think we could outwit them. And there are other ways to get free."

"Like what?"

"Write a letter to your father and let him know you're being detained against your will. I could get that letter to a Welchin sea captain. I promise you troops would arrive on the very next ship to escort you home."

She sighed and slid all the way down the wall until she was sitting on the uneven floor. "And spark an international incident! A pitched battle between Malinquese and Welchin forces! That seems like an awful way to end a grand adventure designed to prove how independent I am."

"I can think of worse ways to end such an adventure," Foley said.

She sighed again. "Like Sarona, I suppose."

He didn't answer, but that was clearly what he meant. She realized—for the first time—that Foley didn't really care about political maneuvering, which prince married which visiting princess, who was named to the throne of Malinqua or Welce or Berringey. All he cared about was the survival of whoever he had been assigned to protect. It was a drastically simple measure of success, she thought. Much simpler than the gauges Corene usually used. A little freeing, actually. *What would I be doing with my life if all I cared about was whether I lived or died?* she wondered.

Not simpering her way through endless dinners in a foreign court, that was certain. At least not the one in Malinqua. The thought was so very odd that she shoved it back down to the bottom of her mind.

"I don't think we're at the point yet where I need to ask my father to send in reinforcements," she said. "But if we reach it, I'm glad to know I can get a message to him through Leah."

"It might be time to see her in person again. To tell her what's happened today."

"I was just thinking that. I'll set something up."

"Good."

They didn't have a chance to say more because a commotion down the hall signaled that a crowd was heading their way. Corene scrambled to her feet, wanting to look calm and composed for the soldiers, but she was surprised to see who led the delegation: Filomara, with Greggorio right behind her.

"She is down there? You saw her?" the empress demanded as soon as she caught sight of Corene.

It was the first time she'd laid eyes on the empress today, so Corene formally bowed her head before speaking. "There is a body at the bottom of the stairwell. It seems to be a woman, and Liramelli thought she recognized the hair and jewelry, but I don't know for certain who it is."

"Open the door," Filomara commanded.

"It's an upsetting sight," Corene said carefully. "You might not wish to see it."

"Open the door!" the empress thundered. "This is *my* home and I will face anything that happens within its walls."

Greggorio had stepped past her and laid both his hands on the door as if confused to find it shut. He looked awful, Corene thought—skin five shades paler than usual, eyes wide and haunted, mouth tensed with the effort of holding something back. Screams or sobs, maybe.

"I'm sorry," Foley spoke up. "The door locked itself again when we shut it."

Greggorio had obviously arrived at the same conclusion, because he had already lifted his hand to run it along the lintel above the door. He came up empty, of course, and Corene watched as he went through the same thought processes they had. He looked at the floor, he bent down to poke through the thick dust in the corners. When he straightened up, Corene thought he looked both puzzled and on the edge of frantic.

"Where's the key?" he demanded.

Filomara issued an order over her shoulder. "Someone fetch Lorian."

Foley answered Greggorio. "We couldn't find it. Steff forced the lock."

"We need the *key*," Greggorio exclaimed. He began digging at the seam between the door and the frame with his bare fingernails. "We have to get to her."

Corene could only stare at him—she had never seen the easygoing Greggorio so wild—but Filomara came close enough to put a hand on his shoulder. "We will get to her soon enough," she said gruffly. "She has waited this long for us."

He shook her off impatiently. "All this time," he said, as if the words were gagging him. "We thought she was somewhere safe and happy, and *all this time*—all these ninedays—down in the dark with the echoes and the rats—"

Well, he's certainly been to the bottom of the stairwell sometime, Corene thought. And he certainly seemed half-mad at the idea that

Sarona had ended her life in such an infelicitous place. She didn't believe he was clever enough to manufacture such distress, which made her think he couldn't have been involved in her death. But maybe, this whole time, Greggorio had fooled them all.

"I am furious that she suffered, and in my home," Filomara said, still speaking in a low, serious voice. "But she is not suffering now. Be calm. Lorian will bring the key."

Greggorio deliberately turned away from her, from all of them. He continued running his hand over the door frame, checking the lintel again, unable to stop looking, searching, trying to find a way past this obdurate checkpoint and down to the dead girl below.

Filomara turned to Corene, her face harsh and set. "Thank you for watching the door until I arrived," she said. "But these are Malinquese matters, and we will deal with them now."

That was unmistakeably a dismissal. Corene was only too ready to go. "Let me know if there's something else I can do—or tell you—or help with," she said, stammering a little.

"If something occurs to me, I will."

Another exchange of nods, and Foley and Corene were slipping past the soldiers and back to the main corridors. "Do you have any idea how to get to our rooms?" Corene muttered. "I'm not sure I can find the way if Liramelli isn't with us."

"I couldn't retrace our steps, but I think I can find the main hall on the lower level," he said, a touch of amusement in his voice. "Surely even you could make your way back at that point."

Indeed, they followed progressively wider and more welcoming hallways until they were suddenly in the grand foyer. It was bright with afternoon sun and bustling with servants and petitioners, and absolutely nothing in its calm, purposeful, well-ordered confines would make you suspect that somewhere on the premises a murderer might be lurking, hoping not to be discovered.

THIRTEEN

"I didn't think you would be here today," Chandran said when Leah showed up at his booth in the morning.

"Neither did I. It turns out the princess would like to visit with me, and this is where she asked me to meet her."

"I am always happy to entertain royalty," he said. "And to have extra hands to do the work. We got a shipment from Dhonsho last night. You can unpack it while you wait."

It sounded like a brusque order, but Leah recognized it as a gift. Dhonsho's primary exports were bright fabrics dyed in luscious colors that reminded her of fruit—plum and lemon and mango and berry—and she loved them. She had been so enamored of a nubby cherry-red shawl that Chandran had actually commanded her to take it as part of her salary for the nineday. Here in mid-Quinnatorz, the mornings were almost cool enough that she could pretend she needed the shawl for warmth, at least before the sun rose too high. She had worn it every day.

The four crates that had arrived yesterday were filled with similar delights—more of that fine, loosely woven material in wide strips of fabric big enough to wrap twice around your body. This time the colors made Leah think of landscapes—grass green, river blue, sunset orange. Each one was finished with a knotted fringe hung with beads that matched the dye. As she lifted the fabrics from the crate, shook out the wrinkles, and folded them back up, the beads of each shawl made small, cheerful clinking sounds.

She really wished she wouldn't have to sell a single one. She would prefer to keep them all for herself.

Nonetheless, under Chandran's watchful eyes, she dutifully put the Dhonsho items on display and made sure that any serious shopper who stopped by had a chance to look them over. By noon, half were gone.

"I don't know how good you are at spying," Chandran observed as they grabbed a quick bite to eat during a noontime lull, "but you have a gift for selling. You have a fine eye for merchandise and the rare ability to make your customers fall in love with whatever you love. You could open up your own booth here on Great Four and be rich within a quintile."

She sipped at her keerza—which, she could hardly believe, she had actually begun to like—and thought that over. "If I became a merchant, I don't think I'd stay in Malinqua," she said. "I'd go back to Welce and open a place in the shop district of Chialto."

His voice was mild but his eyes were keen. "I had formed the opinion you were not eager to return to Welce. Whether or not you had an occupation suitable to your talents."

She shrugged slightly; he was right about that. "Well, one of the reasons I haven't wanted to go back is I haven't had any idea what I might do when I returned," she said. "I certainly don't want to go back to my old life."

"Often one's old life is not an option even if one wished it were."

She poured herself another cup of keerza just so she could ask the question casually while her hands were occupied with something else. "How about you? Would you return to Cozique?"

"No."

That was unvarnished enough that she couldn't help sending him a quick, quizzical look. "Wouldn't, or wouldn't be allowed to?" she asked.

"Wouldn't be allowed to."

Now she straightened up, blowing on her hot drink, and making no more attempt to hide her curiosity. "A crime or a scandal?" she asked.

"Some people would call it a crime."

"And would you take the same actions again if the same situation were to arise?" she asked.

"I would."

She refused to ask another question; he would either tell her or he wouldn't. So she just sipped from her cup and watched him. He returned her gaze for a moment before allowing a small smile to touch his lips and then looking away. "Perhaps it is the fact that I have operated outside the law that makes me appreciate its parameters so deeply," he said.

"That's funny," she said. "Being judged by the inflexible standards of society is what has made me want to live outside it."

"But then, we are different in so many ways," he said. "If you could, you would go back and change your actions. I wouldn't. I would change the situation that led me to act, but I don't regret what I myself have done. You do."

It was annoying how well he read her. During the past five years, Leah had grown fond of the idea that she was mysterious. She wondered if everyone else found her as transparent as Chandran did.

"For good or for ill, neither of us can revisit the past," she said. She gulped the last of her keerza and set down the cup; she'd spotted a trio of wealthy-looking women headed straight for their booth. "And so here we are in Malinqua for the foreseeable future."

"I am, perhaps," Chandran said. "You'll be back in Chialto within a quintile."

She barely had time to give him a glance of surprise before the customers descended, and she was showing them music boxes and scarves and delicate trinkets. He was wrong, of course—if she ever returned to Welce, it would be when she was old and tired, empty of both sorrow and rage. But what spooked her was that Chandran had an eerie way of being right about things. Why would he think she was on the verge of going home?

The bright afternoon was so late that it had almost changed into its sober evening attire by the time a delegation from the palace arrived. Leah spotted Corene's distinctive red hair the minute her group rounded the corner and began a slow promenade down the row of stalls. There were only a handful in the royal party this time—Corene, a diminutive Coziquela girl, the sturdy-looking boy who must be Filomara's miraculous grandson, and the guard named Foley. With an airy wave of her hand, Corene directed the other two to some wonder at a nearby booth, then she and Foley came directly to Chandran's.

"We don't have much time," Corene said without preamble as soon as Leah stepped over to greet her. She spoke in Welchin and very quietly. "Melissande won't be distracted for long."

"What's happened?"

Corene gave her a swift look. "I suppose you've heard the news from the palace."

It was one of the things Leah liked about the princess; she wasn't shocked or offended by the notion that people gossiped about royalty. She actually seemed to count on the idea that information would precede her.

"The body of a young lady was found in some underground passage. I heard about it right after I got your note."

"I want to know what people are saying."

"Some think she was killed by a royal lover—most likely Greggorio," Leah answered. "Others think the empress did away with her because her nephew was too fond of the girl and Filomara wanted him to marry elsewhere. That theory isn't as popular, though, because most people idolize Filomara."

"What else?"

Leah glanced around, but the Coziquela girl was still out of hearing distance, trying on bracelets at another stall. "A jealous rival disposed of her to clear the field."

Corene nodded. "So far, all of these are ideas that have crossed my mind as well—and, I have to think, Filomara's. But none of them feels exactly right to me."

"Other people are saying she probably killed herself," Leah added.

Corene nodded again. "That's what everyone at the palace is hoping happened. Filomara has called in some of her—her—biological experts, and they're supposed to be studying the body, trying to figure out how she died. And if it wasn't by suicide—"

"She was murdered," Leah finished up. "And you'd better get out of Malinqua as fast as you can. The minute your father hears of this—"

"He'll send the Welchin navy to bring me home," Corene said. "I know."

"If you're ready to go, I can get you to a ship this afternoon," Leah said. "You can walk out of the Great Market and straight to the harbor and sail out tonight."

"I'm not so sure," Corene answered. "A handful of the empress's men accompanied us here and they're waiting at the main entrance. I don't think they'd let me sail off without a goodbye."

"Then give me a day or two to plan, and we can outmaneuver them."

Corene was silent a moment. "It might not be necessary," she said. "If Sarona killed herself, it's still really awful, but I'm not in danger."

Leah scanned her face. "You don't want to leave," she said.

"I'm torn," Corene said. "I realize that things have become very strange at the Malinquese court, which makes me think I should walk away right now. But I also have the feeling that I haven't come to the end of the adventure yet, which makes me want to stay." She laughed ruefully. "Or maybe I'm just not ready to go back to Welce."

Leah could certainly understand *that*. "Well, just let me know. I'll find a way to get you out of here—whether or not the empress wants you to leave."

"That's good to know," Corene said.

There was no more time to talk, because Filomara's grandson and the Coziquela girl had arrived at the booth, bickering in a friendly way. "This Steff, he has no taste at *all*," the Coziquela princess complained to Corene. "If the situation ever arises in which he needs to purchase a gift for me, you must be on hand to advise him, or it will be utterly hideous."

Steff was grinning. "I don't know why you'd think I ever *would* need to buy you a present," he said.

"Because women love gifts. It is so obvious it does not need to be stated."

"They do," Corene agreed. "Melissande, did you see these beautiful shawls? Do you think we should buy one for Liramelli? She was so sad."

"These arrived just yesterday from Dhonsho," Leah said, deftly unfolding a blue one and holding it up to Melissande's face. "They're exquisite. I own one myself and have thought about purchasing another one. Perhaps two or three."

Melissande turned toward the little mirror on the counter and admired the way the fabric perfectly matched the color of her eyes. "From Dhonsho? Then we must get one for Alette as well."

"There's a good idea. And one for each of us, too."

"But of course."

"That blue looks very good on you," Leah said to Melissande. "These friends of yours—what would be their best colors?"

"Liramelli always wears black or white but she is so pale she could hardly choose worse shades," Melissande said frankly. "This green, perhaps? I think she needs something vivid."

Corene had wrapped a purple scarf around her head and was studying herself in the mirror. Leah wouldn't have thought the color would suit her, but, in fact, it was stunning against her flaming hair. "Yes, and maybe that bright yellow for Alette? She's from Dhonsho," she explained to Leah. "Her skin is dark brown and she looks best in warm colors."

"Good, now *that's* settled," Steff said in a voice of utter boredom. "Can we go look at something else? *Anything* else?"

Corene made shooing motions with her hands. "Leave. We'll catch up with you. You're too annoying."

It took another few minutes for the royal party to sort through the rest of the merchandise, pay for their purchases, and move on. They had hardly taken three steps away when another group of expensively dressed women descended on the booth, and Leah was kept busy until the market shut down at sunset.

"A good day," she observed to Chandran, when they finally had time to count the money and lock up the cabinets for the evening. "You might want to order more of those shawls."

"Dhonsho products always sell well. I think because they are so colorful," he said. "Despite the fact that the Malinquese seem to strictly curtail color in their own fashions. Or maybe for that very reason."

"I never saw much Dhonshon merchandise in the Plazas in Chialto," Leah said. "When I open my shop back home, I'm going to import half my items from Dhonsho."

"Will you be back here again tomorrow?" he asked.

"I don't think so. I have to keep a couple of appointments. The day after, though."

"I'll look for you then."

. . .

When the next morning dawned sullen and damp, Leah almost changed her mind and headed to the Great Market because it was more pleasant to spend a wet day under a roof than walking the streets of the city. But she'd been lax lately; she needed to check in with her usual contacts just to remind them of her existence.

So she headed to the Little Islands to visit the friends she had carefully cultivated during the last few years. Her first stop was a small, aromatic shop filled with imports from Dhonsho. The windows were always covered with swooping swaths of jewel-toned fabrics so that the air seemed full of colorful shadows. The place was a maze of tables and shelving units holding baskets of merchandise—jewelry, scarves, buttons, children's toys, figurines, goblets, wrapped baked goods, dried fruit, and bottles of liqueur. Hundreds of items hung from the ceiling on long red ribbons—big glass globes, bunches of dried flowers, complex pieces woven of sticks and yarn in fantastical patterns. It was impossible to wander through the narrow aisles without feeling like you were going to knock something over or hit something with your head, but Leah was fascinated by all the exotic items available and usually managed to visit every display rack before she left.

The owners were a wrinkled old woman, her daughter, and her two granddaughters—and possibly assorted husbands and sons, though Leah had never seen any men working at the place. They were part of a sizable Dhonshon community that resided here in the international district and kept some of their native traditions alive, though many of them had never set foot in their home country. Some time ago, Leah had learned that the old woman had emigrated here more than thirty years ago, when her daughter was fifteen; the two younger women had never left Malinqua.

"You'll have to take them to visit sometime," Leah had said when she discovered this, but the old woman had given her head an emphatic shake.

"It is a bad place for women," she said. "We will not be going back."

Leah was popular with all four of the shopkeepers, mostly because she'd performed a kind act three years ago. Their landlord was a miserly

Malinquese bachelor who hated all foreigners, despite the fact that most of his tenants fell into that category. He had never bothered to learn Dhonshon or even Coziquela, so most of his attempts to communicate with his renters consisted of shouts and pantomimes. On this particular day, he was yelling at the four women to tell them he was raising their rent because they always turned it in a nineday too late. Naturally they didn't understand him, but he was so angry that they feared he was about to evict them. Leah had stepped in to act as both translator and mediator—*If they pay their money on time, will you forgo the raise?*—and the women had been grateful ever since.

Today only the youngest girl, Teyta, was on hand, yawning through a slow wet workday. "It is so boring here," she complained to Leah.

"Do you mean in your shop or in all of Malinqua?"

"Both!" Teyta said with a laugh. "I want to sail to Cozique and open a shop in the famous jewel district. They say you can get rich in one day."

"What they say and what is true might be two different things."

Teyta sighed. "Well, even if I didn't get rich, at least I would be living in Cozique."

They only chatted a few minutes before another customer came in, this one Dhonshon and looking like she was ready to buy. "I'll be back some other day," Leah said with a friendly wave, and slipped out into the rain.

She made a few more stops before she ended up at the Welchin café where she liked to spend the most time. The scents and the foods were pleasingly familiar, and the gentle sound of spoken Welchin washed over her like a benediction. She used to get homesick whenever she dropped in on this place, but now she found its familiarity to be comforting instead of distressing.

It was no more crowded here than it had been at the Dhonshon shop, so the owner poured fruited water for both of them, then sat down with Leah for some gossip. They discussed recent news out of Chialto, then shared complaints about the horrible food the people of Malinqua seemed to consider delicacies. "That zeezin, I thought it would burn my tongue clean out of my head," the woman grumbled. "Who ruins good meat with something like that?"

The owner didn't have any useful tidbits to relay, though she did mention that one of her promised shipments was late. "Probably time to change my supplier—he's coru, you know, and has never been reliable—but you'd be surprised at how few torz farmers you can find who want to ship overseas."

"Maybe he just wants more money."

The café owner laughed. "That would be true of a sweela man, but coru? He probably just got distracted."

About an hour later, Leah had reason to think it wasn't the supplier's fault at all.

T he rain had started to fall steadily enough to be miserable, so she'd wrapped herself in her red shawl and then layered on a hooded cape that was more or less waterproof. Still, she was both wet and irritable as she made her way down to the wharf, keeping her eyes on her feet as she sloshed through puddles and rivulets that made the uneven avenue no better than a streambed. She wasn't the first patron to track mud and water inside Billini's bar; the floor was almost as wet as the street outside.

Still, the place was mostly empty since bad weather had kept many regular customers home. Leah sat on a stool up at the front counter, nursed a beer, and commiserated with Billini on the day's lost profits.

"Maybe tomorrow will be better," she said. "Sun and a fair wind."

"It hardly matters," he groused. "In a nineday, I'll be almost out of supplies and fighting with all the other taverns for the few shipments that get through. Maybe I'll just close the place down for a half a quintile and head to the mainland to visit family."

"Wait, I'm confused. Why will you be out of supplies?"

Billini snorted. "Didn't you notice the wharf this afternoon?"

Leah had been too preoccupied with watching where she put her feet to lift her gaze and stare out at the water. "What about it?"

"There's hardly a ship in port. Because of the Berringey blockade."

FOURTEEN

The days following the discovery of Sarona's body were so somber that Corene sometimes felt the whole enormous palace was sinking into the ground, weighted by grief and uneasiness. Preparations for the big celebration continued, as it was barely three ninedays away, but everyone felt bad about planning a party alongside a funeral. The formal evening dinners were sparsely attended, with Filomara skipping about half of them and various other family members choosing to take their meals elsewhere on random days.

"This is almost as bad as the time Aravani died," Jiramondi said one afternoon as he tutored Corene in her Malinquese lessons. "I mean, I was only ten, but I remember how oppressive it was. No one wanted to evince the slightest joy in anything, no matter how trivial, for fear of offending Filomara. It felt like no one spoke above a whisper for a whole quintile."

"I've been trying to figure out who's genuinely sad and who's horrified because it's such a dreadful thing to happen and who's just pretending," Corene said.

One corner of Jiramondi's mouth curled up sardonically. "That's my very practical Welchin girl speaking," he said.

Corene shrugged. "I didn't know her, so I can hardly be in mourning. But I find it interesting to watch everyone else."

"And what have you determined?"

"Greggorio is really sorry she's dead. He genuinely liked her."

"Probably too much for my aunt's comfort, but I agree."

"Filomara—found her problematic when she was alive, but even more problematic now that she's dead."

Jiramondi looked slightly amused. "Again, I'd say you're right. Who else?"

She looked him straight in the eye. "You didn't care for her much. And Garameno despised her."

Jiramondi hesitated a moment, and then nodded ruefully. "She was a difficult and unlikable girl. I don't know if you've ever come across someone who's been blessed with every gift, and who doesn't show a scrap of gratitude about it. Sarona just assumed that she deserved to be beautiful, to be wealthy, to be well-connected. She didn't care that other people have struggles—if she noticed them at all, it was to look at them with scorn. She didn't have an ounce of compassion or empathy."

"Of course I've known people like that," Corene said. "*I* was like that, at least when I was younger—and until I faced a few disasters of my own." She thought about it a moment. "I might still be more like that than I'd want to admit."

Jiramondi sat back in his chair and regarded her with a half-smile. "Now that surprises me," he said.

She smiled back. "That I'd realize it about myself? Or admit it?"

"That you'd think it's true. You're much more aware of other people than Sarona ever was."

"Maybe," she said. "But I never liked people that much. And they never liked me."

Jiramondi rested his chin on his fist and continued to regard her. "But they don't repulse you because they're different. Sarona was often repulsed."

"Who's different? Different in what way?"

He smiled. "And that's what I mean."

"Because Garameno is in a wheelchair, for instance?"

"Exactly. He's not—" Jiramondi searched for a word. "A whole man. Which, to someone like Sarona, made him abhorrent. But you don't notice the wheelchair."

"Of course I notice it," Corene said. "I just don't care. What interests me about Garameno is how clever he is. And how close he is to Filomara. And how very well-informed he is about everything that happens in Malinqua. *Those* are the things that define Garameno, as far as I'm concerned."

"And you aren't repulsed by *me*," he said.

"By—?"

He spoke a Malinquese phrase that she didn't recognize. When she looked puzzled, he offered the definition in a slow, deliberate voice. "A man who has sex with other men."

"Oh, that. *That's* not what I find interesting about you," she said. "What intrigues me is how smoothly you maintain good relations with everyone in the palace. Few people actually dislike you. Most people trust you. But they don't notice how skillfully you're managing these relationships. Your brand of charm is so subtle they don't realize how you're actually using it."

Jiramondi blinked at her. "What a very different way of looking at my existence, to be sure. Mostly I imagine that I'm frantically waving banners and organizing conversations to distract people from thinking about the things in my life they consider repulsive."

Now she was the one to lean forward and study him. "Here's what I don't understand," she said. "How does anyone *know* these 'repulsive things' about you? It's not like you go around the palace kissing footmen or staring longingly at handsome young boys. At least not that I've ever noticed."

He nodded. "I try to be circumspect. But I was discovered once—in a most unambiguous situation—and the circumstances were widely reported. I was too proud to lie and claim I'd been taken advantage of."

"Who discovered you?"

"Lorian. Who, as you know, cannot keep a secret from my aunt, though I begged him." He shrugged. "He's never liked me much, so I think he was glad for the chance to try and ruin my life."

"Why doesn't he like you?"

"He's always *hated* my father. Hated all of Filomara's brothers, actually, except Morli. So he's never liked Garameno, either, which has always been a comfort to me."

She grinned, but said, "So Lorian found you and told Filomara. What did she say? The empress has a lot of faults, but this doesn't seem like the sort of thing that would bother her."

"No, it didn't seem to change her opinion of me one way or the other—but others were in the room when he made his report. The prefect, for instance. You might notice that Harlo is not one of the people I've managed to charm. He considers my—weakness—to be so monstrous that he can barely stand to look at me when we're in the same room."

She'd witnessed that prejudice for herself. "Well, I'm sorry you've had to deal with such reactions from some of the royal court," she said. "But for people like Melissande and me, it doesn't matter."

"Melissande told me that in Coziquela, the word they use to describe men like me is *sublime*. I don't know the word in Welchin."

"There isn't one."

"Because such a thing is unmentionable?"

"Because nobody cares. You think I'm being very tolerant and good-hearted, but I never knew anyone who thought twice about such a thing. Maybe if I'd been raised differently I'd be shocked, but it's kind of hard to get worked up about it now."

Jiramondi laughed out loud, the sound so unexpected and so welcome after these last dreary days that Corene laughed right along with him. "You're right—I've given you too much credit," he said. "You're probably as shallow and small-minded as the next girl, you just had a better upbringing."

"Oh, I wouldn't say that. I was raised by a woman who noticed and cataloged everyone's deficits," Corene said cynically. "Not because they revolted her, but because she might need to exploit them at some point in the future. My father makes it a habit to know every man's weak spot, too, but he's usually not planning to use it against the other man. He just wants to know when and how that person might fail him."

"That must have been a delightful household."

"They didn't live together. And there were plenty of other influences at court that helped shape me, for good or for ill. But I don't think

I became a nice person—well, as nice as I actually *am*, which isn't as nice as I should be—until I started spending time with my sister and my stepmother. And I learned that you don't have to scheme and you don't have to outsmart people and you don't have to be *better* than everyone else all the time. You just have to be you, even if *you* aren't perfect."

"Now there's a lesson Sarona never learned," Jiramondi said. "She only liked perfect people."

"Do you think she actually cared about Greggorio? Or did she just think he was the most likely heir to Filomara's throne?"

"I think it was all the same thing to her. He's always been the most likely heir because, of the three of us, he's the closest to perfect—the reasons she liked him are the reasons Filomara still favors him. Did she actually love him? I don't know. But I don't think it would have pained her soul to marry him. As it would have pained her to marry Garameno or me."

"Even if you'd been named the heir?"

"Maybe even more so then," he mused. "Because the bitterness of our—drawbacks—would have poisoned the sweetness of her life."

"Well, you've convinced me," Corene said. "I'm glad she's dead."

But gladness was in short supply throughout the rest of the palace. At Filomara's request, Liramelli and Greggorio traveled with the body to the estate Sarona's parents owned some fifty miles from Palminera to attend the funeral as the empress's representatives. Corene could not imagine how strained conversation must have been during that long, uncomfortable ride. She could only be glad she hadn't been in the carriage.

Like Corene, Alette was a stranger to Malinqua and had never been friends with Sarona, so she could hardly be weighed down by grief over the other woman's death. In fact, during the next nineday, Alette showed as much animation as Corene had ever seen. She loved the yellow shawl Corene and Melissande had brought her from the Great Market, and she started wearing it every day. She showed up for every meal, she occasionally joined the other women for strolls through the garden, and she attended the impromptu evening sessions Corene had started hosting in her room just to chase away the gloom of the dinner conversation.

It was an odd group, Corene had to admit—bubbly Melissande, exotic Alette, matter-of-fact Steff, and watchful Foley. And herself. She wasn't sure she could think of a single adjective she'd want for her own description.

They spent much of their time playing penta, of course. Alette had proved a surprisingly quick study, winning the first few hands so decisively that they couldn't help but accuse her of cheating. She had shown her rare smile and said, "It is very similar to a game we have in Dhonsho. My sisters and I played it often."

"And did you always win?" Steff inquired, raking up the cards and shuffling them again.

"Of course not. My sisters were all very good at the game."

"You'll have to teach us Dhonshon games when we get tired of penta," Corene said.

"Tired of penta? But is such a thing possible?" Melissande demanded. Of all of them, she was least engaged by the card game. But, of course, she couldn't bear to be excluded from any social gathering, so she endured it.

Steff dealt the cards and they all studied their hands. "That fellow was here again to see the empress," he said idly.

"We have no idea who you're talking about," Corene said. "What fellow?"

"Renalto. The one who runs some biological lab—you met him, Corene. The one who tested my blood."

Melissande feigned alarm. "Tell us quickly! Are they testing you again? Have they decided you are an imposter after all?"

He grinned. "No—well, not that I know of, at any rate. Apparently people at his facility studied Sarona's body before it was sent home, and he was here to tell Filomara what they'd determined about how she died."

He fell silent, studying his cards again, seeming unaware of the fact that the rest of them were staring at him.

"Well?" Corene demanded. "What *did* they determine?"

He looked up, surprised. "Oh, I don't know. She sent me from the room."

Corene made a growling noise in the back of her throat. "You are the most *useless* man."

Steff shrugged and laid down the low cards in the suits of fish and skulls. Everyone else showed their own low cards, and Melissande took the bid.

Foley spoke up while they played the first round. "If training yard gossip is correct, these scientists decided that Sarona took her own life," he said. "They found a knife near the body and evidence that the arteries in her throat were cut. Jaggedly and badly, which made them think the wounds were self-inflicted."

Melissande shuddered delicately. "I could not do such a thing. I could not abide the pain."

Corene carefully did not look at Alette, who had already proven she was willing to take her own life. But the Dhonsho girl didn't seem to mind suicide as a topic. "There are drugs that they say will kill you quickly and easily," she said. "But the people I've seen who died that way didn't look peaceful to me. Bleeding to death isn't so bad. You grow tired and then you sleep. It doesn't hurt as much as you might think." She played a card. "It's living that is sometimes too painful to endure."

Corene leaned over to briefly lay her hand on Alette's forearm. "I wish you hadn't lived a life that made that true."

Alette gave her one long, serious look. "Thank you," she said.

Steff tapped a card against the table, frowning. "That's not right," he said.

"What's not right? Your card? Alette's life?" Corene demanded. "You're always so obscure."

He put the chosen card back and played another one. "Sarona couldn't have killed herself."

"There is no possible way you could know that," Corene answered.

But Foley was nodding. "I thought the same thing."

"But why?" Melissande exclaimed. "What evidence could you have?"

Steff glanced at Foley. "There wasn't enough blood."

"Exactly," Foley said.

"I admit I did not stand there gazing at the body for hours, but I saw plenty of blood," Melissande declared.

"She was wearing a white jacket. She was covered with a white blanket," Steff said. "If she'd cut her own throat, the blood would have soaked everything. I've slaughtered enough livestock on the farm to know how that goes. There was blood on the jacket, but the blanket was almost clean. She was killed someplace else, then taken down the tunnel."

Foley was nodding. "Most likely she was killed in the palace. If you live here and you end up with a body on your hands, you don't have too many places to dispose of it. Since we know from experience how hard it is to leave the grounds without being seen."

"But then that means—that means—" Melissande could not seem to get the words out.

"She was murdered," Corene said flatly.

Steff nodded. "The more I thought about it after we found the body, the more convinced I was."

"But who killed her?" Melissande said.

"Well, that's the question, of course," Steff replied.

"I don't think it was Greggorio," Corene said. "Though he would be the obvious suspect."

"He is too kindhearted," Melissande agreed.

"He's too weak," Alette said sternly. When they all gaped at her, she nodded emphatically. "It takes a great deal of nerve and conviction to kill someone. I do not believe Greggorio is that strong."

"I suppose in a way that's a compliment," Corene said doubtfully.

"In a way," Alette said, equally doubtful.

"And I don't think Filomara killed her," Corene said.

"Not with her own hands, no, but could she have ordered such a thing done?" Melissande asked. "I do not think *she* is too weak to flinch at murder."

Alette was nodding, but Foley shook his head. "She didn't do it," he said. "The body would never have been found if the empress was responsible. She's the one person who *could* have gotten a corpse off the premises—*aided* by the guards, not stopped by them."

"A most excellent point!" Melissande approved. "So we have now eliminated two suspects."

"Though I wouldn't have been surprised to learn Filomara *wanted* her dead," Corene said.

Melissande nodded. "Yes, because she disliked Sarona's relationship with Greggorio," she said. "I do think Greggorio is the key here. He might not be the killer, but someone at the palace didn't like how close he was to Sarona. He paid attention to her—so now she's dead."

Alette played an unexpected trump and elicited groans from everyone else at the table. Her voice was placid when she said, "If that's the case, then the next person to be murdered will be me."

Shock created space for a brief, airless silence, and then they all spoke at once. Corene was the one who managed to talk the loudest. "What do you *mean?*" she demanded.

Alette laid down a high horseshoe, and everyone numbly followed suit, still staring at her. "Greggorio has been very kind to me," she explained. "Until these last few days, he was the only one at the palace I thought might be a friend. It was not a—what is the word you use?— a boy-and-girl thing between us."

"Not romantic," Melissande murmured.

"Exactly. Merely, he saw I was unhappy and asked how he could help."

"He carried messages for you," Corene guessed. "That's how you got news from home that Filomara hadn't read."

"Yes."

"That *was* kind," Melissande agreed. "But I myself did not realize there was any kind of special bond between you, so perhaps it is not widely known."

"You're not jealously trying to win yourself a crown," Foley reminded her.

Her smile was blinding. "But I am!"

Corene frowned at Foley. "You're saying that Jiramondi and Garameno are the most likely murder suspects."

"There are other people who covet the throne," he said quietly. "The empress's brothers, for instance."

"Yes, I always overlook them because they are never here at court," Melissande admitted. "But it seems they have always been interested in the succession."

"Very interested," Corene said. "Jiramondi told me that everyone thinks Filomara's two oldest brothers poisoned each other in a fight over the throne."

"But there are many others equally invested in the succession," Foley went on. "Such as the prefect."

"Liramelli's father?" Steff said in outrage. "That's an insult!"

"I like Harlo, too," Corene said to him. "But we have to put him on the list of possibilities."

"No, we don't! We don't have to put anybody on the list! It's not up to us to *make* a list!"

She watched him steadily. "It is, if we want to survive this particular game. If someone wants to dispose of all rivals to the throne, there's another list and your name is at the top of it."

He threw his cards down, but his expression grew a little calmer. "I don't mind being in danger so much, but I can't stand wondering if any of my friends are killers."

"Really?" Melissande said softly. "You believe you have made friends at the Malinquese court? I spent most of my life in the Coziquela palace, and there might be five people there I would trust with my life. This is not your father's circle of steadfast friends, my dearest Steffanolo. These are not people who will come to help you if your barn blows down or your winter crops fail. These are people who would burn your barn and salt your fields and laugh when you lose everything you love."

This time the silence was longer and more profound as everyone considered what exactly Melissande had lived through to bring her to that bleak conclusion.

"Well, that's cynical," Steff said at last. "I wonder that you can convince yourself to stay, then, and keep maneuvering to win this crown for yourself."

"Because no court is any different," Melissande said sadly. "It would not matter where I went."

"There is life outside the royal courts," Steff answered.

Her voice was even sadder. "Not for me."

"We're straying from the main point," Corene said, her voice a little gruff. "If Sarona was murdered—"

"Well, she had to be," Steff interrupted.

"Then there is a killer living at the palace. And if he killed her because he—or she—wanted to control who will sit on the throne next—"

"Then the four of us are in danger," Melissande summed up.

Corene looked at Foley, whose habitually solemn face looked even more somber. "It might be time to leave," he said, and she nodded slowly.

"I'm staying," Steff said instantly. "I don't know yet what exactly my place will be in Malinqua, but the empress wants me here and I feel as if I belong. As if I have a part to play. I think we can discover who's behind the attack and take care of the danger that way."

"Well, I might go," Corene said. "*I* don't want to be murdered and thrown down a stairwell."

"You will find it difficult to leave," Alette said in her usual calm way. Her gaze was focused on her cards, and Corene assumed she would make one more devastating play. "The port is closed."

"*What?*" they all cried in unison.

She looked up in surprise. "Greggorio told me before they left. The harbor is virtually deserted."

"But why?" Corene exclaimed. "Because of Sarona?"

"Oh, no. Because Berringey has declared war on Malinqua."

It was infuriating and difficult to have to acquire information from scattered and unwilling sources, Corene discovered. She missed living in Darien's household, where everything worth knowing was always learned first. Darien was annoyingly closemouthed, of course, but Zoe divulged information freely and most of the servants were happy to act as Corene's spies.

In Malinqua, no one felt obligated to share the truth with Corene. She had to piece it together from the bits of knowledge she could extract from Emilita and Liramelli's parents, and supplement it with what Steff learned from Filomara and what Foley picked up from the soldiers he trained with among the royal guard.

Indeed, the king of Berringey had declared war on Malinqua, which apparently happened with some regularity. The empress had been expecting it. In fact, half the city had—and most merchants and homeowners had laid in supplies against hard times to come. No one expected the "war" to amount to more than a few skirmishes in the waters that lay a few miles off Palminera, but just in case, Filomara had thrown a tight net around the harbor and shored up fortifications along the mountainous region some five hundred miles to the west where Berringey and Malinqua shared a border.

"Leah tells me there's a smuggler's haven where goods can make it in and out of the city," Foley reported two days later. "But from the sounds of it, that's not a particularly safe exit. You'd have to slip out in a small boat and hope to connect with a larger vessel in deeper waters—and then hope to not get fired on or captured by Berringese warships. Yesterday, Leah said, two smaller boats were set on fire and only half the passengers made it back to shore. All things considered, you're probably better off here for the moment."

Corene found herself cast in turmoil and uncharacteristically undecided. Part of her wanted to leave *right now*, shake off the poisonous gloom of the Malinquese court and return to the familiar dissatisfactions of Welce. Part of her was curious to see what would happen next in Palminera, no matter how frightening or dramatic it was. And part of her, oddly, was reluctant to leave her new friends behind: Melissande, Liramelli, Alette, even Jiramondi—and, of course, Steff. She was unused to having friends, even ones she knew as little as she knew these five. At times she thought everyone else in her life had been family or adversary. Sometimes both.

"I suppose I'm safe enough as long as you're close by," she said at last. "At least no one's likely to slit my throat and shove me down to the storeroom."

"Unless they slit my throat, too."

She grimaced. "Thanks for that thought! Well, at least our corpses will keep each other company."

He offered the briefest of smiles. "Seriously, I think there is a danger here at the palace. But I think the danger is greater outside its walls."

She slanted a sideways look at him. "Is it time to write my father and beg for rescue?"

"You could, but Leah assures me she has already sent messages to Chialto. I would imagine half of the Welchin navy will be on hand within two ninedays."

"I can leave *then*, I suppose."

"I think you won't have much choice."

Back in her father's hands, under her father's protection. A failed adventure behind her and a pointless existence before her. Corene knew there were disasters in Alette's life—and apparently Melissande's as well—but from her perspective, her own situation didn't look much more appealing.

Still, better than being murdered, she thought.

"Till then—I suppose we just go on as we have so far," she said.

"With more care, perhaps," Foley said.

"And infinitely more questions."

She sprung some of those questions on Jiramondi the next day during their language lesson. She had improved enough at speaking Malinquese that she could read and understand complex passages, but she had trouble when she encountered unfamiliar words. She'd started bringing short lists to their tutoring sessions, and he would define them and walk her through the pronunciations.

This time she waited until the end of their lesson before producing five new words. "I overheard a few conversations in the halls, and these are the phrases that kept coming up," she said. "I might not have spelled them right."

"Let me see," he said, taking the paper from her hand. "Blockade . . . warship . . . battle . . ." His voice trailed off and he gazed at her ruefully.

She tried to keep her own expression guileless, but it had never been her most convincing look. "It all sounds very ferocious," she said.

He sighed and laid the paper down. "What do you know?"

"Berringey has declared war on Malinqua, the Malinquese navy is patrolling the waters, and nobody has even *mentioned* it to me. Or any of your other royal guests, as far as I can tell."

"We didn't want you to be alarmed."

"I find it even more alarming to be lied to."

"You're safe as long as you stay inside the walls."

"Unless Berringey defeats the Malinquese navy and destroys the harbor and comes storming through the city, setting the whole place on fire."

"That won't happen. You're safe here," he repeated.

She decided to push him, just to see what he'd say. "I don't feel safe. I feel like it might be time to return to Welce."

"You can't leave," he said.

"Because I can't get past the Berringese blockade?"

He didn't answer, just began rearranging the papers and books on the table. She waited a moment, feeling a growing sense of consternation.

"Or because the empress won't *allow* me to leave?" she asked quietly.

He glanced up quickly enough to meet her eyes, and then dropped his gaze.

"So it is as it seems," Corene said. "The empress's men are so assiduous not merely to keep us from harm but to keep us *here*. And why is that, I wonder?"

He just shook his head. Corene leaned back in her chair, crossed her arms, and surveyed him. Her mind was racing; she was startled to find that she was more intrigued than dismayed.

"So we're hostages—Alette, Melissande, and me," she mused. "But hostages for what?"

Again, he didn't answer, so she continued thinking out loud, "I don't know how Melissande's mother will react, but as soon as my father hears that I'm being held against my will in the middle of a war zone, he will send the Welchin navy here with all speed."

"Yes," Jiramondi said.

Corene straightened up so quickly she felt the bones in her spine snap in place. "You *wanted* Welce and Cozique to send their warships!" she exclaimed. "You're tired of Berringey's constant petty attacks and you thought a show of force would discourage them once and for all from harassing your borders."

"But we're a small nation with no additional resources for war," Jiramondi said tiredly.

"And when Filomara made the rounds, looking to drum up military support, none of the other nations of the southern seas were interested," Corene supplied. "So she found a way to *get* them interested."

"Yes."

"But you can't think that will work," Corene said. "If you're holding us captive, my father and Melissande's mother will join with the Berringey army, not yours!"

"Maybe they would," Jiramondi said, "if that's the way the situation was presented to them."

"But since you are monitoring all our communications—"

"Yes."

"All they know is what you tell them," Corene finished up.

"Yes."

"Although you must be aware that I can find ways to communicate with my father in secret," she said. "And I presume Melissande must have similar channels open to her mother."

"No doubt," Jiramondi said. "But it doesn't matter what you tell them *now*. The Berringese navies are already here. If you are at risk, it is from Berringey, not Malinqua. They *have* to come to our aid."

She sat back in her chair and regarded him, still so surprised that she couldn't summon outrage, though that was, she knew, the proper reaction. "You'll start a war that embroils four nations of the southern seas—and for what?"

"To push back hard at Berringey," he said. "To give ourselves a little breathing room against a most aggressive neighbor."

"Who came up with this strategy? Filomara?"

He was silent.

"She can be crafty, I know, but this seems more convoluted than her usual style," Corene said. "Was it Garameno? Oh, I saw you flinch when I said his name. So it was. Were you in the room as this plan was being hatched?"

"No," he said, as if he couldn't help himself. "I thought it was a terrible idea."

"So then is the whole notion of a royal marriage simply a ruse?"

"That's the beauty of the plan," Jiramondi said. "*Both* parts of it are true. You're collateral *and* you're potential marriage partners."

"As long as we don't realize the bit about being collateral. Which would probably make all of us less interested in being marriage partners."

Jiramondi stared at her hopelessly. "Right."

"You must realize that I'll repeat our entire conversation to Alette and Melissande."

A ghost of a smile touched his lips. "They won't care, of course. You were always the only one who would be offended."

She was about to offer a hot retort, but a moment's thought convinced her he was right. Melissande would merely shrug her dainty shoulders—*Well, each one of them was an imperfect husband all along, so this hardly matters*—and Alette had no illusions to begin with. She had always expected to be the lowliest game piece on a complex and brutal board. She had always expected to be misused.

"I am beginning to hate you all," Corene said.

"Really?" Jiramondi replied. "I would have thought you would have hated us from the beginning."

Corene could hardly wait to repeat the entire conversation to Foley the first chance she got. Which wasn't until later that evening when dinner was over and everyone had finally scattered. She motioned Foley to follow her inside her room, then flung herself onto the settee. He more gracefully sat in a chair across from her, and listened attentively while she poured out the tale.

"Now many of the empress's actions make more sense," Foley said when she was done. "But it's still outrageous."

"My father will be furious," Corene said. "I know ships are already on the way, but I don't think I'll share this information until I'm safely onboard. It would only make matters worse."

"*You* don't seem as angry as I might expect," Foley said.

Corene considered. "I'm disgusted more than angry," she admitted. "And part of me is not even surprised. This is always how schemers behave at court—*any* court. Always looking for the slim advantage, and not caring who gets hurt in the process. It's so distasteful. I'm starting to think I don't want to marry a prince after all."

"Maybe you don't want to marry one from Malinqua," he said. "But there's a prince or a high-born lord somewhere in your future."

"I like that future less and less."

"You're just tired," he said. "You've run headlong toward that future ever since I've known you."

"Well, I think it's time to slow down and think about it a little harder," she retorted. "Some people never marry, and they have very good lives. Maybe I'll be one of those people."

Foley looked doubtful. "Maybe."

She was tired of talking about Malinqua and her own increasingly dismal prospects, so she changed the direction of the conversation without even trying to be subtle. "What about you?" she asked. "Are you one of those people who might never take a wife?"

He was silent a moment, then he shrugged. "Maybe," he said again.

"But royal guards are allowed to marry, aren't they?"

"Of course they are. Or no one would ever sign up to be a royal guard."

"So that isn't something you'd want sometime?" she asked. "A little house, a pretty wife, a few kids running around in the gardens, picking all the flowers and knocking over the wheelbarrows?"

He grinned at the description but shrugged unenthusiastically. "I guess. Sometime. It seems awfully settled."

"But you're such a settled kind of man," she argued. "So calm and steady."

He looked affronted. "You make me sound boring."

She laughed. "I didn't mean to! It's just that you're such an orderly person. I'd think you'd want an orderly life."

He shook his head. "Maybe that's why I don't mind when there's chaos churning around me. It makes my world considerably more interesting. If I'm on my own, life is too dull."

"Well, I think there's plenty of chaos when you're raising children," she pointed out. "They're always making messes and getting into trouble. Zoe says that she's not so much raising a daughter as making sure Celia doesn't inadvertently kill herself."

"From what I've seen of small children, that's a good description," he agreed.

"And since your whole job for years and *years* has been to make sure people don't come to harm, you'd be an excellent father."

"I hope so," he said, still without enthusiasm.

"Of course, you'd have to find the right wife first."

"Not quite ready for that."

"But if you were," she prompted. "What would she be like?"

He looked at her helplessly a moment. She could see him wondering how he had ever allowed her to get him on this topic to begin with. "I haven't given it any thought."

"Well, what kinds of girls have you been attracted to in the past? Tall? Short? Plump? Thin? Talkative and friendly, or quiet and shy?"

"I haven't—there have been different—I don't think this is even something we should be talking about," he floundered.

It was a rare treat to see Foley at a loss, and she pressed the advantage. "Let's imagine a tall girl with blond hair and a quiet manner. Is that the kind of woman you would like?"

"You've just described Josetta."

She laughed. "I know. But would you?"

"You know the answer to that."

"So, not elay," Corene pursued. "I don't see you with a torz girl. Too much like you. Then your life would be *really* boring."

"Thanks," he said sarcastically.

"Maybe a hunti wife? She'd like you because you'd always stand firm and provide support when she needed it. Though, again, that marriage might be a little dull."

She could tell by his expression he could see where this conversation was going and didn't like it. So he tried to outmaneuver her. "I'd have to go with coru, I suppose. All the girls I've ever liked have been women of blood and water. Endlessly changing and endlessly fascinating."

She made her face limpid with innocence. "But you never wanted to stay with any of those girls, did you?" she said sweetly. "Obviously, you need to take a sweela lover."

But he was ready for her. "Sweela girls only play at love—that's what everybody says," he answered. "Not a good match for a torz man. He'd give her his whole heart and she'd just break it and toss it aside."

"No, she wouldn't," Corene said indignantly. "Not if she was the *right* sweela girl."

"Oh, of course. The sweela girl who lives in the little house and raises a garden and leads a simple life," he responded. "Who doesn't miss the excitement of court and the attention of the titled lords who come to visit. *That* sweela girl?"

Corene hunched her shoulders. "You make me sound very shallow."

He affected surprise. "I didn't realize we were talking about you."

"Well, we started out by talking in generalities, but then you got specific," she said with great dignity.

Now Foley grinned. "I don't think it does us any good to try to come up with a description of my ideal wife," he said. "Either I'll meet her or I won't, and I'll realize it's her or I won't. Either way, I think my life will be pretty good."

"But don't you want that?" she asked, and even she could hear the wistfulness in her voice. "Love? Someone who waits for you at the door, someone whose day isn't complete unless she sees your face? Someone who will love you even when you're angry, even when you're ugly, even when you don't love yourself? Doesn't everybody want that?"

He was silent so long that she felt a skip in her heartbeat. His face was still shuttered, but she thought his eyes looked sad. "Is that what you think you'll find in your own marriage to some royal heir?" he asked softly.

She hunched her shoulders again, protectively this time, as if bracing for a blow. "No, of course not," she said, trying to sound matter of fact. "I was talking about ordinary girls. The kind I'm never going to be, remember?"

He watched her a moment. "You'll never be ordinary," he said at last. "But everyone deserves that kind of love."

"But you won't go looking for it and I can't be expected to find it," she said, managing a wisp of laughter.

"Maybe you'll be surprised," he said. "I hope so."

"Maybe you will be, too," she said.

He nodded and came to his feet. "I've had a lot of other surprises," he said, heading for the door. "So maybe."

She stood up and followed him so she could lock up behind him. "I've had surprises, too," she agreed, "but most of them weren't that nice."

He put a hand on the door, hesitated, then turned back to her. "One thing—" he began, and then abruptly shut up.

She stepped closer, feeling strangely breathless. "What? 'One thing' what?"

He made a slight, controlled gesture. "If you do marry some prince. And if he isn't what you expect. What you hope. If he's worse than that, if he's *awful*. You can let me know. It doesn't matter where you're living, what country you're in. Send word to me and I'll come for you. I'll get you out of there, I'll get you home. I'll make sure you're safe."

As if her heart suddenly pumped out molten blood, she felt heat spread from her chest through every part of her body. Her toes and fingers tingled and she knew her face flushed red. But she smiled at him. "That's good to know," she said softly. "You can bet I'll take you up on your offer if I have to! No matter where I am and who I've taken for a husband. I'll know I won't have to stay. I'll know I can count on you."

"Always," he said.

"There haven't been too many other people I could always count on."

"There haven't been too many other people I've made promises to."

"Then I'm even more grateful."

There was more to say—there had to be, though Corene couldn't think of a single word—and anyway, Foley didn't stick around to hear what she might come up with when she finally organized her thoughts. He just nodded once, very businesslike, and stepped into the hall, closing the door firmly behind him. She was left staring at the place he had been standing, feeling her blood still burning like liquor in her veins, and wondering what it might be like to someday be rescued by Foley.

FIFTEEN

Since the air at the palace was suffocating, Corene spent part of every day outside in some excursion: shopping at the Great Market for accessories to wear to the masked gala, for instance, or visiting the small Welchin temple in the Little Islands that Leah had told her about. She never went alone, of course. Foley was always at her side, though he managed to be taciturn enough that she couldn't find an opportunity for another one of those deliciously unnerving conversations about the kinds of people they might marry.

He wasn't her only attendant. Malinquese guards inevitably escorted her, and the other women usually accompanied her as well. Occasionally Steff came along, and even Jiramondi joined them for the expedition to the temple.

Jiramondi had been right when he predicted that neither Melissande nor Alette would be disturbed to learn they were hostages in Malinqua. At any rate, neither of them seemed to blame him for their circumstances. Despite her best efforts, Corene also found it difficult to hate him, though she couldn't resist taking little digs at him whenever an opportunity presented itself. For instance, she scoffed out loud when he drew blessings at the temple and they turned out to be patience, honor, and triumph.

"*One* of those at least doesn't apply to you," she said with a sniff, but he merely smiled and tossed the coins back into the barrel.

She found her own blessings even more unnerving: courage, courage, and courage. She threw them all back before anyone could ask her to decipher them.

They had all been glad, upon returning from the temple outing, to find that Liramelli and Greggorio were back from their travels. However, their presence at the dinner table didn't do much to dispel the gloom that had shrouded the dining hall in recent days. Greggorio looked drawn and haunted, as if he hadn't bothered to eat much for the past nineday, and when he did, his meals were attended by ghosts. He had taken a seat beside Alette at the half-empty table and the two of them held a brief, low-voiced conversation that everyone else pretended they were not trying to overhear. Corene couldn't answer for anyone else in the room, but she couldn't catch a word.

Liramelli looked less haunted but equally sad, and barely bothered to answer Jiramondi's kind attempts at conversation. Neither Garameno nor Filomara was present, and Corene suspected that meant they were taking their evening meal together in the empress's private quarters, hatching some new plot. Even so, it was hard to be sorry they were missing.

"Come to my room after the meal—I have some things to show you," Corene invited Liramelli as they all rose from the table. She nodded at Steff, Melissande, and Alette, and the other three followed her from the dining room.

Foley stayed in the hallway as the five of them entered Corene's suite. "I've been shopping," she said to Liramelli as she shut the door. "I've bought such pretty things for you!"

Steff appeared horrified. "You're not going to sit here and talk about *clothes* all night, are you?" he demanded.

"Maybe, and maybe we shall talk about other exciting things, too, but you will not be in the room to hear because you are a silly boy who is afraid of fashion," Melissande said.

"I'm not afraid of it, it's *boring*!" he exclaimed. "I thought we'd play penta or talk about something that *mattered*."

Liramelli offered an exhausted smile. "Maybe I can see the pretty things tomorrow," she suggested. "When I can appreciate them more."

Melissande drew Liramelli down next to her on one of the sofas, while the other three settled in chairs nearby. "Do you want to tell us about your journey?" Melissande asked. "Or will that only make you more sad?"

A slight shudder shook Liramelli's shoulders; weariness made her pale, plain face even paler and plainer. "Greggorio scarcely spoke the whole time we were in the carriage," she said. "I started babbling, just to fill the silence, just to distract him, because he seemed to be in so much pain. And we'd been traveling for about two hours when he suddenly said, 'I thought she left me. I was angry with her. I almost hated her. And all this time—' And then he started crying." She shook her head. "It was horrible. I hugged him and tried to say nice things, but what kinds of things can you say that will do any good?"

"None, but of course you have to *try*," said Melissande.

"Then at her parents' house it was even worse. Everyone in mourning, everyone blaming themselves for not realizing that Sarona hadn't just run away."

"See, that's the part I don't understand," Corene said, frowning. "Where did everybody think Sarona would *go*? If she'd run away from Greggorio, wouldn't she have sent a note to her parents? If she'd run away from her parents, wouldn't she have gotten in touch with Greggorio? If her parents thought Filomara had shipped her off somewhere, wouldn't they have come to Palminera and caused a commotion? *Somebody* should have known where she was."

"That's the saddest part of all," Liramelli agreed. "Everyone believed she had left *them*. They assumed she *had* told someone else— someone she actually cared about."

"Thus we see very plainly the perils of being a woman with no true friends," Melissande pronounced. When Liramelli made a faint protest, Melissande shook her head. "You cannot pretend she was a nice person just because she is now dead. Everyone has said she was vain and manipulative—which Greggorio never realized, but then we all know he is a stupid man—and her murderer took advantage of that fact. He gambled that everyone would assume Sarona had confided in someone *else*. And he was right. Or she, of course."

"Well, let me say right now that I don't plan on running off without a word to anybody," Steff said. "So if I vanish in the middle of the night, come looking for my body."

"*Steff!*" Liramelli exclaimed.

Melissande was nodding. "I do think there are people at court who would like to see you dead," she said to him. "You cannot be too careful."

"The last time I ran away, I left a note," Corene said. "So I'm with Steff. I'll let you know if I'm planning to disappear. And I'll take Foley with me."

Alette spoke up in her smoky voice. "I would happily leave without a word if I thought I could get safely out," she said. "But if I thought any of you would worry, I would try to let someone know before I slipped away."

"Please do," Corene said. "Or leave a clue behind. A secret message."

"Yes! A code that only the five of us know!" Melissande cried. She pointed at Alette, who, as usual, was wearing her yellow shawl. "Leave that tied in a knot in the middle of your bed."

Alette pulled the edges closer to her heart. "Oh no. This is the one thing I would be sure to take with me."

"Your blessings. Leave them behind on your pillow," Melissande suggested. "Corene, you must go through your little bag of coins and give us each the blessings we drew the other day."

"I would, but I don't have extras," Corene objected. "We can find cheap replicas in the Little Islands."

"That will not do us any good if one of us decides to run away tonight."

Corene laughed. "Then throw some Malinquese coins on your pillow and the rest of us will understand what you meant."

"That'll work," Steff said. "But I still don't plan to run away."

"I don't think you could if you wanted to," Corene said with a sigh. "So we may as well find ways to entertain ourselves."

"I have thought of the best idea for tomorrow's outing," Melissande announced. "We shall visit the white tower. We intended to go many ninedays ago before—well—our plans changed."

The others murmured their assent while trying hard not to glance at Alette, but Corene gave the Dhonshon girl a straight and level look. "Yes, I would love to visit the tower," Corene said. "But *you* have to promise you won't do anything drastic, or I won't let you come."

"*Corene!*" Liramelli murmured, but Alette actually smiled.

"I will behave quite properly," she said. "You will not need to worry about me at all."

The visit to the white tower became more of an expedition than Corene would have liked, since it seemed that *everyone* wanted to join them, even Greggorio and Garameno. She supposed the activity would be good for Greggorio, who still looked shocked with grief, but by the time they added Garameno and his attendant, there were ten of them setting out. Accompanied, of course, by twice that many royal guards and surreptitious Dhonshon soldiers that Alette quietly identified as her father's men.

"There's so many of us we could practically invade another country," Corene muttered to Foley as they assembled in the courtyard.

"Or defend ourselves against foreign armies," he replied.

She sighed. "Which, unfortunately, is more likely."

Today they had dispensed with the carriages and rode horses instead, though Corene wasn't sure who had made that decision. Steff was a natural rider, of course—probably because of all those years spent around farm animals—and the other three women were equally adept on horseback. Corene had never spent much time in the saddle, since her mother despised unnecessary activity and her father was the consummate city man. But old King Vernon's first wife had insisted that the princesses learn every noble skill, and she'd taken them out for long ninedays in the country to practice riding and hunting. Corene had been delighted at the invention of elaymotives, which didn't require horses; she wouldn't mind if she never saw a horse again for the rest of her life.

Still, she managed to control her animal creditably enough as they all gathered in the courtyard. She was interested to see that, with the help of his man, Garameno was able to clamber aboard and strap himself tightly into the saddle, where he looked extremely comfortable. She guided her piebald mare in his direction.

"Just from the way you sit, I can tell you're an excellent horseman," she greeted him.

He smiled over at her—*down* at her, actually, which was an odd sensation. She was so used to him looking up at her from his chair. But she could tell now that he was a taller man than she had ever realized, with wide shoulders and powerful forearms. In fact, from this angle, she could see that he was built very much like the athletic Greggorio. "I love to ride," Garameno admitted. "Whenever I'm in the country, I pick the best horse in the stable and race as fast as I can go."

About half the empress's guards clattered out of the courtyard, and the royal party fell in behind them—Liramelli and Steff in the lead, Garameno and Corene at the back of the column. Foley was just behind them, and the rest of the royal soldiers took up the rear.

"You're not afraid the horse will stumble and throw you?" Corene asked. "It might be tricky for you to remount."

Garameno's eyes gleamed; she wondered if it had been indelicate to point out that Garameno might face challenges another rider might not. Then she remembered what Greggorio had told her on her very first evening at the palace—it was a riding accident that had left Garameno so gravely injured. So it *had* been an indelicate question, though now she wished she'd asked a different one: *Are you afraid every time you climb back in the saddle?* She would be terrified, she was sure. Though she was probably just stubborn enough to do it again anyway.

When Garameno replied, his voice was unruffled. "I don't go alone, of course," he replied. "I would advocate that nobody should."

"No, I am just clumsy enough to fall and hit my head," she agreed. "I would never go riding by myself. Actually, I never go riding just for pleasure since it's not something I'm good at."

"And yet you look completely at ease on horseback."

She laughed. "You're just being gallant."

"People accuse me of that so often," he murmured, which made her laugh again.

"Normally that's not my adjective for you," she agreed. "Clever. Crafty. Maybe even scheming. In so many ways, you remind me of my father."

"You flatter me."

"I wasn't trying to."

He smiled. "Oh, I forgot. You ran away from your father."

"That's what happens to people who try to control everyone around them," she said. "They turn everyone into a rebel."

"I don't try to control people," Garameno said. "Sometimes I try to control circumstances."

"It ends up being the same thing."

"More benign, I would think."

"I'm not sure I would agree."

He turned his head to survey her. His eyes were cool and assessing; again, she noticed how different he seemed when he watched her from horseback. "But then, you speak as someone who doesn't bother to exercise any control at all," he said softly. He was smiling but it wasn't a particularly pleasant smile. "Over your temper—your tongue—even your wild red hair."

When she laughed, she could see it surprised him; he had expected to make her angry. "And I thought I had been so well-behaved here in Malinqua."

"So far," he said. "But something about you always suggests the possibility you will throw a tantrum."

"That's what so many people think about me," she said cheerfully. "But I learned self-restraint in the *cradle*. I know exactly what words are dangerous to say and what emotions I'd better not show if I want to survive at court." She leaned a little closer, over the gulf that lay between their two horses as they jogged along. "So if I behave badly, I do it on purpose. Not because I can't help myself—but because I don't care about the consequences."

He continued to watch her a few more moments in silence, and Corene took the opportunity to glance around. Until this point, they had covered familiar ground, taking the straight road that led to the iron gates. Their party was so large that most of the rest of the traffic had pressed to either side of the street to allow them to pass. The majority of the onlookers watched with curiosity and even excitement, waving to the royal party and calling out some of their names. Corene saw Jiramondi and Greggorio wave in response; Garameno seemed too intent on her to pay attention to the crowds.

Just now, they were trotting past the gate, leaving the relative safety of the walled city, and the royal guards drew a little closer on all sides. Liramelli called something out to the lead rider and the whole party turned north, toward the gleaming white tower with its scoop of moon resting at the top.

"I think you do care about the consequences," Garameno said at last. "If you make a fuss, it's because you want to be noticed. You don't care if people are angry at you. You only care if people are ignoring you."

That was a blow straight to the gut, but Corene didn't allow her reaction to show. Instead she favored him with a slight, quizzical smile. "So I'm not a rebel, you think, merely a spoiled child?"

"More interesting than that," he said. "Someone capable of abandon."

"I think I liked it better when you were being gallant."

He laughed. "I intended it as a compliment."

"Did you?"

"I don't take you for granted, Princess Corene. That's all I'm trying to say."

It wasn't; he was trying to warn her, though she wasn't sure of the precise message. Maybe he just wanted her to know that he was paying attention. That he knew she didn't mind stirring up trouble—and he didn't mind being ruthless in quashing it. *So what happens when the girl capable of abandon meets the man who tries to control every situation?* she wondered. *Who wins, who loses? Is the man overwhelmed, or does the girl disappear?*

And that led her to the next silent question. *What was Sarona capable of—and did Garameno try to control* her?

But when she replied, her voice and her words were demure. "I'm glad you don't take me for granted," she said. "I like it when people realize I'm in the room."

"Yes," he said, "I'm sure you do."

By this time their cavalcade had turned onto a wide boulevard leading toward the tower. Up till now, all of Corene's excursions had been through the southern portions of the city, so she looked around with interest. The basic architecture was similar, most of the buildings being only two or three stories high, and most constructed of wood or stone in red, white, or marbled colors. But here everything looked crisper somehow, as if the stone hadn't had time to wear down with decades of use.

It seemed a reasonable time to change the subject to something much more conventional. "This part of town seems cleaner and fresher," she observed. "Is it newer?"

"Yes, by about a hundred years," Garameno said. "When the city was first laid out, the castle was built at the northernmost edge in the center of the labyrinth. Everything farther north was open land. At that time," he added, "there were dozens of nomadic clans that roamed in the flatlands and hills." He waved vaguely in the direction of the tower. "Occasionally they'd form some uneasy alliance and elect a temporary leader and attack the smaller towns and homesteads. Because there were miles of open land north of the palace, the royal watch could see the raiding parties for hours before they arrived and they could always assemble troops to greet them. The clans never mounted a successful attack against the palace."

"Sounds exciting," Corene commented. "So when was it safe to start building the city up this way?"

"Oh, the clans died out decades ago. They say there are still remnants up in the mountains between Berringey and Malinqua—wild men and women who live by no law but their own—but they haven't been a real presence for at least a hundred years. As the land grew more settled, the city stretched northward. The inexorable march of civilization."

"And what about the white tower? Was it built before or after the city came this far?"

"Before," said Garameno. "I understand it was even more spectacular then, especially at night—this lone beacon of light surrounded by miles of emptiness, almost like a star fallen to the middle of the ocean. There are paintings of it, back at the palace, if you'd like to see them. Stunning, actually."

"Yes, that sounds most impressive."

"There's a whole gallery of paintings of the landmarks of Malinqua. There's a plain west of the city where the grass is always purple. No one knows why. When it's transplanted, the colors gradually shift to green. They suspect some mineral in the soil, but even our eminent scientists haven't been able to isolate it. Anyway, there must be several dozen paintings of that, as well."

"I'd like to visit that spot someday."

"I hope you shall."

For the rest of their ride, he divided his time between describing other local beauties and pointing out key sights along their route— several of the scientific institutes that Filomara was so proud of, the homes of two well-known artists, a music school, a couple of open-air markets that were not nearly as big as the more famous venue to the south. Corene was heartily sick of Palminera's attractions by the time they finally arrived at the white tower.

It appeared to be roughly as big as its red counterpart, its base the size of a bedroom suite back at the royal palace. The soldiers deployed around it while the royal party gathered at the entrance, a wide rectangular opening twice as high as a man.

"I suppose you plan to climb to the top?" Garameno asked Corene.

"I suppose I do."

"Then I will await you here. Of course."

She nodded and swung down from the saddle, already a little sore from the unaccustomed exercise. Most of the others in their party had dismounted as well, though Jiramondi and Melissande stayed on horseback.

"I do not have the slightest desire to traipse up *endless* stairs and begin gasping for breath and look altogether ridiculous," Melissande explained. "All of you go. Go. We will amuse ourselves in some manner. Perhaps we will debate what we should wear to the empress's festival."

"Yes, because I am always interested in discussing fashion," Garameno said sardonically.

Jiramondi was amused. "But there are so many questions to answer!" he exclaimed. "A partial mask or one that covers your entire face? Clothing in your usual style so that everyone knows who you are, or an entirely different sort of ensemble, so no one will guess your identity? These are important matters."

"I am so glad you agree," Melissande said.

Corene laughed and waited until all the others who wanted to make the climb had dismounted from their horses. Foley was among them. He didn't say so, but Corene was sure it was because at the *last* tower, the excitement had occurred at the very top, while he had waited below. He did not want to be absent if anything dramatic occurred again.

All in all, six of them stepped from the outer sunshine to the inner shadows and looked around as their eyes adjusted to the change in light. This tower was essentially a mirror image of the southern one, with a similar wood-and-metal stairway winding up and up and up the tall spire. The lighting was the same as well—a translucent tube that traced a thin line of illumination all the way to the distant top.

But despite the similarities in construction, the place had an entirely different *feel*, Corene thought. The fire at the crown of the red tower had generated enough heat to raise the temperature inside the whole column, and the light it had thrown down through its glass petals was flickering and warm, especially as it played off the rough cinnamon walls. But the smooth white stones of the northern tower seemed to absorb light, not play it back, and the fixed glow that filtered down from the white crystal was as chilly as starlight. The whole place felt cold as winter. Corene suddenly wished she'd brought a heavier jacket.

"It's different here," Alette said.

Corene nodded. "I was thinking the same thing."

"I like the flame tower better," Liramelli agreed. "Although sometimes if I'm in a certain mood—if I want to think something through very carefully—I find that this is a good place to come. It's very still. You can focus your mind."

"Not my mind," Corene said. "The place just makes me cold."

"You'll warm up fast enough once you start climbing," Steff said. He jerked his chin at Greggorio. "Want to race to the top again?"

Greggorio looked more animated than he had at any time since Sarona's death. "It's the only reason I came along. I'm taking the outer edge this time, remember?"

"Oh, I wouldn't forget that."

They positioned themselves at the bottom of the stairwell, each of them with one foot on the first step, jostling each other good-naturedly. "Someone give us the signal to start," Steff called.

"Are you ready?" Corene said. "Then—*go!*"

They took off with whoops and curses, their boots pounding on the wood and metal. Foley tipped his head to critically watch their progress, but none of the women could be bothered to care.

"They're crazy," Corene remarked.

Liramelli sighed. "I wish I had that much energy."

"Well, if you did, you'd use it for something more productive," Corene answered. She waved toward the stairs. "You two go first. Foley and I will come after you."

"Are you sure? I climb pretty slowly," Liramelli said.

Corene laughed. "So do I."

Alette didn't argue, just put her fingertips against the curved wall and began the laborious ascent. Like the stairwell at the red towers, this one had no outer railing, and Liramelli clearly wasn't comfortable without a handhold, so she followed Alette, her own hand brushing the wall. Corene waited until Liramelli had cleared a few steps before beginning her own climb. Foley fell in step beside her.

She glanced over at him. "You're not afraid of falling off the edge?"

He shook his head. "I tend to have a pretty good sense of balance." He glanced up, where they could glimpse the nimble forms of Greggorio and Steff bounding up the stairs. The sounds of their laughter and their heavy footfalls still drifted down to the rest of them, but more faintly now. "That may change when we're about halfway there."

"Yes, that's about when I started getting dizzy in the other tower," Corene agreed.

"You don't have to make the climb," Foley told her. "Just to prove you're not afraid to do it."

She laughed a little breathlessly. Great, only a few steps up and she was already panting. "I don't do *everything* just to prove a point."

He smiled faintly. "My mistake."

"I'm curious," she said. "I want to see what makes this tower different."

"And what's your impression so far?"

"I think Josetta would like it."

"It does have an elay feel to it," he agreed.

"But *I* find it a little spooky. I don't like the light. I think it would give me a headache to be here very long."

"Well, I don't expect we'll linger."

They didn't talk much more during the rest of the climb, which seemed to take forever. Corene couldn't shake the idea that she was running out of air, as if she was nearing the peak of some windswept stony mountain where the atmosphere was almost too thin to breathe, and with every step she took, the oxygen seemed to grow scarcer. Beside her, Foley wasn't struggling at all, and both Liramelli and Alette seemed to be climbing at the same sturdy, determined pace, so Corene assumed she was simply imagining the pressure building in her lungs. That didn't make the experience any more pleasant.

At least it grew easier to see the closer they drew to the top. The white light spilled over the edges of its metal cradle so that, as they climbed upward, they seemed to be moving straight into a phosphorescent fog so dense Corene could almost feel it settling against her skin. Her hand seemed pearled with white—as she assumed her face did—as Foley's did when she glanced over at him.

"You look like a ghost," she told him, managing to inhale just enough air to speak.

"So do you," he answered. "And your hair is glowing. Like a fire that you see through a frost-covered window."

She would have laughed except she couldn't spare the breath.

Finally, finally, they reached the upper limit of the stairwell, and Greggorio and Steff were on hand to pull them through the trapdoor. An impudent wind swirled around them at this height, making the air even colder, but Corene didn't mind because it delivered air to her famished lungs. She wrapped her hands around the thin railing that crowned the tower and just stood there a moment, trying to restore her balance and slow her heartbeat.

"Who won the race?" Liramelli asked.

"I did!" Steff replied. "I think whoever's on the inside always wins."

"You should race somewhere else," Liramelli said. "Along a flat surface. Where neither runner has an advantage."

"The point is the challenge of going up the tower," Steff told her. "A regular race wouldn't be nearly as much fun."

Corene let their words wash over her, but didn't take part in the conversation. Once she'd caught her breath, she turned to study the glowing heart of the tower. It was bigger than she'd expected, fully as tall as she was, a great white globe of quartz that appeared to have been cut in half and securely nested in a metal base. Its rounded surface was smooth as glass, but in its milky depths she could see faults and fractures that added complex internal layers. The eerie white emanation didn't fluctuate like gaslight or fire, though Garameno had once told Corene that the light was produced when the crystal had absorbed enough heat. She leaned over far enough to touch the slick stone with her fingertip and found the globe cool to the touch. She could not entirely repress a shiver.

Turning away from the quartz, she gazed at the vista below. Just as it had from the crown of the red tower, the city looked calm and somewhat surreal, like a painted or imaginary place. She strained her eyes to see the harbor, wondering if she could spot the blockade, but all she could make out was a haze of infinite blue and specks of color that might be naval ships and might be reflections off the water.

More intriguing was the view toward the north and west. Although, as Garameno had said, the city had expanded enough to engulf the tower, it petered out only a few miles past it, devolving into small, isolated neighborhoods that appeared to be half town and half farmland. Beyond those outposts of civilization, the land opened up to what might be rocky prairie—vast sweeps of empty space that sprawled toward a faraway serrated horizon line. Those were the mountains separating Berringey and Malinqua, Corene guessed, unless her eyes were playing tricks on her and she couldn't really see that far. But Garameno had clearly been right; any enemy hordes racing across these plains would have been visible for miles. No wonder the clans had never mounted a successful invasion.

No, to do any real damage, an adversary would have to attack by sea.

She was still staring at the distant horizon when Alette came to stand quietly beside her. The other girl also appeared to be studying the jagged gray line that seemed to mark the end of the world. "So that way lies Berringey?" she asked.

"I think so."

"It doesn't seem so very far away."

"Maybe that's what happens when you can see your neighbors," Corene remarked. "You want what you think they have."

Liramelli moved carefully around the circular walkway to join them. "I'm too cold to stay up here," she said. "I'm going back down."

"I'm right after you," Corene said. "Magnificent view, but I've seen enough."

The descent was quicker than the climb and accomplished without incident. Emerging on ground level into the open air, Corene was surprised to find that the temperature felt at least ten degrees warmer.

"I don't think I'll need to climb that tower again," she observed to Liramelli. "It's such an odd place."

"Garameno and Jiramondi love it," Liramelli replied.

"Really? Garameno's been to the top recently?"

Liramelli nodded. "He usually goes up once or twice a year. They have a relay team to carry him up the stairs—so, of course, after all that effort, he stays for a couple of hours."

Corene glanced at the cousins, currently having a private colloquy from horseback while Melissande politely waited out of earshot, looking bored. Soldiers were fetching the horses that had been tethered a few yards away while the six of them were in the tower. Greggorio and Steff were engaged in what seemed to be a good-natured argument, while Alette had wandered in the direction of a small shop that appeared to sell baked goods. Corene couldn't blame her; she was suddenly hungry as well.

"I can see why Garameno didn't want to be hauled up on someone's back while the rest of us were running up and down the stairs, but I'm surprised Jiramondi didn't come with us, if he's so fond of the place," Corene said.

"I think he doesn't enjoy the experience when a lot of other people are around," Liramelli replied. "Trust me, the white tower has an entirely different feel when you're the only one at the top."

Corene supposed that was true, but she couldn't imagine that she would want to *intensify* the experience, so she didn't intend to find out. "Well, I'm glad I got to see it, but once was enough. But I'd go back to the red tower any day."

Liramelli smiled. "That's because you're a—What's your word?— *smeela* girl."

"*Sweela*. And yes."

"Sometimes I think—"

Her thought went unspoken. Greggorio tore past them at a run, his voice raised to shout a single word.

"*Alette!*"

SIXTEEN

Corene spun around to see what was happening and loosed her own cry of horror. Two men had grabbed Alette—one gripped her by the shoulders, one by the knees—and they were awkwardly running toward a cart where two more men were waiting. Alette was writhing furiously in their hold, kicking and clawing, but it was clear she was overmatched. Corene saw her bright yellow shawl trampled on the ground outside the bakery.

"Alette!" Liramelli shrieked, and then they were all chasing after her, those on foot, those on horseback. Jiramondi and Garameno were the fastest, thundering by so recklessly Corene had to jerk Liramelli out of the way of the flying hooves. Foley was just seconds behind them, already mounted. Corene saw the gleam of something metallic in his hand, and it looked far deadlier than the tool he'd lent Steff to pry open the door to the storerooms.

Behind them came a flurry of royal soldiers, also armed, then Steff, and finally Melissande.

"What's happening?" Liramelli shouted up at her, because someone on horseback had a much better view of the action than those on the ground. "Can you see?"

"Greggorio has reached her! He is *punching* one of the other men—Oh, he is so angry! And the second man, he has had to release Alette to fight back. She is on the ground— No! There is a third man with her, he is dragging her away—but Jiramondi is there, and, and—Foley! He has *leapt* from his saddle, he has a knife in his hands, I think, and he is—there is a lot of blood suddenly, I cannot tell who is bleeding—"

"Is it Alette?" Liramelli said anxiously.

Is it Foley? Corene wanted to ask. Her stomach was suddenly a twist of pain. It was even harder to breathe than it had been at the top of the tower.

Suddenly the mounted soldiers shifted positions, and Corene could see straight past them to the ongoing fight. It was true—both Foley and one of the attackers were covered with blood, and Corene thought both of them must be wounded. Foley's injury didn't seem to be slowing him down, though, since he moved and slashed with an easy grace that forced the other man to fall back two steps, three, five.

"They look like Dhonshon men—do you see?" Melissande demanded.

"Her father's soldiers?" Liramelli asked.

"It would seem so. Awful creatures!"

Several of the royal guards also had leapt from their horses and waded into the fight, obscuring Corene's view, but reassuring her, too: Surely with so many soldiers to take on a handful of men, Foley was not at risk. Jiramondi and Garameno remained on horseback, circling the fighters and shouting directives. "Don't kill them! We want to take them alive!" Corene thought it might be too late for that.

"There's Greggorio!" Liramelli gasped and started running.

Indeed, Greggorio had escaped from the churning mass of bodies and was stumbling back toward the tower, carrying a limp Alette in his arms. With a last glance toward the melee of the fight, Corene dashed after Liramelli, Melissande trotting beside her.

Greggorio didn't stop until he'd slipped inside the tower—maybe a place of safety, maybe not—and laid Alette gently on the stone floor. In seconds, the three women were kneeling beside him, all of them frantically patting Alette's hands, her knees, any part of her they could reach. Greggorio had planted himself right at her shoulder and was brushing the dirt and blood from her face. Her eyes were closed, leaving her face a dark, blank mask. She lay so still that Corene was not certain she was even breathing.

"Alette, can you talk to me? Are you hurt? Say something," Greggorio begged.

Her eyelids fluttered, lifted, dropped, lifted again, to reveal those startlingly blue eyes. She took a deep shuddering breath. "Those men—" she whispered.

"They're gone. They're being taken care of," Greggorio amended.

"They—" She didn't seem able to complete the sentence. "They were—"

"Probably following us from the minute we left the palace," Greggorio supplied.

Melissande, who was all the way down by Alette's feet, leaned forward. "They were dark-skinned like Dhonshon men and each of them worse a hawk symbol on his sleeve. That's your father's crest, isn't it?"

"Yes," Alette said on a sigh.

Corene squeezed Alette's hand. "Tell us where you're hurt. You seem to be having trouble breathing. Do you think you broke a rib?"

"I saw one man try to strangle her," Liramelli said. "Maybe he bruised her throat."

Alette was silent a moment, as if she was trying to marshal her thoughts. Then, "Help me sit up," she said and tightened her grip on Corene's fingers.

Greggorio moved behind her for support and they gently maneuvered her into an upright position. She blinked slowly a few times, then looked straight at Greggorio.

"Thank you," she said somberly. "You saved my life."

"I saw them take you," he said. "I happened to be looking that way. They were so fast—another two minutes—"

"I was careless," she said. "I should never have stepped away from the guards."

"You sound better," Liramelli said hopefully. "Are you all right? Is anything broken?"

Alette nodded. "I feel stronger. But my head hurts. My side hurts. I don't know if I'm just bruised or—"

"We shall get you back to the palace and examine you," Melissande said firmly. "At any rate, you do not appear to be bleeding, for which I am very grateful! Blood is scary but bones will heal."

Corene came to her feet. "I hear horses outside. I'm going to see how the fight went."

Indeed, the whole cavalcade of soldiers and royal heirs had made an untidy return to the open area at the base of the tower, and everyone was milling around, awaiting a decision on what to do next. Two quick glances told Corene what she most wanted to know: Foley was once more on horseback, looking battered but essentially whole, and the four attackers were dead. Their bodies had been slung across the backs of several rather skittish horses whose erstwhile riders held their reins and attempted to keep them calm.

Garameno spotted Corene and edged his horse over. "How is she?" he asked sharply.

"Bruised but otherwise unhurt, or so it seems," Corene responded. She gestured to the corpses. "I thought you wanted to question them?"

"We did," Garameno said. "But they made it impossible to take them alive."

Jiramondi urged his horse closer so he could join the conversation. "We can guess at their motives even without an interrogation," he said. "Alette's father seems to have decided it is a liability to have her in the Malinquese court. We might need to restrict her to the palace from now on."

"Or provide a better guard," Garameno said grimly.

"I suppose you can let her decide which she would prefer," Corene said. She wasn't so sure that Alette would consider confinement to the palace a better fate than death.

"Can she be moved? Can she travel?" Jiramondi asked. "Or should we send someone to fetch a carriage?"

"She can travel," came Greggorio's voice from behind them, and they all whirled around.

He was leading Alette out of the tower, one arm supportively around her waist; her head rested against his shoulder, but her eyes were open and alert. Her jacket had fallen open a little, and against her brown skin Corene could see darker bruises forming on her throat.

"I'll carry her," Greggorio added.

Garameno wheeled around. "Bring his horse!" he shouted.

The next few minutes were a flurry of activity as the remaining horses were fetched and most of the people currently on foot scrambled into their saddles. Once Greggorio was mounted, Foley handed Alette up to him, and she sat across his lap, leaning her cheek against his chest. Her eyes were closed again.

The soldiers had gathered around the royal party in a tight phalanx and they were starting to move slowly south when suddenly Alette stirred and sat up. "My scarf!" she cried. "My scarf—where is it?"

"What does that matter?" was Garameno's irritable reply, but Corene and Melissande instantly pulled on their reins and guided their horses through the line of guards, back to the site where Alette had been snatched. Melissande was the one to swing down and pick up the crumpled length of yellow fabric.

"It is dirty and— Look at that, a muddy footprint, right in the middle! But I do not think it is actually torn," was her assessment. "Such a fortunate thing!"

They rejoined the ranks and the whole group finally got under way, heading south, toward the walled city and the relative safety of the palace. Corene ignored Liramelli and Steff, who glanced around as if looking for her, and worked her way through the unwieldy mass of riders until she made it to Foley's side.

"How badly are you hurt?" she demanded.

"Not very. Cut on my arm, cut on my shoulder, probably a bruise on my thigh."

"You have to let me see when we get back to the palace."

The look he gave her was full of amusement. "I don't think I do."

"What—you're too modest to let me see you half undressed?"

"Partly. And partly I don't think you have any experience binding a wound, so what's the point?"

She was affronted. "You'd let *Josetta* tend your injuries."

His amusement deepened—but behind it she saw some other reaction, harder to decipher. Surprise, maybe. "She never had to."

"But you *would* have let her."

"She had training in a sickroom."

"It's just that—when I saw you fighting him—when I saw the *blood*—I thought—well, I thought—"

"I'm not going to get myself killed and leave you undefended in a foreign land," he said softly.

He had switched to Welchin, just in case anyone could hear them over the clatter of hooves and the low murmur of conversation. She did the same. "I wasn't thinking about *me*," she said, low-voiced but indignant. "I was afraid for *you*. You were suddenly in danger and there was nothing I could to do help you."

He was smiling again. "Well, I'm grateful you realized that, at least," he said. "I wouldn't have put it past you to come running up with a rock to clout one of those fellows in the head."

"If I'd seen a rock, I might have done it," she agreed. "But don't change the subject."

Now he sighed. "What's the subject?"

"I was terrified for you. And I'm so grateful you're all right. And I hope I never have to see you put in danger again."

He was silent a moment, his eyes apparently fixed on the road before them. Then he turned his head and gave her a straight, sober look. "In the future, I won't risk myself for anyone else but you, if you like," he said. "I rode to her aid today because I thought she was important to *you*. To spare *you* from the tragedy of her death. Was I wrong?"

Strange that such a quietly delivered speech could make her backbone prickle and her hands grow suddenly chilly on the reins. "No," she said quickly. "That was exactly what I wanted. Please keep her safe anytime you can. Alette and Melissande and Liramelli and Steff. All of them."

A glimmer of another smile. "And Filomara's nephews?"

"They can take care of themselves. Well, unless it's *easy* to help them. Unless all you have to do is punch someone in the nose."

He laughed out loud and she laughed with him, but somehow she felt the conversation hadn't gone exactly as she'd planned. But she didn't know what else she would have wanted to say, what she would have hoped to hear.

All she knew was that when she'd seen him covered with blood, fighting for his life, her heart had almost stopped. She had had the clearest, starkest realization: *I can't live if something happens to Foley.*

She didn't know what to do with such a thought. It was too big, too unmanageable, to unfold and examine with calm attention. So she crumpled it up as small as it would go and crammed it into the back of her mind, and urged her horse forward so she could ride beside Melissande all the way back to the palace.

Their party made quite a stir as they rode into the courtyard and instantly began calling for aid. Steff slid off his horse, tossed the reins to a footman, and said, "I'll tell my grandmother what happened," before striding inside. Corene caught the resentful looks that Garameno and Jiramondi threw after him, but Greggorio was so focused on Alette that he didn't seem to notice.

Melissande and Liramelli and Corene huddled in a disconsolate group in the courtyard and watched the rest of the party disperse. "I do not think I shall go on any more expeditions to Malinqua's famous towers," Melissande decreed. "There is always too much excitement, and always of a most unpleasant nature!"

"Always involving Alette, if you've noticed," Corene said.

"Ah—so if we exclude her from her plans, we should have very quiet outings," Melissande said with a nod.

"We can't exclude her! We've just now become friends!" Liramelli exclaimed.

Corene patted her shoulder. "She was joking."

"It is how I try to come to terms with the terrible events of the day," Melissande explained.

"I want to talk to her and see if she's all right, but I just know the physicians won't allow us into her room," Liramelli said.

"No, I am sure they will want her to be kept very quiet," Melissande said. "So we must wait until after dinner and then we shall sneak in. And if they have left anyone behind to nurse her, we must get rid of those people so we can talk to her in private."

"If she feels like talking," Liramelli said.

"After a day like this? I'd want to talk," Corene said. "Come on. Let's all get changed for dinner."

The meal was strained, since the prefect, the mayor, and other city officials were present and Filomara had forbidden anyone to speak of

Alette's adventure in the presence of others. So conversation was circumspect and meaningless, but at least it was brief. Filomara ate quickly then rose to her feet, signaling for Steff, her nephews, and the city administrators to join her for an extended conference. As the room emptied out, Corene and Liramelli and Melissande made good their escape.

"And now to check on Alette," Melissande said.

A slender maid and a stout woman who might have been a nurse had been installed in Alette's room, and they made a valiant effort to stop the visitors at the door, but there wasn't really much hope of that. Liramelli spoke to them with quiet authority and Melissande with insistent charm, while Corene just brushed past them to step inside.

"We were told to keep everybody out," the young maid said anxiously.

"You tried, but we have been completely uncontainable," said Melissande, who followed close on Corene's heels. "We promise not to stay for long!"

They sailed through the main room and into the smaller space that served as Alette's bedroom, closing the door on the protesting servants and throwing the lock for good measure.

They found Alette curled up in a window seat, gazing out at the city lights visible against the night sky. She was wearing some kind of diaphanous nightgown mostly covered up by a blanket that she appeared to have borrowed from the canopied bed. The room was in semidarkness, with only one faint wall sconce giving off any light, and it was difficult to see her expression as she turned toward them.

But her voice was unmistakeable. "My friends," she said warmly. "I had hoped you might come."

They crowded around her, bending down one at a time to hug her, casting around the room to find chairs to drag over to the window.

"How are you?" Liramelli demanded. "How badly are you hurt?"

Before she could answer, Corene threw a hand out and nodded meaningfully toward the door. "Speak softly," she said, her own voice not much above a whisper. "And in Coziquela. They are undoubtedly listening at the door."

"And they undoubtedly speak Coziquela," Melissande retorted, but she, too, kept her voice low.

Liramelli leaned closer. "Where are you hurt?"

Alette's right hand lifted to touch her throat, a spot on her chest, her left knee. "Bruises here and here and here, but the physician said nothing was broken."

"Well, that is something we must be thankful for!" Melissande exclaimed.

"You must have been terrified," Liramelli said.

"Yes. I thought I was going to die there."

Corene frowned. "There was a cart. Maybe they were only going to kidnap you."

Melissande threw her an incredulous look. "*Only* kidnap her?"

"No, I mean—of course that would have been horrible, but—"

Alette shrugged. "I heard them shouting at each other. One said, 'Kill her!' and the other said, 'Not here!' I don't know why."

Liramelli was nodding. "There's an old superstition. If someone is slain within the shadow of the towers, the killer will die within three days. You can stand with your back to one of the towers and walk out as far as its height in any direction, and you will find there has not been a murder committed within that circle for two hundred years."

"That is most intriguing. In a grotesque sort of way," Melissande commented.

Corene was still frowning. "But would Dhonshon assassins know that particular myth? I mean, I've been here half a quintile and I never heard that story. And would they *care*?"

"Oh, those men were not from Dhonsho," Alette said.

They all peered at her in the dark. "They were not?" Melissande said. "But the color of their skin—and the insignia on their clothes—"

"Yes. I misspoke. Their heritage is Dhonshon, but they were not my father's men. Not sent by him to kill me."

"How do you know?" Liramelli said.

"The one who held me by the arms—he kept shouting in my face and I could smell the zeezin on his breath."

"Zeezin? So?" Melissande said.

But Corene remembered a conversation she'd had with Jiramondi during her very first dinner at the palace. "Dhonshons use zeezin in funeral rituals, yes?" she said. "They wouldn't *eat* it."

Alette nodded. "Exactly. These men were probably born here in Palminera, and raised here. They are more Malinquese than Dhonshon."

"You don't think your father might have hired them to—to hurt you?" Liramelli said. Corene noticed that she couldn't bring herself to say the words. *Your father might have hired them to kill you?*

Alette permitted herself the smallest smile. "My father would never work with strangers. And never with someone who did not love Dhonsho with every drop of blood in his body."

"But then who hired these dreadful men?" Melissande demanded. "And why hire Dhonshons? It makes no sense."

"It makes perfect sense," Corene said in a hard voice. "Someone from Malinqua wants Alette dead. But he—or she—wants it to look like Alette's father killed her. That way there can be no outrage directed at the Malinquese crown."

Liramelli covered her mouth with her hands as if to hold back a cry; Melissande sank back in her chair, nodding thoughtfully.

"Yes, of course. You are absolutely right," Melissande said.

Liramelli dropped her hands, but her face was still etched with horror. "But it *doesn't*," she cried. "Who in Malinqua would want to kill Alette?"

"Oh, that's right—you were at Sarona's funeral when we had this conversation before," Corene said. "We think someone in Malinqua didn't like the fact that Greggorio was so close to Sarona—was afraid that he might marry her—and that's why she was killed. Greggorio's been very kind to Alette, too, and apparently somebody noticed that."

"He was especially kind this afternoon," Melissande said, her lovely voice surprisingly grim. "He was the one who first realized she had been attacked, so he clearly was watching her. And he raced over to help her, without so much as a dagger in his hand. If someone is looking for evidence that Greggorio feels affection for Alette—"

"He got it today," Corene summed up.

Alette looked down at her hands, but the other three stared at each other in mounting distress. In the faint light that sifted in through the window, Corene could see Melissande's mouth set in a thin line, Liramelli's face growing increasingly anxious.

"If you're in danger because you're close to Greggorio," Liramelli said, her voice rough with worry, "it is someone at the palace trying to kill you."

"Yes," Alette said.

"Which means you're not safe at the palace," Liramelli finished up.

"I know."

"But *who?*" Liramelli demanded. "If it's someone concerned with the succession—"

"Which is everybody," Corene put in.

"You would have to suspect Filomara's brothers, even though they live far from court—or Jiramondi or Garameno—"

"Or high-ranking officials who might care a great deal about who is next to sit on the throne," Melissande said gently.

Corene watched as Liramelli realized what that meant. The other girl stiffened. "Not my father," she said coldly. "Never my father."

"No, of course not," Melissande said in a soothing voice, though they all knew there was no *of course* about it. "But someone who is close to the crown and wants to influence who wears it."

"Well, we don't know who it is," Corene said. "What we do know is that Alette is not safe and she can't stay alone in this room."

Melissande turned to give a long, thoughtful look at the locked door. "Servants have been left behind to guard the room tonight, but will they be able to keep out a determined assassin?"

"Or are *they* the assassins?" Corene said.

"Corene!" Liramelli exclaimed.

But Melissande was nodding. "Yes, yes, we must suspect anybody, and there is no reason a woman cannot be a murderer," she said. "Who better than a nurse, in fact? She probably is familiar with every kind of poison on offer here in Malinqua, and she would certainly know where to slice an artery—"

Liramelli lifted a hand in supplication, and Melissande kindly desisted.

"We will insist that the maid and the nurse leave when we do," Liramelli said. "And Alette will lock the door behind them."

Melissande shook her head. "If a warrant for her execution has been signed by someone in the palace, a locked door won't keep a killer out."

"She can stay with me," Liramelli said, and then flushed angrily when Melissande and Corene just looked at her. "Even if my father were a murderer—which he's *not*!—he would hardly kill someone in his own suite! Who was sharing a room with *me*!"

"She can stay in my rooms," Melissande said.

"Or mine," Corene added.

"Mine," Melissande said gently. "I am sure your father would want to avenge your death, should you and Alette both be murdered in the night, but I am not so sure Welce possesses the military might to make it possible. Whereas Cozique could sink Malinqua's navy in a day and burn this city to the ground—and everybody in the palace knows it. I think I am the person who is least at risk, which means Alette will be safest in my care."

It was a good argument. Corene nodded, and Liramelli turned her head to look unhappily out the window.

Melissande frowned. "I am a little afraid, however," she said. "The Malinquese are so fond of poison—someone could slip a toxin into her food. I could do nothing to stop it."

"That won't happen," Corene said confidently. "If she dies by poison, it will be obvious someone at court wanted her dead. She must be killed by violence for this to look like a Dhonshon assault."

"Most excellent reasoning!" Melissande decreed. "I am reassured."

"I thank you all for your great kindnesses, but you do not have to do so much for me," Alette said softly. "I do not fear death. I will join my mother and my sister and so many others in the afterlife. It must be a better existence than the one I am living now."

"You might not fear it, but you don't want to die," Corene argued. "I saw you today—you fought with your attackers. You wanted to break free. You weren't ready to die this afternoon—and we won't let you die in this room tonight."

Alette's smile was sad. "I might have fought, but I won't keep fighting," she said. "What do you think I am living for? There is no place for me in Malinqua, and there is no place for me in Dhonsho. I do not belong in this world. I will let death escort me out."

The other three women protested strongly at that, still trying to speak softly enough that the servants couldn't decipher their words through the door. Corene finally was able to make her voice heard above the others.

"You *do* have something to live for," she said. "You said so. Someone in the city who loves you."

"Cheelin," Alette said, the name sounding almost like a prayer in her soft voice. "I will never see him again."

"You will," Corene said. "I'm going to figure out how to get you out of here."

Despite the resistance of the nurse and the maid, they packed up some of Alette's clothing and prepared to move her to Melissande's room. They made quite a procession as they paraded through the halls, Corene thought—Alette still in her nightclothes and blanket, all of them carrying baskets and bundles, the servants trailing behind, still remonstrating. Both Alette and Melissande had rooms on the third floor, though some distance apart, so at least they didn't have to contend with stairwells. And they only encountered two other people in their travels, both of them startled housemaids. Corene figured the story of the migration would be all over the palace in less than thirty minutes. The thought amused her.

"You do not mind sleeping in the maid's room, do you?" Melissande asked. "It is much smaller than the main bedroom, but I think it will be quite comfortable. I insisted on a separate suite for my own maid," she explained as they began finding places to store clothes and shoes. "I have so many clothes with me that I needed the extra room."

"I will be most comfortable there," said Alette. "I cannot sufficiently express my gratitude."

"Nonsense, it shall be very much fun," Melissande said.

Liramelli's next words were lost in a yawn. "I'm sorry," she apologized. "But it's been such a long day."

"It certainly has," Corene agreed. "I'm off to bed myself. I'll see you all in the morning."

After a few more moments spent saying farewell, Corene and Liramelli headed off together, parting at the stairwell to seek their own quarters. But instead of going to her room, Corene crossed the hall to stand outside Foley's door. She took a moment to reassure herself that she was utterly calm, not at all emotional, and then she knocked.

He answered within seconds, concern already on his face. "Did something happen at dinner?" he asked.

She stepped inside and looked around curiously before answering. The room was brighter than Alette's had been, but not by much. All the wall sconces were lit, but they'd been turned to a low and restful level. She'd barely been inside his room since they arrived at the palace, but judging by the absence of clutter, the same could be said of Foley. Whereas Corene tended to discard shoes and clothing and other oddments around her room, carelessly crumple the bedsheets, leave armoire doors open and letters scattered on the sofas, Foley kept his room so neat he might not even live in it. The only sign of occupation was a brass kettle and a single cup of liquid steaming on a small table.

"Are you drinking keerza?" she demanded.

"I am. I've developed a taste for it. What happened?"

"I can't believe that. Keerza is horrid."

He shrugged and just watched her.

She looked around again. "Are you always this neat? Don't you ever just kick your boots off and forget to hang up your jacket?"

"I like to know where everything is in case I need it suddenly in the middle of the night."

"That makes sense," she said grudgingly.

"So what's wrong?"

"I came to see how your injuries are."

"Minor. As I told you on the ride back." His eyes searched her face. "Something else is bothering you."

"Alette. She said the men who tried to kill her might have been Dhonshon by blood, but they weren't her father's men. She thinks they were hired by someone at the palace."

Foley's reaction was a small, controlled flinch. "Then she's not safe here."

"She's staying in Melissande's room tonight, but we need to get her out of here."

"We probably should get *you* out of here instead."

"I know," she said. "But I think Alette's in immediate danger and I'm not."

"And the leaving is as dangerous as the staying," he said.

She nodded. "But not for Alette. The staying is worse."

"It will be tricky to get her out unseen," he said.

"I know. But I have an idea. I want to talk to Leah about it. So I want you to take a message to her tomorrow."

He was silent so long that she finally asked, "What?"

"If I'm your courier, I'm not watching over you. Given the events of the past few days, I don't feel comfortable leaving you behind."

"It would just be for a couple of hours."

"A lot could happen in that period of time."

"Fine, I'll go with you. Let the guards follow us all over the city."

"She might be at the market. We could start there."

"Then let's go there in the morning." She took a few steps toward the door, then turned back, grinning slightly as a thought occurred to her. "Of course, anything could happen to me during the night when I'm in my room and you're not watching over me because you're *sleeping*."

She thought he would smile in response, but his face just grew more serious. "I know," he said. "I've thought about that. I could sleep in the hall outside your door."

"I was joking."

"Not much of a joke where Alette's concerned, apparently," he observed. "Your safety becomes more of a concern every day."

She came deeper into his room, closer to Foley, willing to see how far she could push him. "Well, my suite has an empty room where the maid's supposed to stay," she drawled. "I guess you could sleep there."

"And have to tell your father I spent the night in his daughter's rooms?"

"Would you rather have to tell my father I was murdered?"

He sucked in a hard breath. "That's unfair."

"I know." She watched him a moment, wondering what he was really thinking, if she would ever be able to figure it out. Wondering if he ever thought of her the way she was beginning to think of him. "How much danger would you have to believe I was in before you ignored your scruples and stayed beside me night and day?"

He just looked at her a moment. "Your safety outweighs my scruples at all times," he said. "I'd carry you naked from the building if I thought you were at risk. Is that what you want me to say?"

She crossed her arms and tilted her head, her eyes never wavering from his face. "I want you to say—" She thought about it. "I want you to tell me why you took this job."

"Becoming a guard for the royal court of Welce?"

"Accompanying me on this trip."

He was silent.

"Did my father ask you to do it?"

His surprise appeared to be genuine. "I thought your father didn't know you were planning to leave with the empress."

Corene made a rude noise. "My father knows everything."

"I think he likes people to believe that."

"Did he ask you to come with me?"

"*You* asked me to come with you. Don't you remember?"

"Of course I remember. But you didn't need any convincing. Only later did I realize you said yes so quickly because you'd been thinking about it already. And that you'd probably been thinking about it because my father said something to you like, 'Corene's getting ready to bolt. Will you follow her?'"

"That's not the way it happened."

"Then how *did* it happen?"

He clearly didn't want to answer, but Corene waited in silence, still watching him closely. Finally he gave an infinitesimal shrug and said, "It was clear Josetta's life was changing. With Rafe at her side, she would not need me to shadow her everywhere she went—in fact, I felt I was proving to be something of an encumbrance."

"Though you came in pretty handy every time *Rafe* was attacked," she reminded him.

His smile was brief. "Yes. But there were always other guards on hand to watch over him."

He fell silent again, as if this was a complete answer, and she finally had to prompt him. "So?"

"So I went to your father and said he should consider giving me a new assignment."

"And he said, 'Very well, how about my troublesome oldest daughter?'"

Foley said nothing.

"He *didn't* say that?" Corene prodded.

"No."

He obviously wasn't going to volunteer a scrap of information, but it seemed he would answer direct questions. "What *did* he say?"

"He asked if I had an assignment I would prefer."

"And you said?"

"I said yes."

"And what was it?"

He just looked at her.

Corene felt her mouth fall open. "You *asked* to be assigned to me?"

"It seemed like it would be an interesting job," he said. "I'd been around often enough when trouble arrived and you were in the middle of it. More than once I'd thought you needed a bodyguard even more than Josetta did."

Corene found herself trembling a little. The reasonable answer hadn't been the one she'd wanted. *What answer did I want?* "When exactly did this conversation with my father occur?"

"A few days before Rafe's cousin tried to kill him."

"I would have thought *that* event would have made you change your mind," she pointed out.

"Maybe it would have, if the day had gone differently. But the way it ended—" Foley shrugged again. "It seemed like Rafe was out of danger."

"So when I came to you—asking if you would accompany me—you'd already been assigned to me. You would have come along even if I *hadn't* asked."

For the life of her, she couldn't keep the dejection from her voice. The whole thing had seemed like such a grand adventure, such a magnificent gesture of recklessness, but she had been a little afraid to set off all by herself. Securing Foley's attendance had been doubly sweet. She had not only upended the traditional order of things—something always guaranteed to annoy her father—but she had also found the one companion who could make her feel safe on the journey. She had been both irresponsible and responsible at the same time.

Except she hadn't been. Except she hadn't outsmarted her father; she hadn't won Foley over. She had merely behaved as they expected. She had fallen in with their plans.

It was enough to make her want to flee from the palace in the middle of the night and board a foreign ship bound for any destination—she didn't care which one—just to prove she had the nerve to do it. *Courage.* That was what the blessings kept showering on her. Was it time to live up to the attribute?

Of course, it was going to prove mighty hard to escape from Malinqua, what with royal guards following her like malevolent shadows, and Berringey ships blockading the harbor—

Foley's voice interrupted her self-pitying thoughts. "No."

She'd already forgotten what she'd just said. "No what?"

"No, I hadn't been assigned to you. Your father hadn't yet decided whether I should be transferred from Josetta's detail. As you say, she and Rafe were having a pretty eventful time of it."

Her spirits lifted immeasurably at his words. "You defied my father to come with me?"

This time his smile lingered a little longer. "I did."

"What did you think? When I came to you that night, when I asked you to travel with me? Did you think I was being foolish? Being wild? Did you think about going to my father and telling him what I was planning?" A thought occurred to her, for literally the first time. "*Did* you go to him? Did he know I was going— Did he *let* me go?"

"I didn't tell him," Foley said—the quickest answer he'd given all night. Apparently the accusation touched his honor. "I never said I would be his spy."

"But what did you think?"

"I thought—" He hesitated, watching her, as if not certain how he should phrase his words. "I thought you had spent so much of your life in your sister's shadow that it would be good for you to stand in the sun somewhere else. I thought you had spent so much time as a pawn in the royal court—"

His voice trailed off and he shook his head. It was a moment before Corene realized he was actually angry. She could guess what memory still sparked his rage.

"When I was eleven," she said softly. "When King Vernon tried to marry me off to the viceroy of Soeche-Tas."

He nodded. "Later I realized that Darien Serlast would never have allowed that to happen, but at the time . . . at the time . . ." He shook his head again. "I would have been happy if Zoe had drowned everyone at court that day."

"Well, she almost did," Corene said practically.

"That was the first time I realized you needed a protector every bit as much as Josetta did." That faint smile was back. "And nothing that's happened since then has changed my mind."

"So you came with me to be that protector," she said softly, "and because you thought I was right to go."

"Yes."

"I'm glad you did," she said. "I don't think I would have been brave enough to leave if you'd said no."

He glanced around the room, but she thought that he was really imagining the whole palace. "Given the situation you're in now, I'm not so sure it was the right choice after all."

"Probably not," she agreed. "But neither of us could have known that then."

"When you see Leah tomorrow," he said. "Talk to her about getting *you* out of here as well as Alette."

"All right," she said. "We'll go to the market in the morning. Right after breakfast. And if Leah isn't there—we'll find her somewhere."

"Sounds good."

There seemed to be no more to say, but Corene found she didn't want to leave the room. She was ruffled, on edge, wanting to get back to her room to think over Foley's words, wanting to stay and make him say more. She didn't know what she wanted. Begrudgingly, she took the few steps necessary to reach the threshold.

"Lock your door once you're in your room," Foley said.

"I always do." Smiling slightly, she turned back to look at him. "Let me know if you change your mind. If you want to stay in the maid's room and guard my sleep."

This time he was ready for her. "When the situation is dire enough, that's what I'll do."

Not until she had opened the door and taken one step into the hallway did she offer a parting shot. "Sometime, when you want to hear the answer, ask me why I invited you to come with me to Malinqua," she said. She didn't wait to see his reaction. Just closed the door behind her, quickly crossed the hall, and let herself into her own room. Shutting and locking the door, she found herself unable to move another inch inside the room. She stood there in utter darkness, trembling, leaning against the door for support, until it seemed half the night had passed.

SEVENTEEN

Leah's conversation with Corene did not go at all as she had expected—although she supposed that was typical of a conversation with the princess. The two of them huddled behind the curtain at Chandran's shop and whispered in Welchin, a language that was quite suitable for expressing surprise.

"You want me to spirit someone *else* out of the city? Not *you*?"

"She's in more danger than I am."

"Your father might not agree."

"Right now I don't care what my father thinks. Will you help me?"

Of course she would. Staying in Corene's good graces was part of her job. And this little adventure was unexpectedly appealing—in a stupid, crazy, dangerous way.

"The day after tomorrow, then?" Corene asked as she lifted her hand to pull back the curtain.

"I might need more time. Two days after tomorrow."

"We'll meet you then."

Leah ushered Corene out of the stall and watched as the princess mingled with the rest of the shoppers and faded from view. Then she turned to Chandran.

"I need the rest of the afternoon off. And the next couple of days."

He was silent a moment, studying her. When he spoke, his voice was troubled. "I understand that the atmosphere at the palace is toxic. But if the princess is attempting to leave undetected, her options are not good. The illegal ports are not safe."

"I know. She's not leaving."

"And yet she has a commission for you. A dangerous one, I take it."

Leah spread her hands. *What isn't dangerous?*

His next words surprised her. "Do you need my help?"

"It's a kind offer," she said. "But I don't think so."

"You don't trust me."

"I don't trust anybody. And you did try to poison me once."

He smiled. "But that is how things are done in Malinqua."

"If I ever do need help, I'll turn to you," she said. "If it makes you feel better to know that."

"It does," he said. "Whatever task you're engaged in, stay safe."

The words warmed her all the way to her toes, a useful response to the chill of the day. It was no use reminding herself that she'd known Chandran less than a quintile—and that he might be an even better undercover agent than she was. He could be spying for Filomara or the Coziquela queen or any other nation with full coffers and a curiosity about its neighbors, but she had come to believe in him. She knew better, but that hadn't stopped her. She couldn't decide if trusting Chandran confirmed she would always be a fool or proved that there might still be hope for her bruised and suspicious heart.

She made her way to the harbor and paused a moment to study the scene. With the blockade in place, it seemed oddly empty and strangely quiet. Where there were usually close to a thousand ships lined up along the wharf, and hundreds more hovering off in deeper water, today there were only fifteen ships snugged up against the docks. Most of them were small, fleet vessels that could outrun the heavy Berringese destroyers patrolling the waters. Few of them would carry much cargo, except the most precious and the most expensive; most of them would trade in information instead. Just as precious and equally expensive.

Leah drew her jacket closer against the chill and followed the narrow, twisting roads that spoked off the harbor with no discernible pattern. She was looking for a specific address that Corene had supplied, though she doubted the princess knew just how dicey this particular neighborhood was—filthy, tumbledown, stinking of fish and garbage and urine. It was the district where the most transitory of visitors resided: the sailors on land for a single night, the women and boys who serviced them, the thieves and pickpockets who preyed on them. Leah had stopped at her own quarters to change into her oldest clothes and sturdiest shoes, and she'd loaded up on weapons she could tuck into a pocket or a waistband. She kept one knife in her left hand, pressed against her thigh but ready to use. In a locale like this, it was not possible to be too careful.

She finally found the place she wanted, a two-story building with broken shutters, peeling wood, and a front door that sagged off its hinges. Judging from the stench boiling out through the door, there was nothing resembling plumbing inside and none of the inhabitants cared. Or someone had died here in the past three days—and none of the inhabitants minded that, either.

Leah didn't care how important this was to Corene, she wasn't stepping inside.

She backed up a pace so she stood in the middle of the cramped street and lifted her head to shout toward the second-story window. "Cheelin Barlio of Dhonsho!" she called. "I need to talk to you!"

There was silence from the building. Silence from every sad, sorry, secretive structure on the street.

"Cheelin Barlio!" she called again. "Looking for Cheelin Barlio!"

From an open window a few buildings down, someone threw a rock and growled out something that might have been a curse and might have been a warning. The rock was so badly aimed that Leah didn't even shift position in response.

"Cheelin Barlio! I need a word with Cheelin Barlio!"

She'd figured it could take thirty minutes for someone to get annoyed enough to come out and either help her or shut her up, so she was pleasantly surprised when, ten minutes after she started shouting, the sagging door was pushed open and a man stepped into the street. He was Dhonshon, with brown skin, black hair, and eyes the color of copper. He looked perfectly capable of defending himself against a hostile world.

He was about five inches taller than Leah, well-muscled, and holding his own dagger, which he made no attempt to conceal.

"What do you want?" he asked.

His Coziquela was perfect. Not only that, he was dressed in clothes that looked as if they had been washed sometime within the past nineday, and the stench of his living quarters didn't cling to him when he stepped close to Leah. This was a fastidious, educated man who didn't belong in a hovel; he belonged in a mansion.

"I have a message for you from a woman of sage and saffron."

The code phrase elicited the right reaction. Cheelin stiffened, straightened, and looked swiftly up and down the narrow road. No one appeared to be near enough to overhear—no one appeared to be *alive* anywhere else on the street—but he still drew a pace closer and dropped his voice to a whisper.

"What message?"

"She is ready to leave," Leah replied, just as softly. "She will meet you in three days at a place you specify."

Cheelin's face lit with excitement, then narrowed in worry. "How? How will she get out of the palace? I heard a rumor of an attack yesterday—"

"Not just a rumor. Truth. It is the reason she is ready to take the risk. Do you have a route to safety?"

"Yes. If she has a route to freedom."

"Where shall I bring her?"

Cheelin stepped back a moment to study Leah. "How will *you* get her from the palace?"

"Others will bring her to me. We have a plan."

"Why would you help her? Why would they?"

"Because they care about her," Leah said sharply.

"I don't know that I can trust you. That she can."

"You don't," Leah agreed. "But here are the facts. We are bringing her out of the palace two days after tomorrow, and either you meet us or you don't. If you do, you have to sneak past Malinquese guards and Dhonshon renegades and Berringese warships and who knows what other hazards as you try to find a safe haven for both of you in some other country. If you don't meet us, she'll probably be dead within a nineday. You choose."

His face showed a mix of emotions—hope, fear, distrust, fatalism, and a small vulnerable light that Leah had to assume was love. Leah didn't know much of Alette's story, but Cheelin looked like he had formerly been a man of some wealth, some social standing, some pride. Yet here he was squatting in a fetid shack, working, starving, hoping for the slightest chance to whisk his beloved from danger. He might distrust Leah and fear greatly for Alette's safety, but he would not fail them. Not this man.

"There is a neighborhood south of the red tower," he said. "Not very prosperous. There's a stable yard where hundreds of horses are kept. People come and go all day and no one pays any attention. I have friends there. That's where you should bring Alette."

"I know the place. We'll be there."

"What time?"

Leah shook her head. "I'm not certain. Probably early afternoon. We'll be coming from the Little Islands area, but—"

"It's best to walk, if Alette can go so far on foot," he interrupted. "You are less likely to be noticed."

"That's what I thought. But it will take us a few hours to cover the ground."

"I am worried about her feet," Cheelin fretted. "Her shoes—they are always so fashionable and flimsy."

Leah couldn't help a small smile. "I'll tell her friends to make sure she's wearing something practical."

"She'll be so afraid— Does she even know you? And she will be looking over her shoulders, startled at every sound—"

"She will be less afraid to leave than to stay," Leah said gently.

"Yes," Cheelin said, nodding firmly and straightening his shoulders. Leah imagined he was taking on burdens, gathering his strength. "And she will know she is coming to me. And then all will be well."

"Yes," Leah echoed. "I think all will be well, indeed."

Next she went to the Little Islands, to the Dhonshon shop run by the four women she had befriended. The youngest, Teyta, was yawning and sulking as she folded fabrics and straightened the merchandise. "Finally!" she exclaimed when Leah walked in. "Someone interesting to talk to! I am so *bored*!"

Leah smiled. "How would you like to do something exciting? And earn a little money besides?"

"Really? I would *love* it!"

"It might be dangerous," Leah warned.

"I don't care! I would do *anything* to get out of here for even half an hour."

"Have you ever been to the palace?"

"Maybe a dozen times. Sometimes the cook orders special ingredients from our shop and we deliver them when they come in. Is that it? You want me to take something to the palace?"

"Well," said Leah, "not exactly."

Even when Leah outlined the plan, Teyta didn't lose her enthusiasm. Leah never mentioned Alette's name, but she would bet Teyta had guessed who else was involved in this caper, which probably added to her excitement.

"I know I should ask permission from your mother," Leah said after they had gone over the details a few times. "But I'm afraid she'll say no."

"Pooh," Teyta said, tossing her head. "I'm a grown woman. She can't tell me what to do."

"Sometimes mothers can tell their daughters what to do until they're both very old women."

Teyta laughed. "Then I shall ask my grandmother to order my mother to let me go! My grandmother has very strong feelings about—" Teyta hesitated, no more interested in using names than Leah was. "About Dhonsho," she ended lamely.

"I'll be back tomorrow to make sure you haven't changed your mind."

"I won't."

Since she was so close, Leah swung by the Welchin café for some fruited water and a little gossip. The shop owner looked inexpressibly relieved to see her.

"Leah! I have been hoping for three days that you would come by," she said, pouring a glass without even being asked.

Leah felt her eyebrows arch. This was new. The shop owner had always been the most casual and comfortable of Leah's contacts, full of news but never full of urgency. "Didn't I leave you an address where you could get in touch with me?"

"Yes, but that was more than a year ago and of course I lost it! But I told him you come by at least once a nineday, so you would be here eventually."

"Told him? Told who? Did someone leave me a message?"

"No—he's waiting for you himself. I have a room upstairs that I rent sometimes, though it's been a couple quintiles since I had a paying tenant."

"So somebody's looking for me and he's *here*?" Leah felt sparks of uneasiness flicker down her spine. "Who is he?"

"I'm not sure, but he's from Welce. And I think he has a lot of money—at any rate, he's been very openhanded."

"But he didn't tell you his name."

"He told me *a* name, but I don't think it's his."

"How did he know to find me here?"

"He said that a ship captain told him about this place."

"Huh." That made Leah a little less suspicious. She had, in fact, given this address to Captain Ada Simms, so her secretive visitor might simply be a shady character here to offer a smuggling deal. Which made her wonder . . . "Your visitor just arrived from Welce? He made it through the blockade?"

"Apparently so. He hasn't said much about the trip except that it was a real adventure."

Leah gulped down the last of her water. "Well, then. I guess I'd better go see what he wants."

Just then the front door opened and a family of five came in, chattering in Welchin. "Can you just take yourself upstairs? He's in the last room at the end of the hallway. I'll see you later!"

Leah nodded and made her way to the back of the shop and into the kitchen—which smelled like sugar and bread and home—and from there to the narrow stairwell. She still felt premonition skittering along her backbone, so she held the banister with one hand and her favorite dagger with her other. This man might have been sent by Captain Simms, but that didn't mean he wasn't a scoundrel.

Only four doors opened up off the short hallway, which was dimly lit by small windows at either end of the corridor. Leah was tempted to stand outside the last door and shout at the occupant to come out—as she had with Cheelin Barlio—but she figured the shop owner wouldn't appreciate the ruckus. So she knocked instead and listened to the *thump* and rustle on the other side of the door. Footsteps approached.

She expected a suspicious interrogation from the mysterious boarder, but instead he flung the door open and spread his arms in a warm greeting. He was already smiling. "Leah!" he roared. "It *is* you! Of all the places for you to go to ground!"

She just stared at him. He was a stocky man in his middle sixties, with a ruddy complexion, a ready laugh, and curly red hair about half surrendered to gray. Oh, but she knew so much more about him than the facts of his appearance. As long as he was in the room, someone was bound to be talking—usually him—and almost everyone was likely to be entertained. He was smart, warmhearted, scheming, unreliable, lovable, infuriating, and kind. He was the sweela prime, and there was no one she would have been more surprised to see in Malinqua.

"Nelson Ardelay," she said blankly. "What are you doing here?"

He took her arm and pulled her through the door. "Come in, come in. Are you hungry? I was just about to eat."

"I think I'm too stunned to choke down a morsel."

He grinned and shepherded her over to a small table, where he had, indeed, laid out fruit compote, fresh-baked bread, and other appetizing items. "Well, then you can just sit and watch me chew," he said as they sat down.

"I'm serious. What are you *doing* here?"

Nelson tore into a piece of bread. He was the kind of man who could talk with his mouth full and yet somehow not be annoying; he had so much to say that he couldn't wait to get the words out. "We have been hearing some very disturbing rumors out of Malinqua. Darien wanted to send a navy straightaway to bring Corene home—but there was some question about how easily a navy might force its way in. So he thought to send an ambassador first, someone who could analyze the situation and maybe talk some sense into the empress."

"So he picked you," Leah said dryly.

Nelson grinned. "Well, I *can* talk," he said modestly.

"You certainly can. But if you're here to negotiate, why are you hiding like a fugitive?"

"I thought I'd try to see how the land lies before making a grand entrance at the palace. See how much danger Corene is in."

"Some, I think," Leah admitted. "But I don't think she's greatly afraid."

"No. Well, she's not a fearful girl in general."

"So you really have a navy at your back?"

He gestured vaguely toward the ocean. "Fifty ships. Out to sea far enough to not seem threatening—though I assume Filomara has caught wind of them by now."

"I haven't seen any warships in the harbor. How'd you get through the blockade?"

He grinned. "I came in with a merchant trader who knew a less—shall we say—obvious route. She's the one who told me how to find you, in fact."

"So I figured. Though how Captain Simms got in touch with you to begin with—"

"Oh, it's all very convoluted," Nelson agreed. "But apparently you talked to her some ninedays ago, and claimed you knew Kayle Dochenza. And she asked Kayle, and Kayle shared the news with me, and then he told Darien and—" He shrugged. "Once Darien knows something, all the pieces fall in place."

She sighed. "And Darien knows everything."

Nelson regarded her steadily. "He knew where *you* were, at any rate, which is something I would have liked to know for a long time."

"Really?" she said tiredly. "You even noticed I was gone?"

"Of course I noticed! And inquired discreetly, though the trail went cold very quickly once it meandered through Darien Serlast's office." For a moment Nelson's cheerful face looked grim. "There are many things I admire about our regent, but I do not believe he always knows best in every single situation. I am still angry with him for not telling me where you were—or rather, where he had sent you."

"I asked him not to tell anyone. I didn't want to be followed. And argued with. And reminded."

"Well, you've been gone five years now. I would think some of those memories would be a little less painful by now."

Leah gave a ghost of a laugh. "And you would mostly be wrong."

Showing admirable and uncharacteristic self-restraint, Nelson didn't reply. He simply took another bite of bread and watched her, waiting for her to ask the question she had wanted to ask somebody, anybody, for the past five years.

"So how is she? How's my daughter?" she finally said.

Nelson would know, of course. He was the girl's grandfather.

EIGHTEEN

When the day came for them to set out on their expedition, Alette was the calmest one of all. Liramelli was trying to maintain her usual stoic demeanor, but she kept dropping things and bumping into walls, betraying her deep nervousness. Melissande fluttered even more than usual, making minute adjustments to her own toilette then hovering around the rest of them to straighten a shawl or smooth down a wayward curl. Corene snapped at everyone: *Do you have to be so restless? Don't break anything else!* Not even Melissande reproached her for her tone.

But Alette merely sat quietly in the middle of Melissande's room and waited for the minutes to tick by. She was dressed in traditional Dhonshon clothing—a vivid tunic in what Corene considered the sweela colors of red and yellow and orange, overlaid with the yellow shawl Alette wore every day. But she had complemented this ensemble with sturdy, rather ugly shoes that looked suitable for walking across a continent.

"What did you tell Jiramondi when he asked if he could come with us?" Liramelli asked. She'd posed the same question at least twice already.

"I said today is a Welchin holiday on which only women were

allowed into the temples," Corene replied. "Which is why Steff couldn't come, either. And then he asked if Foley was coming and I said yes, but we wouldn't let him inside the temple. Which we won't," she added.

"But Jiramondi is very smart, you know," Melissande said, worried. "He might be in the library even now! Looking up Welchin customs! He will realize you were lying to him."

"Maybe, but by then it will be too late." Corene glanced once more at the clock, which finally, miraculously, showed the correct time. She had approached Lorian last night to ask him to arrange for transportation. *The other women and I would like to go to the Little Islands in the morning. Could you have a carriage ready?* She didn't say *a carriage and a dozen guards* because Lorian would take care of the guards all on his own.

"Finally. Let's go."

They headed out the door, the rest of them wrapping themselves in their own colorful shawls as they went. It was partly symbolic—wearing Dhonshon clothing as they plotted a Dhonshon escape—and partly practical. Foley was the one who had alerted Corene to this detail.

"When you're following someone, you can't always see his face," he had explained. "So you look for physical markers that you can spot at a distance. Height. Coloring. An unusual piece of clothing. If you wear certain colors, you make life a lot easier for the guards who are trying to keep you in view."

Good to know. They would offer Filomara's official soldiers and skulking assassins a veritable *rainbow* of targets. They wanted the guards' job to be very easy indeed.

No one impeded them as they wended through the corridors and out the front door of the palace, chatting as casually as they could. Corene could tell that her own laugh was high and strained, while Liramelli couldn't bring herself to laugh at all. But soon enough the four of them were seated in the open carriage and it was headed out at a brisk pace. Foley was on horseback beside them, and a dozen guards ranged before and behind. Corene figured they'd pick up any murder-minded escorts once they were a few blocks from the courtyard, but she wasn't going to bother to look for them.

"What a very nice day we have for our outing," Melissande observed nervously. "Sunny and not at all cold! We could walk for hours if we had to."

Corene glared at her. "Fortunately, we won't have to."

"No! Of course not! Such a lovely carriage the empress has provided."

"I believe the weather is supposed to get much chillier tomorrow," Liramelli said in her serious way. "Even stormy. Clouds rolling in tonight."

"Clouds! Yes. One will hardly be able to see the moon tonight if there are clouds," Melissande rattled on. When Corene gave her another minatory look, Melissande added, "Oh, but I *prefer* moonlight, of course. It makes everything so pretty."

"Why don't we just enjoy the sunlight and not talk so much?" Corene suggested.

Liramelli sat a little straighter. "Perhaps I should act like Garameno for this trip, and point out interesting sights," she said. "You see that tall building—the gray one with the tile roof? That's the archives for the history of the city. One of Garameno's favorite places."

"One of the reasons Garameno is so very dull," Melissande murmured.

Liramelli's travelogue took them through the rest of the journey, which seemed to last for hours but was really less than one. Despite her impatience, Corene felt a surge of panic when the carriage crossed into the Little Islands and pulled up in front of the Welchin temple. It was time! Was she ready?

"Here we are!" she announced, her voice too cheery. "Let's go in and pull blessings."

Foley helped them out of the carriage while the royal soldiers redistributed themselves in a loose ring around the temple. At least five of them were close enough to overhear when Melissande exclaimed, "There is a note on the door!" before she looked around guiltily, wondering what she might have betrayed.

"Oh, yes—it's just reminding everyone that today is the women's holiday, and no men are allowed inside," Corene answered in a loud voice. In fact, she knew before she read it what the note would say in Leah's clear, steady handwriting: *The temple will be closed for a few hours this morning to complete some minor repairs. Please visit us this afternoon.* She and Corene had devised this simple ruse as the best way to make sure no strangers were in the temple when the royal party arrived. The note was in Welchin, of course, which meant that the guards couldn't read it, which meant that Corene could translate it however she wanted for their benefit.

Alette spoke up for almost the first time since they'd climbed in the carriage. "But *we* may enter," she said, and pushed through the door.

Inside, the light was soft and inviting, and the place was empty except for two people—Leah and a young woman who was a complete stranger. She had Dhonshon coloring and was about Alette's age, but otherwise the women didn't look much alike. Her hair was shorter and curlier, her eyes were a pale green, and the shape of her face was rounder. And she didn't wear Alette's perpetual look of haunted sadness, but instead greeted them with an expression of delight and astonishment.

"This is Teyta. A friend of mine," Leah said. "I don't actually know everyone else's name, but this is Corene and this is—"

"Best not to say it out loud," Corene interposed.

"No need. Princess," Teyta whispered, and made a complicated gesture that was clearly meant to denote great respect.

Alette shook her head and whipped off her yellow shawl. "Not today," she answered.

Leah stepped between them. "Quickly," she said. "I don't know that we have much time. Even though the sign's been up since dawn, people have been coming to the door and knocking all morning. I never realized how many people in this city wanted blessings."

"Perhaps someone should guard the door, just in case," Corene said. Melissande and Liramelli hurried over to lean their backs against it, their feet planted as if to resist the incursions of a whole army.

Corene paused to drop coins in the tithing box—a couple of quint-golds, far more than she'd usually donate, but today was a special occasion. They needed the blessings of all the elements.

Teyta and Alette didn't waste any time. They both stripped down to nearly transparent underdresses and then swapped clothes, keeping only their own shoes. Corene had to admit that Alette looked much less like herself when she was wearing Teyta's outfit instead of her own. It was still brighter than the typical Malinquese ensemble, but a more sober blue shot through with streaks of green and yellow. Teyta had thoughtfully brought a thin, woven scarf in the same muted blue, and Alette draped this casually around her head and shoulders.

Teyta, meanwhile, looked every inch Dhonshon royalty in Alette's flame-colored dress and sun-yellow scarf. The two women were about the same height and of similar build, though Teyta's figure was more lush than Alette's. *Because she hasn't been on a steady diet of misery,* Corene thought.

When they were both fully dressed, Corene came over to study them. "Good," she said. "I can't believe what a difference the clothing makes."

Leah's gaze flicked between the two women. "The biggest difference is their eyes," she decided. "The princess's are so *blue.*"

"No one will notice that from a distance," Alette said.

"No, but when we arrive at the palace, someone might," Corene said. "Anyone we encounter in the hallways—"

"I'll just pretend to be sick," Teyta said, closing her eyes and swooning in Corene's direction. "You'll have to help me up the stairs."

"I'd have Foley carry you up, but then people would really start worrying. The empress would even send this annoying woman who claims to be a nurse. *She'd* know you aren't Alette."

Leah turned to glance at Corene. "She won't be able to fool anyone. She can't join you at dinner, for instance—"

Corene shrugged. "Alette skips meals half the time anyway. No one will be surprised when she isn't there."

"All this time you thought I was being unsociable when I was merely laying the groundwork for my escape," Alette said in her usual serious voice. It was a moment before Corene realized she was joking.

She laughed. "Very clever of you!"

There were voices outside and a tentative knocking at the door. Liramelli put her finger to her lips and she and Melissande leaned more purposefully against the wood. After a moment, they heard the sound of voices retreating.

"We can't wait much longer," Leah said, looking a little worried. "Are we done? Can we go?"

Corene glanced around. No stray bits of clothing on the floor, no dropped jewelry that would betray who had so briefly taken shelter there. "I think so."

"Five minutes more," Alette said. "I would welcome a blessing from your temple to see me on my way."

Corene could see that the thought of lingering even a minute longer made Leah want to scream, but who could decline the opportunity for a blessing? "Of course," Leah said courteously.

Alette stepped closer to the barrel and plunged her hand in. "First, I will pull coins for each of you—my benefactors. My friends."

Checking to make sure the door was securely locked, Melissande and Liramelli hurried over. Teyta looked on with bewilderment and curiosity. "I'll explain later," Corene told her.

It only took a few moments for the coins to be drawn and distributed, though Corene and Leah had to translate for everyone. Corene tried not to sigh when courage was bestowed upon her, and Leah looked sardonic when her blessing turned out to be hope. No surprise that Melissande received charm and Liramelli steadfastness. It was clear that Alette was most pleased by the blessing she drew for Teyta—the elay glyph of kindness.

"I think you must be a very kind person," she said, "to do such a remarkable thing for me."

"She is," Leah said. "Now, we must go."

"No, no—we must all draw blessings for Alette before we send her on her way!" Melissande exclaimed. She was already stirring the barrel, already had a coin in her hand, offering it to Corene.

"Travel," Corene said with a smile. "That seems about right."

In quick succession, they also showered Alette with hope, love, luck, and triumph. "Most propitious!" Corene exclaimed in a low voice.

"Indeed, I don't see how they could be better," Liramelli agreed. "*Surely* this means you will be successful on your journey."

Impulsively, Corene threw her arms around Alette. "Oh, how much I wish you would be able to tell us if you make it to safety! Write me, if you can. Send the letter to Darien Serlast in Chialto. The news will eventually find me."

She was a little surprised that Alette actually hugged her back. "I will. You will hear from me. I *will* make my way to freedom."

There was another knock on the door and the sound of someone trying the lock. "*Please* will you go?" Leah begged as soon as they heard the footfalls move away. "The princess and I have a great deal of ground to cover—and *you* have a tricky deception to carry out. It's time to get started."

"It is," Corene said. She reached out to squeeze Alette's hand, one last silent farewell. "Stay here for at least fifteen minutes after we leave. Sit on the red bench as if you are meditating yourself into balance. No one will bother you at the sweela station. We will draw the guards as far away as we can."

Liramelli looked at her. "You don't want to go straight back to the palace?"

Corene shook her head. "That's where we're most likely to be discovered. I want to stay away as long as possible to let them get far away."

"Good," Leah said, nodding. "Go. I'll talk to you later." Her face changed abruptly—almost comically. "I forgot! Corene, I *have* to talk to you. Tomorrow, if possible. Can you come to the market?"

"I can unless Filomara's thrown me in the dungeons for this little escapade. Did something happen?"

"Sort of. Just come to the market. But go now. *Go!*"

Corene checked briefly to make sure Teyta was securely wrapped in the yellow shawl, then pulled open the door and ushered the other women before her. She didn't even glance back at Leah and Alette before she stepped into the sunlight, blinking at the change from the dimness of the temple.

"What a pretty day it is!" she said brightly. "I'd love to go to the red tower and look out over the city. What do you say?"

"Oh—I was just thinking how nice that would be," Liramelli said. She was a terrible actress, incapable of saying the words in an unforced manner, but Corene wasn't sure she was any better herself.

Melissande, no surprise, was a natural. "Yes, of course, you know how much I love climbing to the top of the towers! But I had the most delightful thought. Could we perhaps stop somewhere and pick up food to carry with us, so that we might have a nice meal once we have made our way up?"

"Liramelli?" Corene asked. "Is there someplace we could buy food?"

"Yes—there's a whole street of vendors just a few blocks from the tower. Let's do that!"

So they directed the coachman to drive them halfway across the city, following the beacon of the jeweled flame dancing on top of the southern tower. The soldiers fell in place around them, none of them seeming to pay much attention to the occupants of the carriage. When they reached the district where dozens of small vendors camped out in their carts, hawking an amazing variety of foods, Liramelli and Corene left the others in the carriage and climbed out to reconnoiter. Foley dismounted to follow them through the crowded street, and three of the soldiers did the same. The rest clustered around the carriage, looking around alertly.

"All went well?" Foley murmured when he drew close enough to Corene.

"So far."

"The tower is an excellent idea."

"I'm glad you agree."

They loaded up on breads and fruits and meat pies and things Corene couldn't identify but that Liramelli assured her everyone would like, and then they clambered back into the carriage. It took some time to navigate the vendors' alley, and part of Corene wanted to shriek with impatience. She had to remind herself that it was a good thing to be blocked at every corner by old women slowly crossing the street or riderless horses patiently awaiting their masters. They were in no hurry to get back to the palace—they were as safe now as they would ever be.

It was well past noon before they finally made it to the red tower, and they were all hungry by then. And a little irritable with the strain of constant vigilance. Well, Teyta didn't seem irritable in the least. She was clearly enjoying every part of this expedition—the ride in a well-sprung carriage, the prospect of good food that she hadn't had to cook or pay for, and, of course, the ongoing charade. A couple of times Corene had to whisper a reminder to cover her face with the shawl. Probably not one palace guard out of a thousand would remember that Alette had blue eyes—but just in case that one guard was part of this detail—

Teyta was less thrilled with the adventure once they disembarked from the carriage and she realized that Corene really intended for them all to climb to the top of the tower. "But—it's so very high up," she protested weakly.

"It is," Corene said. "Just think how good your appetite will be once you've had all that exercise!"

Foley went with them, of course; he even carried most of the food, since the rest of them had little energy left to do more than heave themselves up the stairs. Melissande complained for the entire climb—which only proved, Corene thought, that she was in excellent physical condition. Otherwise, she wouldn't have had the breath to grumble.

As for herself, Corene felt stronger with every step she took up. The temperature rose as they grew closer to the blaze, but that only fed her energy. She was a child of fire, after all: wayward and unpredictable and sometimes dangerous. She could wreak havoc or she could beat back the darkness; it was all in how she chose to employ her intelligence, her skill. She might allow herself to be controlled, but only when it suited her own ends. She must never forget that she had the power to forge her own destiny.

Where is all that coming from? she thought with a silent laugh. But she didn't mind. She felt good, she felt strong—she felt, for the first time since she'd arrived in Palminera, like she had done something that mattered.

Liramelli was the first to climb through the trapdoor and she called encouraging words to Teyta, who was struggling. "Just a few more steps—that's right—and here you are! Now catch your breath and look around. I know you'll agree the effort was worth it."

Melissande was a step behind them. "What? Here already? I could climb twice as far!" she exclaimed.

"Perhaps you can *run* down when we're on our way back," Corene said, climbing up beside her. "And then run back up!"

"Yes, a most appealing plan," Melissande said.

"But first we eat," Liramelli said. "I'm utterly starving."

They all dropped to the hard wooden surface of the landing, Foley situating himself right at the trapdoor in case anyone came up looking to offer harm. A steady wind carried away just enough of the heat to make the temperature tolerable—and anyway, they were all so hungry that they couldn't be bothered to complain about the fire. They all tore into the food as if they might not get another meal for the rest of their lives. The hot dishes were cold by now, the fresh ones wilted, but none of them cared.

"Nothing has ever tasted so good," Melissande pronounced. "No, not the finest banquet in Cozique! It is sumptuously delicious."

"My mother doesn't like us to eat street food, but this is wonderful," Teyta agreed. Corene noticed that Teyta tried a little of everything except the meat pie with zeezin. Clearly her grandmother had taught the next two generations the prohibition against that funereal spice.

Once they'd finished their meal, Corene insisted that Teyta stand at the railing and take in the vista below them—the toy-sized houses and horses in the streets nearby; the shadow of the sea in the distance; the chiaroscuro arrangement of the palace labyrinth, light and dark nestled together. "Wasn't I right? Isn't the view worth the effort of the climb?"

"It is pretty impressive," Teyta admitted.

"Yes, exceedingly grand," Melissande added. "But myself, I am not enough enamored of the scenery to want to climb up these steps ever again. And I am starting to grow very warm. Is it time to climb back down?"

Liramelli started gathering leftovers. "I think it is," she said. "We have to get back. I have a great deal to do before dinner."

"Yes—how shall we manage dinner?" Melissande asked as she came gracefully to her feet.

"Alette has been in your room these past few nights, hasn't she?" Corene asked.

"She has. But whenever she doesn't join us for a meal, the empress sends servants with a tray of food. And depending on who the servant is—"

She might realize that Teyta is an imposter.

Corene frowned. "Then perhaps neither of you go down to dinner tonight," she said. "When the servants come, you can answer the door and say Alette is sleeping. Say you both feel unwell and you decided to stay in."

"That should work," Liramelli said. "But how do we get Teyta *out* of the palace? They'll stop her from leaving if they think she's Alette. And when they realize she's not—"

Teyta, who should have been far more nervous than she appeared to be, merely smiled. "My mother and my sister are coming quite early in the morning to make deliveries to the kitchen," she said. "I'll be downstairs awaiting them and I'll walk out when they do. No one will notice that there is one more Dhonshon in the group."

"If it is that simple, we should have sent Alette out with Teyta's family!" Melissande exclaimed.

"No, because if the guards stop Teyta's family tomorrow, they'll find only Teyta," Liramelli said. "But if Alette had tried to escape with them—"

"It still feels very dangerous," Melissande said. "I cannot help but worry."

"Worry won't help anybody now," Liramelli said, following Foley as he lowered himself to the stairs. "We just have to act our parts."

They got a chance to do that sooner than they expected. They had barely settled themselves in the carriage when they spotted a group of five riders approaching the tower on horseback. Corene had barely registered that three of the riders were wearing palace livery when Foley leaned over and spoke in a low, sharp voice.

"Royal guards. And Garameno. He'll want to speak to you."

"Oh no!" Liramelli cried, instantly looking around as if there might be a place to run. "Has he seen us?"

"Of course he has," Corene snapped. "Teyta, draw your shawl closer. Shut your eyes. Lean against Melissande as if you're ill."

Teyta had barely complied with these directives before Garameno hailed them, drawing his horse alongside their carriage.

"I see we all had the same idea on this fine day," he greeted them. "Had I known you were coming here, I would have petitioned to accompany you."

Liramelli fidgeted in her seat, but Corene spoke with what she hoped was indifferent calm. "It wasn't our original destination. First we headed to the Welchin temple down by Little Islands. Coming here was a last-minute thought."

His attention had been caught by Teyta's mournful form. "What's wrong with Alette? She didn't attempt—" He kindly did not complete the sentence.

"No, we think she may have eaten something that disagreed with

her," Corene said. "We stopped to pick up food along the way and—"
She shrugged.

Now Garameno glanced at Liramelli. "You didn't take them to
Tower Alley, did you?"

She looked guilty. "I did! But we were careful about what we
bought—at least I thought we were."

He shook his head, looking faintly amused. "The sickest I ever was
in my life was the time I ate fried meat strips I bought off a cook in
Tower Alley," he said. "I threw up until I thought my bones would be
the next things I vomited. And if I remember correctly, *you* had a similar experience."

Liramelli managed a wan smile. "Yes—Greggorio and I both were
sick on more than one occasion. But that was ages ago! Surely they're
all different vendors by now!"

"Different vendors, same effects," Garameno said. "How are the
rest of you feeling?"

"I was fine until you started talking about vomiting," Corene said.

"I admit, my stomach has been feeling just a tiny bit unsettled,"
Melissande said in an uneasy voice. Teyta gave a small moan, and
Melissande drew the girl closer. "But at the moment I am most concerned about Alette. Can we not simply go home now, as quickly as
possible? I want to get the poor girl to bed."

Garameno waved carelessly and backed his horse from the carriage. "I'll see you all tonight at dinner—or perhaps not!"

Liramelli and Corene waved back; Melissande just patted Teyta's
hair and murmured reassurances into her ear. Corene waited until the
tower was a good distance behind before she spoke in an excited voice.

"That could have been a disaster, but I think it was a stroke of luck,"
she said. "Now he will believe us when none of us come down for dinner."

"Well, I really think I *could* throw up, so I don't know that I was
lying," Liramelli said.

"Oh, you should have done it—right on his shoes!" Corene
answered. "That would have convinced him."

"Can I sit up now?" Teyta asked, her head still on Melissande's
shoulder.

"Better not," Corene decided. "I'm sure some of the soldiers report directly to Filomara. Let's not give them any reason to doubt our story."

They had always known that the diciest part of the whole day would be their arrival at the palace doors, and Corene found herself growing increasingly tense from the minute they passed through the gates of the inner wall. Her stomach felt like it had been clenched in an iron fist, and as they turned into the courtyard and came to a gentle stop, she felt that grip tighten and twist.

Footmen streamed from the door, but Corene didn't wait for their assistance. She leapt from the carriage, ran to the decorative bushes that lined the nearest wall, and vomited up her lunch. A retching noise to her left informed her that Liramelli was right beside her, doing the same.

As she knelt before the bushes, waiting to see if she would be overtaken by another bout of nausea, she heard Melissande's imperious voice behind her. "No, I do not want to be helped up the stairs, and neither does Alette. We are in a very precarious state and if you jostle us, you will be sorry. Merely stay out of our way and let us get to my room. Thank you."

Corene heard the rustle and creak of people disembarking from the carriage, then light footfalls fading away as Melissande led Teyta into the palace, then the sound of wheels and horse hooves as the carriage drove off. More footfalls, these drawing closer, and she felt a hand on her shoulder.

"Can I help you to your room?" It was Foley.

"I'm not sure I can stand."

"I can carry you."

"I think if you move me, I'll just throw up all over you."

"That wouldn't bother me."

She managed a ghost of a laugh. "Well, it would bother *me*. Just let me stay here another minute."

She took a couple of slow, shallow breaths then tried lifting her head. That wasn't so bad. She was even able to glance around to take in the scene. Liramelli had managed to come to her feet with the aid of Lorian, who fussed over her with the solicitude of a beloved uncle. He led her to the door, where other footmen waited, but Corene didn't see if he handed her over to anyone else.

She turned her head just enough to address Foley in a low voice. "Melissande and—and Alette?"

"Through the door with no interference. I didn't watch to see how far they made it. I'm more concerned about you."

"I'm not the key player in this particular drama."

"To me you are."

That was nice to hear, though still inaccurate. Corene put out a hand and Foley gently pulled her to her feet. Nausea roiled through her stomach again, but she waited and it passed. "Let's try it," she said.

The walk from the courtyard through the door took impossibly long, and the path from the door to the stairwell seemed like a mile. Corene came to a halt before placing her foot on the first step and gazed up at the endless staircase.

"I'm not sure—"

"I know," Foley said. He bent and picked her up, cradling her against his chest as he slowly ascended.

Corene closed her eyes as her head swam and the steady motion made her stomach clench again. But in a moment the dizziness subsided and all she was aware of was her cheek pressed against the rough cloth of Foley's jacket. The shape of his body and the scent of his skin. It was almost worth being sick to experience the pleasure of being in Foley's arms.

This was not the first time he'd carried her somewhere. Even in her wretched state, she found herself wondering if he remembered that.

It had been during the winter she and Josetta were away from the Chialto court, hiding out in case anyone else wanted to harm them. They had been traveling the country in the company of two itinerant traders, friends of Zoe's, and Foley had been with them. Of course Foley had been with them. Those were the days when you never saw Josetta unless Foley was three steps behind her.

Jaker and Barlow had been at a small town off the main road, finding buyers for their merchandise, but they'd left Corene and Josetta at the campground with the wagon. The day had been cold but sunny, and it was a rare treat to not be trapped in the rocking wagon all day, covering the interminable open miles of the western provinces. So they'd gone off for a slippery walk across an icy meadow, reveling in the sunshine and the exercise, and Corene had tripped and fallen and twisted her ankle.

She'd tried not to cry—because she was twelve years old now and people were finally starting to treat her like an adult and Josetta was finally starting to like her after all those years of despising her—but she couldn't help it. She was in too much pain. "I'm sorry, I'm sorry," she said over and over as Josetta carefully straightened her leg and felt along the bruise and pronounced, with great relief, that she didn't think anything was broken.

"Sorry about *what*?" Josetta finally said, but not in a mean way. It had taken Corene that long to realize Josetta never said anything in a mean way. Josetta was barely fifteen herself, scrawny and big-eyed and nervous and worried, but there was something so steady about her. You felt like you could hold on to her if you were going under.

"I'm sorry I fell—I'm sorry I'm crying—I'm sorry I'm so horrible—" She sobbed out all the words.

Josetta had left off poking at Corene's foot and scooted over until she could take Corene's shaking body in a close and comforting hug. "I'm not sorry about any of it," she said. And even though her words didn't exactly answer Corene's confession, Corene understood Josetta's meaning: *Terrible things have brought us to this point, but here we are and you're my sister and I love you.* Corene hadn't had the words for all that when she was twelve, but she had never forgotten the feeling. Josetta was the first person who'd ever loved her just for existing, without requiring anything from her, even that she be lovable. Coming to that realization had been one of the profoundest moments of Corene's life.

"But I can't walk back to camp," she hiccuped.

"It's all right," Josetta replied. "Foley will carry you."

And he had, matter-of-factly scooping her up in his arms and moving with great care through the snowy landscape. Corene was at the age when she had just started to notice boys—the handsome soldiers in the royal army, the promising sons of the Five Families who came to the palace on public days—and she practically adored Foley. He must have been twenty at the time, and he could have stood in for her ideal—a tall, quiet man who never bothered boasting about the fact that he was extremely good at the job he had chosen to do. He wasn't handsome in the well-groomed way of the rich boys she saw every day, but he had strong clean features and a serious face that became merry when he laughed.

And there he was, holding Corene against his chest, carrying her as if she weighed nothing at all. She'd never forgotten the thoughts that had circled in her excitable, pain-hazed, twelve-year-old brain on that day. *I love Foley. I will love him forever.*

And here he was again, holding her carefully against his body, carrying her as if she was sweet and precious cargo. Was he devoted to her or was he just too stubborn to allow harm to come to her while she was under his protection? Did he watch her so closely because she was an assignment or because she was a woman?

I shouldn't get sick. I shouldn't get hurt. I think such impossible things when I do, she thought. But she buried her face more deeply into his shirt, took in another breath, inhaling his scent again.

The palace stairwell, unlike the one at the tower, seemed much too short.

Someone had alerted the servants, so Emilita was awaiting them in Corene's room. The little maid clucked in sympathy as Foley placed Corene on the bed, then she practically pushed him out the door.

"I will take care of her now," she said in Malinquese. Corene didn't have the strength to protest. She lay on the bed, feeling her stomach cramp again, and knew she wasn't done with the day's miseries yet.

But in her right fist she clutched a small object, and now she opened her eyes just enough to get a look at it. An ordinary silver button, round and a little tarnished. It had been on Foley's jacket, and it had come off in her hand as she clung to him for support.

She knew she should give it back to him in the morning. But she was pretty sure that she wouldn't.

NINETEEN

The early evening was pretty uncomfortable, but by midnight Corene felt her body relax, and she fell deeply asleep. When she woke up, bright sunlight announced that late morning had arrived with its usual brassy insistence. She felt pummeled and somewhat giddy, but otherwise good. And she was starving.

She'd just emerged from the bathing room, freshly cleaned and dressed, when there was a tentative knock on the door. Liramelli stood on the other side, wan but upright, and carrying a basket of fresh-baked rolls.

"If you will ever again trust my recommendations on food, I brought you breakfast," Liramelli said.

"This is exactly what I wanted," Corene said, ushering her in and settling them both at a table. "How are you feeling?"

"Better than yesterday." Liramelli shuddered. "I'm so sorry—"

"Like I said, I think it was lucky," Corene interrupted. "It didn't feel like it last night, but since we had no trouble getting Teyta into the palace—" She gave the other girl an inquiring look. "Unless you know something that I don't."

Liramelli shook her head. "I went by Melissande's room before I came here, but her maid said no one was there. I don't even know if either of them got sick or if they were both just pretending."

"I haven't checked on Foley, either," Corene said guiltily. *So much for love.* "Though he seemed fine when he left last night."

"I think you and I were the only ones who ate the meat pie," Liramelli said. "Melissande doesn't like zeezin and Teyta wouldn't eat it and I don't know about Foley. But I'm pretty sure that's what made us sick."

Corene crammed the last of a roll in her mouth and grinned. "I saw Lorian helping you into the palace with his own two hands," she said. "He didn't even seem to worry that you might throw up on him."

Liramelli smiled faintly. "I've always been his favorite. Unless Greggorio's in the room, and then *Greggorio* is his favorite. He always knew we were sneaking around the palace, getting into rooms where we shouldn't be going, but he never reported us to Filomara."

Though Lorian had taken the first opportunity he had to describe *Jiramondi's* illicit activities to the empress. Corene shook her head; thoughts for another day. She came decisively to her feet. "We have to find Melissande," she said. "I have to know what happened."

The minute she opened her door, Foley opened his as well. He looked perfectly normal, perfectly rested; the jacket he wore had no missing buttons. "You seem better," he said. "Both of you."

Liramelli blushed and murmured something indistinguishable, but Corene answered, "I *am* better, thank you. What about you? Did you ever get sick?"

He shook his head. "Must have eaten different things."

"Do you know anything about—"

Before Corene could complete her sentence, Liramelli touched her arm. Melissande was hurrying down the long corridor, and she was alone.

"Inside," she murmured, and the four of them quickly reentered Corene's room, locked the door, then huddled together near the farthest wall, so no eavesdroppers could overhear.

"Teyta is gone," Melissande breathed. "We got up very early this morning and crept down the hallways to the kitchen and waited there for what seemed like a very long time. Do you have any idea how many people come to the palace in the morning? Before it is even light?" Even through her whisper, her voice sounded aggrieved.

Liramelli was amused. "Dozens."

"Hundreds! I would say that is a great vulnerability of the palace, but Teyta assured me that there are always soldiers lined up along the kitchen path, watching everyone come and go."

Corene made a circling motion with her hand, indicating that Melissande should get to the point. "So, Teyta and I loitered in the hallway until we saw her mother and sister come in with packages. Then I stepped into the kitchen and was very charming and apologetic but explained how hungry I was since I had missed my dinner and could somebody find some crust of bread for me to eat? And while I talked to the cook and the undercook and everyone else on the kitchen staff, Teyta slipped over to be with her family. And as they left, I stepped outside as if I merely wanted fresh air. But I watched as Teyta and the others casually walked past the guards and kept going, down the paths and out of sight." She took a deep breath. "And nobody stopped them for as long as I could see. I think they are safely gone."

Corene and Liramelli gave very quiet squeals of glee and threw their arms around each other, practically dancing where they stood. Foley didn't join the celebrations, but he grinned broadly as he watched them.

"We will have to go by Little Islands soon and find out for sure," Corene said. "But I think we've done it."

"Now if only Alette and her young man have managed to find a boat to safety," Liramelli said.

That silenced them all and brought the worry back full force. *If only we could know,* Corene thought. Alette and Cheelin might be prisoners of an enemy ship or dead on the ocean floor. Unless Corene and the others heard for certain otherwise, they would always be left to wonder.

"She left a message for us," Melissande added.

"She did? What kind of message?" Corene asked.

"After I left the kitchen this morning, I went to her suite. I am going to tell everyone that I sent Alette back to her own room sometime in the night, so I wanted to make sure the bed looked like it had been slept in.

The place was very tidy, so I pulled out clothes and shoes and dropped things on the floor, and did many other small things. When I went to pull back the covers, I found these."

All this time, she had been holding something in her hand—what looked like a scroll of colorful fabric. Now she unrolled it to reveal three squares of cloth, each about the size of Corene's hand, one purple, one green, one blue. In the center of each, embroidered in fine gold thread, was a blessing glyph.

"She made these for us," Melissande said, and now her quiet voice was gilded with tears. "Remember we promised that if we ran away, we would leave behind our blessings so the others knew we had left of our own accord? She did not leave *her* blessings—she left ours."

Corene felt her own throat close up. "The blue one says charm," she told them gruffly. "Obviously Melissande's. The green one is loyalty. Liramelli's. The purple one is mine. Courage."

Melissande distributed them and Liramelli held her scrap of cloth briefly against her cheek. Corene saw the fabric get stained by a tear before Liramelli folded it and tucked it into a pocket.

"She got to safety. I have to believe that," Liramelli said quietly.

"Me, too," Corene said. "She'll let us know."

Foley spoke up. "Still, the longer you can keep her disappearance quiet, the farther away she will get."

Melissande nodded. "I thought of that. I locked her door when I left. And then in case anyone came to *my* room looking for the key, I buried it in the kitchen garden."

"You've had a very busy day, and it's hardly even started!" Corene exclaimed.

"I know. And I am almost faint with hunger."

"Liramelli brought me some rolls, but I'm hungry, too," Corene said. "Let's go downstairs and find food."

It was dinnertime before Corene heard anyone ask directly about Alette. She and Melissande and Liramelli had done their best to avoid conversations with members of the royal family—even Steff—forgoing their usual language lessons and penta games and other group activities. Instead, they'd all claimed lingering effects of illness and kept to their rooms or taken solitary walks in the garden to pass the time.

But they all made it to dinner, since Filomara had let it be known that various city officials would be on hand and she expected all her guests and relatives to attend. Corene thought the meal might not go well, so to bolster her spirits she put on her favorite Welchin tunic and trousers, wrapped her purple shawl around her shoulders, and slipped Alette's embroidered blessing in her pocket. *Courage,* she thought.

Once she made it to the dining room, she was far from pleased to see Bartolo and Sattisi already there, making one of their mercifully rare appearances. Also at the table were Liramelli's parents, the mayor, and a handful of other dignitaries.

Corene managed to secure a spot between Steff and Jiramondi, so she actually enjoyed herself for most of the meal. Jiramondi teased her about her recent escapade and then recounted his own miserable episodes in Tower Alley.

"Why does anyone ever go *back* there?" Corene demanded.

"Because you might go ten times every year and only get sick once every three years," he said. "Because the food is cheap—and it's usually good—and it is fun to do something so unstructured. And to gamble that *this* time it will go well."

"I don't think *I'll* go back ten times," Corene said.

It appeared that Filomara had been auditing their conversation, though she sat five places removed from them at the head of the table. She leaned forward and said, "No, and you would be wise to never return. I cannot believe any of my nephews took you to such a place."

"It wasn't us," Jiramondi said. "Just Liramelli."

Who cast her eyes down. "I'm truly sorry."

"Well, no lasting harm done, since everyone has recovered," Liramelli's father said.

Greggorio glanced around the table. "Not Alette," he said. "I haven't seen her all day."

Everyone looked Melissande's way. Though it hadn't been openly discussed, everyone knew where Alette had been sleeping lately. And, Corene thought, everyone probably knew why.

Melissande was the picture of innocence. "I sent her back to her room in the middle of the night," she said. "It is not an entirely pleasant thing when two people are sharing a suite and both of them are— indisposed."

Greggorio frowned. "And no one's checked on her all day?" He pushed his chair away from the table, but Filomara frowned him back into place. She lifted a hand and glanced at the doorway, nodding at the shadowy figure who stood there. Lorian, Corene supposed. She didn't hear the sound of footsteps moving away, but she was sure someone had been dispatched to Alette's room. She tightened her fingers around her fork and took another bite. Better finish her meal now while she still had the chance.

"Before you had the unfortunate encounter with the meat pies, you had a most pleasant day, or so my daughter tells me," said Liramelli's mother, Mariana, obviously trying to lighten the mood. "There is a Welchin temple at the Little Islands, she said? Tell me what that's like."

That was an easy conversational gambit, and Corene gratefully took it. She described the ritual of the blessings and then gestured at Filomara. "The empress drew blessings when she was visiting in Welce earlier this year."

"Oh, do tell us," Garameno drawled. "Which attributes were bestowed upon my aunt?"

Filomara unexpectedly answered before Corene could. "Endurance, power, and surprise," the empress said. "I was not happy with that final one—until the surprise was revealed a few moments later." She nodded in Steff's direction and her face softened into what passed for a smile. "That I had two living grandsons."

"Yes, an excellent revelation," the prefect agreed. "I am looking forward to grandchildren myself."

Liramelli seemed embarrassed and stared down at her plate. Mariana replied gaily, "Not *quite* yet, however."

"I went to the Welchin temple about a nineday ago," Jiramondi said. "In case anyone is interested, my own blessings were patience, honor, and triumph."

"Not the ones I would have expected," Garameno murmured.

"That's exactly what I said," Corene replied with a smirk. "I would be quite curious to see which ones *you* pulled from the barrel."

"Well, then—" Garameno started to say.

But he was interrupted by Lorian's sudden entrance. "Majesty, she is gone."

For a moment, it was as if no one in the dining room heard or understood the significance of his words. The room still buzzed with the ordinary undercurrent of chatter and clatter: Melissande was laughing with Harlo; Liramelli was explaining something to Sattisi. Only Filomara and Garameno looked up sharply when Lorian spoke.

"Gone?" Filomara repeated, frowning. "Not in her room? Where then?"

"No one knows. Her maid has not seen her since yesterday. I will make inquiries with the rest of the staff."

Now Jiramondi caught wind of the conversation. "Who's gone? What are you talking about?"

"Alette isn't in her quarters," Garameno said.

Jiramondi didn't look too concerned. "So? Is she in Melissande's room? Or in the library or the garden? There are hundreds of places she could be."

Melissande broke off her private conversation. "Alette? She wasn't in my suite when I came down to dinner, but I suppose—" She shrugged.

Greggorio was on his feet again, and this time Filomara's scowl didn't cow him. "I'll look for her. I know the places she likes to go."

He pushed past Lorian and out the door. Filomara nodded at her steward. "Send the servants out. Search every room."

That'll take some time, Corene thought, sipping her water. She wondered if it would be possible for someone to hide for days—quintiles, even—in some of the half-abandoned reaches of the palace. The sixth story, for instance, or the tunnels beneath the storerooms. *Definitely the tunnels,* she decided. *Access to food, access to water. You'd go mad, but that might be better than whatever you were facing aboveground.*

She took a deep breath and said, "I don't know why you're so worried."

Filomara gave her a hard look. "I'm worried because she was recently ill and she is under my protection, and I don't want her to be lying somewhere in a dead faint."

Corene sipped her water again, eyeing the empress over the glass. "But you know she has to be somewhere on the premises," she said.

"None of us can leave without soldiers following us, can we?" She gestured around the table. "I mean Melissande and Alette and me, of course. Steff, too, probably. I'm not sure."

Now everyone at the table was so quiet that the *clink* of Melissande setting down her fork sounded louder than cannon fire. Filomara didn't flinch.

"I have an armed escort every time I leave as well," the empress replied. "My subjects are loyal and loving, but there are always dangers. I would hope no one of any prominence ever travels the city unattended."

"I tried it once—just to see," Corene went on. Her voice was polite, almost casual. "I was chased through the city by royal guards, but I eluded them. I saw them pounce on a woman with some violence just because she looked like me. They didn't seem bent on my *protection* so much as my *capture*."

Filomara narrowed her eyes, considering how to answer. Harlo spoke first. "Filomara, is that true? They are under protective guard?"

"They are representatives of foreign nations and their lives are precious," Filomara snapped. "If harm came to any of them, we would instantly be at war—with yet *another* nation! Of course I have them watched! How could they possibly object?"

"I do object," Corene said. She couldn't resist glancing at Garameno. "I have never liked it when anyone tried to control me."

"You have been treated with every kindness," the empress ground out. "Shown nothing but courtesy. If you wanted to leave, you had merely to say so. But you have never been prisoners here."

"No, we've been hostages," Corene said calmly. "You hope to embroil our home countries in your stupid war with Berringey."

There was a small outcry at that from Harlo and Mariana and even Bartolo. Filomara just gazed stonily back at Corene.

"If that is the case," she said. "I have been successful. There are Welchin naval ships a few miles out from the harbor and Coziquela ships are on the way."

"Really? Coziquela soldiers come to avenge me?" Melissande said. "But how romantic!"

"Not to avenge you," Filomara snapped. "To keep you safe from Berringese invaders."

"But the Berringese have done nothing to harm me," Melissande pointed out.

"Neither have I!" Filomara exclaimed. "I have kept you here, but I have kept you safe! Your own parents would have done the same!"

"Clearly not," Corene said. "My father allowed me to leave the country against his expressed wishes. He might be watchful, but he's not a jailor."

"Or perhaps he's not as careful as he could be with the things that really matter to him," Filomara shot back.

Corene laughed. "As careful as *you* are?" she demanded. "You sent your youngest daughter to Berringey to be murdered."

"That's a lie!" Filomara cried. She slammed her open hand on the table and everyone pushed back as if they wanted to run from the room. But no one did. Everyone sat, frozen with horror, staring between the two of them. "I sent her to Berringey to marry a prince!"

"Who you knew very well might be sacrificed, along with his whole family, if certain circumstances arose," Corene said. "You gambled with her life. And you did it knowing exactly what the risks were."

Filomara was on her feet now, shaking with wrath. She had such presence, even with her small stature, that she seemed to tower over them. "I *loved* her," she said in a low, furious voice. "I gave her the greatest opportunity of her life."

Corene stood more slowly. "And yet Subriella is dead. And Aravani is dead," she said, knowing she sounded ruthless, sounded cold. She didn't need to hear Steff murmur her name in a shocked voice to realize that. But she went on unheeding. "And ever since then, it has been nothing but lying and scheming as every single member of your court vies to be named your heir."

Filomara's worn, sad face creased into a grim smile. "*You* would know something about that. You have fought for a crown at your court and at mine."

"I'm done now," Corene said simply. "I want to go. Malinqua is too poisonous. Palminera is too dangerous. I don't want to be the next corpse that shows up in this scramble for a throne."

There was another outcry at that, this one louder. "What do you mean by that?" Garameno demanded.

She glanced down at him. "Count the bodies," she advised, just as Foley had suggested so many ninedays ago. Why hadn't she listened to him? "Subriella. Aravani. Aravani's daughters. Two of Filomara's brothers. Sarona. And now possibly Alette. *Someone's* trying to clear a path to the throne and make sure there are no inconvenient bastards sired by careless heirs. I don't want to get in the way."

Now the low murmur around the table was of consternation and denial. Corene could only make out a few phrases. *But it was an accident! . . . A fever! . . . Nobody could have known about Berringey . . . Donato and Morli killed each other, everybody knows that . . .* But she watched as a few faces registered doubt, horror, speculation. *Could it possibly be true?*

Filomara's hand slammed on the table again, bringing them all back to shocked silence. "Do you think I haven't *noticed*?" the empress roared. "Do you think I *overlooked* the graves of my daughter, my granddaughters, my girls that I loved?" She swept a hand out as if she would sweep the room clean of murmuring ghosts. "Morli dead—and then Donato dead—*not* the same night, as everyone supposes, but two days apart. Who mixed those poisons?" Her finger stabbed at Garameno. "Your father?" She pointed at Jiramondi. "Yours?" She went around the room, gesturing at the mayor, at Harlo, even the stunned Sattisi. "You or you or you? Do you think I have not taken what steps I could to protect the heirs that I have left? Do not come here, little Welchin girl, and think to school me on the finer points of treason. I was old and bowed with grief before you were even born."

"And I am young and in fear for my life," Corene said deliberately, shutting out any twinges of pity. "I want to go home."

"How I wish I could send you there," Filomara spat out. "But I do not want *your* death on my conscience as well, and it is not safe to let you set sail from the harbor."

"Well, then," Corene said. "I suppose I'll have to gratefully accept the escort of your soldiers whenever I leave the palace. Maybe they'll keep any schemers at court from trying to kill me."

That unforgivable remark elicited a chorus of gasps and exclamations, though she was pretty sure she heard someone mutter, *"Don't be so sure."* Steff, probably. She didn't think she'd manage a better exit line, so, inclining her head in an ironic gesture of respect, she pivoted on her heel and stalked out.

She was almost pushed down the hall by the explosion of conversation that erupted as she left. She could feel her heart pounding; the argument had been both exhilarating and unnerving, but she thought she'd handled her part well enough. Melissande would certainly tell her later if she hadn't.

She was so tightly wound that she flinched a little when Foley unexpectedly fell in step beside her. "I didn't realize you'd stayed at the door for the whole meal," she said as an excuse.

"It seemed wise," he answered. "Things have been so unsettled lately that it's hard to gauge where disaster might strike next."

"You heard my whole performance?"

He nodded.

"What did you think?"

He glanced at her. "I couldn't decide if you were trying to turn the subject away from Alette's disappearance—or throw the whole court into turmoil with accusations of murder."

"A little of both," Corene admitted. "If everyone has something else to think about, maybe they won't look for Alette so hard. Or, at least, they won't look for her outside of the palace. They'll be hunting for bodies in dark closets."

"You've just drawn the highest degree of attention to yourself," he said quietly. "You're more at risk now than you've ever been."

She laughed. "I think I'm *safer* than I've ever been. If I die now, I've just *proved* there's a killer at court. This person has only succeeded for so long by being very careful."

"Maybe," he said. "But maybe you've made the killer so angry that he or she just wants you dead."

A few more moments and they were at the door to her room. Corene glanced at Foley as she put her fingers on the handle, surprised to see a look of uneasy indecision on his face.

"What is it?" she said.

"Your safety," he said. "Always your safety."

"Ah." She opened the door but didn't step inside. "You're wondering if it's time you slept in my room."

"Yes," he admitted.

She gestured across the threshold. "Plenty of room."

"Plenty of scandal."

"My father is immune to scandal, or haven't you noticed? Josetta was sharing a bed with Rafe long before anyone even knew he was royalty, and Darien never blinked."

"Josetta isn't his daughter."

She ignored this. "You can't possibly think my *mother* would object. She sees all men as means to an end. To be used however the situation dictates."

He watched her a moment, his face troubled. "You're not usually so cynical."

"Yes, I am."

"You *pretend* to be," he said. "But you usually don't mean it."

"I mean it," she said, "I just wish it wasn't true."

"What you said tonight—did you mean that?"

"Which of the many things I said?"

"About being done. About wanting to go home."

She couldn't decide if she should nod or shake her head. "Yes and no. I'd like to leave Malinqua, but I don't want to go home. I don't know what options that leaves me."

"Plenty of other places in the world."

It was nice to feel her face lighten in a smile. "Yes, we could head to Yorramol! And join Alette there, maybe."

"If you went to Yorramol, you might never come back," he said.

"Or come back so changed no one would recognize me."

"I don't think anyone ever changes that much, except in stories."

"I think I'd recognize *you*," she said softly. "No matter how much you changed."

He shook his head. "I'm always the same."

"Maybe because you want to be," she said. "I'd like to be different."

"Would you? Different in what way?"

She raised her hands as if she could scoop the right words out of the air. "Less angry. More certain. Happier. Nicer. And I wish I didn't care so much about—" She didn't complete the sentence.

He tipped his head to one side, as if trying to figure it out. "Your father loves you, you know. You don't have to win his affection."

"That's not it," she said. "Or that's only part of it. I want him to be proud of me, but I want it to be because I'm doing something that *matters*. I always thought I had to be on a throne somewhere—in Welce or Malinqua or somewhere else, who knows?—because that's what I was trained for. But I'm starting to realize I don't even like court life. All the scheming, all the intrigue. I like the parts where we talk about international trade and alliances between nations. I don't like the parts where someone wants me dead if I flirt with the wrong person." She sighed. "And I definitely don't want to marry any of the potential heirs to the Malinquese throne. This trip has been a mistake from start to finish."

"Maybe you didn't win yourself a crown," he agreed. "And maybe you didn't win your father's approval. But you achieved one thing that's really important."

"What's that?"

"The same thing I achieved when I moved from my father's house to Chialto," he said. "You altered the trajectory of your life. You didn't know what you would find at the end of the road, but you knew you wanted to be on a different road than the one stretching out before you."

That was so accurate she could not, for a moment, think of a reply. "Are you glad you left your father's farm?" she finally asked.

"I am," he said. "What about you?"

"I'm glad you left the farm, too," she answered.

"That wasn't my question."

"Really? I misunderstood."

His half-smile was back, but he slowly shook his head. "I don't believe you did."

She laughed. "At any rate, I'm glad you're here in Malinqua to keep watch over me—particularly after my remarks tonight. I imagine Filomara isn't the only one unhappy with me right now."

"And we're right back to the beginning of our conversation," he said. "Trying to figure out how to keep you safe."

She kept her face innocent. "Only one way to truly ensure my safety."

"I know." He squared his shoulders. "I'll get my things."

. . .

It was both delightful and unnerving to have Foley alone in the suite with her. She felt giddy and a little breathless, thinking how near he would be, wondering what he would wear as he sought his bed, wondering what *she* should wear and if she should take the opportunity to present herself to him while she was clad in only a flimsy nightgown. *Oh, Foley, I heard a strange noise and it frightened me . . .*

She decided that she'd caused enough scandal already tonight; she should behave with decorum in her own bedroom. So she put on a thick robe that covered her from throat to ankle—it was more chaste than some of her dinner ensembles—and paused to bid him good night after she washed up in the bathing room. She was surprised to find he didn't plan to ensconce himself in the maid's room, which he considered too far from the entrance. Instead he had made a pallet for himself right in front of the door to the hallway. "That way no one can get in without tripping over me," he explained.

"Unless they climb in through the window," she said, just to tease him.

"Too high to do without a rope, and the walls are too slick to manage it without special tools," he replied.

"Are you serious? You've thought about that?"

"Of course I have."

"You're even better at your job than I thought you were."

"Somehow that doesn't sound like a compliment."

She laughed. "It is! I don't know why you always doubt me most when I'm being completely sincere."

He eyed her for a moment and didn't answer. She laughed again and pulled a chair close to where he had settled on his pallet. "So I have a question for you," she said in a chatty tone.

He looked even more doubtful. "What," he said, his voice flat.

"How often have you spent the night in a woman's room?"

He rolled his eyes and rested his back against the door. "How often have you been told your behavior is inappropriate?"

"More times than I can count!" she retorted. "So is that your answer, too? More times than you can count?"

"I think you knew I wouldn't answer the question when you asked it."

"But I want to know."

"But I don't have to tell you."

She flounced a little, not easy to do on a hard-backed chair. "Well, then, how often did you spend the night in *Josetta's* room?" When he looked even more annoyed, she hastened to add, "Just watching over her! Keeping her safe! I wasn't implying anything else."

"The situation never arose," he said.

She allowed herself to look unconvinced. "Really? That's odd. I thought—" Her voice trailed off.

"Why? What did Josetta say?" he asked, caught briefly off guard.

"Well, I just thought—I mean, it always seemed that you were so close—or at least, *Josetta* felt close to *you*—"

"That might be," he said. He seemed to be thinking over how to frame his reply. "I suppose it's not uncommon for a young woman— who has been very sheltered—to sometimes find that she's—that she thinks she is—" He started over. "A man who has agreed to guard her with his life might appear in a somewhat romantic light—"

Corene could hardly contain her delight. "I knew it!" she exclaimed. "Josetta offered herself to you, didn't she? She always said there was nothing between the two of you, but I always thought she liked you more than she'd admit."

Now he seemed alarmed. "I didn't say that."

She shrugged, guessing at what must have happened. "Josetta approached you, but you turned her down with talk about guards and assignments and duty. And being the sweet, polite, good girl that she is, Josetta meekly nodded and turned away. Is that what happened?"

"Nothing happened," he said.

"Huh," she said. She resettled in the chair again, but really it wasn't made for lounging around and having conversations about love. She couldn't get comfortable. Or maybe she just couldn't relax. "Well, I'd still like to know the answer to my original question."

"What question was that?" he asked wearily.

"About all the girls you've been in love with."

"I've been too busy to fall in love."

"No one's that busy."

"Maybe it's just that I love my job."

"Right now your job is me," she said.

His face stilled. His body stilled. He just looked at her. Corene felt herself freeze in place on the unforgiving chair as she stared back at him.

"That's right," he said, finally, slowly, not looking away from her. "And my job is to keep you safe. From any hazards that might arise— even the ones you create yourself."

Her chin lifted at the reprimand. *You might throw yourself at me, but I will guard you from the consequences of your reckless behavior.* "Are you really that good?" she asked softly. "You can save me from my own indiscretions?"

"I won't have to," he said. "You're too smart to put yourself in harm's way."

"Unless I don't think I'm putting myself at risk."

"Oh," he said, "I think you always know exactly what the risks are. You like to *play* with fire, but you won't let it burn you."

Abruptly, she came to her feet, feeling oddly shaky. She wondered if Foley was half as unnerved by this conversation as she was. He still sat utterly motionless, watching her with a coiled attention. *Yes. Probably just as unnerved.* But far more determined to remain unmoved.

"I'm not so sure," she said, moving toward the bedroom but glancing back at Foley. "What's the point of being sweela, after all, if you can't handle a few flames?"

The farther away she got, the more Foley seemed to relax. "What's the point of being torz," he retorted, "if you can't remain steadfast and strong?"

That made her laugh, which made him smile in return. "I feel like I should warn you that this conversation isn't over," she said.

"You don't have to," he said. "I know you well enough by now to realize that on my own."

She gave another laugh, this one interrupted by a yawn. Foley's smile grew wider.

"Go to bed," he said. "You're exhausted."

"I shouldn't be so tired. I've only been up a few hours."

"You were in pretty bad shape yesterday. I'm surprised you've stayed on your feet this long."

She yawned again. "You're right. I'm going right to sleep. I'll see you in the morning." Her hand on the doorknob, she suddenly remembered a detail that had slipped her mind. "Oh, no! I promised Leah I'd come see her today! She has something to tell me."

"I sent her a note this morning when it was clear you weren't going to be leaving the palace. I said you'd try to get to the market tomorrow or the next day."

"Excellent. I wonder what she wants, though?"

"I guess you'll find out in the morning."

TWENTY

Breakfast was about as awkward an occasion as Corene could remember in her entire life, and there had been plenty of unpleasant meals in the court at Chialto. Garameno, Jiramondi, Sattisi, and Bartolo were the only ones in the dining room when she walked in. She cursed herself for not going by Melissande's room on her way, but she'd been too hungry to make the detour.

Bartolo glared at her so hard that she almost turned tail and ran out, but then she summoned a radiant smile and marched right past him to the food laid out on the sideboard. No one spoke as she loaded her plate and sat down as far from the others as the table would allow. She tried not to feel self-conscious as she lifted her first forkful and started to chew.

"You've managed to work up an appetite, I see," Garameno said in a level voice. "More than some of us have done."

She took a sip of keerza to wash down the food. "If you find my presence irksome, you could advise the empress to send me home," she responded politely. "I'm sure she'd listen to you. You have such influence with her."

Bartolo snorted in disgust. "I suppose you find your food tastier when it's seasoned with insults," he said.

"It's actually freedom that tastes best to me," she shot back.

They all looked up hopefully when they heard footsteps coming down the hall, but when Steff stepped through the door, things didn't improve. "Oh," he said, clearly at a loss. "I thought everyone would be done with breakfast by now."

"More examples of Welchin courtesy," Jiramondi murmured.

"Well, the room usually *is* empty by now," Steff said. He didn't let the icy atmosphere prevent him from filling his plate and sitting across from Corene, and he didn't let the audience prevent him from speaking his mind. "You should apologize to my grandmother. I can't believe you said such things."

"I won't apologize. I should have said them sooner. Or *you* should have."

He sent a quick glance up the table to where the other four were obviously listening. "Maybe she should have heard our suspicions about a murderer, but the other things? About her daughters? That was awful."

Corene shrugged and ate a piece of buttered bread. "I guess I'm just an awful person."

"That was my own conclusion," Garameno said.

"She isn't usually," Steff said, unexpectedly firing up in Corene's defense. "She just isn't *careful*. But last night she was trying to be mean, and I don't know why."

Bartolo came to his feet and threw his napkin to the table. "Because she thinks cruelty is amusing," he declared. "As only fools and children do." And on that dramatic line, he stalked from the room. Sattisi scrambled to her feet and followed behind him.

Garameno backed his chair from the table and smoothly maneuvered it to the door. "I think you had an agenda," he said quietly. "But I don't think you're about to share it."

"I think I was pretty clear," she said. "My agenda is to leave. If I'm unpleasant enough, I figure someone will help me go."

"If you're unpleasant enough, someone might confine you to your room," Garameno said.

"Better than cutting my throat and throwing me down the back stairwell," she said cheerfully.

Garameno gave no answer but a muted sound of disgust and wheeled himself through the door. "Wait!" Corene called. "Has there been any news of Alette?"

Garameno shook his head and kept going, so she looked over at Jiramondi. Who also shook his head.

"No," he said, "and my aunt is most concerned."

"I imagine she is! So I suppose she's had servants check the empty rooms—and the tunnels below the palace—"

"And the kitchens and the servants' rooms and the gardens and the mazes," Jiramondi supplied. "I expect all the living quarters to be searched within the next nineday, in case someone thinks they are *helping* Alette by hiding her."

"You can search my room anytime," Corene said. "I'm not harboring her."

"I didn't mean you."

Steff had been pretty focused on his food, but he looked up to find both of them watching him speculatively. "*I* don't have her," he exclaimed. "Servants are in and out of my room all the time! Ask them!"

"No, Greggorio seems more likely," Jiramondi said on a sigh. "I imagine his room is among the first ones that Lorian had searched."

Corene toyed with her food. "Is there any thought that she might have just *left*? Escaped the soldiers somehow and slipped out of the city?"

"I would wish that were the case, but it's hard to see how," Jiramondi replied. "And even if she got past the palace guards and the gate guards—where could she go? I don't believe she has friends in the city, and there are few ships to give her passage out."

Corene laid down her fork. "What will Filomara tell her father?"

Jiramondi offered her an unhappy smile. "I have no idea. My guess is she will wait until he *asks* about his daughter. Which he has not done lately due to the fact that the Berringese navy is blockading our harbor."

"And due to the fact that he does not seem to feel much affection for any of his children," Corene added. "But if he believes she has been harmed at your hands—or disappeared while under your care—he might have the excuse he needs to join this war."

"You're right!" Jiramondi replied, feigning astonishment. "I hadn't thought of that!" He came to his feet and gazed down at her for a moment. "How fortunate we are to have you here to point out all the things we otherwise might have missed."

She stared back at him, unrepentant. "Send me home," she said. "And bumble on in your own way without me."

Jiramondi laughed and left the room without making any other answer. Corene stifled a sigh and turned her attention to Steff. "I don't think Jiramondi likes me anymore."

Steff shrugged and spoke casually through a mouthful of food. "You did something, didn't you?"

It was a second before she registered that he had switched to Welchin and that his voice was too soft to carry beyond the edge of the table. "What do you mean?"

He gave her a look. *You know exactly what I mean.* "You're not upset enough."

She exhaled on the ghost of a laugh. "And here I was thinking the same thing about you."

"I'm not because you're not. And Liramelli's not."

"I'm trying to be. It's hard to know how I would behave if—" She shrugged.

He swallowed a long gulp of keerza, glanced at the empty doorway, and said, "Is she safe?"

"I hope so. Hard to know for sure."

He nodded. "Let me know if you ever do."

"I will."

"But you still shouldn't have been so dreadful to Filomara last night."

"Then they should let me go home."

"This isn't a good time for leaving the city. The blockade."

"There must be some ships getting in and out," she said. "I want to be on one of them."

A shadow at the door pulled her attention that way a moment before Lorian stepped noiselessly inside. "The empress wants to see you," he said in his formal way. "Both of you. Immediately."

Steff crammed a last piece of bread in his mouth as he came to his feet. Corene summoned an uncaring, disdainful expression, but in truth she felt anxious. Filomara probably wanted to express her deep displeasure over Corene's display last night, and Corene didn't imagine the experience would be enjoyable. She was glad Steff would be there—even if she did think he might take Filomara's side.

Silently they followed Lorian down the halls to one of the formal receiving rooms on the second floor of the white wing. Corene took a quick look around as she stepped in, noting the usual plain furniture and severe colors; this was not a place designed to put a visitor at ease. The only bit of softness was supplied by the view of the gardens through the huge windows on the back wall. Corene squared her shoulders and turned to face the empress head-on.

And almost tumbled over in surprise when she realized there was a man standing next to Filomara—and she knew him.

"Nelson Ardelay!" she exclaimed, flying across the room to hug him. He laughed and met her halfway, collecting her in a hard embrace that drove the breath out of her body. "What are you *doing* here?"

"Looking for you, of course."

Steff didn't know any of the primes very well, but he knew enough to come over and offer a bow. "Good to see you," he said.

"And good to see you!" Nelson replied. "How have you fared as the young prince practically returned from the dead?" As he spoke, he scanned Steff's face for whatever he might read in its expression. Well, he was doing more than that, Corene knew. As the sweela prime, Nelson had a deep affinity with fire, but he also had an uncanny ability to know what other people were thinking. He claimed he couldn't actually read minds, but it was hard to lie to him, hard to keep him from knowing how you really felt about something. Right now he was probably trying to assess how comfortable Steff was here at the Malinquese court, no matter what Steff might say.

"It's been wonderful," Steff said, glancing over at his grandmother, whose stern face did not lighten at his words. She was displeased with Nelson's sudden appearance at her court, Corene realized, which made Corene even happier that he had arrived. "I've learned so much—met so many amazing people—"

Nelson clapped him on the shoulder. "Will we ever be able to lure you back to Welce?"

Steff smiled. "Not for a long time, I think."

Corene touched Nelson's arm. "But really," she insisted. "Why are you here?"

Filomara finally spoke up. "Yes—why and *how* are you here? My own ships have had trouble making it through the Berringese blockade."

"Well, you know, when you have a navy at your back, you tend to get one of two responses," Nelson said affably. "People either fire at you or they leave you alone. Turned out they decided to leave us alone."

"Really? My officers haven't reported any Welchin naval ships coming close enough to the harbor to engage with enemy vessels."

Nelson smiled. His eyes were bright with deviltry; he was enjoying himself, Corene thought. "Maybe it was just their presence in deeper water that made the Berringese think twice about attacking us," he said. Corene supposed he had come in through an illegal port and that that was why Filomara was so annoyed, but it seemed obvious he wasn't going to admit it. Just to make *sure* she was annoyed. "But you should be happy I made it through! Since my ship captain was carrying cargo you had expressly ordered from Welce."

Corene could see Filomara's irritation war with her curiosity, but she didn't have to unbend enough to ask what he meant. Steff did it for her. "What cargo?" he asked.

Nelson threw his hands wide. "A smoker car! Direct from Kayle Dochenza's factory! I understand it's being delivered to the palace later today."

"Oh, that's great," Steff enthused. He turned to his grandmother. "You'll like having an elaymotive. I can show you how to drive it."

"Or I can," Nelson said warmly. He glanced around as if trying to gauge how many spare bedrooms the palace offered. "If you want to put me up here, we can work in a lesson or two anytime you have a free moment."

"I'm delighted that the elaymotive has arrived, but not even remotely interested in learning how to operate it," Filomara said in a cold voice. "And naturally you must stay here. I'll have Lorian find a suite for you close to Steffanolo and Princess Corene. Do you also need a room for your attendants?"

Nelson waved a hand. "Oh, I knew that Malinqua wasn't much of a place for pomp, so I traveled alone," he said. "Didn't even bring a valet."

"Or a guard?" Filomara asked with some disbelief. When she had visited the Chialto court, she had brought a hundred soldiers and refused to stay at the palace unless thirty were housed there with her.

"Well," he said, still smiling, "there's the navy."

"Hardly within call, if trouble arises," the empress pointed out.

He spread his hands. "Call me an optimist," he said. "I'm not expecting trouble."

Filomara glanced at Corene, then back at Nelson, clearly nonplussed. She'd expected the Welchin ships to show up, Corene realized, but she hadn't planned for a high-ranking ambassador to slip through the cordon and land on her doorstep. She'd planned to do all her negotiating through a blockade, emphasizing the danger that Corene might be in if the navy didn't come to her assistance. The fact that Nelson could arrive unescorted and unannounced took away one of her high trumps, but it also slipped a wildcard into her hand. Because now he was effectively a prisoner in her house as well—except he didn't seem to regard himself that way. Which meant he might be planning another play that she couldn't figure out how to counter.

It was giving Corene a headache just to try to think like Nelson and Filomara. So she decided to see what would happen if she set an explosion. "Well, there's been plenty of trouble so far," she said. "I don't think you should move into the palace. If you've got a ship ready, I'll leave with you this morning."

That caught Nelson's attention. Steff protested and Filomara snapped, "Don't be ridiculous." But Nelson gave her a keen look and said, "If you're in danger, let's go now."

"She's not in danger," Filomara said testily. "Things have been unsettled here, but the princess has never been at risk."

"You can't leave now," Steff said. "The celebration is two days away! You have to be there!"

"Celebration?" Nelson repeated.

"A gala to formally mark Steffanolo's appearance in Malinqua. We have been planning it since he arrived, and I expect it to be a most impressive event."

Nelson raised his eyebrows at Corene. "I do like a party," he said. "But it's up to you."

Truth be told, Corene hated to miss the event, so she was willing to stay. Anyway, mostly what she'd wanted to do was rile everyone up, and she'd succeeded at that.

"Yes—very well—we'll stay for the gala," she said, making her voice sullen. "But right after that? We can leave?"

"We'll see," said the empress.

"We'll go," said Nelson.

"Good," Corene said. She slipped a hand under Nelson's elbow and tugged him toward the door. "Let's talk. I have so much to tell you!"

The day was chilly but clear, making a walk in the gardens pleasant once they stopped to put on heavier jackets. Corene wanted to show Nelson the maze, but he wouldn't set foot in it. He found a spot in the middle of an herb garden where nothing grew higher than their knees and there was nowhere for an eavesdropper to hide. The two of them sat on an ornamental carved bench while Foley stood about twenty yards away, scanning all approaches.

"Now," Nelson said, sounding much more serious, "what's going on here?"

She gave him a succinct version of recent events while he listened closely, nodding from time to time. It was always so refreshing to talk to Nelson; he could follow the thread of a story, no matter how convoluted, and he never needed anything explained twice.

"Yes, I would say it's time for you to leave Malinqua behind," he said when she finished her recitation. "But is Steff safe to remain? Or should we kidnap him for his own safety?"

"Do you have the resources to kidnap him?" she countered. "You *appear* to have come empty-handed."

He grinned. "I could probably arrange something."

"I think Steff is smart enough to make up his own mind. And he stands to inherit wealth and property here, even if he isn't named heir. He has good reasons to stay."

"I'll trust your judgment on this. We will leave him if he wants to be left."

"So tell me your part in all this," Corene said. "Why are you here?"

"Since the day you left, your father has been debating whether to send someone after you," Nelson said.

Corene scowled. "He *has*?"

Nelson frowned her down. "Don't get sulky on me. Of course he has. And of course he's been watching you closely since you arrived."

Corene sighed. Leah was only the most visible of Darien's spies. He might have twenty more that she would never even know were nearby.

"When we got word of Berringese forces sailing into the harbor, he began to grow truly alarmed. That's when he marshaled his own navy—"

"Which is *exactly* what the empress wanted him to do!"

Nelson nodded. "And then, since I was coming anyway, he asked me to play ambassador and get a true read of the situation if I could. And I must say," he added, "the true situation is as convoluted as they come. Royal hostages, foreign wars, homegrown coups— It's hard to sort it all out."

"I've been thinking about it," Corene said. "I think there are at least two factions at work. I think Filomara came up with the idea of importing foreign brides for her nephews—and then, if necessary, keeping them as pawns to win military support from Cozique and Welce. But I think someone *else* is trying to control the succession by getting rid of rivals."

"Who do you suspect?"

She shook her head. "Everyone at court could have a favorite."

"Well, who is the person most likely to be named heir?"

She thought it over. "Generally speaking, I think everyone expects it to be Greggorio. He's well liked and he looks the part—and good advisors could compensate for the fact that he's not very smart."

Nelson grinned appreciatively at the description, but just said, "So someone is trying to push him out of contention?"

She shook her head. "I think someone is trying to *keep* him in contention. Aravani and Subriella were the most likely heirs—until they died. Filomara's brothers were the next likely heirs—until two of them died and two were banished. Garameno—but he was incapacitated. Jiramondi—" She considered. "I'm not sure anyone ever thought he was a viable candidate."

"So, how does that explain the dead girl? The one thrown down the underground passage?"

"Someone didn't want Greggorio distracted," she explained. "Until he started flirting with Sarona, everyone assumed Greggorio would marry Liramelli."

"The prefect's daughter," Nelson said, nodding. "An ideal pairing. So, Sarona would need to be eliminated to keep Greggorio free to marry Liramelli."

"Alette had to be gotten rid of, too, for the same reason."

Nelson gave her a keen look. "So who do you think is trying to shepherd Greggorio to the throne?"

Corene wrapped her arms around her shoulders and hugged herself against the chill. "The most obvious person would be the prefect or his wife," she said. "Working together or independently."

"What do you think of them as suspects?"

She shook her head. "I like Mariana a great deal—Harlo a little less so—but I don't know either of them very well. And anyone whose family has survived at court for generations—" She shrugged.

"Is capable of playing a deep game," Nelson finished. "Anyone else you favor for murder?"

She managed an unhappy smile. "If it's not someone trying to put Greggorio on the throne, then I'd have to pick Garameno as the plotter," she said. "He's clever enough to plan a careful coup that takes years in the making. And he's an excellent candidate for the throne—the oldest of his generation, and the smartest, too. But his injury makes him less appealing to most of the people who matter."

"It also makes him less likely to be the killer if he was a victim of the killer's machinations," Nelson pointed out.

"True. Unless the accident was really just an accident. And he was so enraged by the cruelty of fate that he decided to eliminate all his rivals."

"So if Garameno is cold-bloodedly murdering anyone higher in the lists than he is— How did he react to Steff's appearance at court?"

"Of the three nephews, Garameno has been the least welcoming and Jiramondi has been the most," she said, "but *none* of them were pleased to see Steff."

"Which brings me back to my earlier point, but with a little more urgency," said Nelson. "It's not safe for Steff to stay."

She nodded. "I know. And yet—I don't know that he's in real

danger unless he's named Filomara's heir, and I think that's unlikely to happen." When Nelson looked skeptical, she said, "He's a stranger. He knows nothing about the people or the country. If someone had sailed into Welce last year and proved to be Vernon's grandson, would the primes have blithely turned the country over to him to govern?"

Nelson shook his head. "Obviously not. But we might have been willing to marry off this mythical offspring to you or Josetta in order to combine *his* bloodline with *your* deep knowledge of the culture. If I were backing Steff as a candidate, that's exactly what I'd do—find him a bride among the high-ranking nobility. The prefect's daughter, for instance."

Corene nodded. "If that's the case—if whoever is running this grand scheme is doing it on behalf of Liramelli—then Steff is actually safer than anyone."

"Which brings us right back to the prefect and his wife."

Corene nodded again. "Or other politicians who support Harlo. There are dozens of factions among the nobles and I honestly don't know the players well enough to guess who might be capable of pulling off something this big."

"Layers and layers," Nelson agreed. "There always are. Well, it's a puzzle, sure enough, and a fascinating one. But once you leave—" He shrugged. *Not your problem anymore.*

"Do you really think you can get me out of here? Filomara seemed pretty certain you're just as trapped as I am."

"I have more resources at my back," he drawled. "And systems in place that will trip an alarm if I do not make certain appearances every day. Filomara can't afford a war on *two* fronts. She wanted the Welchin navy here to support her, not to attack her. She'll let us go. Once I have concluded my business—"

That reminded her of something he'd mentioned at the very beginning of the conversation. "Wait—you said you were coming to Malinqua anyway. Why?"

"One of those amazing coincidences. I happened to be with Kayle Dochenza when he was approached by a remarkable woman—a sea captain, it turns out, the most robust and redoubtable creature. She wanted him to verify the identify of a woman she'd met in Malinqua, who claimed to be a friend of Kayle's."

"Leah," Corene guessed. "She's a spy for my father."

"Leah, indeed. Kayle read the letter she produced, told the captain, 'Yes, she's exactly who she says she is,' and then handed the paper to me."

"Why?"

"Because he knew I've been looking for Leah for five years."

"What? *Why?*"

"Because that's how long ago she ran away."

Corene shouldn't have been so surprised. It had always been clear that Leah was gently bred—she might be working as a shopgirl and spy in Malinqua, but she moved and spoke like a woman of noble birth. And if Darien had known her before she turned to espionage, it made sense that Nelson did as well. In fact, Nelson had probably sought Leah out even before he came to the palace. *That* was what Leah had wanted to tell her, Corene guessed—that the sweela prime had arrived in Malinqua and was ready to upend all their lives. "Why did she run away? How well did you know her?" She appraised him frowningly. All the sweela men—the Ardelays in particular—were notorious for their flirtations and affairs, but Leah was barely half Nelson's age.

He laughed at her expression and held up his hands in self-defense. "*I'm* not the one who took her for a lover," he said. "It was Rhan."

Rhan was Nelson's youngest son, a man of indiscriminate affections and irresistible charm. One of Corene's favorite people in all of Welce, as it happened, though he couldn't be trusted for a minute. "Rhan. Of course. So he seduced and abandoned her—"

"You would have to get his version of the story to be certain of that," Nelson said gently. "But all accounts agree that there was a baby girl born of the union."

"Ah," Corene said. "Poor Leah. But did she bring the baby here? She hasn't mentioned a daughter."

"No," Nelson replied on a sigh. "Taro offered to care for the child—"

"Leah's related to *Taro Frothen*?" He was the torz prime, one of the most powerful men in all of Welce. Corene couldn't believe it.

"She's his niece."

"If she's part of the Five Families, she must have been at the Chialto court pretty often. Why haven't I ever met her before?"

"You probably did, when you were much younger. She looks much different than she used to—she's changed her hair and her style of dress. I might not have recognized her myself except that I was searching for her."

"I still can't believe that a daughter of the Five Families is living in the slums of Palminera."

"I believe when Darien proposed the move she would have preferred any situation that took her out of Rhan's vicinity."

"And now?"

"Now I am hoping to bring her back with me. I think perhaps the heartache will have faded enough that she will be willing to resume her old life again. And perhaps be a mother to her daughter—who could use one."

Corene tried to remember who had been on the premises whenever she had visited Taro's property during the past five years. There were always people clustered around the torz prime—he collected them as easily as other people collected shells or coins. "So Taro and Virrie are raising Leah's daughter? I wonder if I ever met her."

"Many times," Nelson answered. "Her name is Mally."

Now Corene was so shocked she almost fell off the bench. "She's the decoy princess? The one who's been standing in for Odelia all this time?"

Nelson nodded. "The one whose life changed forever when we realized Odelia was not fit for the throne. She will always have a home with Taro, and he's the man I'd want raising *my* children if I wasn't around, but the situation is far from ideal. Mally has no place at court anymore. No parents looking out for her. What is to become of her? Leah should come home and care for her daughter—and so I told her."

"Well, Rhan should care for her as well," Corene said. "Shame on him to ignore her all this time!"

"It is not entirely his fault," Nelson said. "He could hardly show a partiality for her if she was masquerading as Odelia—not if we wanted the fiction to hold. Nor could I single her out, nor any of us related to her by blood. It nearly killed my wife to know she had a grandchild that she could not kiss and make a fuss over."

"Well, I suppose that makes sense," Corene said reluctantly. "But I will still scold Rhan the next time I see him."

"I think you should," Nelson said. "He has behaved very badly in all this."

"It is what one expects of an Ardelay."

Nelson laughed. "It is indeed."

"But tell me what's going on in Welce! Zoe's letters are so haphazard you can't really tell what's happening, and Josetta is too kind to dwell on scandals. So tell me everything. Who's in trouble? Who's in favor? When will Darien be crowned?"

You could hardly find a better person than the sweela prime to pass on a quintile's worth of gossip, and they spent a very enjoyable twenty minutes while he shared the latest news. But there was one name noticeably missing from his report.

"You've said nothing about my mother," she said when he was done. She was proud of herself for keeping her voice so level.

He gave her one quick, keen glance. "I thought you must have gotten her news directly from Alys."

Corene shook her head. "Not a letter. Not a word."

"Ah. Well, then, I suppose you don't know she's moved out of Dominic Wollimer's house and petitioned to dissolve the marriage."

"I didn't, but I can't say I'm surprised." It had seemed clear that Alys only married Dominic because she thought his heirs would be in line for the Welchin throne. That was why she'd gotten pregnant, too. Once the primes had decided Darien should be the next king, Alys had no incentive to stay with her husband. Corene took a careful breath. "I suppose such a separation will make it difficult on the baby, once it's born."

"Ah," Nelson said again. "Sadly, she miscarried a few ninedays ago. Shortly after you sailed, in fact."

Shortly after the primes chose Darien. "Miscarried?" Corene repeated.

"That's what she claimed."

For a moment, she just stared at him. Nelson made no effort to look away, just held her gaze with steady compassion. He knew what she was thinking, of course: *How lucky I am that the whole royal court was excited about my birth, or I might have been "miscarried," too.* All these ninedays mired in Malinquese politics, and Corene had almost forgotten how ugly life could be back in her own palace. Or at least, in her mother's household.

"How challenging for her," she said at last. "I hope she recovers soon from the loss."

"Yes," he said. "Well—I think she already has."

When Corene was silent, Nelson slapped his hands on his thighs and then came to his feet. "So!" he said, a little too heartily. "I think we are all caught up and agreed on our next steps. We will stay for this celebration and we will be gone the next day. We will leave Steff behind to maneuver his way among his bloodthirsty relatives, but we will take Leah back with us. And if Filomara tries to stop us—well, she will see that Welchin soldiers are fiercer than she expects."

"Yes, it sounds good," Corene said, her words ringing somewhat hollow in her ears. She was ready to leave Malinqua behind, but not at all eager to return to Welce. She knew she was tired of court life, but she didn't know what to replace it with, and nothing awaiting her in Welce held any particular appeal. Then there was the matter of Foley. Once she was back in Chialto, would he disappear from her life? How would she hold on to him? How would she convince him that if she wasn't a princess, she could love wherever she chose? What if he convinced *her* that he thought of her only the way he'd thought of Josetta— as someone to protect, not someone to love? Wouldn't Welce be even drearier then? It was all she could do not to sigh out loud.

"Don't worry," Nelson said, sensing her dissatisfaction, though she hoped he hadn't correctly interpreted the cause. "Everything will be fine once we're home."

TWENTY-ONE

That night's dinner was the most enjoyable meal Corene could remember since she'd arrived in Palminera. There was something about the presence of the sweela prime that loosened people's tongues and made them want to talk, made them vie with each other to tell their stories. Nelson listened, he laughed, he asked incisive questions until every one of them sat back with a little glow, believing that they had *finally* been heard and understood. Some capricious chance had put Melissande next to Nelson at the table, and their delight in each other's company spilled over to everyone else in the room. Corene even caught Bartolo smiling once or twice, and she couldn't remember ever witnessing that before.

Quite a change from breakfast, she thought.

After the meal, Lorian came to the doorway and nodded at Filomara in a silent communication. She came to her feet and asked Nelson to withdraw with her for private conversation—then, after a moment's hesitation, included Steff, Garameno, and Harlo in the invitation. Corene caught the look of desolation on Jiramondi's face, quickly masked; Greggorio didn't even seem to notice he'd been excluded.

Corene glanced swiftly at Melissande and Liramelli, jerking her head toward the door, and they both nodded. Five minutes later they were all ensconced in Corene's room, while Foley retreated to his own quarters.

"I love him!" Melissande exclaimed, flinging herself onto a sofa. "Nelson! You could talk to him for *years* and never get bored!"

"I liked him, too," Liramelli said. "But I think he would be exhausting to be around for any length of time."

Corene laughed. "Both statements are true," she said. "He is the personification of all the sweela traits."

"So, is he really here to take you away from us?" Liramelli demanded. "I'm not ready for you to go! I'll miss you so much."

"Yes, I am very sad to think of you leaving," Melissande said.

"And I am sorry to leave the two of you, but it is time I was gone," Corene said firmly. "I think, after last night, even Filomara will be happy to see the last of me."

Liramelli groaned and buried her face in her hands. "Last night! All those things you said!" She looked up, her expression serious. "My father was so upset. He and my mother stayed up talking for hours. He said he had never put events together that way, that it took an outsider to see a pattern all of them had overlooked."

"So now he thinks there might truly be a murderer on the loose in the palace?" Corene asked carefully. *And he doesn't think it's himself?*

Liramelli nodded. "He says he will talk to the empress about initiating an investigation. But who can be trusted to lead it? Anyone close to the throne could somehow be involved."

"It is very unnerving," Melissande agreed. "At the same time, it is a little bit exciting."

Liramelli sighed. "I think I would prefer it if life was duller than this." She looked over at Corene with a doleful expression. "When you and Nelson Ardelay leave—are you taking Steff with you?"

"No," Corene said. "He wants to stay."

Liramelli brightened immeasurably at that. "That's something else my father said. Steff is the one person we know who hasn't been scheming for a throne for the past twenty years. We could trust *him*, if nobody else."

Melissande lounged back on her sofa, one hand idly playing with her hair. "I think our little Liramelli has an attachment to Steffanolo," she said. "She can hardly say his name without blushing and stammering."

Liramelli rewarded her by doing both. "That's not—that's not true! I mean, of course, I do like him, he's—he's very pleasant to be around—"

Melissande sat up and spoke more briskly. "He is a perfect prospect for you in temperament and heritage," she said. "If you like him, all the better. I think your father should petition *now* for you to marry him."

Now Liramelli's face was scarlet, but she tried to carry on as if they were merely having a political conversation about advantageous alliances. "My father wants to see an heir declared before he marries me off. He still thinks it might be Greggorio."

"Whom you could also wed, but there would be nothing but heartache there, if you loved him," Melissande said. "He will not be faithful to his wife."

"Which wouldn't bother *you*, I suppose," Liramelli said a little spitefully.

Melissande laughed. "It wouldn't," she agreed. "But Greggorio and I would not suit. He finds me unfathomable and I find him—tedious."

Corene was curious. "Who *would* you marry, given a choice of heirs?"

"Jiramondi," Melissande answered promptly. "I like him, and we wouldn't interfere with each other. Whereas Garameno—" She considered. "I suppose we would tolerate each other. But he thinks I am a flighty girl, which makes me want to behave badly and—you can see we would quickly wear on each other."

Liramelli's face was troubled. "My father says—well, of course I am not supposed to repeat it—my father says Garameno will never be emperor because he cannot produce heirs of his own."

"According to the gossip I have heard, the accident damaged his legs but left him functional in all other areas," Melissande said delicately.

"Yes, apparently, but there was some—some test all three nephews had to undergo. To prove they could actually father children. And Greggorio and Jiramondi passed, but Garameno did not."

Melissande threw her hands in the air. "Oh, this is endlessly entertaining! You Malinquese and your *tests*! Do you not know how many bastards have sat on the thrones of the southern seas before your scientists devised their precious examinations? Kings and queens have been unfaithful since the day the first one was crowned! It does not *matter* if a man may sire children or a woman may bear them. Someone will always step in to make sure another child is born."

Corene was laughing. "As I am living proof," she said.

Melissande turned her bright eyes toward Corene. "So if *you* were choosing," she said, "which of Filomara's heirs would you want?"

She tried to close her mind to it, but the image of Foley would not be banished from her thoughts. Not a royal match, of course. But more and more, as these chaotic days unfolded, her ideal of the perfect man. Faithful. Capable. Devoted. Someone who didn't try to control her, who didn't want her to comform to some picture of her that he already had in his head. Someone who made the world safe for her so she could explore it.

She didn't see how she would ever muster the desire to spend her life with any other man.

Melissande was watching her with interest, and even Liramelli—not nearly so attuned to others' moods as Melissande—was regarding her with speculation. Corene forced an unconvincing laugh. "I would create havoc throughout the court by picking someone everybody despised," she said. "Some lord's bastard son or exiled nephew. Just to stir things up."

"Yes, that does seem very much in keeping with your personality," Melissande agreed.

Liramelli came to her feet, rubbing her hands against her trousers as if to brush away the quirks of the conversation. "Well, things will be very stirred up over the next few days," she reminded them. "The party is only two days away!"

Melissande rose also, yawning. "It will be very exciting," she said. "I am looking forward to it indeed."

The two women exited, still talking idly, and Corene shut the door behind them. Then she stood there, silently, waiting until their voices faded down the hall. Another minute of silence, while she still waited—another.

Then the sound of another door opening and closing, a soft step, a quiet knock. She opened the door and gestured to Foley to come inside.

"You should always issue a challenge first, to make sure you know who's on the other side," he scolded as she secured the lock behind him.

She smiled at him, hoping her expression was casual, hoping he couldn't hear the mad galloping of her pulse. "I didn't have to," she said. "I knew it would be you."

The next two days no one did anything except think about the party.

For some time now, construction crews had been in evidence around the palace—in the courtyard, in the gardens, even in the grand hall and ballroom—measuring all the public spaces and assembling scaffolds and structures of mysterious purposes. Finally, as they hammered and sawed and shouted and cursed and lifted various frameworks into place, it became clear what they were creating: a detailed miniature representation of the city, with all its landmarks spread around it in minute and charming detail. A great stone basin was built and then flooded to represent the sea; small sailboats and paddlewheels were set upon it to provide rides for children and lovers. One cluster of vendors' booths stood in for the Little Islands, and another for the Great Market. A walkable labyrinth with head-high walls represented the giant maze that led from the iron gate to the royal palace. It would be filled with entertainers who would recite stories or sing songs or tell fortunes to anyone who strolled the looping path.

"I admit, I'm starting to get excited about this celebration," Corene remarked when she toured the grounds with Liramelli and Steff and Melissande the day before the event. "At first, you know, I thought, 'A party just to honor Steff? How much fun can *that* be?' But now that I see all the trappings—"

Steff shoved her good-naturedly on the shoulder. "You're just jealous because no one ever threw a party to celebrate *you*," he said.

"I want to see what they've done around back," Liramelli said.

"Not me—I am tired and going back to my room," Melissande said. "I want to be entirely rested so that tomorrow night I may enjoy myself for the festival."

Steff elected to keep exploring with Liramelli, but Corene accompanied Melissande inside. They had to dodge workmen stringing banners from the high ceilings and detour past women wrapping ribbons around the banisters of the grand stairwells.

"I have two lassenberries left and I will share one with you if you want," Melissande said, so Corene followed her down the twisting corridors to her third-story suite. She glanced back only once to make sure Foley was behind them. He was, of course, though he didn't follow them into Melissande's quarters.

They were barely inside the room with the door shut before Melissande said, "I did not want to say anything in front of Liramelli, but I have gotten word from my mother."

Corene nodded, unsurprised. "She knows about the Berringese blockade? The empress's plans to involve Welce and Cozique in this petty war?"

"Yes, and she is not happy about it. I believe she plans to summon me home—perhaps in some dramatic fashion."

Corene raised her eyebrows, but Melissande didn't elaborate. "Are you ready to go back?"

Melissande produced a fatalistic shrug. "It is so very complicated! My mother made it clear that if I did not secure a marriage for myself while I was here, she would arrange one for me the minute I returned. She is convinced that marriage might make my behavior—" She thought about the right words. "Less scandalous."

Corene grinned. "I do wonder exactly what you did that was so bad you had to be exiled."

Melissande spread her hands. "Small romances! Nothing hundreds of women do not engage in every day! But married women, as she likes to point out, have more license in their actions. So she is busy lining up candidates for me and I'm sure she plans to have me married within a quintile."

"Is that what you want?"

Melissande made a graceful gesture eloquent of uncertainty. "I like the idea of the freedoms that come with married life. I do not like having little say in my choice of partner. But I believe my mother and I can come to terms."

"So we all flee Malinqua and Filomara's grand plans," Corene said.

"She deserves to be fled from."

"I am sorry for Liramelli, though. I'll miss her—and I think she'll miss us."

Melissande smiled. "Oh, but she and Steff will make a match of it, don't you think? That should be some consolation."

"I hope they will. They seem ideally suited." Corene laughed. "Though more suited in Welchin terms. She's elay and he's coru. Wind and water are natural allies. But I don't know how the Malinquese would describe them. I mean, I don't know which one would be fire and which would be ice."

"No, the Malinquese are so very precise and conventional in how they view the world," Melissande agreed. "They do not allow for the subtleties that come with a multifaceted perspective. They think every-thing is either one way or another."

Corene held her hands up side by side. "Flame or ice. Sun or moon. Open-hearted or closemouthed."

"Man or woman."

Corene dropped her hands. "Well, that *is* true, I suppose."

"Nonsense, there are people who do not truly seem to be either, but just *are*," Melissande argued. "And certainly just because you are one does not mean you can only be made whole by fitting together with your opposite. There are men who love men, and women who love women, and men and women who love *both* men and women. You would need many towers all over the city to represent anything so complex."

Corene was starting to guess why Melissande's mother might con-sider her daughter's behavior scandalous. "Do you?" she inquired. "Love women instead of men?"

"In addition to," Melissande said. "But how could I not? Those small hands and delicate cheeks—that soft skin—and there is some-thing about the scent of a woman's body—"

Corene blinked at her. "I can honestly say I've never given any of that a second's thought."

Melissande offered up her naughty smile. "You might *try* thinking about it," she suggested, taking a few steps closer. "You might find it delicious indeed."

Melissande now stood only inches away, close enough for Corene to catch the fragrance of her lemon perfume. Corene didn't back away, so Melissande lifted a hand and placed her fingertips on Corene's cheekbone, slid them down to Corene's pointed chin. They were about the same height, so Corene found herself staring straight into Melissande's night-blue eyes.

"If you're brave enough," Melissande said, "you can see what it feels like to kiss a woman."

Corene smiled. "I don't think it requires bravery," she said. "Just curiosity."

Melissande lifted her eyebrows in a question, and Corene shrugged slightly in response. The feel of Melissande's mouth on hers was pleasant and warm, light pressure, soft skin, a sense of honey and satin. A moment or two, no longer, then Melissande drew back. She lifted her eyebrows again, and once more Corene responded with a shrug.

Melissande laughed. "So you did not mind it, but you did not grow flustered with excitement."

"Is that what's supposed to happen?"

Melissande took her arm and drew them both down to a little sofa on the side of the room. "You've never kissed a man, either? Now *that* I find truly shocking."

"Oh, I have. A few. Mostly at parties, and mostly when they were drunk, and I didn't mind *that*, either, but I didn't—" She didn't know how to articulate it. "But I didn't *care* about it. I didn't get breathless. I didn't suddenly start tingling all over my body, as they say in the romances—"

Melissande was shaking with gentle laughter. "Then you've been kissing the wrong people—men *and* women," she said firmly. "There is only one solution, of course! You must kiss many, many people—ones you know well, and ones you scarcely know at all—and keep on kissing them. I promise you, one day you will feel that tingle, that *hunger*. You won't want to stop. It doesn't necessarily mean this person is right for you, or even good for you, but at least you'll get a taste of desire."

Corene couldn't stop it: Foley's image took shape at the back of her mind. *I think I'd feel that hunger if he ever kissed me,* she realized. *I feel it now.* Something in her expression must have betrayed her thought, because Melissande's gaze was suddenly keen and searching.

"Oh, but there *is* someone who stirs your blood," she said softly. "You just have not had the nerve to speak up."

"It's more complicated than that."

"It's always less complicated than you think," Melissande assured her. "So—who? Someone at court? Not Steff, surely, or any of Filomara's nephews. Not a woman, I suppose?" Corene shook her head. "No, then, I wonder if—" Melissande sat up straight and practically clapped her hands together. "Foley! Of course! Most excellent choice. Your first lover should always be someone who adores you."

Now Corene was blushing as hotly as Liremelli had the night before. "Foley doesn't adore me," she said.

"Ah, but you adore him, do you not?" Melissande asked. When Corene only shrugged and laughed and looked away, Melissande said, "You do. I can see you do. But does he know how you feel? He is not the kind of man to make a move without encouragement. Well, he is not the kind of man to try to seduce someone he has been charged to protect. Hmmm. That might be problematical." She tapped her chin with her finger as if trying to solve a particularly complex puzzle.

Corene laughed again, pushing herself to her feet. This conversation was wreaking severe havoc on her nerves. "At the moment, I think we have plenty of other things to focus on," she said.

"We do," Melissande said regretfully. "But there is always time to think of romance."

"Perhaps tomorrow will be romantic!" Corene said as she headed for the door. "Everyone dressed in finery and wearing masks and drinking too much. So many possibilities!"

"Yes," Melissande replied. "I am quite looking forward to it."

Foley fell in step beside Corene as they headed back to her room, but she didn't have much time to feel jittery at the notion that he would be following her inside, because she already had visitors at her doorstep—Nelson and Steff.

"Well, *there* you are," Nelson said grumpily. "I've been wanting to talk to you all day."

She unlocked the door. "I'm astonished to find Steff here with you," she said. "I left him touring the gardens with Liramelli, and I was sure they'd be down there till midnight."

Nelson sent Steff a quick appraising glance, but Steff only grinned. *Don't think you can hide the state of your heart from the sweela prime,* she wanted to warn him—but then she realized that Nelson could read her own emotions just as clearly. It made her want to pull a scarf over her face.

Instead, she nonchalantly waved them over to a grouping of chairs and they all sat. "Anyway, I thought *you* spent all day with the empress, practicing your diplomatic skills," she added.

"Part of the day," Nelson said. "It turned out I wasn't as diplomatic as I could have been. I told Filomara that she was at fault for all the turmoil in her court because she should have picked a clear successor long before now."

"Oh, she hates being told she's done anything wrong," Steff said. "I bet she didn't like that."

"No, she didn't."

"And it's particularly ironic coming from *you*, since the primes changed their minds about fourteen times when they were trying to decide who should be the next ruler of Welce!" Corene exclaimed.

Nelson grinned. "She would have pointed that out, I'm sure, if she knew all the details."

"Did you actually manage to accomplish anything with all your talking?"

"I think so. She's agreed not to keep us from leaving and I've agreed to talk to Darien about trade sanctions against Berringey," Nelson said. "But we don't import much from Berringey, so I don't know that our sanctions will have much impact. She needs to enlist Cozique if she wants to do real damage."

"Talk to Melissande in the morning. She's more astute than she seems."

"I could tell she had an excellent brain," Nelson said, nodding.

Corene let that pass. "But from what I can tell, her mother's just as likely to break off relations with Malinqua after this little stunt Filomara has pulled."

Nelson stretched out as if he was ready to stay and gossip all night. "You think the people in your own court are a bunch of plotters and backstabbers, and then you go out into the world and you see the same petty, jealous behavior everywhere else—writ large—even worse and with more dire consequences," he said. But he spoke with relish, as if he enjoyed every minute he spent watching the human pageant.

Steff stirred. "But it shouldn't be that way," he said earnestly. "We should all try to be better people than we are. My father used to say that all the time. And kings and queens should try harder than anybody."

"They should," Nelson agreed, "but they usually don't. One of the prerogatives of power is to misbehave—because no one can stop you when you do. Many an upstanding man or woman has ascended to the throne, vowing to be moral, to be honest, to be faithful—and almost every single one of them has failed. Because it is so hard to be good when it is so easy to be bad."

"My father isn't bad," Corene said. "He's one of the exceptions."

"So far," Nelson said. "But he hasn't actually been crowned yet."

"Even once he is! He won't ever be *evil*."

"No, I think he's as true as they come," Nelson agreed. "But there will be times he might—let's say—take advantage of his resources. Use his influence to see one man ruined and another one exalted. Enact his own kind of justice outside the official system. He's done it already to punish Dominic Wollimer."

"Who's Dominic Wollimer?" Steff asked.

"My mother's husband. Soon to be former husband, I hear," Corene said. She was breathing a little fast. "What did Darien do? No one ever told me anything."

"Really? I'm sure Josetta knows—well, she's the one who told *me*." Nelson shrugged. "Darien bought up certain debts that Dominic owed, invested in companies that Dominic was part of—essentially found ways to disrupt or control every source of income he has. He hasn't bankrupted the man yet, but he's made it plain he *could*. And he will. It was very much a personal vendetta, not a political one, but once you reach Darien's level of power, the two are intertwined."

"Why doesn't Darien like him?" Steff wanted to know.

When Corene didn't answer, Nelson did. "Because he hurt Corene. And Darien wanted Dominic—and every single person in Welce—to know that anyone who harmed his daughter would suffer immensely in return."

Corene felt a little light-headed. She had always wanted proof that Darien loved her—well, there it was. Oh, he'd *said* it many times, and Zoe had insisted that he did, but Corene had always found it so hard to believe. She'd always thought he had just been stuck with her—the bastard daughter he'd sired in an attempt to serve his ailing king—the tiresome, unfortunate, and permanent link to the woman he hated above all others. He'd done right by Corene because he was hunti and because he was Darien. He'd taken her in, shielded her from her mother, given her money and clothes and a place to live. But she'd considered herself a burden, a responsibility, and Darien Serlast already had way too many of those.

But if he actually loved her—

"That doesn't sound so bad," Steff said.

"Oh, well, he also threatened to kill Dominic if he ever touched Corene again," Nelson said casually. "No, maybe the word he used was 'destroy,' but I think it was pretty obvious what he meant."

"Now *that's* not right," Steff responded.

Nelson shrugged. "That's the prerogative of power," he said again. "If you're ever named king of this corner of the world, I hope you're able to resist putting your personal concerns above your temporal duties—but I bet you're not."

"I probably won't be king, though. Emperor, actually. So we'll never know."

Nelson surveyed him with a smile. "But maybe we will."

The two of them stayed another hour, though Corene was heartily wishing them gone long before then. She wanted to think over what Nelson had said about Darien. She wanted to review the scene in Melissande's room—not the kiss so much as the conversation that had come afterward. *He is not the kind of man to make a move without encouragement.* She wanted Foley to knock on the door and step into the room and listen with grave interest to whatever she might say—

She didn't know what she would say.

Maybe tomorrow. Or after the party. Or on the long, dull voyage back to Welce. Or once they were in Chialto, and she was no longer Foley's assignment, but just a friend. When he could walk away without guilt, abandon her without fear.

When she asked him, *Do you love me?*

TWENTY-TWO

The Great Market was closed on the day of the festival, which was hardly shocking. *Every* commercial venue in Palminera had shut down for the gala designed to celebrate the existence of Filomara's unexpected grandson.

Leah was somewhat surprised to find herself marking that momentous occasion in Chandran's company. She hadn't thought to mark it at all, to be truthful, but when Chandran invited her to join him for the festivities, she didn't have the slightest inclination to refuse. Better than sitting in her lodgings down by Little Islands, watching through the windows, insulated from both the rowdiness and the delight the evening was sure to bring.

Besides, she had something to tell Chandran, and this might be her last opportunity.

She met him in one of the northern neighborhoods, outside of the city wall and well within view of the white tower. This was a part of Palminera she hadn't explored too often, since she found the harbor and the Little Islands districts more congenial. But Chandran seemed quite familiar with the streets and alleys, even with some of the people they encountered as they strolled along. She wondered if he lived in this part of town. She thought it was odd that it had never occurred to her to ask.

"Is every single person in Palminera outside in the streets celebrating?" she demanded as they turned onto yet another avenue jammed with people.

"Probably," Chandran said. "The empress does not arrange too many festivals, not even on changedays, as you may have noticed over the years. Everyone is drawn to the notion of joy. Particularly the sort of joy that can be experienced by consuming food and drink someone else has provided."

As he spoke, they rounded another corner and came across a wide promenade so packed with revelers that it was almost impossible to navigate. It was instantly clear what had drawn everyone here: double rows of makeshift booths and merchants' carts dispensing everything from baked goods to cheap wine. The street was so crowded that it was hard to tell where the lines began or how long it might take to get served, but so far the mood of the mob was patient and happy. Leah thought that could change if supplies ran low or too much alcohol was consumed.

"Might be midnight before we get dinner," she observed.

"Not so long," Chandran said. "I have a few friends here."

He took her by the wrist so they didn't get separated and gently began breaking through the crowd. Eventually he pulled her to a sort of back alley serving one long row of booths, and they came to a halt at one particular station. Here, two middle-aged men and a frazzled young woman were handing out what smelled like meat and cheese wrapped in fried bread. The aroma was so appetizing that Leah was instantly starving.

One of the men caught sight of them but didn't bother to speak a greeting, just nodded at a huge wicker basket near the rear of the booth. When Chandran pulled back the lid, Leah could see a couple of dozen bundles—some of the house specialties, she realized, swathed in paper to stay fresh and in ragged old blankets to keep warm. Chandran put two in a cloth rucksack he'd brought with him and handed Leah a jug of water waiting by the basket.

"I think this is all we need," he said.

"You've thought of everything," she said with a laugh. "Now if there were only somewhere quiet where we could sit and eat!"

He gave her his slight smile. "I have thought of that, too."

They worked their way free of the crowd and continued north on progressively less crowded streets—though none of the routes they took were actually deserted. They'd traveled a few blocks in near silence before Leah guessed his intended destination.

"The white tower? That's where you want to eat?"

He glanced down at her. "There are supposed to be fireworks displays later in the evening. I thought they might be interesting to see from a high vantage point."

She'd never seen fireworks in Welce, but they were all the rage in Palminera when the city held its rare festivals. She laughed again. "What a very good idea!"

She was less enthralled with the idea, however, as they began the climb to the top of the tower. She'd never attempted the task before, and she was unnerved not only by the height, but by the eerie lighting and the impermanent feel of the stairwell. But she was too stubborn to quit or even admit to much discomfort. Only part of that was pride, she realized; part of it was a reluctance to disappoint Chandran.

She was panting for air by the time they made it to the top of the spiral stairwell and she followed Chandran through the rectangular opening of the landing. But once she caught her breath and gazed out at the city, she was instantly entranced. Palminera spread out before them like a field of moving stars. Bright constellations had formed around the vendor stations scattered across the city; an even bigger and brighter one had coalesced around the palace at the center of the universe. From this distance, at this hour, it was impossible to see the shapes of buildings, the colors of houses, but every street could be mapped by the lights flowing from end to end.

"Well, *this* is certainly lovely," she observed.

Chandran had made one full circuit around the huge, glowing crystal, and now he came to stand beside her. "Amazing," he said. "No one else is up here. I thought we might have company."

"No one else is sober enough to make that climb," she retorted.

He laughed and knelt down, spreading the rucksack like a tablecloth and laying out the bundles of food. As she unwrapped her own, she found that it contained not only the main dish, but also a side treat of baked fruit sprinkled with sugar. It smelled even better than the meat.

"A cloth to wipe your fingers," Chandran said, pulling this item out of one of his side pockets. "I neglected to bring goblets for us, I am afraid, so we will have to share the jug."

"I think I can endure the hardship," Leah replied.

The food tasted just as good as it smelled, and they both ate hungrily, speaking very little. Even so, the silence was companionable. *Strange,* Leah thought. *He is the one person I've met in Malinqua I actually regard as a friend.*

As soon as they were done, they pulled themselves to their feet and leaned against the railing, gazing out at the panoply of lights below. Here and there they spotted vivid bursts of color—fireworks, maybe, or young men setting off small explosions—and they speculated about the entertainments being offered to the crowds on the ground. Chandran pulled a spyglass from his vest pocket and they passed it back and forth to get a better view of some of the activities.

"I must say, even though Filomara doesn't entertain often, she does it right," Leah observed after they'd spent about twenty minutes looking out over the city. "An excellent way to welcome her grandson."

"And to bid farewell to you," Chandran said.

Her heart skipped a beat and she looked over at him. In the unwavering white light of the crystal dome, his face looked ghostly and sad. "I've been trying to decide how to tell you I'm leaving," she said. "How did you know?"

"You have always been looking for an excuse to go home," he said. "And now you have found one."

"What excuse? I haven't told you anything."

He shrugged and turned away from her to stare at the shoreline. "My information sources are at least as good as yours," he pointed out. "I know that an important man from Welce arrived in the city a few days ago and has taken up residence at the palace. You have been troubled and distracted lately. It is easy to guess that you know this man and that he has brought some pressure on you to return to Chialto."

"He's my daughter's grandfather," Leah said. "He says she needs me."

"She has probably needed you any time these past five years."

"Probably," she agreed. "But until recently, I didn't think I had anything to give her."

"And now you do?"

"I don't know. I want to find out."

He nodded. "I am glad you are going."

That hurt more than she would have expected; she felt a pain in her chest as if she'd splintered a rib. She drew a careful breath and stared out blindly at the harbor.

She felt him glance down at her. "I think you will never be happy anywhere but Welce," he clarified. "And it has become important for me to see you happy."

That made it easier to breathe, somehow, but she kept her eyes fixed on the distant view of the shoreline. "If you wrote to me, I'd write you back," she said.

"I am happy to hear that," he said, "as I have every intention of writing you."

"And if you get tired of Malinqua, you could visit Welce."

"Does anyone ever tire of Malinqua?" he asked. But when she risked a quick look at him, he was smiling. She focused on the harbor again. "We shall see," he added. "I do not travel as well or as readily as I once did."

"You'd like Welce," she said. "You could set up shop in one of the Plazas. I'd make sure the regent and all the Five Families patronized your business."

That was the closest she'd ever come to admitting how well-connected she was in her home country. She doubted he was surprised, though; she thought Chandran had figured her out the day they met and never had to revise his original opinion. If he was a spy for Cozique, she had just given him an almost irresistible invitation—but she didn't care if he was. She still hoped he would come to Welce someday. There were plenty of other spies in Chialto. What could it matter if one more arrived?

"When do you leave?" he asked.

"Tomorrow or the day after," she said. "It depends on what Corene and Nelson need to do before we set sail."

"Make sure you let me know before you go."

She nodded because it was hard to speak. Her throat was closing and her eyes were watering, so she couldn't see *or* talk. Fiercely she wiped at her face and stared determinedly toward the ocean.

"Look at that!" she exclaimed, surprise clearing up her tears. She pointed. "The harbor's full of ships again! Do you think Malinqua has broken the Berringey blockade?"

Chandran lifted the spyglass to his eye and studied the scene in silence for a moment. When he spoke, his voice was so serious that Leah felt a shiver at the small of her back. "No," he said slowly. "Those are Cozique ships. The city is under attack."

TWENTY-THREE

The day of the party was cold and clear and full of commotion. There were so many workmen tramping through the bottom stories that Corene never ventured down past the third floor, and she spent most of the day in her room. Liramelli showed up at her door just as the noon lunch tray arrived, Melissande right behind her, and the three of them spent the afternoon preparing for the night's festivities. All three maids were on hand with clothing, cosmetics, and accessories, so they spent a most agreeable few hours doing nothing but primping. It might have been the most lighthearted afternoon Corene had spent in Malinqua.

And one of her very last. She tried not to think about that.

"A masked gala seems so very whimsical for Filomara, do you not agree?" Melissande asked as she adjusted a confection of lace and blue velvet over her face. The holes were so large that you could clearly make out the shape and color of her eyes, which pretty much ruined any chance she had of keeping her identity a secret. She had also chosen to wear a dress of dark blue—her favorite color—in a distinctively Coziquela style. Anyone who had ever met her would instantly know who she was. Corene figured that was the point.

"I do agree!" exclaimed Liramelli, who had gone to some trouble to disguise herself. Her delicate mask was formed of silk and feathers, and it covered her whole face, with only small slits in places to allow her to see and breathe. She had even wrapped a dark scarf over her fair hair and commissioned high-heeled shoes so that people wouldn't recognize her by her height or coloring. "Yesterday I heard Garameno and Jiramondi mocking the whole idea of it—saying that because Steff was the unknown heir, everybody else had to arrive in disguise. That's much more subtle than Filomara usually is."

"Maybe it wasn't her idea," Corene suggested. She stood in front of the mirror, making minute adjustments to her costume. Unlike Melissande, she wanted to blend in, so she had worn traditional Malinquese colors and fabrics, just cut in a looser and more fashionable style. Her jacket and trousers were deep gray, shot through with bits of crimson; her mask was attached to a hood that covered her telltale red hair.

"It might have been Lorian's idea," Liramelli said doubtfully. "I know he doesn't seem like a very *festive* person, but he's very proprietary about the palace. Anytime Filomara entertains on a grand scale, he feels like it's a reflection of him personally, and so he often picks the food and the decorations."

"Then I shall have to find him tonight and kiss his dour face," Melissande said. The idea made them all burst into laughter.

Though if anyone would kiss Lorian and find the experience interesting, Corene thought, it would be Melissande.

Finally they were ready—finally the windows showed them dark skies above and tantalizing firelit shapes below—finally it was time for the dinner that would precede the gala. Corene followed Melissande and Liramelli into the hallway, to find Steff, Foley, and Nelson already gathered. Heedless of their party clothes, they were seated on the floor and playing a three-handed game of penta.

"The sweela prime is a cheater," Foley remarked as he gathered the cards and tossed them inside his room.

Nelson laughed and came to his feet. "It's not my fault I can tell when you're excited about a hand and when you're bluffing," he said.

"I would so much like to have that ability!" Melissande exclaimed. "To know when someone is being truthful or telling a lie."

"He has other skills you'd like just as much," Corene said. She was trying not to stare at Foley when he stood up. She hadn't realized that he, too, would dress in party finery, but she supposed that would allow him to trail closely behind her all night without anyone knowing who he was. In addition to the well-tailored Malinquese jacket and trousers, he'd acquired a quarter-face mask, which was just now dangling around his neck, ready to be tied in place. The dark colors and severe style suited him immensely. He looked taller, more powerful, a little dangerous. Out of the corner of her eye, she saw Melissande appraise him and then look Corene's way with a smile. Corene refused to look directly in the other girl's direction.

"What kind of skills?" Liramelli asked.

"He can control fire."

"Really? Oh, that *is* most impressive," Melissande said. She held out her hands, clad in lace gloves so sheer they were scarcely more than blue threads tied around her palms. "Show me. Put a flame at my fingertips."

Nelson grinned. "I can't call fire from nowhere," he said. "I can just make it behave."

"Even in Malinqua?" Steff asked. "For some reason I always thought the powers of the primes didn't extend beyond the Welchin border."

Nelson's grin widened. "Well, I haven't had much chance to experiment since I set foot in Palminera," he drawled, making Corene instantly suspect that he had. "But I think I could do a trick or two if I needed to."

"That might make the party even more exciting," Melissande said.

Nelson took her arm and set off down the hall. "I'll see what I can do."

A buffet dinner was laid out in an oppressively ornate dining hall that Corene had not been in the whole time she'd been in Malinqua. Maybe two hundred people were inside, milling aimlessly around. These were the very elite of Malinquese society, Corene knew—the titled nobles, the wealthy landowners, the political darlings—reveling in the privilege of being invited to this most exclusive of events. Simultaneous celebrations were going on all over the city this night, but the very finest food, music, and entertainment would be found here at the palace, and this was the place where *everyone* wanted to be.

Unfortunately, Corene had only met a handful of them during her stay, and the disguises prevented her from recognizing any of them now. Five minutes after she entered the room, she took an unwary step away from her own party and instantly lost track of Nelson and the others. She stood there a moment, wondering what she should do. A tap on her shoulder made her turn around hopefully to find Jiramondi right behind her. His own mask was barely a strip of silk across his eyes, and he was dressed in his usual style, so it wasn't hard to recognize him.

"You don't have to tell me if I'm right, but you look like the Welchin princess," he greeted her. "And you look a little lost."

"Coming to a dinner in disguise sounded much more fun before I thought about walking into a room full of strangers," she said. "How did you know it was me?"

He grinned. "I recognized Foley behind you."

That made her laugh. "So what's the procedure here? I see food and I see tables, but it doesn't look like there are formal seating arrangements."

"No, since we're all in disguise, it would ruin the fun to know who your tablemates are," Jiramondi explained. "You're supposed to fill your plate at the buffet then sit down next to some random stranger and start flirting madly."

"You don't sound particularly pleased by the notion."

"I hate events like this," he said. "Bad enough when I can see people's faces and gauge how they react to me. But here! Everyone a potential foe and no way of knowing! It's awful."

She glanced around the room. "I don't see Garameno."

"No, he hates masked dinners even more than I do. Because, of course, he *can't* blend in. He'll come down later for the outdoor festivities, though."

"When do those start?"

"Soon," he said, taking her arm. He guided her toward a sideboard piled with dozens of appetizing dishes. "So let's eat something now and recruit our strength."

They'd finished their first plates of food and were considering returning to the buffet for more when there was a huge *boom* from outside the palace. Even before its reverberations faded, people were laughing and jumping to their feet, streaming toward the doors.

"Now we move to the courtyard," Jiramondi said. "Though there will be food available inside all night, and music in two of the salons, for people who want to come in and rest."

"Excellent," she said. "Let's go explore the marvels outside."

Indeed, the courtyard outside the palace had been transformed into a wonderland, far more magical than it had appeared yesterday when all the underlying supports were visible. Strolling through the displays, her hand tucked inside Jiramondi's elbow, Corene couldn't stop exclaiming at the lovely sights. Strings of white lights were wrapped around shrubs, trees, ornamental stands, the false walls of the replica labyrinth—everything—throwing the whole area under a spell of enchantment. In one bend of the maze, performers juggled lit torches and waltzed with mannequins made of fire. In another, acrobats dangled from invisible wires, appearing to somersault and pirouette above the crowd with only air to support them. The boats sailing on the counterfeit sea were bedecked with colorful lanterns that made it seem as if the water was dancing with fairy lights.

"This is exquisite!" Corene said.

"Much more appealing than I thought it would be when it was first described to me," Jiramondi agreed.

She looked over her shoulder to make sure Foley was getting a chance to enjoy all the delights. "Isn't this amazing?"

"Most impressive," he replied.

She turned her attention back to the vista before her and declared, "I want to see *everything*."

They continued on their perambulations, seeing new wonders at every bend in the path: the woman twisting her body into impossible shapes, the man making scarves and birds and even a child disappear and reappear at will, the couple using some kind of glittering fire to paint streaks of color in the air. As they moved from station to station, they were serenaded by different musicians, each one far enough from the others that their offerings did not overlap. Here were three young girls singing in high sweet harmony; here, five men producing amazing sounds from strings and bows. Corene was mesmerized by the circle of drummers, their hands flying with unbelievable speed over the taut skin of their instruments, their insistent rhythms vying with her heart for the pace that would drive her pulse.

Everywhere they went, someone recognized Jiramondi and stopped to pull him aside. Usually Corene would go on a few paces without him, then stand transfixed at the next sight until he caught up. Foley always followed a few steps behind, never close enough for her to draw him into conversation. While Corene watched the drummers, Jiramondi got caught up in a much longer discussion, but she didn't mind. She thought she might just stand here and listen for the rest of the night.

"It's remarkable, isn't it?" said a voice over her shoulder, and she turned with an automatic smile. The man standing behind her was tall and broad-shouldered, but that was about all she could tell, since any distinguishing features were hidden behind a black mask, black hood, and close-fitting black clothing. He even wore gloves to disguise his hands. She knew him, though; she couldn't place his voice, but she was certain she'd heard it before.

"I've never heard anything like them. Are they from Malinqua?"

"Originally from Berringey, I believe, though living in Palminera now. I heard that the empress found them in the Little Islands."

"Where all the most interesting items are found."

He smiled, the whiteness of his teeth breaking the perfect darkness of the mask. "Said by someone not native to this country."

She laughed. "What gave me away? The fact that after all these ninedays, I still can't speak the language very well?"

"That was only one factor," he said, declining to elaborate. "Are you enjoying yourself?"

"Much more than I expected to. Are you?"

"Much more than I expected to," he echoed. "The empress entertains so rarely—and cares so little about ostentation—that I always expect her celebrations to be stingy and small. But this is so open-handed and expansive that I almost find myself wondering where I am."

His patterns of speech were teasingly familiar and, for a minute, she thought she could identify him. *Greggorio,* she almost said aloud.

But that wasn't right. This man had a similar build, but he didn't move with Greggorio's innate grace. And he offered observations that would never have occurred to Greggorio at all.

"I suppose that's the point of a masked event—to make you wonder where you are and who you are and who everyone else is," she responded. "To make you question the things you thought you knew."

"An exercise we should all be engaged in all the time anyway," he said. "Complacency has killed more men than combat."

It sounded like something Nelson would say. But she was certain this wasn't the sweela prime.

"I try not to take things for granted," she said, scanning his covered face, trying to read some recognizable pattern under the opaque fabric.

"It is the human tendency," he said. "The only ones who are able to overcome it are those who live very precarious lives."

"As you do?" she asked.

The smile again, briefer this time. "In the extreme."

She couldn't think of an answer to that, but she didn't have to, because Jiramondi joined them then, shaking his head. "No, I *don't* know how much the empress spent on this extravagant event and if it signals her intention to name Steffanolo as her heir," he said, clearly still irritated by his most recent conversation. "And if I *did* know either of those things, I wouldn't share the information with you. Oh. Hello there. Didn't see you at first."

This last was directed at the man in the black mask, who nodded at Jiramondi and bowed to Corene. "Enjoy the rest of your evening," he said, and glided away into darkness.

"Who was that?" Jiramondi asked.

"I couldn't tell. I thought you might know."

Jiramondi shook his head, then shrugged. "Mysterious strangers taking bold liberties," he said. "Another thing to love about a masked gala."

That made her giggle. She held out her hand and he hooked his elbow around it. "So let's keep walking and see what else we find."

They found the fountain that flowed with fiery liqueur—flames dancing on top of the cups of liquid that were being handed out by very careful servants. They found a tiny cottage built entirely of flowers, though they declined to drop on their knees and crawl through it, as many of the younger guests were doing. They found a man sculpting images from ice and a woman playing a flute and a troupe of actors performing scenes from well-known comedic productions.

They also found another half dozen people who wanted to draw Jiramondi aside and share an observation or air a grievance. Corene guessed he was wishing he'd taken more trouble to disguise himself. *Maybe I'll suggest that he go back to his quarters and find a hat or a hood that shadows his face,* she thought. But when she looked around to check on him, she couldn't find him anywhere. The motion of the crowd had pulled her too far away from him, or his latest petitioner had dragged him to some shadowy spot to have an even more private conversation.

She stifled a sigh and lifted her chin and kept walking, though the lights and the performers and the sights didn't seem quite as magical when she was viewing them by herself. Foley insisted on remaining a few paces behind her, guarding rather than accompanying her, which made her feel even more solitary. She kept scanning the masked faces of the people who passed by, sure she would find Melissande or Liramelli or Nelson somewhere in the crowds, but so far they remained elusive. She wondered if they were all together somewhere, enjoying themselves so much that they didn't even realize she was missing.

Disconsolately, she paused by a knot of people who were watching a man juggle knives and oranges, deftly changing his grip each time the opposite item fell into his hand. "Any bets that he'll cut himself?" asked a man standing beside her. He wore a blue cape and a matching mask; his voice was unfamiliar. No one she knew, she was pretty sure.

"No," she responded. "He wouldn't be here if he was that clumsy."

"Too bad. Seems like the kind of crowd that would enjoy blood."

An odd thing to say. She edged away slightly. "Oh, I wouldn't think so," she said. "It's a pretty civilized group."

He closed the gap. "On the surface, maybe," he said. "But you don't have to scratch too deep to find the savage underneath."

All her instincts were warning her of danger, and again she stepped away. "I don't intend to scratch anyone," she said.

Again he followed. "And if someone scratches *you?*" he murmured, lifting a hand as if he would stroke her cheek.

She drew breath to scream but before she could utter a sound, Foley was there, knocking the man to the ground. It happened so quickly she couldn't track the motion. One moment, menace; the next, chaos. All around her were gasps and shouts and coiling bodies as people drew back and the man in the blue cape jumped to his feet.

"If you—" he began with a snarl, and Foley knocked him down again. He moved so quickly, so fluidly, it was as if he only waved or gestured, but the man was sprawling before them, coughing with pain. This time he stayed down, shaking his head and moving his hand along his ribs as if to feel for broken bones.

The bystanders were muttering now, trying to decide if they should intervene, trying to determine who was at fault. Any more uproar and royal guards would appear, Corene thought.

But she didn't want to prolong this scene. She grabbed Foley's wrist and tugged him away. "Come on." The man on the ground didn't cry out anything melodramatic like *Stop them!* and none of the nearby watchers felt impelled to pursue them, so within a few steps they were out of sight, lost in another bend of the maze.

"Thank you," Corene said. She was tired of him stalking along behind her, so she held on to his wrist; she was pleased when he made no move to pull his arm away. "There was something unnerving about him."

"I could tell he made you uneasy. And when it looked like he was going to touch you . . ."

She shivered. "I'm glad you were watching me."

"I'm always watching you."

I'm glad of that, too. Instead she said, "We've *looked* at all the wonders, but we haven't *tasted* any of them. Let's go try something! You choose. What looked good to you?"

He glanced down at her, his eyes crinkling in a smile behind the mask. "The brew that was on fire," he said promptly.

She felt laughter bubble up. "I know exactly what you're thinking," she said.

"Do you? And what's that?"

"You're thinking, 'I'm a guard and she's royalty. What I want should have no influence on what we do. But she's stubborn enough to insist, so I may as well avoid the argument and speak up.' Is that right?"

Now he was openly laughing. "Close enough. Though I also spared a second to think, 'I'd just pick the safest option, but she wouldn't believe it, so we'd have the argument anyway. So I may as well tell the truth.'"

She slid her hand up to the bend of his elbow and turned toward the fountain, but now he wouldn't budge. "What?" she said.

He disengaged his arm. "You can't promenade through the festival with me like I'm some kind of lord."

"Why not? Nobody knows who you are. Nobody knows who *I* am, when it comes to that."

"Because I'm a guard and you're royalty," he said, giving her own words back to her.

She played a trump to see what it would get her. "But there are so many people," she said. "I'm afraid."

"No you're not."

This time she didn't take his wrist or elbow; this time she reached for his hand, and twined her fingers through his. He made as if to pull away, and she tightened her grip. Obviously he could get away if he wanted, but he hesitated.

"You don't want to break my fingers," she pointed out.

"I need both hands free," he said, his voice uninflected, "in case someone attacks you."

"If someone attacks me," she promised, "I'll let go."

"Corene—"

That was it. Just her name. But it stopped her. He never called her by name—never formally addressed her, really—and she was trying to recall the last time he had needed to get her attention. Did he say "Majesty"? "Princess"? Did he just wave a hand? She couldn't remember.

"Why did you come with me to Malinqua?" she asked softly. They were standing midway between two displays of light, so they could see each other, but not clearly. And anyway, there were the masks. But she would bet he could read all the emotions on her face. She wasn't making any attempt to conceal them.

"I told you that the last time you asked."

"Because you thought I needed a protector."

"Yes."

"Why did you want to be that protector?"

He didn't answer.

"You never asked me," she said, her voice even lower, "why *I* wanted *you* to come with me on this trip."

With one quick twist, he broke free of her hold. But he didn't move away. "Because you thought I was skilled enough to do my job." When she started to speak, he interrupted. "That *has* to be the only reason. I can't *do* the job if you say other reasons exist."

She listened to that closely. He was trying to hold his voice steady, but there was a raw undertone that she found very interesting. "You mean, you'd resign your post?" she said. "You'd leave me alone in Malinqua?"

"You won't be staying in Malinqua," he said stiffly. "I would ensure you made it safely home."

"And *then* you'd resign?"

"If my presence was detrimental to your well-being."

"What if your *absence* was detrimental to my well-being?"

"I doubt that situation will arise."

"It will. It has. We're in that situation already," she said.

"If that's the case, then this assignment has already been too long," he said firmly. "As soon as we're back in Welce, I'll ask your father for another post."

"And if I tell my father that I don't feel safe with any guard but you?"

"I will explain to him that I fear you've grown too attached to me. I think he'll be happy to see my services redirected."

"I hope I don't find ways to get myself in real trouble when we're back in Welce and you're not around to protect me," she said. "Think how awful you'd feel if you learned something bad had happened to me because you weren't there."

He just looked at her for a moment, his face entirely unreadable behind the mask. "I feel certain you are too sensible to take dangerous risks just to prove a point."

She allowed herself a small smile. "Well, we won't worry about Welce until we're back in Chialto," she said. "For now—let's go sample some of that fiery punch that you admired so much." Again she tucked her hand inside his elbow. And this time he didn't bother protesting or pulling away.

He wants to be a hunti stone, she thought, as they moved through the throngs of people, dodging the drunk ones, smiling at the happy ones. *But he has a loyal torz heart. I must turn coru and wear away at him, drop by drop, until he is completely exposed. And then I will be the sweela girl who sets us both on fire . . .*

It was such a delicious thought that it made her shiver. He glanced down in concern. "Are you cold?" he asked.

She shook her head. "No, I'm perfectly fine."

They found their destination with no trouble and accepted servings of flaming brew from the footman. Corene had to release Foley to hold the cup in both hands, and she admitted to a little trepidation as she lifted it to her mouth. Foley was watching her, his own glass poised, his eyes narrowed with amusement.

"Are you as brave as you pretend you are?" he asked.

"Are you as impervious?" she retorted, and downed the liqueur in one long swallow. The flame flicked harmlessly at her nose; it was the hot spices that scorched her throat on the way down. She felt her eyes water and her tongue burn, but the taste that lingered was smoky and sweet. "Powerful," she managed to choke out, "but I like it. Not for every day."

Foley was sipping his more cautiously, even appearing to roll a mouthful across his tongue. "Probably singe away your sense of taste if you had it too often," he said. "But I like it, too."

They finished off the potions and handed their glasses back to the servers. "Now where?" Corene asked. "What else did you want to see?"

"There was a knot of people on the front lawn," he answered. "I couldn't tell what they were looking at, but they all seemed pretty impressed."

"Let's go find out."

They strolled around the outer edge of the temporary labyrinth to the very front of the palace grounds, where a throng of people had indeed gathered around some mysterious attraction. A half dozen lanterns hung from nearby poles, but the crowd was so thick that Corene couldn't tell what they were examining by the cheerful light. Trying to be polite about it, she pushed her way forward, squeezing past lovers and drunkards and squirming children.

When she got close enough to see the prize, she laughed and waved Foley closer. "A smoker car!" she cried. "Nelson *said* there was one on the boat that brought him over."

A few of the admirers overheard her and crowded closer. "What did you call it?" asked someone she took to be a young man. She could see a thin beard covering what portion of his face wasn't disguised by his three-quarter mask.

"A smoker car. An elaymotive," she replied. "It runs on compressed gasses, so it doesn't need a horse. It was invented by a crazy man who lives in Welce."

"Is it fast?" asked a man.

"Three or four times as fast as a horse, I think."

"Is it dangerous?" asked a girl. "Could it catch fire? Explode?"

"I don't think that happens anymore."

"Any*more*? It *used* to?"

"Well—a few times—"

The first young man spoke up again. "Can you drive it?"

She glanced back at Foley. Oh, how much she wanted to say yes. The truth was, she could, but she wasn't very good at it. Barlow and Jaker had taught both her and Josetta, and she'd practiced a few times on her father's vehicles. This one was one of the smaller models, roofless and compact, made to carry only four people and only in good weather. She could probably maneuver it around the palace grounds without knocking down too many spectators. Of course, she had no way of knowing if there was any fuel in the tanks; it might not even be operational.

But if it was—Foley could drive an elaymotive. She'd trust *him* to tool around the fairgrounds without killing anyone. She raised her eyebrows at him in a silent question, but wasn't surprised when he shook his head. Stealing someone else's property wasn't on Foley's list of acceptable behaviors.

"No," she said regretfully. "I wonder if the empress imported a driver along with the car."

"*I'd* like to learn to drive it," the bearded young man said.

One of his friends answered him, and pretty soon Corene had lost the crowd's attention. She could tell it was making Foley edgy to have her standing in such a mob, so she apologized her way back out through the press of people and took his arm again. He didn't even bother protesting.

"That was fun," she said. "What else would you like to see?"

"What's around back?"

"Let's find out."

They skirted the outer edges of the displays until they made it to the back lawns of the palace. Here among the flower and vegetable gardens, the layout was much less formal. No labyrinth replica, just clusters of furniture and banks of candles set up amid organized activities. These included everything from archery contests to foot races, which meant the mood was more boisterous and it was harder to hold a conversation. Corene supposed that was a relief to Foley, but she didn't mind. She kept her light grip on his arm with one hand, and with the other pointed out sights he might have missed.

They'd never caught up with Nelson or Melissande, Steff or Liramelli, but now she rather hoped they didn't. She was enjoying herself much more without them. She did catch a glimpse of Lorian, prowling through the gardens with a trio of footmen at his back. He wasn't masked, and his face was drawn in its usual serious lines; he appeared to be patrolling the festival to make sure everything was going smoothly, and he looked ready to dispatch servants to fix anything that went amiss.

"Do you want to try your luck in the archery contest?" Corene asked Foley, but he shook his head.

"I'm not very good with a bow. Better at close combat."

"Maybe they have wrestling matches somewhere."

"Maybe I wouldn't want to be distracted."

She rolled her eyes, but she didn't press. She would save her persuasions for when they mattered.

The crowd thinned out and the noise died down as they moved farther and farther from the palace. The night grew darker as well, since there were only a few lanterns hung from low branches or clustered around arrangements of benches.

By the time they reached the hedge maze at the back of the property, they appeared to have left every other fairgoer behind. Lorian apparently hadn't expected many people to walk the maze when there were so many other delights to explore, because he had barely bothered to light it. Corene could spot a single white lantern glowing in the very center of the maze—probably swinging from the doorway of the gazebo—and four more were hung at strategic spots to shed dim illumination across all of the tangled pathways. Even so, the walk would be mostly in shadow.

"Let's go to the center," she said, tugging Foley toward the opening in the tall shrubbery. "Maybe there's something special set up in the gazebo."

"And maybe there isn't," he said. He resisted a little, to show his disapproval, but he allowed her to pull him inside.

Corene moved swiftly through the well-trimmed greenery, remembering the pattern—one left and then a series of right turns. Foley followed close behind her, so silent she looked back twice to make sure he was still there. As soon as she made the final turn to the central clearing, she saw that there was indeed a lantern hung from the gazebo, and by its light she noticed two things: All the colorful summer flowers had disappeared, and someone was there before them.

Two someones, actually, and neither of them standing. One was stretched out before the little fountain, lying on the stone apron with ominous stillness; another was kneeling beside him, a hand on the first one's chest. Both wore dark clothing and full face masks. The one on his knees turned to look at Corene as she started forward with a cry of distress.

"Is he hurt? What happened to him?" she exclaimed, dropping beside them.

"I don't know. I just found him like this," he replied.

At the sound of his voice, she glanced at him sharply, though she couldn't tell anything by looking. It was the man she had encountered earlier, the one who was dressed all in black and had spoken of complacency and risk. Alarm sent a runner of fire down her spine and she turned her head to make sure Foley was there. Yes. Of course he was.

"Is he hurt?" she asked again, her voice warier.

The stranger nodded slowly. "I think he's dead."

She sucked in a sharp breath and touched her hand to the injured man's lips. She could feel no air coming in or out.

"Who is he?" she whispered.

The masked man hesitated before saying, "I don't know."

She wondered if that was true. She could peel the mask off, but if he was a stranger to her, his face would tell her nothing. She pushed back to her heels and looked around for clues. If he had come all the way to the center of the maze, perhaps he'd had a reason. Perhaps he'd thought this would be a safe place to cache a weapon or a document or a bag of stolen jewels—

A slight breeze set the lantern to dancing, and its moving light illuminated a shape just a few feet away. She narrowed her eyes, trying to make it out in the shadows, and Foley stepped closer.

"Corene," he said. "It's Garameno's wheeled chair."

"Garameno!" she exclaimed, and scooted closer to the body. "Oh no, no, no—"

"You shouldn't—" the stranger began, but he was too late. Corene had already teased up the bottom edge of the mask and now she rolled it over the dead man's chin, his nose, his brow, his hair.

For a moment, as she gazed down at him, his features didn't make sense. The slack jaw was too slim, the cheekbones too smooth. This wasn't Garameno.

"Greggorio," she whispered.

TWENTY-FOUR

Corene stared down at Greggorio's pale face, feeling as if the world had tilted and would never right itself again. "I don't understand," she said.

Foley was at her side, pulling her to her feet. "You don't have to understand. Just go find a guard. Then the empress."

The stranger also stood, brushing his hands along his trousers as if to scrub away the scent of death. "Not yet," he said, his suave voice sounding suddenly urgent, a little desperate. "Let me work out what happened first."

"Why should *you* figure it out? Who *are* you?" she demanded.

"It doesn't matter," Foley said, trying to drag her away even as she planted her feet. "We have to go get help."

Suddenly the man grabbed her other arm in a grip that bruised, and for a moment Corene was stretched between them. "Stay," he growled. "This is more complicated than you realize."

Foley swung his free hand to punch the stranger hard in the chest. The man grunted and released Corene just as Foley flung her across his body, back toward the path of the maze. "Go!" he roared.

Corene stumbled a few feet forward from momentum before spinning around. She'd finally recognized the voice. "Foley!" she cried. "*That's* Garameno!"

Garameno had recovered his balance and was poised on the balls of his feet, looking as if he wanted to run or pounce. "Something's wrong here," he said, still in that urgent voice. "I don't know why anyone would kill Greggorio."

She stared at him. "You're standing—you're moving so freely—"

"Maybe he doesn't need the chair," Foley said.

"Maybe he killed Greggorio."

"I didn't!"

"Corene, *go*! Get help," Foley ordered.

"No, stay and *listen* to me," Garameno pleaded. "It's true, I don't need the chair—but that's not the point right now—"

She came a step closer, still staring. "You don't need it at *all*? Then why—all these years, *pretending*—"

"I had my reasons. But tonight I left it back here so I could walk the fair without being recognized—"

"So you could find Greggorio and *kill* him!"

"*I didn't kill him!* Maybe nobody did! There's no blood—maybe he just fell—"

"There are bruises. Around his neck," she whispered. She had seen them when she peeled back the mask.

As if he couldn't help himself, Garameno started toward her, only to be shoved violently back by Foley. "I didn't hurt him!" Garameno shouted over Foley's shoulder. "I found his body when I came back for the chair! That's the truth!"

He lunged forward again, and this time Foley knocked him to the ground with a blow that left Garameno gasping with pain. "Go," Foley commanded with such intensity that Corene dumbly nodded. "I'll keep watch over him."

She turned around and blundered into the ill-lit maze. She was so stunned and confused that at the second or third turning she paused, trying to remember if she was supposed to take a left or a right. Panic threatened to overwhelm her and she fought it down. *Stay calm, stay calm.* She was still deep in the maze, so she should still be making lefts. All lefts until the very final turn—

While she followed the twists and tangles of the maze, her mind scrambled down equally intricate pathways. Garameno could walk! Why had he spent so many years pretending otherwise? It made no sense. It was clear his disability had practically knocked him out of the running for Filomara's throne. Why would he disqualify himself that way? Unless he wanted people to perceive him as vulnerable and weak— while he plotted against all of the other contenders.

He could have killed Sarona and carried her body underground. He most certainly could have hired Dhonshon soldiers and sent them after Alette. And Corene had no trouble believing that he could have strangled Greggorio tonight and left him for dead.

But there the probabilities petered out, like a maze pathway leading to a dead end. It seemed impossible that he would have been the one advising Filomara to marry Subriella off to her murderous Berringese husband. Equally unlikely that he could have poisoned Aravani and her whole family—he would have been only fifteen at the time. But when his two uncles died a few years later, he would have been about twenty, an age when he was certainly old enough, and ambitious enough, to start coveting the crown.

Corene came to a stop to catch her breath and get her bearings. Maybe Aravani's death had truly been due to illness, and maybe no one had advised Filomara to send Subriella off to Berringey. Maybe it wasn't until Filomara's daughters were dead that Garameno started eyeing the throne with so much longing. Maybe chance eliminated his first two rivals, and only then did Garameno decide to start improving his odds . . .

He was smart enough to plot a whole series of murders. That she believed without question. But ruthless enough? Cruel enough? She wouldn't have thought so. *But I have been wrong about so many people in my life,* she thought.

One final turn and she was out of the maze, sucking in air as if she'd been underwater, blinking at the festive lights as if she'd been feeling her way through an underground passage. *I can see again,* she thought idiotically.

Her next unbidden thought: *What if Garameno was telling the truth?*

What if he hadn't murdered Greggorio?

Say he'd left his wheeled chair at the heart of the maze so he could walk freely through the party, unrecognized by anyone who knew him. She could understand why that would appeal to him, and the maze made a perfect hiding place. Once he had had his fill of the fair, he returned to the gazebo—to find his cousin dead.

But what would have brought Greggorio to that isolated place during the height of the celebration? The very fact that it was isolated, she decided. Greggorio had never recovered his usual good spirits after learning of Sarona's death; he'd been even more subdued once Alette disappeared. He might not have been enjoying the party at all, though he'd dutifully made an appearance to please his aunt. But when the lights and the laughter became too much for him, he sought out a place of silence and solitude. She could still hear Liramelli's voice in her head. *Greggorio and I used to come here all the time . . .*

At the heart of the maze, he found his cousin's chair. Corene tried to imagine the sequence of events that had happened next. Maybe he paused a moment to wonder why the chair was there when Garameno was nowhere in sight—or maybe, being Greggorio, he didn't even wonder. He just saw a place to sit, and he sat. Maybe practiced wheeling himself around the fountain once or twice. Heard a noise in the bushes—looked up just in time to see a masked stranger creeping up in the patchy lantern light. He probably grinned—being Greggorio. *Hey, look, this is kind of fun,* he might have started to say, moving his hands to the big wheels.

But before he could get the words out, the assassin strangled him.

The attacker must have believed it was Garameno in the chair, Corene decided. She had only recently realized that the two cousins were about the same build, the same height, and if you couldn't see their faces—

But that meant someone had tried to kill *Garameno* tonight.

Who would have wanted to do that?

She began hurrying through the crowd, her feet gaining momentum as her thoughts picked up speed. Garameno was at risk for the same reason any of the cousins were at risk—because he was a candidate for the throne. Corene wouldn't have said he was the likeliest of the three, and yet in many ways he was Filomara's favorite, the one she relied on for advice and counsel. Just the other day, Filomara had invited Garameno to join her private conversation with Nelson Ardelay after dinner—a mark of favor that had been witnessed by almost everyone who had any interest in the politics of the succession.

For instance, the prefect had been at dinner that night. And Harlo had always staunchly backed Greggorio for heir—and he'd always wanted his daughter to marry Greggorio. Harlo would have a strong motive for making sure Garameno was scratched from the list.

The fairgrounds grew brighter with lamplight as Corene drew closer to the main activities. They grew denser with people, too. She tried not to be rude as she pushed through the crowds, scanning silhouettes briefly to see if she could recognize faces through their layers of disguise. The thought almost made her laugh out loud. *All people conceal themselves,* she thought cynically. *And I never recognize anyone's true heart.*

If Harlo had murdered Greggorio thinking he had killed Garameno, he would be wild with desperation when the truth came out. He might betray himself by his level of shock and horror and guilt. On the other hand, in recent days Harlo had seemed mighty interested in Steff as a suitor for his daughter's hand. Maybe he'd gotten rid of the wrong nephew, but he wouldn't care too much as long as Liramelli could wed Steff and still take the throne.

It was too confusing. Corene had been bred to such scheming; her mother commonly thought several steps ahead in whatever game she was playing, trying to devise her best strategy. But Corene didn't have the energy for such machinations. She didn't have the iron will to ignore the short-term consequences in favor of the long-term gains. She wasn't ruthless enough to forget about the people who might be hurt so she could get what she wanted.

It was a surprise to her, really. She'd always thought she would be.

She moved through a circle of light and careened into a short woman, knocking her backward. "I'm so sorry," Corene apologized. "Are you all right?"

The woman giggled and grabbed the arm of a friend. "I've been tripping all night," she said gaily. "Do you want some wine?"

"No—thank you—I've got to find someone," Corene answered and hurried on. Back through patches of light and darkness, back through drunk and happy crowds. *Back to turmoil,* she thought, *when all I want is order.*

There was no choice—she had to enter the palace and see if the servants could locate Filomara or Lorian. She was already nervous about how long she had left Foley alone with Garameno. Foley was a soldier, and armed, and clearly able to defend himself—but she had *no* idea what Garameno was capable of. And she was willing to bet he was armed, too. On the thought, she started to run.

Then the crowd parted and, like a gift from a conjurer's hand, Lorian appeared. As before, he was striding through the throngs with great purpose, flanked by footmen. The mastermind of the festival, the beating heart of the royal palace. If anyone would know what to do, it would be Lorian.

He saw her running in his direction and courteously turned her way. "Princess Corene," he greeted her, though she was still wearing her mask and hood. Probably he had made a point of discovering what every high-ranking guest was wearing. "Do you need assistance?"

"Lorian," she panted. "You've got to find the empress. Greggorio's— Greggorio's dead."

He had reached out a hand to steady her, but his grip tightened painfully on her arm. His sharp face grew even sharper in the patchy light. "*What?* Greggorio is *dead?* That can't be."

"I found his body—in the maze," she said, still gasping for air. "Lying by Garameno's wheeled chair, as if he'd fallen to the ground and tried to crawl away."

"By Garameno's chair?" Lorian repeated. "Then it's Garameno who's dead."

"I took off his mask. I saw his face."

"It has to be Garameno," Lorian repeated. "It has to be."

She suddenly remembered something that Liramelli had told her. *Greggorio was always Lorian's favorite.* Right now, Lorian seemed in shock, unable to believe a terrible truth. She wished she could soften the blow, but there was no time. *Someone* had killed Greggorio, and if it wasn't Garameno—

"I'm sorry," she said as kindly as she could. "Greggorio is dead and I think someone murdered him. There are bruises on his body—"

With a suddenness that sent her reeling, Lorian almost flung her away from him. "You're wrong," he snarled. "It's *Garameno* who was strangled."

He didn't stay to argue, just spun on his heel and raced for the maze, knocking fairgoers out of his way with brusque impatience. Caught by surprise, the three footmen followed in a disjointed, uncertain manner, trading glances that betrayed their astonishment.

Corene stared after him, her mouth open in stupefaction. She'd never seen the imperturbable Lorian so rocked off balance. But the death of any heir would undoubtedly unsettle the steward, who guarded the whole compound as possessively as if it belonged to him alone. Though he had seemed more distraught by the notion of Greggorio's death than Garameno's. *It's Garameno who was strangled,* he had snapped.

I didn't say he was strangled, she realized. *I said he was bruised.*

She supposed the only bodily bruises that were likely to lead to death were ones around the neck. Strangulation was a logical assumption to make.

More logical if Lorian had been the one to do the strangling.

That thought stopped her heart and froze her to the ground, unmoving even as other partygoers jostled past her.

If someone was trying to smooth Greggorio's path to the throne, Lorian had certainly been in a position to do so. Just two nights ago, he had been standing at the door as Filomara invited Garameno to join her conference with Nelson Ardelay. He might have resolved at that very moment to eliminate Garameno as a contestant, and tonight offered him the perfect venue.

And he could have orchestrated every other disaster with equal ease. He could have murdered Sarona and set soldiers on Alette. Much earlier than that, he would have had ample opportunities to do away with Filomara's brothers if he was afraid they would challenge her for the throne. Would he have murdered Aravani? Suggested Subriella's ill-fated match in Berringey? Possibly. If he had been convinced either girl would make a bad ruler. If he had believed it was in the best interests of Malinqua to see a male emperor next on the throne.

For the past thirty years, Lorian could have fancied himself as a kingmaker, pulling strings and directing events to control the succession.

Everyone knew he had a fondness for Liramelli and was devoted to Greggorio—but no one realized just how far his affections went.

If he had strangled Greggorio thinking he was Garameno . . .

Foley's there, she thought in a panic. *Foley's watching over Greggorio's body and he'll think Lorian is there to take the situation in hand. But Lorian will be crazed with grief. And Foley will realize why and Lorian will kill Foley—*

It didn't matter that Foley was a trained soldier with an athlete's body and an outlaw's array of weapons, while Lorian was an aging servant with soft muscles and no fighting skills. Corene was sure that Foley was in danger. She flung herself back through the crowd, back toward the dark corners of the property, back toward the maze of lies and treachery and murder.

She had gone maybe thirty yards when she saw the mob before her swirl with disruptive motion as determined figures cut through the fairgrounds, heading in her direction. "There she is!" she heard a voice call out, and she realized that the lead figure was pointing at her.

At first she thought it was one of Lorian's footmen and she stuttered to a halt, wondering if she needed to run in the other direction. Then she realized it was a royal guard, and he was followed by three more, and they were all pushing through the crowd, shoving aside bodies and knocking over decorations in an effort to get to her.

She definitely needed to run.

She spun around and dove through a mass of revelers, ducking under outstretched arms and skidding around large men who were too bulky to push aside. Someone spilled one of those flaming drinks on her and she felt fire flash down her spine as a woman nearby screamed *She's burning!* But either the tiny blaze was quickly extinguished or she absorbed it through her sweela skin, because it didn't harm her. She only ran faster.

Behind her she heard gasps and cries of alarm, the occasional sounds of thuds and crashes, and she knew the soldiers were still in pursuit. She was in the main part of the fair now, and everywhere she looked the paths were brightly illuminated; unless she could find a place to duck and hide, the soldiers would have no trouble keeping track of her. *But I don't have to make it easy for them,* she thought. She needed to create some misdirection.

There—a young woman was so focused on flirting with a man selling spiced oranges that she didn't realized she'd dropped her scarf, a filmy strip of spangled white fabric. Corene bent down as if to fasten an errant shoe buckle and snatched the scarf as she straightened up. Once she'd moved a few yards away, she paused long enough to wrap it around her head and throat. It was a flimsy disguise, but it might turn away the attention of the guards who would be watching for a woman wearing a gray hood and mask.

She continued on, a little more slowly now. The guards would look for someone who was running, so she must appear to be just another fairgoer, relaxed, happy, and eager to see the next attraction. Then she had to make her way to someplace safe. Or she had to find Filomara.

The trouble was, she couldn't imagine a place that would be safe. And she thought that Filomara might not trust Corene's version of events, but take Lorian's word instead—which didn't bode well for Corene's safety even if she found the empress.

Who would believe me? Who could help me even if they did believe me? she wondered as she paused to watch a pair of acrobats do flips and cartwheels. *Who has the power and knowledge to circumvent Lorian?*

She could think of only one person: Garameno. Who might very well be dead now, after all, if Lorian had summoned soldiers to accompany him through the maze.

Garameno dead—and Foley with him?

She stifled a sob.

Maybe Jiramondi could help—maybe the prefect. Both were steeped in court politics; both would instantly grasp the significance of Greggorio's death. If she could find them, if she could convince them—if she could manage to find allies before Lorian or his soldiers caught up with her again—

She turned toward the front doors of the palace and practically into the arms of a royal guard. As she stumbled and almost fell, he raised a hand to steady her. "Thank you," she murmured and stepped away.

Maybe it was her accent, even though she spoke so quietly; maybe it was the furtiveness with which she moved. But his head whipped around and he stared down at her. "Who are you?" he demanded, motioning to one of his colleagues nearby.

She took a step back. "I'm—"

"It's the Welchin princess!" the other guard cried. "Lorian wants her detained!"

She whirled around and dashed away.

There was a shout behind her, and then another; a woman screamed and something crashed to the ground with the disastrous sound of breaking glass. Corene just put her head down and ran, shoving people out of her way, tripping over the ones who didn't move fast enough, and leaping over prone bodies and decorative obstacles. Twice more, to her right and behind her, she heard the voices of royal soldiers calling to each other: *Stop her! Stop the princess!*

She had no idea how Lorian had alerted the guards so quickly, what he had told them to make them believe she was dangerous. She had no idea how long she could outrun them. She had no plan. She had no hope. Her breath burned in her chest and her heart beat so hard it hurt. Her only coherent thought was *They will catch me and I will die.*

But she didn't stop running.

Suddenly the crowd thinned out and she lifted her head long enough to get her bearings. She was on the far edge of the front lawns, almost to the limits of the fair. If she had had any chance of losing herself among the spectators, she had lost it now; there was nowhere left to hide. Maybe she could just keep running—down the straight, wide road that led to the wrought-iron gates—then past the gates—then out into the city itself, down to the docks, where she could fling herself into the ocean and swim all the way home to Welce—

She would never make it past the iron gate. Soldiers there would stop her, grab her, turn her over to the ones who were chasing her now. The ones who were so close she could hear their pounding footsteps, their cries of *I see her! I see her! There she is!* The ones she was too exhausted to outrun—

And then she saw it ahead of her on the lawn, only a few lingering admirers still clustered around it, touching its gleaming metal surfaces and its foreign dials and gauges. The smoker car. A gift directly from Welce to its most prodigal princess.

She managed a last burst of desperate speed, plowing through the young men gathered around the elaymotive, scattering them with her wild gestures and frantic cries. She vaulted over the low door and slammed her palm against the ignition button before she was securely seated on the front bench. The engine growled to life with a guttural roar that was the sweetest thing she'd ever heard.

She heard the soldiers yelling behind her—heard the fairgoers nearby squealing with alarm—but she had no attention left for anything but the elaymotive. It lurched like an angry demon when she threw it into gear, shuddering so badly she was afraid she might have killed the motor. Then it shot forward, barely missing a couple who dove out of its path, and jounced over the uneven ground as Corene tried to remember how to steer, how to feed fuel consistently through the lines. She was going too fast as she hit the curb that divided the lumpy lawn from the smooth surface of the main road, and she almost pitched over the open side of the vehicle. But she hung on grimly, turning the wheels sharply to keep the elaymotive on the pavement.

And then everything was fine.

The road stretched out, graded and level, straight for the main gate. The celebration was winding down, so traffic was starting to pick up— carriages, horsemen, even pedestrians clogging the way—which meant Corene couldn't stomp on the accelerator and race toward the gate like she wanted to do. But she could squeeze the little button that loosed a sound like a foghorn and caused horses to panic and pedestrians to leap aside, clearing a path for her down the middle of the street. She burned with exhilaration every time she blasted the horn and some other startled horse dragged its cart off the road. She could hear commotion behind her, but it faded fast. Within minutes, she had left the sounds of the palace behind.

The gate came up quickly, before she'd had time to plan. She didn't know what she'd do if the metal grill was closed; she didn't think the elaymotive would survive if she just tried to crash straight through. But that turned out not to be the problem. The gates were open—but a row of guards stood shoulder to shoulder, barring her passage with a human blockade.

She had never in her life even thought about killing another person, but she would run them all down if she had to.

She blasted the foghorn again, twice, three times, and pressed down on the accelerator, so she felt like she was hurtling through a noisy tunnel of sound and wind. It was clear she wasn't going to stop. And it was clear the soldiers realized it—they split for the two sides of the road, shouting as she roared past. Some of them threw things at her—rocks or knives, she wasn't sure—but their aim was bad or her speed was good, because a few objects thudded against the car and then she was out of range.

Free of the palace! *Safe!*

Oh, but this night was full of hazards.

She couldn't slow down, because she knew the gate guards would quickly mobilize to pursue her. But she couldn't keep up this hectic pace, because she didn't even know where she was going.

And because within a half mile of the gate she rounded a curve and came smack upon a roadblock. How could she have forgotten? The entire city was one giant celebration. Directly in her path was a collection of vendor's booths and happy citizens, clapping along to loud music and toasting each other with sloppy glasses of wine. There was no way to smash through that obstruction without killing a dozen people and probably destroying the elaymotive.

Cursing under her breath, she backed up the smoker car and turned down a smaller cross street that was quieter, darker, and much less crowded. On this back road, there was so little public illumination that she had trouble seeing what lay ahead of her, so she had to radically reduce her speed for fear of running over some helpless bystander. Not until then did she remember that Kayle had installed lighting systems on the newer models of the smoker cars, and she tried various buttons and switches until two side lamps on the front bumpers sprang to life.

She proceeded cautiously anyway because now she could see all the dangers nighttime had concealed from her—uneven surfaces, strange objects discarded in the middle of the road, holes in the pavement. And people. Standing on the side of the road, hanging out of windows, staring at her. She had to hope she was able to cover a lot of ground because the guards would have no trouble figuring out where she'd gone.

For the next ten or fifteen minutes, she drove randomly, still with no destination in mind; her only goal was to put as much distance as possible between herself and the palace. Every time she came to another noisy knot of celebration, she changed course and found a different route. She wasn't even sure what direction she was headed anymore. Which way was the palace? Which way the sea? If she could find the Little Islands, she might be able to locate Leah, and surely Leah would know a safe place to go. Leah would be able to get a message to Nelson—or even to Darien—or perhaps to some of those Welchin warships hovering just off the coast.

But would Leah know what had happened to Foley?

This time, the sob escaped. Corene put a hand against her mouth, trying to push back the cries, but it was no use. Where was he? Had Garameno managed to hurt him, had Lorian and his soldiers dragged Foley down like a criminal? Surely not; surely Foley was too strong, too clever, too alive to danger. Too *alive*. He had promised Corene he would not leave her alone in a foreign land, he would keep her safe, and he couldn't do that if he was dead. He wouldn't betray her that way. He would be faithful to the end of the world itself.

He was alive, he had to be. As soon as he realized Corene was missing, he would come looking for her. Where could she go that he would be sure to find her?

The red tower.

During that adventurous day when they had tried to outrun the palace guards, Foley had said, *If we ever get separated . . . go to the tower of fire and I'll find you there*. At the time she hadn't been able to imagine a reason she would ever leave him behind, but Foley was always thinking in the most drastic terms about what might go wrong. He would outwit Garameno, he would elude Lorian, and he would come to the red tower looking for Corene. She had to meet him there.

Fortunately, it was never difficult to locate the petals of fire blooming along the horizon, and they were particularly vivid against the midnight sky. Judging by the tower's location, Corene was farther east than she would have thought, and not as far south. She would need to work her way southwest, tracing an indirect route through the busy streets. But that was better than just driving at random. She backed up the smoker car and made a ninety-degree turn to enter a lane headed more or less in the direction she wanted. The flames waving from the tall tower seemed to be motioning her forward.

It took another twenty minutes of wrong turns and backtracking before she found herself on a relatively straight path toward her destination. This part of town was blessedly quiet, too, with fewer parties spilling into the street and almost no other traffic to complicate her journey. She felt a sense of relief so strong it was almost euphoria when she finally pulled up in front of the tower. She was here. She was safe. Foley would find her.

If Foley was still alive.

He had to be. She had to believe that.

She climbed out of the smoker car and then just stood there for a minute, wondering what to do next. Wondering what was happening back at the palace. Wondering if the celebrations were still going on throughout Palminera. Here it was eerily quiet, and she could almost believe the whole city had given one collective yawn and curled up to sleep. She stood on tiptoe and peered back the way she'd come, trying to glimpse movement or overhear sounds of reveling.

Well, of course, if she climbed to the top of the tower she would command a view of the entire city and perhaps she could draw better conclusions about what might be happening. As soon as she had the idea, she thought, *I'm too exhausted to make that much effort.* Indeed, her whole body felt strained and sore from the mad dash across the palace grounds. But she was also filled with a buzzing energy, an adrenaline-fueled restlessness; she didn't think she could just stand there, staring blankly into the empty dark, without losing her mind.

"All right," she said under her breath, "I'll climb the stupid tower."

The minute she stepped through the cavernous door she heard the quiet hissing sound of gas traveling through the fuel lines. The lighting seemed even dimmer than she remembered, and the stairwell more insubstantial. She gazed at it uncertainly for a moment, noting all the places metal planks had been brought in to reinforce the worn wood. She knew absolutely it was strong enough to bear her weight, but at the moment it looked like it might collapse under the slightest pressure.

Either climb up there and see *or stay down here and fret,* she told herself sternly. And because she hated to picture herself as timid and anxious, she strode over to the stairs and determinedly began her ascent.

The rhythm, the effort, the sense of having a goal all steadied her, and she felt lighter and more sure of herself the higher she went. As before, she felt the heat build to an oppressive intensity the closer she came to the top; the whuffling sound of the whipping fire drowned out her own labored breath.

Then she was on the uppermost stair—through the opening— standing on the top platform of the tower. Behind its stained-glass petals, the fire leapt and crackled with a manic energy. *It knows how wild this day has been for the city it watches over,* Corene thought. A ridiculous notion, but she couldn't shake it. She wondered if the white ghostlight in the northern tower shone even more brightly, more balefully, on this eventful night. She glanced in that direction, to see the moon-colored stone glowing like a fallen star. But maybe it always looked like that.

Slowly she circled the perimeter, leaning away from the heat of the fire, trailing her hand along the warm metal of the top rail, trying to get her bearings. There—that splash of light and color, full of moving shapes and shadows—that must be the palace. That must be where the celebration was turning into a wake, where the fairgoers became mourners as news spread of Greggorio's death. And possibly Garameno's death.

And possibly Foley's.

He's not dead.

She stared through the darkness in the direction of the royal residence, willing herself to see faces, bodies, details across the cluttered miles. She couldn't make out anything, of course. Just those streaks of light that seemed to waver like candle flame—a trick of her own watering eyes, no doubt.

She shook her head and looked impatiently away, scanning the rest of the city for any indication of excitement. Scattered across the whole grid were smaller clumps of activity, outlined by what she took to be torchlight and gas-fed streetlamps. Even as she watched, a few of those were extinguished, and then a few more. It must be well past midnight, she thought. While some parties would undoubtedly continue till dawn, the more sober, reasonable men and women would be seeking their beds by now, thinking about the workday that would be starting in a few hours.

The revelers on the wharf didn't seem ready to call it quits, though. The whole curve of the harbor was lined with lights, some moving, some still. It took Corene a while to realize that the ones in motion came from ships out on the water, where there appeared to be dozens of vessels crowded around the docks. She wondered if this meant the blockade had been lifted or if private citizens had just taken the opportunity to launch barges and fishing boats and carry the celebration out to sea. Indeed, it looked like some kind of special display was happening at the harbor, because she saw gaudy eruptions of fire and caught the echoes of distant booms. It reminded her of the light shows Darien would hold at the Chialto palace on changedays.

She leaned over the railing, trying to get a better view. Actually, now that she was paying closer attention, the booms didn't sound so friendly; they reminded her more of cannon fire. And those blasts of light might not be harmless bursts of color, but destructive explosions instead. She could feel the metal of the railing scald her hands, but she clung to it a moment longer, straining to hear, straining to see.

Below her a voice spoke in a sharp, excited tone, perfectly audible despite her distance from the ground. "There she is! At the top of the tower."

Her heart bounded and she shrank back, trying to see down without making herself so visible. How could she have forgotten that she was prey for some of the night's hunters? She could make out four or five shapes on the ground below, shadowy and indistinct in the darkness. But she didn't need a good look to know who they were—guards from the royal palace. Sent by Lorian to retrieve her.

Or kill her.

Surely not. She was a princess from an ally nation. Surely no matter how many Malinquese heirs Lorian had eliminated, he wouldn't dare harm a foreign national. Though he had been perfectly willing to murder Alette, and Alette hadn't known his terrible secrets. Staring down through the bars of the railing, Corene thought she could see the glint of metal in the soldiers' hands as they lifted their edged weapons. These men were not here simply to subdue her.

She backed toward the fiery heart of the tower, her hand at her throat, feeling the heat of the great blaze licking along her neck and scalp. She thought she could hear the sound of boot heels striking against the cobblestones, ringing against the metal of the bottom rungs. She was trapped. Only one way down, and that one blocked with soldiers with nothing but ill intent. She swallowed a sob.

Two ways down. She remembered the day Alette had leapt to the railing and paused there, ready to fling herself to the ground below. Corene didn't think she had the nerve to do that—to run to the arms of death even if it chased her from another direction. If she was going to die tonight, she would die fighting.

How could she fight? She had no weapons. Just her bare hands and the clothes on her body.

And the fire at her back.

There was only one way down the tower—but only one way up, too. A soldier had to poke his face through the trapdoor to the platform, and only one man at a time could make it through. It wasn't much of an advantage, but it was the only one she had.

She could hear them now—louder, closer—footsteps clambering up the stairs. She stood tense, frozen, listening, trying to gauge by the echoes how many soldiers were ascending, how far they had made it up the spiral. Two, she thought; halfway—more than halfway.

She unwound the spangled scarf she had stolen from the careless fairgoer and dropped it at her feet. It was too insubstantial for her current purposes. Then she stripped off her gray jacket, a close-fitting garment of warm, heavy weave. There was a seam down the back that ended with a decorative pleat. She took hold of each half of the pleat and jerked with all her strength, ripping the jacket into two pieces.

Two weapons.

She tossed one aside. Then she sidled up to the stained-glass panel, as close to the heat as she could stand, and dangled the other piece into the edge of the fire. The fabric caught almost instantly, a yellow flame climbing up the woven ladder of cloth. Just in time—she heard voices only a few feet away. She spun around to see a soldier's head pop up through the opening, and he looked straight at her.

"I've got her!" he bawled to someone below.

She flung the burning jacket right into his face.

He shrieked and clawed at the flames licking along his skin. Her throw had been lucky or he was badly positioned to defend himself from such an unconventional attack. His own jacket almost immediately caught fire, and his hands were busy beating at the flames, but now his sleeves were burning, and even his hair. The narrow opening kept him trapped in place—he couldn't pull himself up to roll on the floor, he couldn't see well enough to drop down to a lower step. He kept shouting and cursing and flailing his arms, and Corene ran over and kicked him repeatedly in the face.

He collapsed backward then, disappearing down the hole, and she heard more shouts and commotion as his falling body knocked into someone below him. She couldn't make out what the thuds and clanging might mean—was he tumbling all the way down the stairwell?— but she knew the next soldier would be right behind him. She snatched up the other half of the jacket and thrust it into the fire.

The second soldier was no smarter than the first. He shoved his head and torso out of the trapdoor, bracing his hands on the platform as if to push himself all the way through. This time, Corene was standing behind him, and she kicked him in the back of the head so hard that his skull smashed against the floor. In the seconds that it took him to recover, she looped the burning jacket around his shoulders, where it instantly caught his own clothes on fire.

His screams were horrifying to hear, and she backed away from the trapdoor as he writhed and shrieked and tumbled out of view. She could hear the sound of his body knocking against wood and metal as he somersaulted back down the circular stairwell. *I did that to him,* she thought. *I crippled or killed another human being.* She had never had to consider how desperately she would behave under extreme circumstances, just exactly what she would do to keep herself alive.

Apparently she would do anything, no matter how appalling.

She clenched her fists. And she would do it again, and again, till she burned her last item of clothing or she set the final man on fire. Unfortunately, it was likely she would run out of wardrobe options before she ran out of soldiers. She could undoubtedly rip her trousers in two, but her thin undergarments would go up in flames the minute she dipped them into the fire. Then she would be nude and completely vulnerable to attack from any soldier—any predator—if she didn't freeze to death as the night air chilled around her.

I don't know what to do, she thought.

Below, there was a sudden burst of noise—raised voices, clashing metal—and she ran around the perimeter of the platform, trying to peer down. Had more soldiers arrived? Were any of them her allies? That was definitely the sound of blade against blade, but it was all too possible the newcomers hadn't come to rescue her. They could easily be thieves roaming the streets on this night of easy pickings, and the disorganized band of royal soldiers had proved too attractive a target to resist. But the fight had that intense, sustained sound of professionals battling to the death, and Corene felt her hopes start to rise. Maybe Garameno had survived. Maybe he had sent his own troops after her—for undoubtedly Garameno had spent years cultivating palace guards and officers who were loyal only to him. And if Garameno was alive, surely Foley was alive—and Foley, of course, had known where to find Corene on this disastrous night—

"Foley!" she shouted, not sure if her voice would carry over the clangor of combat. "Foley! I'm up here! At the top!"

No one answered, unless a renewed frenzy of fighting could be considered an answer. Hoping to get a better view, she gripped the railing more tightly and bent so far over it that she almost tipped herself off the platform. The huge door in the base of the tower admitted a wavering square of light that flowed over the ground, and in that square she could see black silhouettes feinting, parrying, and falling back. It was like watching a shadow show created by the spinning of an enormous lantern, and Corene felt herself grow dizzy from the imagined motion. Another pair of fighters clashed and disengaged, clashed and disengaged, but she couldn't tell if she should celebrate or despair because she didn't know who was winning and who was losing. She tightened her grip and leaned over another inch, hoping to make the shadows seem more solid within the bright light.

It shouldn't be so bright. The tower's interior illumination was a tube of faint gaslight that spiraled up the wall, casting only an eerie glow. That deep yellow color was too vibrant, too intense, full of its own shivering shadows—

"Oh no," she whispered.

She yanked herself upright and ran to the trapdoor, falling to her knees and thrusting her face through. Heat and color soared up at her, decorated with bits of ash and the smell of roasting wood.

The stairwell was in flames.

TWENTY-FIVE

Corene pushed herself to her feet and backed away from the trapdoor as if it were a rabid animal that had suddenly focused its mad eyes on her. This was her fault. She had doomed herself with her own frantic actions. One of the soldiers she set on fire had lain too long against those wooden stairs, and the dry tinder had caught with an eager elation. The great chimney of the tower would pull the blaze upward in a matter of minutes, the fuel of the stairway laying a direct track to Corene. The wooden platform itself was hardened to almost ironlike density, but it wouldn't resist the siren call of flame for very long. How could it? After centuries of lying so quietly, so tamely, next to the prismed cauldron of fire, it would abandon itself to flame with joyful immolation.

Corene was about to be burned alive.

Behind her, she felt the thin barrier of the railing stop her retreat. The metal was even hotter now; she could feel its muted brand through the cloth of her trousers. The air around her was clogging with acrid smoke. Soon it would be almost impossible to breathe.

She couldn't do it. She couldn't give herself over to the conflagration. She would turn elay and fling herself into unsupported air; she would become torz and smash into the unforgiving earth. She was a sweela girl but she could not meld herself with fire.

She turned around and stared down, trying to nerve herself to make the leap.

"*Corene!*"

The voice was so hoarse that at first she didn't recognize it, but that hardly mattered; clearly someone was here looking for her.

"I'm on the top of the tower!" she shouted back. "Where are you?"

"You have to get out! *Now!*" came the answer.

Below her. Standing in the square of rippling yellow light. The shape of a man she would recognize from any vantage point in the world. "Foley?"

"Yes!"

"Foley! You're alive!" For a moment—despite the heat, the peril, the many shocks of the night—she felt herself filled with an almost insane happiness. "I'm so glad! I'm so glad!"

"Corene, you have to come down—the tower is on fire!"

Somehow, it didn't seem so terrible to die if Foley was still alive. It was illogical, but this night wasn't made for logic. It was as if she could bear anything as long as he survived. There was practically a lilt in her voice as she called back, "Foley, I can't come down—the tower is on fire!"

Another shape heaved itself into the brilliant light. This one was burlier, shorter, moving less freely but with a certain latent power. "You can make it out of there," this figure called up to her. "I'll hold back the flames."

"Nelson!" That crazy delight swirled through her again. They were both alive; they were both here to save her. Suddenly the whole night seemed brighter, and it wasn't because of the raging fire. "But are you sure?"

"You'll be safe enough," Nelson shouted. "Just come on down the stairs."

Even as he spoke, she could feel the air around her radically cool. The molten light rising from the trapdoor turned faint and ghostly; even the leaping flames within the stained-glass blossom dropped so low she could hear the buzz of the gas feeding through its tube, though the fire was not completely extinguished.

She took a deep breath. *I can do this,* she thought. *I can walk through fire. I can live through this night.*

Nonetheless, it took all her will to crawl to the trapdoor and drop her legs blindly through the opening, feeling for the first stair with her toes. The minute her thin slippers touched the step, she yelped and curled her legs back up. The metal of the plank was so hot it seared her soles.

"What's wrong?" Foley shouted. The men must have stepped inside the tower the minute she disappeared from view at the railing; the timbre of his voice echoed differently off the smoke-filled interior walls.

"I burned my feet. The stairs are hot."

"I can't do anything about that," Nelson bellowed. "You'll just have to be brave."

"Courage," Foley called. "Remember. That's always been your blessing. Show courage."

She took a deep breath and lowered her legs again, biting her lip against the stinging pain. Maybe if she moved really quickly, running from stair to stair, her skin wouldn't have time to blister. She put all her weight on her feet and dropped through the trapdoor to land in a crouch on the top stair.

The dying fire had filled the tower with smoke and reduced the ambient illumination to almost nothing; she could barely see three yards in front of her, and the stairway circled down into an ominously impenetrable fog. She swallowed a whimper of terror and braced her hand against the wall.

Courage, she thought, and rose shakily to her feet.

It wasn't possible to run down the stairwell, after all. The swirling smoke not only made it difficult to see the descending steps, it drifted around her face and resulted in a sort of poisoned vertigo. She focused on her feet and took first one stair, then another, each time trying to find the original wood instead of the supporting metal. That worked until she placed her weight on a plank of wood, and it gave way beneath her. She shrieked and pitched forward, her hands outstretched to break her fall, while her leg smashed through the shattered lumber almost to her knee.

"Corene! Corene! What happened?" came Foley's instant cry.

Painfully, she pushed herself back to a sitting position and extricated her leg. It was scratched and bleeding and prickly with splinters, but it could have been worse, she supposed. It could have snapped in half.

"My foot went through a stair and I fell!" she called back. "I think I'll be all right."

"I can't come up after you," he replied. "You have to come down."

She tried to stand, but the battered leg buckled under her and she hurriedly dropped back down. Very well, she'd descend on her buttocks, the way very young children did. At the back of her mind, a question circled: *Why can't Foley come up the stairs?* She didn't ask, because both possible answers were terrifying. Either he was too hurt to navigate the steps, or the stairwell was too compromised to hold his weight. In which case . . .

She didn't feel as dizzy in the seated position, so her pace actually picked up as she continued downward. But the air grew denser with smoke, harder to breathe, and the stairs were increasingly dangerous—full of charred holes where the wood had burned away, many planks still smoldering with sullen fire. In multiple places she had to rise briefly to her feet and step carefully down on the remaining metallic skeleton, because all the wood was gone.

"Where are you? How far down?" Foley called.

"I can't tell. I can't see to the bottom. Can you see me?" She tried waving her hand through the gritty haze.

"I don't know. Maybe. Just keep coming down."

"If Kayle was here, he could blow all this smoke away," Nelson grumbled.

This time Corene had to swallow hysterical laughter. If she was going to start wishing for impossible things, she'd wish for something a lot more useful than the elay prime. For instance, a handrail or a rope or an intact set of stairs. She bumped her way down two more steps.

"Where are you now?" Foley asked.

This time she did laugh. "I still don't know."

"Just keep talking to me," he said. "It helps me gauge the distance."

"What happened at the palace?" she asked breathlessly. It took a lot of effort to shout and scoot down the stairs at the same time, especially when the air was so thick. "Garameno didn't kill Greggorio."

"I know," Foley said. "How did you figure it out?"

"Because I found Lorian—"

"Lorian!" Foley exclaimed. "But he—"

"I know! When I told him about the body, he got—got—so crazy—"

Nelson's incredulous voice came next. "The murderous steward? *That's* who you told?"

"Well, I didn't know he was murderous until he sent soldiers after me—"

"And that's why you ran?" Foley asked.

She giggled, and then she cursed when her backside landed on a particularly hot sheet of metal. She hurriedly descended to another step, but it wasn't much better. The fire had apparently started at the base of the stairs and roared its way up; it would get dicier and dicier the closer she got to the ground. "I didn't run, I *drove*," she corrected him. "I stole Filomara's smoker car!"

"We found it outside the tower," Foley said. "That's when we knew for certain you were here."

"Very smart," Nelson added. "Kayle would approve."

Corene paused to catch her breath and try to assess where she was. She could hear the others more clearly now but she still couldn't see them; she might be the equivalent of three or four stories up. *On the roof of the Great Market,* she thought, her spirits rising. *You can climb down that far.* "But how did *you* find out about Lorian?"

"He came running through the maze with soldiers at his back, screaming, 'Kill them! Kill them!'" Foley said dryly. "I drew the logical conclusion."

"Oh no! How many soldiers? How did you fight them off?"

"Four soldiers, as well as Lorian. Garameno and I could retreat to the gazebo and make a stand, but it was hardly much cover."

"Can he fight? Really?"

"I'm guessing there are a lot of things young Garameno can do," Nelson put in. "As soon as I met him, I could tell he was concealing a big secret, but I don't read foreigners very well, so I couldn't guess what it was."

"He can fight," Foley confirmed. "But he didn't have to. Because moments after Lorian arrived, another set of soldiers came running through the maze—"

"Garameno's troops," Corene said. "I knew he must have some."

"He'd sent his man after them the minute he found Greggorio. They made quick work of the soldiers."

"And Lorian?"

Foley was silent a moment. "On his knees by Greggorio's body. Holding him. Weeping. I've never seen anything like it."

Corene came to her feet to navigate another mostly nonexistent stair and felt the whole structure shudder beneath her. She held her breath until the shaking stopped, clinging to the red stone with her fingernails—as if that could possibly help—then eased down one more step. Her heart was pounding so hard it was difficult to keep her voice steady.

"So what did you do with him?"

"I didn't need to do anything because more royal guards started pouring through the maze. Hacking their way through, really—just leveling the shrubs. Filomara was with them. I saw her confront Garameno and I decided it was time to come look for you."

"But he found me," Nelson interposed, "because *I* was looking for you. Some fool had gone running through the grounds yelling about a woman stealing the elaymotive, and since it sounded *exactly* like something you would do—"

Corene managed a breath of laughter as she sank back to her buttocks and curled her fingers around the stair. This just felt like the safer method of locomotion. "I was afraid Lorian's men would kill me," she explained, feeling ahead of her for the next step. "So I thought I should—"

The entire stairwell before her ripped from the wall and collapsed in a mighty crash of sparks and splinters and rending metal. Corene shrieked and scrabbled for a hold, wrapping her arms around the final stair still attached to the wall, feeling it pull slowly away from its anchoring. The hot metal burned the skin of her forearms; her feet danced precariously over nothingness. "Foley!" she cried. "*Foley!* It's coming down!" She heard the remaining bolts groan as they scraped through the stone.

"You'll have to jump!" he called. "I'll catch you!"

She felt panic gallop through her chest; she couldn't breathe, she couldn't think. "I can't! It's too far!"

"No, it's not. I can hear you—you're so close."

"I can't see you! You can't see me! I'll just fall straight to the stone and die!"

"You won't," he said, his voice calm and reassuring. "I can hear you. I'm right under you. I'll catch you."

"I'm too high!" she choked out. "I'll fall on you and crush you and *you'll* die!"

"Then take my life," he answered. "Take it. I don't want to live anyway, if you're dead."

She whimpered. "I can't," she whispered. "I can't kill you to save myself."

A section of the stair above her shifted and swung free from the wall, scraping along the rough stone. She shrieked again, almost mindless with terror. Her whole body was dangling from the bottom stair as she clung to the searing metal, but her sweaty hands were beginning to slip. "Foley!" she wept.

"Corene, I see you!" he roared. "Let go before the stairs fall! *Let go!*"

His voice rose to her from directly below. He was still invisible in the swirling smoke, but she had to believe that he was there. The faithful torz heart; the one she could trust with her life. Oh, but she did not want to fall into his arms and smash him against the ground. He would die to protect her, but she would die from the loss.

"I can't," she whispered. "I can't."

He could not have heard her, not through the creaking of the stairs and the snapping of the embers and Nelson shouting something she couldn't make out. But he answered her anyway.

"Corene, I love you," he said, his voice so clear he might have been leaning over to speak directly in her ear. "I won't let you fall."

Courage, she thought, and opened her hands.

Seconds of smoke and cinders and air and *nothing* and then the collision—arms and chest and a hard impact on the stony ground and rolling, rolling, her body entwined with his, no sense of up or down, just pain and motion and terror. Then a pause—a suspension of thought and movement and sound and everything—and Foley's insistent voice against her cheek, his breath against her skin.

"Corene. *Corene.*"

She tried to inhale, choked on the hot air, and didn't speak his name so much as cough it. "Foley! Are you all right?"

"Yes—yes—unhurt, but you—I need to look at you. Sit up, can you sit up?"

"I don't know, I'm so dizzy—"

How could they be alive, both of them? Maybe she hadn't been so high up after all, or maybe she had perished in the fall and this smoky dreamland was where the dead existed. *I didn't think there would be so much pain once I died,* she thought, her senses swimming as Foley pulled her to a sitting position. She felt his hands—his strong, capable hands—run swiftly over her arms, her ribs, her legs, pausing at the shredded skin along her right calf before checking her ankles and feet.

"I don't think you've broken anything," he said, his voice rich with relief. "And your head? Did you hit it when you fell?"

"I don't think so. Everything else hurts, but not my head. And you? You're really all right? You're not lying?"

"I never lie to you," he said.

All around them, currents of smoke swirled like particularly insistent ghosts, but they were in a small cocoon of open air, practically sitting on top of each other, their faces inches apart. She had no idea where Nelson had gone, but he wasn't within the perimeter of this tiny magical space, so he might as well not exist. She lifted her hands—bruised and bleeding and streaked with red where she had clung to the hot metal—and put her palms on Foley's cheeks.

"You said you loved me," she whispered. "Did you say it just so I'd jump? Or was it the truth?"

He watched her steadily. His face was grimed with ash, his eyes rimmed with red from the stinging embers. Or maybe he had been crying. He repeated, "I never lie to you."

"I love you, too. You know that. Or maybe you don't. But I love you."

"I know you think you do."

"Oh, Foley," she said, almost laughing. "You have no idea what I'm thinking."

She leaned in to kiss him. It was a remarkably sweela kiss. He tasted like smoke and ashes and fevered life, like miracles and passion and the embodiment of dreaming. Her skin was hot, or his was, or the very stone beneath their bodies still harbored fire, because she was flushed with heat and her lips burned against his mouth.

"I'm so glad I didn't die," she whispered.

There was a disturbance behind them and an eddy in the hazy air, and suddenly Nelson was standing there, his hands on his hips, his face streaked with soot. "Truly? Right now? *This* is the time you pick?" he demanded. "These stairs could collapse at any minute!"

Foley didn't even bother to look embarrassed as he stood up and helped Corene to her feet. She clutched at his arm, but he didn't show any inclination to let her go. "He's right," Foley said. "We need to get out of here."

She nodded, letting him guide her toward the big square of blackness that must be the wide door. She'd only taken three steps before she had to step over a body on the floor, hidden till now by the low smoke. She caught her breath and tightened her grip on Foley's arm. "Are they all dead?" she asked quietly.

He nodded. "Yes. Four of them."

He had promised he would kill to keep her safe—and expressed the hope that he would never have to do so. *Mostly because I don't want you ever to be so much at risk.* Well, she had been at risk and he had responded as promised, though it was horrible to think about.

"Four," she repeated. "I'm impressed."

"One of them was already dead from the fire I believe *you* set," he said.

She nodded, her throat so tight she couldn't speak. So she had killed a man after all. Sometime soon, she would need a long, quiet moment to think about that.

"And the sweela prime accounted for another one," Foley added.

She swiveled her head to get a look at Nelson. "He *did*? I didn't know he could even hold a weapon."

Nelson's grin was tired. "That's not how a prime slays a man."

"Oh," she said, facing forward again to watch where she was going because Foley was steering her around another dead soldier. Well, she knew what Zoe was capable of. The coru prime could call a man's blood right out of his veins, make it seep through his skin in rivulets of red—though as far as Corene knew, Zoe had never actually killed anybody. Corene didn't know how Nelson would stop an assailant, but she wasn't surprised to learn he could do it. More surprised that he *would*.

There were too many bodies piling up in Malinqua. She was unutterably grateful that none of them were hers, or Foley's, but she was tired of this place. Tired and sad and in pain and ready to sail away.

They stepped through the great door into the clear, cool night, and Corene took one deep breath of sweet air—then felt her feet freeze to the ground.

The tower was ringed with soldiers.

She felt Foley drop her arm and pull a blade; she felt Nelson press closer, bristling with heat and menace. But the soldiers didn't surge forward, brandishing weapons, and neither of her protectors issued a challenge. They spent a brief, tense moment staring at each other in the imperfect light of flame and star, trying to make out faces and insignia. It didn't take long for Corene to realize these men weren't wearing Malinquese livery. In fact—could it be?—was that the small Welchin rosette embroidered on the fronts of their uniforms?

She drew herself up to what she hoped was a regal pose and demanded, "Who are you? Speak now."

The lead soldier stepped forward and offered formal bows to Corene and Nelson. "Majesty," he said. "Prime. I'm Captain Sorren of the Chialto Royal Guard, and these are my men. We await your orders."

She felt Foley relax and Nelson start laughing, but she was too stunned to do more than stare. "Chialto Royal Guard," she repeated. "How did you get here?"

A smaller shape slipped past Captain Sorren and resolved itself into Leah. "You're safe!" she exclaimed, flinging her arms around Corene for a quick hug. "I brought the soldiers. When I realized what was happening—"

"What *is* happening? Why are Welchin troops in Palminera?" Corene asked. Suddenly she registered the intermittent, echoing booms rolling across the city from the direction of the docks; suddenly she remembered the flashes of light she'd seen from the harbor. She gasped. "Are we invading Malinqua?"

"Not us," Nelson answered.

"Berringey?"

"Cozique," Leah said.

Corene felt that the night had left her too stupid to absorb information. "But—why?"

"For the same reason I'm here, and Welchin warships lie a few miles out in the ocean," Nelson said dryly. "Because Filomara has been careless with the safety of her guests."

"Melissande's mother," Corene realized. "She sent a navy to retrieve her."

"So it appears."

Corene gestured at Captain Sorren. "But then you—did you battle the Coziquela navy to come find us?"

"That wasn't necessary," he replied.

Still confused, Corene glanced at Nelson, who was pursing his lips. "Let's say I might not have been entirely truthful with Filomara," Nelson said. "Before I came ashore, I had some conversations with the Coziquela admirals. It turned out we were basically in agreement and we saw no need to fire on each other."

Corene rubbed her temple. Maybe she had been wrong when she told Foley she hadn't hit her skull on the stone. She was starting to get a headache. "So then—what's happening now?"

Captain Sorren replied. "It's been a busy day. Coziquela forces made short work of the Berringey blockade before confronting the Malinquese navy. Welchin ships were not far behind, and we met very little resistance. Coziquela forces now occupy the harbor and by now, I believe, control most of the city. If the empress calls up her infantry, we could see a great deal of bloodshed, but my guess is she will make terms. It's not like Cozique wants anything from Malinqua except the queen's daughter safely returned."

Corene listened closely, nodding a few times. Well, it made sense, but what a disaster for Filomara! Every one of her complex plans in tatters—one of her nephews dead, her trusted steward revealed as a bloodthirsty traitor—and now her city in the hands of a wealthy rival. This night of celebration had turned Palminera to ruins.

"What part did you and Leah play in all this?" Corene asked the captain.

Leah answered for him. "I saw the Coziquela ships in the harbor. I knew that a Welchin warship lay at anchor in the smuggler's port, and I thought you might need your own guards to see you through this night." She took a deep breath. "We were heading for the palace when I saw the red tower go up in flames. I didn't know what that meant—but when the flames suddenly died down, I knew the sweela prime had to be nearby."

Nelson was grinning. "It *is* rather my signature style."

Captain Sorren spoke again. "Now that we've found you, let us escort you back to the ship. There's enough chaos on the water that I'd prefer not to cast off until morning, unless you're in a desperate hurry to pull out."

"We can't leave," Corene said. "We have to go to the palace."

All of them frowned at her with various levels of disapproval. Nelson said, "If you think there's chaos on the *water*, you can bet it's five times worse on land."

"The palace will be nothing but mayhem," Foley added. "No one is there to keep order."

"Best to leave now," Leah agreed, "before things get any worse."

Corene's mouth set in a mutinous line. "I'm not leaving until I know how the situation stands at the palace," she said. "They're my friends— Garameno and Jiramondi and Liramelli. And Steff! And the empress! Her whole *life* has fallen apart tonight. Alette already disappeared and Filomara has no idea what happened to her. I'm not going to do the same thing. I'm going to say goodbye to her—to all of them. And even though you think you can pick me up and drag me back to the ship, you *can't*. I won't go. I'll break down a locked door and I'll jump into the ocean and I'll swim back to shore, and I'll walk back to the palace on my bare feet, if I have to, but *I'm not leaving*."

She was so angry she couldn't read their expressions. She thought maybe Leah and Captain Sorren were eyeing her speculatively, wondering how much she would resist if they tried to kidnap her, but Foley was smiling and Nelson was openly laughing.

"She's sweela, but never forget that her father is the most hunti son of a bitch of all hunti sons of bitches ever born, and she's every bit as stubborn as he is," Nelson said. "I admit I'm curious to see the aftermath of this night's work. Let's go back to the palace."

They formed an actual cavalcade as they navigated the streets back to the royal residence. Foley drove the elaymotive and Nelson insisted on sitting up front, so Leah and Corene crammed themselves onto the narrow bench in back. Nelson had given Corene his jacket to wear, because the night was chilly and she had, of course, sacrificed her own. "I'm never cold," he said when she tried to protest, so she accepted it gratefully. She snuggled into it as she watched Captain Sorren deploy his men—half ahead of the elaymotive and half behind. They were all mounted on horses they'd acquired in some fashion. Corene hadn't asked.

Unlike Corene's first manic dash through the city, this journey took them down streets that were oddly quiet and wholly deserted. All the windows were dark and no one peered out to investigate the noise of their passing. It was as if—through some mysterious but reliable method of urgent communication—every resident had learned of the betrayals at the palace and the invasion at the harbor, and everyone was hunkered down to wait out the consequences of disaster.

It was easier to see on this trip, though; thank the sweela prime for that. Every gaslight on their route flared to sudden brightness as they approached and sank back to a muted glow as soon as they passed. No one even bothered to comment.

Things got livelier as they approached the walls to the inner city, where the gate area shone with an artificially white light that owed nothing to Nelson's careless magic. There were dozens of soldiers camped on both sides of the wall, and in the ample illumination Corene could tell that their blue-and-gold uniforms were neither Welchin nor Malinquese. Captain Sorren was correct: Cozique had control of the entire city.

Their contingent met with a few cursory challenges, but once they were recognized as Welchin, they were waved on without fuss. Corene craned her neck, trying to peer down the labyrinthine alleys inside the gate, but those roads were just as dark and silent as the ones outside the walls. The whole city seemed to be holding its breath.

It was a different story once they made it to the palace grounds, where there was so much activity it was hard to figure out who was doing what. The whole place was a wreck of trampled shrubbery, abandoned furniture, discarded wine bottles, dropped clothing, and spilled food. An army of servants moved through the welter, trying to set things right. Coziquela soldiers prowled the perimeter, but Malinquese guards stood at the palace entrance and took strategic positions throughout the grounds as if daring the foreign invaders to come one step closer. The wide front doors were propped open, admitting a steady stream of traffic both in and out—soldiers, servants, and the well-dressed members of Malinqua's elite.

The first person Corene recognized was Melissande.

Before the elaymotive had even come to a halt, Corene was on her feet, shouting and waving. "Melissande! Melissande!" she cried. She hopped over the low door and ran toward the palace.

"*Corene!*" Melissande shrieked, racing toward her. "I have been so worried! You cannot even imagine!"

They collided just outside the door in a violent embrace and clung together, laughing and crying.

"You do not know—you do not know—so very much has happened," Melissande panted, still clinging to her.

"Greggorio is dead. Lorian killed him. Your mother has invaded," Corene replied, equally breathless.

Melissande exhaled a shaky laugh and released her. "Then you do know. The big things, at least. And when we could not find you—oh, we were so afraid. Lorian admitted that he had sent soldiers after you, but we could not find a body, and we have been *wild* with worry. But we could not find Foley, either, so we were a little hopeful."

By this time, the rest of the occupants had climbed from the car, and Melissande had had enough time to identify their military escort. "I see it is not only my mother's men who have invaded Palminera," she said sadly.

"Welchin troops haven't attacked," Corene replied. "They're only here for me."

"That's exactly what my mother's troops are saying."

"Where is everybody?" Corene demanded. "What happens next?"

Before Melissande could answer, someone else stepped through the door. "Who are you talking to?" Steff asked. "Has there been any word of— *Corene!*"

For the fourth time in this tumultuous night, Corene was swept into a hard embrace, this one almost as crushing as Foley's. Steff's cry brought more bodies through the door, and soon she was being passed from Steff to Liramelli to Jiramondi and back to Steff. It was odd how much she enjoyed the experience; she had never been one to seek out casual contact.

"Enough—enough—let me get my balance," she said finally, pulling herself from Steff's arms but keeping one hand on his shoulder and one on Melissande's. "Can we go somewhere and talk? Then you can tell me everything that's happened."

TWENTY-SIX

Nelson went off to find the empress, but Jiramondi shepherded the rest of them to a small bookroom on the second floor in the white wing. Foley and Leah followed them up the stairs, as did half the Chialto guard, though none of them stepped inside the room. Melissande fussed over Corene, smoothing back her disordered hair and using a delicate handkerchief to brush smoke and soot from her face.

"And your *hands*!" Melissande exclaimed. "They are so *raw*!"

"I'll take care of all that later," Corene said impatiently. She was too tired to stand any longer, so she sank to a chair at a small table, and the other four all followed suit. She demanded, "Tell me everything. Tonight. Lorian. What *happened*?"

Jiramondi nodded and folded his hands before him. He looked thin and exhausted, as if this night had lasted years instead of hours. "Greggorio is dead," he said, the simple words holding pounds and acres and years of silent grief. Corene knew that his emotions must be too complex to sort out easily. Greggorio had been his rival, but also his cousin; she had witnessed between them competition, exasperation, but also affection. Behind the deep shock Jiramondi would be feeling a sense of bewilderment and loss.

"I know," Corene said, glancing at Liramelli. The other girl was leaning back against her chair, eyes closed, cheeks pale with sorrow. Steff reached over to take her hand and Corene saw Liramelli's fingers close convulsively over his. Here was someone else whose loss too big and too complicated to calculate in a single night. "And Lorian killed him. But how did events get to this point to begin with?"

"We're still piecing it together," Jiramondi answered. "And it is so much more complicated than we thought."

"It seems simple enough to me," Corene said. "Lorian started assessing the next candidates for the throne and eliminating the ones he didn't like."

"Maybe, but he wasn't the first," said Jiramondi. "If Lorian is telling us the truth, Morli started this game."

"Morli?" asked Steff.

"Greggorio's father," Liramelli explained, opening her eyes, though she still wore an air of fragility.

"He was the oldest of Filomara's brothers and always believed he should be her heir. But not only did she intend Aravani to take the throne after her, Morli himself was childless."

"Until finally his third wife gave birth to Greggorio," Liramelli said, her voice breaking only slightly when she spoke his name.

"The very year Aravani and her daughters died of a mysterious fever," Jiramondi added.

"Morli *killed* them?" Steff demanded, his voice thick with horror. "Once his own son was born?"

Jiramondi nodded. "Or so Lorian says. Lorian has not admitted that he helped Morli plot the murders—but he was always fond of Morli. Always close to him. It would not surprise me to learn he was somehow involved."

"But then did Lorian kill Morli, too?" Corene asked. "It makes no sense."

Jiramondi sighed and rubbed his forehead. "What appears to have happened is that Morli was murdered by Donato—Filomara's second-oldest brother, who had always wanted the crown for himself. And

Lorian was so heartbroken and enraged by Morli's death that he poisoned Donato just a day or two later."

"Filomara's other two brothers got blamed for the deaths and were banished from the palace," Liramelli said.

"While Lorian remained at court, now convinced that it was up to him to make sure Morli's son was the next one to take the throne," Jiramondi continued.

"Which meant eliminating the other contenders," Corene said. "Starting with Garameno."

Jiramondi nodded. "Yes. Lorian admits that he arranged for the accident that left Garameno crippled."

"Except it didn't!" Liramelli exclaimed, straightening in her chair and regaining a little animation. "All this time—Garameno has been able to walk! He has been completely whole! Why pretend otherwise?"

Corene could guess. "He needed to appear weak," she said. "He needed to seem like he wasn't a threat so Lorian wouldn't try again to kill him."

Liramelli looked confused. "So all this time Garameno knew that Lorian was a murderer?"

"I don't think so," Jiramondi replied. "He had noticed that everyone near the throne was being systematically eliminated, but he didn't know who was responsible for the deaths. So he turned himself into an unlikely candidate so that he would draw no unwanted attention."

"Why weren't *you* eliminated?" Corene asked him.

Jiramondi responded with the ghost of a laugh. "But I was," he said. "Lorian is the one who made sure everyone knew I was . . ."

"Sublime," Melissande supplied.

He gave her a crooked smile. "Yes. Sublime. It was a kinder way to disinherit me than murder, I suppose."

Steff stirred in his chair. "So, really, up until then, Lorian wasn't so bad," he said. When they all looked at him in disbelief, he shrugged. "He killed one person, Donato, who'd already poisoned someone else. He *tried* to kill Garameno, but he didn't succeed—and maybe he wasn't trying to kill him. Just to frighten him. So at that point he wasn't so terrible."

"Unless he was involved in Aravani's death," Corene pointed out. "But even if he wasn't, his murders didn't stop with Donato, did they?"

Jiramondi shook his head. "He had made up his mind that Greg-gorio should take the throne—and he was equally determined that Greggorio should marry Liramelli. Who was also his favorite."

Liramelli was staring down at the table. "When I was a little girl, he would take me anywhere in the palace I wanted to go. He showed me the jewels in Filomara's vault. When ambassadors came from Welce and Cozique and Dhonsho, bringing gifts for Filomara, he would sneak bits and pieces of them for me—sweets and ribbons and jars of perfume. I still have an opal from Yorramol that he brought me when I was seven years old."

"So when Greggorio lost interest in Liramelli," Corene said. "When he began flirting with Sarona—"

"That poor unfortunate girl." Melissande sighed.

"Lorian intervened," Jiramondi summed up. He glanced at Steff. "So now he's up to at least two successful murders, and he starts to think he can control everything. He doesn't like the fact that Filomara still relies so heavily on Garameno. The night Nelson Ardelay arrives, Filomara invites Garameno in to assist with negotiations. Lorian decides Garameno is still considered a viable candidate for the throne and must be eliminated—not just crippled, but killed."

There was a little silence while they all contemplated how badly that plan had gone wrong.

"One thing I don't understand," Corene said finally. "What about Steff?"

"What about me?"

"Why didn't Lorian see *him* as a threat? Why is Steff still alive?"

"Indeed, yes!" Melissande exclaimed. "If I am Lorian, I get rid of Steff the very first nineday he is in the palace!"

Liramelli made a choking sound and clutched Steff's hand even more tightly, holding on as if she could protect him with her own sturdy body.

"I believe he took other steps to try to discredit Steffanolo," Jira-mondi said.

"The men who tested Steff's blood!" Corene realized. "Lorian bribed them to say Steff wasn't related to the empress! I always thought that was Garameno."

"I thought so, too," Jiramondi confessed. "But now I think it was Lorian."

"And yet, another expert certified him as Subriella's son, so the question remains," Melissande pointed out. "Why is Steff alive?"

Jiramondi lifted his eyes to give Steff a long, considering look. "I think because he is an untutored, inexperienced country bumpkin who does not understand the impossible complexities of court life."

"That's mean!" Liramelli cried.

Steff laughed. "It's fair."

Melissande nodded. "We who like Steff see his many good qualities, of course, but it does seem unlikely someone as canny as Filomara would force a crown on his head when he does not seem—entirely—suitable to rule a country."

"So Lorian had no reason to kill him," Jiramondi said. "But that could have changed in a year or two if Filomara started to favor him."

Corene leaned back and surveyed Steff and Liramelli. "Or if Lorian realized that the two of you had fallen in love," she said.

Liramelli snatched her hand away; her cheeks were bright with color. "What? No! We're not—we're just very good friends," she said.

But Steff, grinning, took hold of her hand again and squeezed it so hard she couldn't pull free. "So you think he would have gotten rid of me if he thought I was stealing Liramelli from the rightful heir?" he asked cheerfully.

"I think it's very likely," Jiramondi said.

"Lucky for you two Lorian will be locked up somewhere for the rest of his life," Corene informed them.

Liramelli's gaze dropped to the table and Jiramondi's expression grew more severe. "No," Jiramondi said, "he'll be executed within the nineday. Traitors always are."

It was not the custom in Welce, so Corene couldn't help but be shocked. But when she tried to frame a counterargument, she found it hard to come up with reasons why Lorian shouldn't be put to death.

"I'm sure he doesn't see himself as a traitor," she said softly. "He sees himself as a great patriot who was trying to serve his country by keeping its rulers strong."

"I don't think that's the kind of service Malinqua needs," Jira-mondi replied.

Melissande stirred on her chair. "What happens next?" she asked. "I want so very much to stay and find out, but I am certain I will be leaving very soon. An ambassador from my mother arrived with the navy, but I do not think he and Filomara will have much to discuss. We will sail for Cozique in a day or two."

"And I'll be leaving for Welce in the morning," Corene said, feeling equally dismayed about the prospect. "So you'll have to promise to keep in touch and tell us everything that happens here."

"I'm not much of one for writing letters," Steff excused himself.

"*I* will tell you everything," Liramelli promised.

"It will take some time to pick up the pieces," Jiramondi said. "And I don't know what kind of bargain the Coziquela forces will strike with the empress." He glanced at Melissande. "You might not be leaving after all. Perhaps what your mother will want to ensure peace between nations is a blood treaty. You to marry Garameno."

"Garameno?" Corene repeated.

Jiramondi nodded. "Now that it's clear he's a whole man, there's no impediment to naming him her heir. Greggorio is dead, Steff is—"

"A bumpkin," Corene supplied. She couldn't resist.

"And I am still the abomination with the revolting predilections," Jiramondi finished up. "Garameno is the only choice to become Filo-mara's heir."

"But perhaps the empress will then want Garameno to marry Lira-melli," Corene suggested.

Liramelli practically flounced in her chair. "I don't want to marry Garameno."

"No, and I do not want to, either," Melissande said thoughtfully. "I admire Garameno, but I do not like him very much. I do not want to be tied to him."

She sighed. "And I do not want to be tied to Malinqua. I thought it would be a grand adventure to come to a foreign nation and marry a handsome young heir, but I find the prospect less appealing every day. I miss Cozique so much more than I expected. I want to go home."

"I thought your mother put conditions on your return," Corene said.

Melissande sighed again. "Yes, indeed. She wants me to marry. She will have picked out a suitable groom for me by now, I'm afraid. But perhaps the man will not be so bad. Or we will be able to come to a certain understanding." She shrugged.

"I suppose Garameno will be able to find a bride among the women of Malinqua," Corene said.

Jiramondi hesitated. "I suppose he will," he said. "Though there are stories—they might or might not be true—"

"That he is impotent!" Melissande exclaimed. "Yes, we have heard these tales. But there are many ways for a sterile man to bring children into the world."

"Not in Malinqua," Jiramondi said. "Where, as you know, blood can be tested."

Melissande spoke with great earnestness and not a trace of embarrassment. "Then you will have to overcome your repugnance and mate with a woman at least enough times to produce a royal heir on behalf of the family," she said. "I imagine you will be able to manage it. We are not so repulsive, you know."

Jiramondi looked so nonplussed that Corene burst out laughing and couldn't stop. Steff was laughing, too, and Liramelli—though she looked appalled at the plain speaking—could not suppress a smile. Jiramondi finally wiped the astonishment off his face and offered Melissande a slight bow.

"And, indeed, I'm sure I *could* manage it if I had to, but fortunately, there is another way."

Liramelli was clutching Steff's hand again. "Steff," she said.

Jiramondi nodded. "Indeed, yes. Steffanolo. I think it likely that Filomara will choose Garameno to rule after her—and declare *his* heirs to be the children of Steffanolo's body." He glanced at Liramelli. "If Steffanolo happens to marry someone highly favored by members of the court, that solution will appear all the more satisfactory."

"Oh, I do like that," Corene said. "Very tidy. Filomara's direct bloodline continues, but Malinqua doesn't have to suffer through an incompetent king. Or emperor or whatever you people call yourselves."

"I don't really think I'd be so bad," Steff said. When they all looked skeptical, he grinned. "Well, at least I wouldn't go around *murdering* people. That makes me better than that Morli fellow, at least. And that other one—Donato."

"I remember my uncles very clearly, and you are *much* better," Jiramondi assured him.

"So things are resolved very neatly here in Palminera," Corene said. "Once you get rid of the Coziquela armies, of course, and clean up the bodies, and execute the traitors—"

"Yes, it will take us some time to get back to normal, but then I hope for a period of great calm," Jiramondi said.

"But what happens to *you*?" Melissande asked him. "Everyone else is either dead or has found his place. What about you?"

He spread his hands in an expressive gesture. "I believe I will have some value as an advisor to Garameno. We have always gotten along well enough, and he has few people he can truly trust."

"It doesn't sound like a very exciting life," Corene said.

"After the past few ninedays, I am less interested in exciting and more interested in sane," said Jiramondi.

"You say that *now*," Melissande said. "But in a quintile, you will be wracked with boredom."

"Maybe," he replied. "If that's the case, I'll start looking around for amusement."

"I have a better idea," Melissande said. She had been yawning just moments ago, but now she seemed revitalized. She straightened in her seat and brushed back her dark hair. "You can come to Cozique and marry me."

"I can—*what*?"

They were all staring at Melissande, who was rosy with delight. "It is perfect!" she exclaimed. "There must be *some* sort of negotiations between Cozique and Malinqua, you know, since my mother has invaded your city! We will present ourselves as willing to do whatever it takes to ensure peace between our nations. But in reality, we will be pleasing ourselves. You will be very much liked in Cozique, where we appreciate clever and insightful men. You will not be shocked by my behavior and I certainly will not be shocked by yours. I cannot see a single impediment."

"But he—he will not love you," Liramelli said hesitantly.

Melissande waved this away. "No, but he will like me, and I will like him, which matters a great deal in marriages such as these," she replied. "More than love, perhaps."

"Are you *serious*?" Jiramondi demanded.

"Entirely so! I wish I had suggested this plan days ago, then I could have spent all my hours convincing you! I am afraid there is not much time left now, however, so you must think very hard and very quickly about whether I would be the proper bride for you."

"Marriage to you would solve many of the dilemmas in my life," Jiramondi admitted. "But to move to Cozique—that isn't something I'd considered."

Melissande shrugged. "We could split our time, perhaps—a quintile in Malinqua, a quintile in Cozique. As time goes on, I think you will find yourself happier in my country. But all of that could be arranged later."

Jiramondi glanced from her to the others, his face full of questions and doubt. Liramelli still looked uncertain, but Steff nodded encouragingly, and Corene gave him a wide smile. "I think it sounds ideal," she said. "I can't think of anyone who would object."

"Then I say—" Jiramondi hesitated a moment before plunging on. "Then I say yes."

Leaving Jiramondi and Melissande to talk over the details of their arrangement, the rest of them filed off to their beds. There was still a great deal to discuss, Corene thought hazily, but she was too tired to think things through. Maybe her brain would be clearer in the morning. Well, it was almost morning already. Maybe it would be clearer in the afternoon.

Leah and Foley and Captain Sorren and a good portion of his men followed Corene through all the twisting hallways to her own quarters. "We'll just bivouac in the corridor," Captain Sorren said. That was when Corene realized she would have no good reason to expect Foley to stay in her room overnight to protect her. Tonight of all nights! When they had even more to discuss than Jiramondi and Melissande did! She couldn't prevent herself from glancing back at him and saw, by his faint smile, that he was thinking the same thing.

Well, they would have other days to talk. Other nights to spend together.

"You'll stay in my suite, of course," she said to Leah as she unlocked the door. "There's plenty of room."

"The princess's leg needs attention," Foley spoke up. "She should have had someone look at it already."

"How bad is it?" Leah wanted to know.

"I ache so much all over I couldn't actually tell you," Corene said with a sigh. "But I'm pretty sure the bleeding has stopped."

"Do you have any medical supplies?" Leah asked.

"I've got a few things in my room," Foley said. "I'll take care of her. You go settle in."

And just like that, he managed to get them ten minutes alone.

As soon as they stepped inside his room, he closed the door and opened his arms. She sank against him as if she would melt against his body and re-form herself to his shape and contours. He pressed her against him—supporting her, protecting her, loving her, all with one embrace—and she felt his mouth against her hair.

"Did you mean it?" she said against his shirt.

"Mean what?"

"When you said you loved me."

"What do you think?"

She lifted her head and he dropped a quick kiss on her mouth. "I think you would have said anything right then to get me to jump."

"Maybe I would have," he said, "but as it happens I meant it."

"It's not very nice of you," she said, "to make me almost *die* before you tell me you love me."

That made him laugh. "Well, it's not very nice of you to almost die," he pointed out. "So we're even."

"Will I have to wait till the next time I'm in mortal danger to hear you say it again?"

"I love you I love you I love you," he recited. "So, no."

"Will you still love me when we're back in Welce?" she asked.

That question he didn't respond to quite as quickly. He loosened his hold and pulled her over to a stool, pushing her to sit. "Roll up the hem of your trousers," he said. "I want to get a look at that leg."

"That wasn't an answer," she said, but she spoke to his back, since he had stepped into the second room to fetch his supplies. She sighed and rolled back the fabric of her pants. Well, there certainly was a reason her calf was throbbing with pain. The skin was bruised and torn, and one long gash was a trough of dried blood. "Ow," she said, because just looking at it hurt.

Foley returned and knelt before her. "Try to hold still," he advised as he went to work. First he cleaned the area, then smeared it with ointment, then wrapped it with a bandage. "You probably should have bathed first," he said. "Because you'll want to keep that dry."

She laughed tiredly. "I know I smell like smoke, but I'm too tired to bathe anyway. I'll have Leah help me change the dressing in the morning."

He stayed kneeling on the floor, her foot braced against his thigh, and looked up at her. "Yes," he said.

"Yes what?"

"Yes, I'll still love you in Welce. Will you still love me?"

"Yes," she said. "Ask me sometime how long I've been in love with you. Way longer than you've been in love with me."

A faint smile played around his mouth. "You might be wrong about that."

Surprise sent a jolt of wakefulness through her veins. "Really? How long?"

"You keep asking me. Why I came with you to Malinqua."

"Because—because you were in love with me? *Really?*"

"I don't think I would have admitted it, even to myself. I just knew that when you asked me to accompany you, I was filled with a sense of rightness. And something a little fiercer than that. I thought about it later. I think it was joy."

"I was always so jealous of Josetta. Having you to look after her. Watch over her. I used to try to imagine what that would be like." She smiled. "And it has been even better than I imagined."

He stretched up to give her another brief kiss, then settled back on his heels. "I would have given my life for her," he said seriously. "I respect her, I care about her, I believe in her. But I didn't give my heart to her. I saved it for you."

She set her hands on his shoulders and gave him a serious look. "It will be a little tricky. In Chialto," she admitted. "It will be a while before my father thinks I'm old enough to hold down my own household. But you know how stubborn I am. I won't give you up once we're back in Welce."

He hesitated a moment, then said, "Maybe we shouldn't go back to Welce."

"I've considered staying in Malinqua for a while longer," she admitted. "But I think Filomara has more important things to do than entertain foreign guests."

"There are other countries to visit," he said. "Other places to see."

She blinked at him. Of course he was right. Of course her choices were wider than Malinqua or Welce. There was a whole bright world out there, filled with brilliant courts, scheming nobles, and monarchs looking to shore up their alliances.

"Cozique," she breathed. "We have been trading partners for decades, but no Welchin royalty has visited that court since before Vernon was on the throne."

He was laughing. "And just how do you know that?"

She waved a careless hand. "It used to come up in our history lessons all the time. But I am the daughter of the man who will soon be king of Welce. I think Melissande's mother would be *very* happy to meet me. We can talk trade—but we can talk other things, too."

"You could be Welchin diplomat to *all* the southern nations," Foley suggested. "If you're looking for a role to play with your life, that could very well be it."

Sheer excitement made her laugh out loud. "Yes! Of course, my father might have some thought about which nations I should approach and what kinds of treaties he'd like to sign, but— Foley, I think I could *do* this! I think I would *love* to do this!" She gave him a quick, exuberant kiss on the mouth. "And, of course, you would have to come with me everywhere I went, because a royal ambassador would never travel without her guard."

"I would be happy to travel with you to every corner of the world."

"But we will start with Cozique," she said. "We can set sail with Melissande and Jiramondi."

"Jiramondi?"

She didn't bother to explain, just flung her arms around his neck and hugged him hard. "Yes! We'll go to Cozique within the nineday! Foley, it's *perfect*!"

Predictably, when Melissande heard about this plan in the morning, she was delighted. "Absolutely! You shall come with us when we leave tomorrow. My mother's own ship has been sent to bring me back, and I assure you, the accommodations are most luxurious. You will love Cozique—and, oh, how much Cozique will love you."

Less predictably, Nelson was also enthusiastic about the plan. "Cozique, eh? From everything I hear, you'll fit right in. And sweela souls make the best ambassadors." He tapped his temple. "All that thinking."

Corene was pleased but bewildered. "Aren't you going to argue with me? Tell me I have to come home?"

"Do you want me to?" he inquired. "You know I love a good argument."

"No! My mind is quite made up. But aren't you worried that my father will be angry with you? He sent you here to bring me back."

"It's why he sent me," Nelson agreed, "but it's not why I came."

Corene hit her forehead with the heel of her hand. "Leah," she said. "You came to Malinqua to bring *her* back home."

"That's right. And she's agreed to sail with me in the morning. From my point of view, the journey has been a success."

Corene tilted her head to one side, thinking that over. "Mine, too," she said. "Not at all what I expected, but very much a success."

There were more goodbyes to make—to Liramelli, to Steff, even to Garameno. She still found it odd to see Garameno on his feet, moving decisively around the room, filled with new confidence and power. He looked so much like Greggorio that it made her heart ache—but he was so much himself that she was able to swallow her sadness.

"You've played a dangerous game very well," she told him.

"If I'd played it better, others might not have paid such a heavy price," he replied.

"Maybe the next round won't be so bloody."

"I will do everything in my power to make sure that's the case."

"And you know there's at least one body that's not on your conscience—Alette."

He nodded. "Liramelli finally told me the truth about her disappearance. You saved her from Lorian, perhaps, but I don't know that she survived even so."

"We aren't sure *yet*. But she'll let us know when she's safe. I have to believe that."

He held his hand out in a gesture of respect and farewell. "She was lucky to have you playing the game at her side," he said. "I would hope for such a good partner the next time my own stakes are so high."

And that was as high a compliment as anyone had ever paid her.

Alette's name also came up during Corene's farewell to Filomara. "I suppose I should apologize for spiriting Alette away like that, and then accusing you of letting her be killed," Corene said. "So—I'm sorry."

Filomara accepted that with a nod. Corene thought the empress looked old and exhausted, haggard with grief and disasters. "Thank you for that, at least," she said.

"I hope her disappearance doesn't cause trouble between you and Dhonsho," Corene said, "once her father discovers she is missing."

Filomara permitted herself a wintry smile. "I shall tell him that she took the opportunity to sail away with Melissande," she said. "Let him take on the Coziquela armies if he is bent on vengeance."

Corene couldn't help it; she burst out laughing. She should have known Filomara would find a way to wrest at least a small, bitter victory out of this near total defeat. "That sounds like an excellent plan," she approved.

"So you are leaving in the morning."

"Yes—unlike Alette, I really am sailing with Melissande to Cozique."

It was hard to tell if Filomara meant it when she said, "We hope you will visit us again someday."

But Corene was sincere when she replied, "I will. I have many friends here. And I think I will spend many of my future days traveling."

Filomara gave her a heavy look. "That's a hard, unsettled life. Never making a permanent home."

Corene laughed. "I think it will suit me. But I guess I'll find out."

She said much the same thing to Foley the next morning as they stood at the railing on the Coziquela ship and waved goodbye to Palminera. Half the city had turned out to see them off, or so it seemed. Maybe they were just taking the chance to wish good riddance to the Coziquela ships, which had clogged their harbor for the past few days; maybe they were just on the docks welcoming normalcy back into their lives.

"I suppose it depends on how long we stay in Cozique," Corene said. "But I'm thinking we might want to visit Berringey next."

He glanced down at her. "But you'll want to return to Welce from time to time, won't you?"

"Oh, of course! I imagine I will learn things I will want to tell my father in person—not entrusting them to a letter—and I'm sure there are instructions he will want to give me before I set sail for the next country." She laughed and added, "And, of course, we'll want to go back now and then to remind everyone that they miss us."

He grinned, but his voice was serious. "Your whole family will be proud of you. I'm sure they already are."

She tugged on her necklace and pulled the charms out into the light. "I want to live up to my blessings," she said.

"You've certainly proved you have courage."

"And ever since we decided to go to Cozique, I've felt a great sense of clarity. This is what I'm supposed to be doing."

"Now all that's left is change," he said. "And that's what travel will bring you."

She smiled up at him. "Not too much change. *Some* things will need to stay the same."

He put a hand to his heart. "Forever loyal," he said. "I always live up to my blessings."

She took his hand in hers then gazed back out over the railing. Palminera was receding slowly but unmistakably; soon it would be nothing more than a collection of shapes and colors bleaching out under the high bright sun. She couldn't even make out the twin landmarks—the tower of red, the tower of white—that illuminated the city with their own very different definitions of light.

I'm a sweela girl who is learning to control her own fire, Corene thought. She'd been running away from her life the last time she'd boarded a ship, looking for a place to belong. Now she was running toward it.

Who knew what the next port might bring? She lifted her free hand and waved at Palminera, half in farewell and half in thanks. They would be in Cozique in less than a nineday. She could hardly wait.